the Kingmaker

KENNEDY RYAN

Bloom books

Published by Bloom Books, an imprint of Sourcebooks
P.O. Box 4410, Naperville, Illinois 60567-4410
(630) 961-3900
sourcebooks.com

Cataloging-in-Publication data on file with the Library of Congress.

Originally self-published in 2019 by Kennedy Ryan.

Printed and bound in the United States of America.
VP 10 9 8 7 6 5 4 3

Dedicated to the warriors, dreamers & hustlers who change the world.

AUTHOR'S NOTE

Lennix, this story's heroine, is a proud member of the Yavapai-Apache Nation, an American Indian tribe. Some tribes mark the transition from girl to young woman through a puberty ceremony known by various names. My story pulls from the Western Apache's version of this rite of passage, generally known as the Sunrise Ceremony or Sunrise Dance. *Na'ii'ees*, which means "preparing her," ingrains in young girls the qualities deemed important for adulthood. The completion of this rite holds consequences for the entire community—blessings, health, and longevity. For the four days of the ceremony, the young girl is believed to be imbued with the power of Changing Woman, the first woman, according to the tribe's origin story.

Banned in the late 1800s by the U.S. government in an attempt to Westernize and assimilate Native people, such ceremonies became illegal, necessitating that they be practiced in secret until 1978 when the American Indian Religious Freedom Act passed. This rite of passage is sacred and pivotal in the life and development of many young Yavapai-Apache women. I approached even writing about this rite with respect and reverence and only under the guidance of several Indigenous women to ensure I would not misrepresent this or other traditions. I also consulted a medicine man who oversees these ceremonies to ensure the integrity of its portrayal. Any mistakes are mine, not theirs. In addition, these ladies opened my eyes to the epidemic of Missing and Murdered Indigenous women, which is addressed in this story. I owe a debt of gratitude to the following for their assistance:

Sherrie—Apache/Yavapai
Makea—Apache/Yavapai
Andrea—Yavapai
Nina—Apsáalooke Nation
Kiona—Hopi Tribe, Liswungwa (Coyote Clan)

PART 1

*"My mother was my first country.
The first place I ever lived."*
—"lands" by Nayyirah Waheed, poet and activist

PROLOGUE
LENNIX

THIRTEEN YEARS OLD

My face remains unchanged in the mirror, but my eyes are older.

Older than the last time I stood in my bedroom with its pink canopy bed and the Princess Barbies shoved to the back of my closet. Posters of NSYNC and Britney Spears still plaster the walls, but right now I can't recall one lyric. The songs of my forefathers and their fathers before them fill my head. Ancient songs with words only we know—the songs we had to reclaim—cling to my memory. They ring in my ears and hum through my blood. The ceremonial drum still beats in place of my heart. A woman's spirit occupies this girl's body with my barely budding breasts and baby-fat cheeks. I'm still only thirteen years old, but in the four days of my Sunrise Dance, the rite of passage that carried me from girl to woman, it feels like I've lived a lifetime.

I am not the same.

"How ya doing, kiddo?" my father asks as he and my mother walk into my bedroom. Seeing them together has been a rare occurrence lately. Actually, seeing them together has been rare for a long time.

"I'm fine." I divide my smile between them into equal portions, like I do with holidays and my affection. Split right down the middle. "Tired."

Mama sits on the bed and pushes my hair back with long, graceful fingers.

"The last few days have been hard for you," she says, offering a rueful smile. "Not to mention the last year."

We started planning the Sunrise Dance months ago. With enough food to feed everyone involved for days, gifts, getting the traditional dress made, and paying the medicine man and the ceremonial dancers, it's a long process that is not only exhausting but expensive.

"I wouldn't change a thing," I reply. My knees ache from the kneeling, from dancing on my knees and on my feet. I danced and I sang for hours, led through the words by the medicine man. And the running. I've never run so much in my life, but when I ran in the four directions, I gathered the elements—earth, wind, fire, and air—to myself. I've absorbed them. They're part of me and will guide me the rest of my days.

"I know you're exhausted," Mama says. "But are you up to seeing a few people? They've walked with you the last four days and are all so proud."

Despite the fatigue, I smile. My friends and family rallied around me, not just during the last four days but for the months leading up to my Sunrise Dance. It is a huge deal, not only for me but for the entire community.

"Sure." I run my hands over the supple buckskin of my ceremonial dress and moccasins. "Do I have time for a quick shower?"

The medicine man dusted my face with cattail pollen as part of the blessing near the end of the ceremony. Even though it was rinsed away, I still feel the traces of it and the last four days on my skin and in my hair.

"Of course," my father says. There's pride in his gray eyes. Though not Apache, he was involved with the ceremony and observed every step. As a professor of Native American Studies at Arizona State, though the traditions don't belong to him, he understands and deeply respects them.

"Everyone's eating out front and enjoying themselves," Mama says. "They'll keep while you get clean."

My parents exchange a quick look, seeming to hesitate together. It catches my attention because they're rarely in sync despite having once been passionately in love. My father had been a student studying reservation life. My mom lived on the rez in the same modest house we're in right now. It was fireworks for a while. Long enough to make me.

Maybe the fireworks sputtered. Maybe my parents were too different, my mother wanting to remain on the reservation, connected to her tribe and this community. My father, a rising star in the department when he completed his doctorate, needed to be at the university. They drifted so far apart they broke. Now, I'm their only connection. Things haven't been exactly contentious between them, but they have disagreed a lot lately, mostly about me.

"Today was a landmark for you," Mama says carefully, again sharing that quick look with my father as if she needs reassurance. "You're a woman now. The spirit of Changing Woman has made you strong."

I nod. I've never been that religious. My mother doesn't practice all the traditions, but today I did feel a surge of strength during the ceremony. Somehow I actually believe the spirit of the first woman empowered me. I still feel that zing along my nerves I couldn't shake even after the ceremony ended.

"As you know," my father takes up where my mother left off, "we've been discussing where you should attend school next year."

"You know I love having you here on the rez and in our school," Mama says. "Learning our traditions."

"And you know that I want you to take advantage of every opportunity available to you," Dad adds, his face schooled into a neutral expression. "Even if some of those take you beyond the reservation, like the private school near my house that I believe would stretch you—even better, prepare you for college and a scholarship."

"She can go to college free based on federal funding for the tribes," Mama reminds him. "She doesn't need the private school for that."

"Yes, but statistically only about 20 percent of Native students finish the first year of college," Dad says, "Why not prepare Lennix for what lies beyond the reservation while still keeping her connected to her community? Can't she be prepared for both worlds?"

It sounds reasonable.

And scary.

I've only ever attended the schools on our reservation. As empowered as I feel with Changing Woman's strength, the prospect of something new still intimidates me. This conversation has been my life in many ways. Loved by them both and splitting my life between their two homes.

"There's a lot to consider," Mama says, a little impatience creeping into her low voice. "But the point is, we think *you* should make the decision."

I look from my mother, who is an only slightly older version of me, to my father, whom I look nothing like except for my gray eyes. I carry them both in my heart, though, and I think my greatest fear is actually hurting one of them with my choices.

"We can discuss it more when I get back," Mama says, running a soothing hand down my back. "I'm off to Seattle tomorrow. There's a protest for that new oil pipeline they're proposing. They're so shortsighted. Money today won't mean much when the water is polluted and the land is beyond repair."

"So true," Dad mutters. They are united in their love for me and, though he isn't Native, their passion for tribal issues. "Just be careful."

Some of the old affection I glimpsed between them when I was younger gathers in her eyes. "I'm always careful, Rand. You know that, but there is so much to do and no time to waste. Injustice doesn't rest, and neither will I."

I wish she *would* rest sometimes. There's always a cause, a protest, a pipeline. Something that takes her away. I can't complain, though. She's the person I admire most in the world, and she wouldn't be who she is without that passion for others.

"We'll talk more about this when I get back from Seattle," Mama says. "How's that sound?"

I look between them and nod, a knot of dismay forming in my belly at the thought of displeasing one of them.

They leave me to shower and change, and when I go downstairs, my friends, family, and community overflow from our small living room. The joy on their faces is worth all I've endured the last four days. The Sunrise Dance is a celebration we were denied for years when the government outlawed it. We had to practice it and so many of our traditions in secret. We'll never take it for granted again, the privilege of celebrating in the open. We owe it to ourselves, but it's also an homage to all those who came before us. It's a thread that ties us to them.

Mena Robinson, Mama's best friend, stood as godmother to me during the ceremony, a role that strengthens our bond even more than before. She and Mama could be sisters in appearance but also in closeness.

"I'm so proud of you," Mena whispers.

"Thank you for everything," I tell her, tears in my eyes. For some reason, in her arms, surrounded by everyone who bore witness to my transition from girl to woman, the emotion of the last four days cascades over me.

"Mena, Lennix," Mama calls, glowing and aiming her camera at us. "Smile!"

I grimace, so tired of pictures and of being the center of attention, but Mama takes many more photos. And she hovers, touching my hair, hugging me, forcing me to eat. Her love and pride wrap around me, almost smother me. By the end of the evening, I want to be in my bed and alone.

I should have made Mama take a dozen more pictures. I should have given her a thousand kisses. I should have slept at her feet.

I would have if I'd known I'd never see her again.

"A riot is the language of the unheard."
                              —*Dr. Martin Luther King Jr.*

CHAPTER 1
MAXIM

FOUR YEARS LATER

I AM MY FATHER'S SON.

I'm the spitting image of Warren Cade. Dark, russet-streaked hair with a slight wave just like his. Identical light-green eyes. Same wide stretch of back and shoulders. Toe to toe, nose to nose, we both stand six feet, three and a quarter inches. Notwithstanding the striking physical similarities, beneath our skin, inside our bones—we're the same. Considering my father is one of the most ruthless sons of a bitch you'll ever meet, that should scare me.

"Why am I here, Dad?" I sink into a buttery-leather seat on his company's private jet. "What was so important you had to pull me off campus into this mile-high meeting?"

He glances up from the file on the table in front of him. "Would it kill you to spend a little time with your old man?"

It could kill us both if the last few years are any indication of how we'll get along on this trip. Our clashes are epic. As a kid, I was my father's shadow. "Hero worship" would be a mild term for the way I viewed him. We were inseparable, but as I got older and formed my own opinions, found my own will, the chasm between us grew wider. My father rules our family with the same iron fist with which he runs Cade Energy, the family business. When he tries to rule *me*...it doesn't go as well.

"It's an awkward time," I reply with a shrug. "I'm finishing my thesis and—"

"Why you even wasted your time with that master's program, I'll never know."

I bite back any reply to defend my decision. It made sense when I double majored in business and energy resources engineering for undergrad. That fell in line with his plan for me. Going on to pursue my master's at Berkeley made no sense. According to his timetable, I should have been leading a division in our company by now.

"Let's not go there," I finally say, running an agitated hand through my hair, overlong and almost to my shoulders.

"You need a haircut," Dad says abruptly, shifting his attention back to his file. "Like I was saying, you'll be done with graduate school soon. Time to get back on track."

"I *am* on track." I clear my throat and don't meet his eyes. "And I'm not sure what I'll do next."

A lie. I know exactly what I'll do next. A PhD in climate science, but I'm in no mood to fight. I haven't seen him in a long time. I'd rather talk about the Cowboys' playoff hopes. The Longhorns. His golf swing. Anything other than my career—than our opposing views on what I should do.

Dad's eyes snap up and narrow on my face. "What the hell do you mean you aren't sure what you'll do next? Now that Owen's in the Senate, we need you running our West Coast office, Maxim. You know that."

The note of pride in his voice when he mentions my older brother Owen grates a little. Pride hasn't been in his voice for me in a long time. *Disapproval. Disgust. Frustration.* That's all I've gotten since I told him I'd be going to Berkeley for my master's instead of starting at Cade Energy.

"Dad, I don't know that I'm…" I hesitate. The next words could set off a bomb I'm not sure we should detonate this high in the air. "Maybe I'm not the right fit for the job."

"Not the right fit?" He flips the file closed and glares at me. "You're a Cade. You were literally *born* for the job."

"Let's talk about this later."

"No. Now. I want to know why the company four generations of Cades spent building from the ground isn't good enough for you."

"I didn't say that. I'm just not sure I'm the best person to run a company producing oil and gas. I question the sustainability of fossil fuels as this country's primary energy source. I believe we should be aggressively transitioning to clean energy—solar, wind, electric."

Shocked silence follows my words that are essentially a rebel yell to one of America's most powerful oil barons.

"What the ever-loving *fuck* are you talking about, boy?" he bellows, his voice bouncing off the walls, trapped in the luxurious cabin. "You'll finish that damn useless master's degree and start in our California office as soon as possible. I got no time for this wind and air and whatever tree-hugger horseshit nonsense they've been teaching you at Berkeley."

"Nonsense is believing this planet will run forever on poison. If you'd just listen to my ideas about transitioning to clean energy—"

"Oil was clean enough when it was paying for your fancy education, huh? And your trips and cars and clothes. It wasn't poison then, was it?"

"I wouldn't expect you to notice, but I paid my own tuition," I correct him softly.

Before he can verbally express the disdain on his face, a uniformed attendant peers through the curtain.

"We're here, Mr. Cade," she says.

When my father stands, his knee knocks the table. The file falls, spilling a flurry of papers onto the thick-pile carpet. I bend to retrieve them, stuffing a few back into the folder. Certain words blare from the top page.

Pipeline. Army Corps of Engineers. Ancestral burial grounds. Water rights. Environmental impact.

"Dad." I force myself to look up from the page long enough to catch and hold his gaze. "Where are we, and what are we doing here?"

He doesn't answer for a moment but extends his hand until I reluctantly give him the file.

"We're in Arizona." He grabs his suit jacket from a hook on the wall and slips it on. He's still fit and trim, and that suit costs enough to take ten years off any man. "Laying a new gas pipeline, and let's just say the, uh, natives are getting restless." He smirks at his own joke but sobers when he sees I'm not laughing.

"That memo referenced the Apache," I say with a frown.

"Until you man up and actually run something in Cade Energy, that memo's none of your damn business, but that's why I'm here. If they think their little protest will stop my pipeline, they can think again."

"We're laying a pipeline that disturbs sacred burial grounds?" Outrage and anger almost choke me. Shame, too, that my name is attached to something so heinous. "Will this endanger their water supply?"

"We're laying a natural gas pipeline that will transport half a million barrels a day and create thousands of jobs."

"So no thought for the environmental impact?"

"What about the economic impact?" he counters harshly. "If you did something other than sit at a computer all day *studying*, you'd know what it's like to be responsible for thousands of families. Thousands of livelihoods. To have shareholders demanding a profit. And they care even less about some river on a reservation than I do. It's my job, Maxim."

"Your job should also be ensuring that pipeline doesn't contaminate other people's water."

"I don't have time to argue with you." He heads for the exit. "You can stay here while I handle this or get off for all I care. The worksite's near a reservation, and according to our foreman, those Indian women got some of the best pu—"

"Stop." I swallow my disgust and follow him down the short

flight of steps lowered from the plane. "I don't want to know what your foreman thinks about women."

"Like you don't get your dick wet," he says, his voice caustic.

"Oh, I love women. Too much to disrespect them."

"I should have known better than to send you to Berkeley," Dad mutters, climbing into the back seat of the black Escalade that's waiting for us. "Damn sissy school's made you soft."

"You didn't send me anywhere." I look out the window, watching the desert landscape rushing past as we leave the airfield. "And having actual principles isn't the same as being soft."

"You know what your problem is, Maxim?"

"I'm sure you'll tell me."

"You aren't ruthless enough. You think your brother won that Senate seat worrying about some reservation water supply or burial ground?" Before I can reply, he charges on. "Damn right he didn't. Politics requires balls of steel, and Owen's got 'em."

"Glad you're pleased with one of us," I say through tight lips.

"If you're not a 'fit' for the family business and your delicate constitution isn't suited to politics, what do you plan to do?"

He's not ready to hear what I plan to do, and I'm not sure I want to tell him. I'll let my actions speak for themselves. For me.

"How's Mom?" I ask, shamelessly shifting conversational gears because this line of discussion is going nowhere.

His face softens, the hard planes yielding to what is maybe his one redeeming quality. He adores my mother. It may be the only undefiled thing left about him.

"She's good." He clears his throat and studies the passing landscape as I did, retreating to the scene beyond the window. "Misses you."

"I'll make sure to see her soon."

"It hurt her when you didn't come home for the holidays."

"As much as seeing you and me at each other's throats would have hurt her?"

I regret the words immediately. So much for redirecting our conversation. No matter what I do, it always comes back to this—to me not measuring up, me not pleasing my father, me failing. Him disappointed. Him leveraging money to twist my arm and trying to bend me to his will.

Well, I won't be bent. If he thinks I'm not ruthless, he hasn't been paying attention. Head-to-head, I'd bury my brother. Owen gobbled up every crumb our father dropped, leading him down the prescribed path. Balls of steel? Fuck that. My father practically *bought* Owen that seat in the Senate. If I want to make my own way, I'll have to pay my own way.

And that's fine with me.

"God, Maxim," my father says, his voice low and loaded with frustration. "I thought this trip might…" He shakes his head, letting whatever he hoped for trail off with the unspoken words. "What happened to you? What happened to *us*, son? We used to hunt together." He chuckles and flashes me a reminiscent grin. "Hell, you're a crack shot. You can shoot the wings off a flea. And fly-fishing in Big Horn River."

We cooked our haul over an open fire that night. I silently complete the memory, still tasting the fish and the laughter, the camaraderie that came so easily then.

"And remember that week we broke in Thunder?" he asks.

"That horse was half Arabian, half demon," I recall with a short bark of laughter.

"He was no match for us, though. Between you and me, we broke him in."

An image sears my mind. Thunder, with rolling eyes and a bucking back, his neighing a battle cry. We took turns, Dad and I, that week on our Montana ranch, riding the horse, bridling him, training and taming him until my father could lead him around a fenced circle by a rope, the horse's spirit as subdued as his light trot.

Docile. Broken.

And that's how my father wants me. Trotting obediently, my neck draped with the reins of his power.

"That horse was no match for the two of us. We can do anything together," Dad continues. "Come run Cade Energy with me, Max."

I almost fell for it. When his money doesn't work, he employs his only other weapon: my love for him. He dangles his affection, his approval before me like ripe, low-hanging fruit. Just bite. A tempting trade. My will for his. Do what he says. Be who he wants and he'll love me that way again. But I've seen too much—changed too much. Our eyes, hair, bones, and very natures may be the same, but I've spent years venturing beyond the safety of my father's borders, and it has fleshed me out. It's made a man of me, and the man I want to be is not my father.

I don't respond but keep my gaze fixed through the tinted glass. I'm still formulating a response that won't cause a back-seat battle when we pull up to the construction site.

A few hundred people crowd the plot of desert. Bulldozers and trucks loiter, impotent and silent, each with a dark-haired protester anchored to it. Their arms hook around the necks of the bulldozers, a cast plastering both arms in an unbroken loop. Some are chained to the trucks, impeding any forward movement. Protesters raise signs and link arms to form a line of bodies around the site. Media trucks topped with satellite dishes dot the scene, and well-groomed reporters stand nearby armed with their microphones. Police officers ring the area, sober sentinels with expressionless faces. I can't tell if they're here to protect or threaten. I guess it depends whose side you're on.

"Dammit to hell," my father mutters. "I need those trucks moving."

A vaguely familiar man approaches the Escalade, irritation and anxiety twisting his expression. He stands outside the door, obviously waiting for my father to get out. Dad rolls the window down halfway, not bothering to so much as lean forward. Anger strikes out on the man's face like a snake's forked tongue before he gains control of it and steps closer to the window, his features falsely placid. He looks deferential for a man who barely deigns to acknowledge him.

"Mr. Cade," he says, leaning close enough to the window to be heard.

"Beaumont," Dad responds, his use of the man's name jogging my memory. He's a division leader I met at one of the company picnics held at our Dallas compound. "You said you had this situation under control. I'd hate to see what you consider a disaster."

Beaumont clears his throat and loosens his collar before speaking. "It *was* under control, sir," he says. "We were on schedule. I caught wind of this planned protest yesterday and contacted the office as soon as I heard. I thought they'd send someone. I didn't expect you to come personally."

"I *am* someone," Dad snaps, "keeping you on your toes. I needed to see this shitstorm for myself. Who are all these people?"

"Mostly people from the reservation," Beaumont says. "But some students from local universities showed up, too. As you can see, some have chained themselves to the construction equipment. Some just arrived from the run."

"What run?" I ask from the shadowy corner on the other side of the back seat.

Beaumont's eyes flick in my direction, narrowing before returning to my father's face.

"Uh, sir," he starts, his tone cautious, his expression closing off even more. "We can talk later or—"

"It's all right," my father says impatiently. "You can speak freely in front of him. It's my boy Maxim."

"Oh, yes." Beaumont relaxes and inclines his head to me like I'm some kind of prince and my father his liege. "Good to see you again, Maxim. How's Berkeley treating you?"

"The run?" I ignore the pleasantry and press for the information I requested. "What kind of run?"

"Yes, well, some of them call themselves water protectors," Beaumont answers. "They raise awareness through these marathons. They finished one today."

I nod toward the media trucks. "Seems like they raised some awareness about this pipeline."

"It's a small story in the big scheme of things," Beaumont insists. "Some old Indians and a bunch of kids from the reservation, worried about something that's not likely to ever happen."

"You mean a spill?" I demand. "They're worried their main source of water will be polluted? Is that what you mean?"

Beaumont glances from my scowling face to my father's. The look he gives my dad says it all without him uttering a word. *Whose side is your son on anyway?*

Not yours. That's for damn sure.

"We have the contingency, right?" Dad asks, ignoring the byplay between me and his corporate henchman.

"Yes, sir." A smirk tweaks Beaumont's mouth. "Everything's in place. It will only take one call, and I can—"

"Can you hear me?" someone yells through a bullhorn, slicing into Beaumont's assurances. "Can you see me?"

My father rolls the window down fully, leaning forward to see who's behind that voice. I lean forward, too, and I freeze.

It's a girl. A woman. She's young, but there's power in her stance, in her face. The late daylight loves her, kissing the hollows under the rise of her cheekbones. The wind carries her hair as easily as it carries her voice, whipping the dark strands behind her like a pennant on a battlefield. She seems to command the elements as effortlessly as she does the crowd's attention, standing on a mound of dirt, a hill as her stage. Even if she weren't slightly elevated, she would tower. She's a straight line of color sketched into the desert landscape, transformed by a glamour of dust and sunlight.

"I said, can you hear me?" She repeats loudly, more intensely. "Can you see me? Because I don't think you can."

Her black T-shirt blasts "REZpect Our Water" across the front and tucks neatly into the waistband of a flowing patterned skirt stopping at knee-high buckskin moccasins. She's a perfect blend of past and present and future. A smattering of stars decorates the skin around her left eye, while lines of color fan out from her right.

Stars and stripes.

I find myself grinning at the sly humor painted onto her skin, a wordless commentary on patriotism and colonialism and probably a dozen subtexts I wouldn't know where to start naming.

"I don't think you can," she continues, "when corporations lay pipelines on land we were promised would be protected."

A shout rises from the crowd.

"I don't think you can," she shouts into the bullhorn, "when my ancestors who bled and died find no peace in the very land they sacrificed for because trucks and plows turn over their graves."

The crowd releases a reply mixed with English and a tongue I don't understand but obviously affirms her message, encourages her to go on.

"Four years ago," she says, "on a day like today, my mother left for a protest in Seattle much like this one. She never came back."

She lowers the bullhorn and stares at the ground for a moment. Even from here, I see the bullhorn shaking in her hand when she raises it again.

"Our women disappear," she says, her voice wavering but fierce, "and no one cares. No one searches. No one says their names, but I say her name. *Liana Reynolds.* I didn't have her body, but I had her name, and I came here to sacred ground and whispered it. The wind carried it to my ancestors. I asked them to recover her spirit. To take her home."

She shakes her head, impervious of the tears streaking her face. "I came here to mourn. When it was time for the rite of passage from girlhood to womanhood, I came here to dance. We worship here; we wed here. The ground where you sit, our pews. The trees around you, our steeples. You are standing in our church."

Her voice rings out, commanding and broken. A lone tear streaks through the vibrant stripes around her eye. There are no shouts in reply. No raised fists. Only lowered eyes. Shaking heads as her sorrow takes us hostage.

"And the man elected to represent us," she goes on, her features hardening into an angry mold, "is the one who betrayed us. Senator Middleton, shame on you! You sold our land to Warren Cade. Land we were promised would be protected, you gave away. It wasn't yours to give!"

The air trembles beneath the weight of her words, and like she summoned it, a desert wind, a sirocco, lifts the dark river of hair hanging down her back and tosses it like a mourning wail through the air.

"It wasn't yours to give," she repeats, even more fervently. "Liar. Trickster. Thief."

The crowd echoes back, as if they've done it a thousand times.

"Liar! Trickster! Thief!"

"Is it because you never saw us that you don't care?" she barrels on, and even through the bullhorn, it's a whisper. A barely there question, as if she doesn't want to ask because she already knows the answer.

"Well, see us now," she shouts with renewed vigor into the bullhorn. "Ignore us today when we fight for what is ours—for what was promised to us. We will not be moved. You cannot strip us of everything. You cannot steal the prophecies that light our way."

There are a few shouts in response before she goes on.

"The prophecies foretell a generation rising up to defend, to fight, to recover what was lost," she says, the tears continuing in a single stream from each eye. "I am that generation."

Another collective shout swells from the crowd.

"We are that people who say enough!" Her eyes scan the crowd like a general searching for weaknesses to root out, for strengths to employ. "Say it with me. Enough. No more!"

"Enough! No more!" the crowd responds.

"Enough! No more!"

"Enough! No more!"

"Tu be hi'naah!" she yells, fist in the air.

"Water is life!" The crowd echoes back.

"Tu be hi'naah!"

"Water is life!"

Under the cover of applause, she climbs down the hill and slips into the line of bodies linked at the elbows and blocking the trucks.

"Do it," my father says, his voice hard, angry. "They think they can throw off my schedule? They wanna fuck with me? They don't even know where to start. Make the call."

Beaumont nods and punches a few numbers in his phone before raising it to his ear.

"Move in," he says.

"Dad, what are you doing?" I pin my question to him but fix my eyes on the scene through the window. He spares me a glance, his mouth a stern, ungiving line.

"Balls of steel, son," he says, his eyes slits. "Balls of steel."

The sound of dogs barking jerks my attention from my father's stony expression. A fleet of Dobermans on leashes bounds from trucks circling the site. Officers wearing padded vests face off with the protestors, their expressions blurred by plexiglass face shields.

"Dad, no!"

The words have barely left my lips when the first mist of tear gas invades the air.

"No one will get hurt," Dad says, his eyes trained on the scene playing out. "They have strict instructions to keep order and intimidate if necessary, but no one will get hurt."

"You can't be that naive. Situations like this escalate in the blink of an eye. One wrong move, and there's a shot fired and a dog bites, and you'll have a lawsuit on your hands."

Not to mention the guilt, but I'm not sure my father is capable of that anymore. I never thought his ruthless streak would run this far—would run roughshod over innocent people.

"Lawsuit?" my father scoffs. "Look out this window. Whose side does it look like the law is on?"

I do look out the window, and I'm assaulted by helplessness, guilt, and shame. Several protestors cover their eyes too late against the sting of gas, and they screech, rubbing furiously at the intrusion. Another group advances, positioning themselves directly in the path of the construction truck, in the path of what appear to be rubber bullets. I grit my teeth when I see the girl from the hill in that line. The Dobermans have turned, jaws pulled back from their teeth, and they advance on the protestors.

Advance on *her*.

I don't stop, don't think about the line I'm crossing, about my father, the architect of this cruel chaos. I don't consider my own safety, only theirs.

Hers.

Her words throb in my ears and pulse in my veins.

No more. Enough.

Can you hear me? Can you see me?

I can't unsee the proud line she cut into the horizon on that hill. Can't unhear the heartbroken history she shouted to the wind.

I see you.

I hear you.

I throw the door open, and before I know it, I launch into a run across the dusty land.

I'm coming.

CHAPTER 2
LENNIX

A THOUSAND NEEDLES PIERCE MY EYES. I KNUCKLE-SCRUB MY eyelids, even while knowing from our protest training that flushing with water is the only thing that will help. Preparing for tear gas and *doing* it are two completely different things. Lesson number one in civil disobedience, but I'm not sure any amount of training could prepare me to face a snarling dog, held back by a flimsy leash. I stumble, my eyes clenched tightly against the discomfort, and slam into something hard.

"Sorry," I gasp, reflexively reaching out to put space between me and whomever I plowed into. I ease my eyes open. Backlit by the sun, a man towers over me. Considering I'm in the middle of a riot, growling Dobermans barely kept at bay, tear gas still hanging in the air, and standing shoulder to shoulder with a line of protesters howling in pain and rubbing their eyes, it's bad timing to notice this guy is gorgeous. And that he smells really good.

"Uh…um, hey," I stammer. "I mean, hi."

Idiot. Nincompoop. I just gave a rousing speech that still has my heart twisted and my cheeks wet from tears, but I'm tongue-tied because a hot guy showed up to protest the pipeline?

"Are you okay?" His voice rolls over me, deep and husky with the slightest trace of a drawl. Texas, maybe? Did he come all the way from Texas to join us?

"Uh, yeah." I rub my eyes again. "I will be."

I'm dragged back, figuratively, also literally, kicking and scream-ing, into this nightmare scene with frothy-mouthed dogs and masked cops wielding tear gas.

"Shit!" The curse comes from my right, and a grimace of pain skitters across the face of Jason Paul, one of the protesters and my teacher from fourth grade. He struggles to shake his hand free of a dog's lockjaw bite. My heart leaps to my throat when a growling dog comes right for *me*. The really tall, great-smelling guy jerks me back and out of harm's way but gets bitten on the arm himself before the cop jerks on the leash. I don't have time to thank him for sparing me or to apologize that he got caught in the cross teeth, as it were. I'm shoved forward, my arms wrenched together, plastic handcuffs drawn tight at my wrists.

"What are you doing?" I shout over my shoulder at the officer cuffing me. "This is a peaceful protest. We have every right to be here."

"Private property, lady," he murmurs close to my ear, spite slick-ening his voice. "Apparently your permits weren't in order."

"This is a mistake," Tall and Good-Smelling says when they slip plastic cuffs on him, too.

"You'll get a chance to have your say." The officer shoves him toward a police van. "Call your lawyer."

"Trust me. You don't want my lawyer involved," the guy says, his voice as cutting as the glance he shoots the cop. "Let me go. Let them go, and don't give me that shit about permits. I know what this is."

"This," the officer says, pushing the guy's head down to clear the van, forcing him inside, "is you having the right to remain silent."

Six of us fill the benches lining the van interior, three on either side and facing each other. The cops give us bottles of water to flush the tear gas from our eyes as much as possible. We prepared for this moment, but I don't think any of us actually expected to be arrested. Even if we had, none of us would have done anything differently. Everyone in this van has a vested interest in what happens with that pipeline. It would endanger the reservation's water supply. It would desecrate sacred burial grounds. We all grew up drinking from that stream. Dipping in it for ceremonies that mark pivotal moments in our lives. Each of us has a reason to be here.

Except him.

Now that we're not surrounded by dogs and choking on tear gas, I study him more closely. In all the confusion, I only had time for a general impression of hotness, but now with us both shackled in the paddy wagon, I have all the time for a closer examination. Or at least as long as it takes to get to the police station.

He has one of those magazine faces. Not exactly like a model, but a "someone" face. An "I should know you" face. It's not about how handsome he is, really. Though I can't overstate the impact of dark, mahogany-dusted hair licking around his ears and down his neck. Or his green eyes, the color of the peridot stone we mine in our holy hills. Precious metal eyes. And seriously. The Creator must have used a protractor to achieve a jaw so perfectly angular. But there's something more, like if you get caught up in that face and what is, admittedly, a fantastic physique, all lean muscles and a "from here to there" chest, you'd be missing the whole point of him.

"So you came all the way from Cali for this?" I ask, nodding to the Berkeley T-shirt straining across his pecs.

"Uh, yeah." He shifts in his seat.

"That's great that people all across the country are hearing about the pipeline," Mr. Paul says, smiling at magazine-face man. "And coming to stand with us. Thank you."

"Yeah," he says again. "So how long have you guys been fighting, um…Cade on this?"

He spreads the question to all five of us, but I answer first.

"Last year, Senator Middleton sold the property to Cade Energy," I offer, gritting my teeth. "Of course, as usual, disregarding that it was supposed to be protected. Not theirs to actually sell."

"Their promises," Mr. Paul says, with a bitter twist to his lips, "are worth no more than the paper every treaty they've ever broken was written on. Senator Middleton got this pipeline passed by tacking it on at the last minute to another bill that already had support."

"It was done before we even knew about it," I add. "We started organizing immediately, but at every turn, Cade has politicians, the Army Corps of Engineers, local police, everyone on his side and in his pocket. The worst part is he could reroute this thing."

"What makes you say that?" Berkeley T-shirt asks.

"The original proposal ran the pipeline near a suburb about ten miles north," I answer, "not near a water supply or anything, but the people there didn't want it. So guess what? They didn't get it. They didn't even have to protest. Just said no."

"Guess their voices are louder than ours," Mr. Paul mutters.

"Basically, environmental racism." Berkeley T-shirt sighs and shakes his head.

"No, *exactly* environmental racism," I correct. "But we won't take it."

"We're not going anywhere. We know how to last," Mr. Paul says, a proud set to his head. "We were the last tribe to surrender. We have warrior in our blood."

"What do you mean?" Berkeley asks.

"Geronimo was the last Indian warrior to formally surrender to the U.S. government," I tell him. "He was Apache."

"Wow," Berkeley says. "I didn't know that."

The van comes to a stop, and through the back window, I see the small police station.

I'll be grounded for the foreseeable future. There goes…well, life, pretty much.

My father knew about the run. I founded the sponsoring organization, REZpect Water, an action group for youth water protectors, but I conveniently left out the part where I'd actually be *in* the protest with the dogs and tear gas…and such. When they offer us our one phone call, maybe I'll just pass and live out the rest of my senior year in a holding cell. I could redirect all my college acceptance letters to the police station. That wouldn't raise any red flags, would it? What self-respecting place of higher learning isn't recruiting from the penal system?

"Out," the cop standing at the door barks, her voice rough and impatient, her unibrow dipped into a frown.

The six of us shuffle toward the police station. The officers don't seem bothered by the fact that I'm a minor and take my mug shot without incident. The police station is a small-town operation with one holding cell we're all tossed into together. I don't anticipate these charges sticking. Cade probably just wants to intimidate us.

Good luck with that, you rich prick.

I may not actually live on the rez anymore, but staying with my father in town hasn't made it any less my home. I'd still be living there if Mama…

I shove that thought down to a dark hole where I keep the really painful stuff. Why deal with it now? Save something for the therapist I'll start seeing in my thirties when I finally decide it's all too much to handle on my own.

My mother was murdered? Taken? Stolen?

Gone.

One of those "unseen" women, an unheard voice, whose disappearance wasn't shouted about on the news or fretted over by the world.

And I'll never get over it. Not ever.

There are days when I go a few hours without thinking about it—without wondering what happened to the beautiful woman who gave so much of herself to me and everyone around her. Yeah, there are those days, but not many. Mostly there are a thousand things every day that remind me of her, not the least of which is my own reflection.

"Good to have those off," Berkeley T-shirt mumbles, rubbing his wrists and reminding me of our current less-than-ideal circumstances. I don't know how long they'll keep us in this holding cell.

"This thing hurts like crazy," Mr. Paul says, touching the reddened, punctured skin of his hand.

"You need medical attention." I walk over to the bars and glance back over my shoulder to Berkeley T-shirt. "So do you."

Berkeley. According to that T-shirt, he's probably already in college. Yeah, he's already a *man*, not a *boy*. My dad would strangle me and maim him.

"I don't think I'll lose it." He nods to his injured arm, one corner of his mouth tipping up.

Focus on first aid, not his lips.

"Hey!" I yell through the bars. "We need a first-aid kit in here."

Unibrow takes her sweet time ambling toward the cell.

"You rang, m'lady?" she asks. Oh, the sarcasm is thick with this one.

"Yeah. We have two people here with dog bites, thanks to the Cujos you turned loose on us." I point a thumb over my shoulder. "Thought I'd do you a favor and spare you a lawsuit. You're welcome."

She eyes Mr. Paul, who cups his hand, and then she glances at Berkeley. She lingers there, taking in the fully spectacular male specimen he is.

Can't blame ya, girl.

"I'll get a first-aid kit and some antibiotic," she finally says before turning on her heel to leave.

"You're a real Florence Nightingale," I shout after her and turn back to the crowded cell. Another van has brought in more of the protestors. It makes my heart heavy, seeing my friends and neighbors behind bars like criminals. We don't steal. We don't disregard the law and break our word. That is what has been done *to* us since the first ship docked.

"Stars and stripes, huh?" Berkeley asks from the bench against the wall.

He's the only person here I've never seen before. I walk over and take the empty spot beside him.

"'Scuse me?" I ask, resting my back against the wall and pulling one knee up while I wait for him to clarify.

"Stars." He gestures to one side of his eye. "And stripes. On your face. Is that on purpose?"

Sharp. Observant. He does attend Berkeley. Stands to reason.

"I never claimed to be subtle," I say with a tight smile.

"Yeah, I picked up on the not-subtle part at the protest," he says with a straight face, but with eyes twinkling the tiniest bit.

I don't feel like discussing my complex relationship with this nation's forefathers and their twisted definition of "we the people." I settle for the simpler answer to his question. "The stars are for my second name," I tell him.

"Second name?"

"A medicine man came through our reservation when I was a little girl and gave me my second name: Girl Who Chases Stars."

"Wow. That's some name."

"Tell ya a little secret." I lean closer. "I think it may have been rigged."

"Rigged?"

"When I was little, I wanted to be an astronaut. Well, at first I wanted to be a clown."

"Obviously. Who didn't?"

"You, too?"

"No, they're creepy as fuck. What a weird kid you were."

"This we can all agree on." I laugh, surprised that I *can* laugh in a jail cell having this strange conversation with a guy I met not much more than an hour ago. "So around five or so, I decided I'd be an astronaut instead. Everyone knew it, so maybe the medicine man was simply giving the people what they wanted, so to speak. Chicken, egg. Earth, moon."

"So if Girl Who Chases Stars is your second name, what's your first?"

"Lennix. With an 'i' because I know you're thinking 'o.'"

"Lennix." He rolls the syllables around on his tongue, and something about the way he seems to test the name, taste it, sends a shiver down my spine. I've never been around a guy like him before. *Correction*. A man. The guys at school leave me cold—cold and uninterested and unimpressed. This guy? Warm, interested. Way impressed.

I'm distracted when the cell door opens and a woman teeters in on skyscraper heels. Her blue wig is longer than her dress, which I'm sure was a cocktail napkin in another life. I think I've seen her a few times on the rez and in town, too. She's Native, and I bet if you sandblasted her makeup off, she'd be quite pretty.

The cell door bangs closed behind her, and she scowls, her gaze roaming the crowded cell and stopping on Berkeley. A smile creeps over her lips, and she takes the empty-ish spot on his other side, bumping his neighbor over with one curvy hip to make room for herself.

She drags her eyes over all the things I noticed right away—his lean muscles, strong chest, and dark hair. When he stares back at her, letting her look her fill, I want to rip that blue wig off her head and stomp on it.

Real mature.

"Well, well, well," she drawls, licking her glossy red lips. "Ain't you something?"

To Berkeley's credit, his eyes never drop to the breasts bulging at the deep slit of the microscopic dress's neckline. He looks at her unblinkingly, almost as if waiting for her to go on.

"Didn't expect to find the likes of you in here," she says. "Must be my lucky night."

She reaches up toward his face, but he catches her wrist before she touches him. Her long talon-like nails hang inches from his jaw. With what looks like some gentleness, he pushes her hand back and drops it.

"Oh, it's like that?" she demands, the dark eyes hard and glassy like pebbles. "Your loss. I could do it like you never had it before."

"I'm all set," he finally speaks, a small quirk at the corner of his lips, "but thank you."

"You think you are." She leans forward until I'm sure her poor neckline will rip open any minute now. "Ever had your dick sucked with Pop Rocks?"

Berkeley coughs into his fist, but I detect the smile he's hiding. "Excuse me?"

"Pop Rocks," she says with a smile wide enough to reveal a missing tooth near the back. "The candy. It's one of those 'kids, don't try this at home' kinda things. You need a professional for it."

"Um, I don't…use professionals," he says. "So I wouldn't know."

She flicks a glance over at me and narrows her eyes. I narrow mine right back, a silent dare to mess with me. She rolls her eyes and stands with a flourish, making sure to run those gold-tipped talons over her body before walking across the room and sitting down beside another unsuspecting man.

"Well, well, well," she drawls to him. "Ain't you something?"

Berkeley makes a choked sound, and I swing a glance back his way.

"What are you laughing at?" I ask, even though my lips are twitching, too.

"Pop Rocks," he whispers, grinning. "Who knew?"

We're both sitting on the bench, leaned back, our shoulders shaking in silent laughter. Humor crinkles the edges of those beautiful eyes, and I'm suddenly sad I'll probably never see this man again. I know it's crazy. We've only shared a few words in not much more than an hour, but I'm the kid so often trapped between worlds, split in two and finding my place. On rare occasions, you come across someone who just gets you, and you don't have to figure out your place. Wherever you are is okay.

I think he could be a "wherever you are" person.

His laughter fades, too, and I don't know how long we stare at one another, but the seconds stretch into a perfect tension. Not uncomfortable at all. It's a just-right tautness that draws between us and sends fireflies over my tingling skin, lighting me up.

"Did your *daddy* know you were protesting today, Lennix?" Mr. Paul asks.

His pointed question shatters the tension and scatters the fireflies. Berkeley blinks, looks away, and folds his arms over his chest. Mr. Paul flicks a suspicious, avuncular glance between Berkeley T-shirt and me.

Wow. I think calling my elementary school teacher a cock blocker goes a little far since I'm barely flirting with this stranger, but still… Did he have to bring up my "daddy"?

"Uh, he knew I was speaking today, yes, sir," I reply.

Not exactly what he asked, and the look he gives me says he knows it.

"Will your father be upset that you protested?" Berkeley T-shirt asks.

"Probably." I release a not-so-long-suffering sigh. "He's super-protective since…" *Since my mom disappeared.*

She left like she had a dozen times before, off to a protest in Seattle, and then…nothing. And ever since, my father has tried to roll me in bubble wrap and cotton, but I'm not having it. He's right. This world is not a safe place, but playing it safe all the time is not how I make that better.

"Sorry about your mom," Berkeley says.

I glance up to find sympathy darkening his eyes to forest green. I'd forgotten he would have heard me talk about her today.

"Thanks." I swallow the hurt and helplessness that lodge in my throat when I think about Mama. "Anyway, my father's really protective now. This will probably get me grounded for weeks."

Man. Way to sound like a twelve-year-old in front of the finest man you've ever encountered in real life.

"Grounded?" His dark eyebrows sky rocket. "Exactly how old is the Girl Who Chases Stars?"

Well, so much for the short-lived not-flirtation we've been enjoying. He's probably like us. Someone behind bars who shouldn't be. I seriously doubt he wants messing around with an underage girl to land him here for good.

Smart guy.

Resigned, I drag out the one word I know will shut this down. "Seventeen."

CHAPTER 3
MAXIM

SEVEN-FUCKING-TEEN?

She's jailbait. And I'm literally already in jail.

While I've been wondering if it would be too awkward now that we're both out of handcuffs to ask her out, she's been sitting over there completely underage.

Shit and double shit. I'd be arrested *again* for the things I was imagining while she sat across from me. She doesn't look seventeen. Someone should pop a warning label on this girl.

It's not her appearance. It's the things she said at the protest. It's the gravity in her eyes when she looks at you. I don't know how to name the color of her eyes—have no idea what I should call them. No way are they just gray. They are silver eyes. Not just the color, but the metal. Tough and tried and smelted beyond her years into this indescribable hue. Metal and mettle.

"You're, um…very mature for your age," I finally manage, surreptitiously inserting an extra inch between us on the bench.

"My godmother says I'm an old soul."

At least something is of age.

Jesus, the girl's not even a freshman in college, and I'm getting my master's. I may be a lot of things, but a perv isn't one of them, at least under typical circumstances.

The Girl Who Chases Stars is not typical circumstances. She is atypical. Unusual. File this under "won't find another like this one." I bet those high school idiots have no idea how to handle her. A part of me really hopes they don't.

"It's not fair," she says, tilting her head slightly and sending a river of dark, pin-straight hair swinging behind her. "You know both of my names, and I don't know yours. I've literally been calling you by your T-shirt in my head for the last hour."

I hesitate, hopefully not long enough for her to notice. I'll never see this girl again. Hell, I probably won't see any of the people in this holding cell again, but they've left a crater-like impression on me. Her most of all. I'm ashamed of my last name—ashamed of my father and how he's like every other entitled son of a bitch who has stolen from them, disregarded their rights, and diminished their humanity. Cade is a name that opens doors and closes deals, but I want nothing to do with it today.

"Maxim."

"Like the *Gladiator* movie?"

"That was Maximus."

"Still. It means 'the greatest,' right? That's a lot to live up to."

"Let's just say my parents had high hopes."

"Had?" she probes, those indefinably gray eyes searching my face. This kid is *so* not a kid.

She's a kid, asshole. Remember that or get comfortable behind bars.

"I think I'm kind of a disappointment," I admit, forcing my mouth into a casual grin at the sympathy in her eyes. "It's okay. They've disappointed me, too. It's a family trait."

"I'm sure they're proud of you," she insists. "I mean, if my kid traveled from California to Arizona protesting for indigenous people, I'd make bumper stickers with his face on them."

Yeah, about that...

"Lennix Moon," one of the cops who booked us yells. He opens the barred door and gestures for her to go out into the corridor.

"Well, that's me." She laughs and casts an if-I'm-not-mistaken wistful glance my way.

"Yet another name?"

"Middle name." She stands up and smooths the golden skirt. "Lennix Moon Hunter. Quite a mouthful, huh?"

I'm still scrubbing my mind of the dirty thoughts I had about her mouth *before* I found out she was seventeen. Out of the question.

"Well, goodbye and good luck." I extend my hand for a parting handshake.

When she takes it, her fingers feel small and sure in mine. Our skin conducts a charge between our palms. That volt hits me somewhere between my chest and my stomach. I wonder if I'm imagining it, but when I look up, her eyes fix to that one point of connection. She glances up, a mixture of curiosity and pleasure right there to match mine.

Except she's seven-fucking-teen, and there is no place for pleasure or even more than the vaguest curiosity between her and me.

I drop her hand abruptly, breaking the electric link.

"Nice meeting you, Lennix Moon."

Our stare holds an extra second. I dropped her hand, broke that connection, but it doesn't seem to matter. There is still something linking us. She seems to know it, to feel it, too, because even with the cop waiting at the open cell door, even with her father out front presumably ready to ground her, she's still standing here looking at me, a question mark hanging in the charged air.

"Lennix, your *daddy's* waiting." It's the guy who was talking with us earlier. He's glaring a narrow-eyed warning my way.

I drop my glance to the holding cell's dirty cement floor.

"Oh, yeah," Lennix says and clears her throat. "Guess I better go. I'll, uh, see you later, Mr. Paul."

I don't look up again but watch from beneath lowered lids as her moccasins take her out of the cell and away. It feels like I missed something or never had something that I'm sure would have been good. I know it's unreasonable because I met her no more than an hour ago. We've had one conversation. Some people leave an impression. Lennix Moon Hunter has left more than an impression. She's left her mark on me.

And it's shaped like a star.

"I'm prepared to forgive you."

These are the first words my father has spoken since he "collected" me from the police station in town. I'm glad the other protesters had all left by the time the officer came and called for "Cade." Even though I'll never see them again, I didn't want that name clinging to me like slime. When I climb into the back of the Escalade, my father sits with folded arms and a ticking jaw, his head turned away from me. His outrage fills the air-conditioned space. His fury and mine silently wrangle as we head toward the airfield.

I ignore his ridiculous opening line and swallow my irritation and indignation to respond. "Are you flying me back to Berkeley? I have shit to do."

The frosty look on his face cools even a few degrees more. It's his subzero face.

"What the hell were you thinking?" he demands, the anger he's checked roaring, snapping in my face with teeth. "Do you have any idea how much damage you could have done? What a black eye it would be for Cade Energy if anyone had realized who you were? That my own son protested *my* pipeline?"

"I agree with you there. I wouldn't want anyone to know I'm a Cade either."

"Boy, it's your damn future I'm protecting," he thunders, veins straining to get out through the skin of his neck.

"Taking away sacred land? Endangering a tribe's water supply? Stealing all over again from people who have been done wrong by this country at every turn? That's not my future, Dad. I don't want any part of it."

Hurt flashes through his glare, and for a moment I feel bad, but then I recall the stinging eyes of those in the cell with me. I see the dogs biting Mr. Paul. I touch the bite on my arm that was intended for Lennix. My father's hurt is a shallow, temporary thing compared to how they have and will continue to be wounded. His is mostly dislocated pride.

"Well, you won't have a part of it then, but there's nothing you can do to stop it."

"Do this, and I'll never work at Cade Energy."

"Are you threatening me?"

"I'm not threatening you, Dad. I'm saying if you go forward with this pipeline, there's no chance in hell I'll ever work with you."

He stiffens, his eyes slits of reptilian green.

"We didn't need you to build this company, and we won't need you to keep it. I'll be damned if you'll manipulate me into anything. You wouldn't know how to run a business if your life depended on it. That's the problem, you ungrateful welp. You've had the Cade name all your life. You don't have what it takes to make it without it."

"Oh, like Owen became a senator without using the Cade name? Give me a fucking break. He's your puppet. Your hand is so far up his ass, you have to wipe for him."

"You're jealous of your brother's success. That's pathetic, since you won't do what it takes to succeed yourself."

"I *am* doing what it takes to succeed. I have been. You just haven't cared because it's not your plan."

"You don't have a plan, boy," my father sneers. "What plan is that? Saving whales and Indians? Walk away from me, and we'll have something the Cade family has never had before." He fills his pause with deliberate cruelty. "A failure."

I let his words hurt. I let myself feel the full weight of his contempt and his disappointment. His eyes gleam darkly like volcanic glass. Even in defeat he looks simultaneously frigid and like he might drown you in hot lava at any second.

"I won't fail." My words carry no bravado, only confidence, because I have every intention of proving him wrong.

"You will," he counters with as much certainty. "You are unsalvageable."

Unsalvageable.

I should have known he'd find a word that went beyond disowned. Beyond disgraced. A word that would cut to my core character as if it was something he'd tried to save and failed miserably. And now there's no hope.

The car comes to a stop. Our fight has frosted the air. Tension coats the interior of the car. I'm surprised the windows haven't fogged.

We both exit our respective sides. The Cade jet idles on the tarmac, awaiting my father's bidding like every other subject in his kingdom.

He starts walking, stopping to turn when he realizes I'm not with him.

"Come on," he snaps. "I have more important things to do than indulge your temper tantrum."

"You have never paid one tuition bill," I say, not addressing his insulting words. "Never paid my rent or room and board. And you haven't even noticed."

The look on his face should bring me some satisfaction, but it only reiterates how little he cares about me as a person; he hasn't seriously concerned himself with the details of my life because I'm not where he wants me to be.

"Grams left me a little money that I received when I turned eighteen, if you remember," I say with a painful, wry smile. "Not much by your standards, but it lasts if you're careful. I've been on my own for years and doing better than fine."

"You wouldn't last a year without my name." His thin smile relishes the probability of my failure.

"You know what? I might fail. I might end up broke, but I'll be my own man. It'll be hard, but I'm determined to make a life for myself that has nothing to do with the Cade name."

And then I see it on his face, in his eyes. This is the moment that breaks us. It comes as suddenly as the gargantuan icebergs I've been studying. One moment, whole and solid, and the next, severed into two distinct walls of ice estranged from each other. That's what we are. Separate. Frozen.

"Say what you really mean, Maxim. It's not just the name or the company you want nothing to do with, is it?"

"I want nothing to do with *you*. You're not cutting me off, Dad," I tell him, slinging the words like stones catapulted over a wall. "I'm the one cutting you off."

I have no idea where we are. The airfield is in the middle of nowhere, but I turn away from my father and his private planes and corrupt kingdom and start on a path I can't even see in front of me. I don't exactly know how I'll do it, but I'll prove him wrong, and all while leading a life free of him and his expectations and his constant disapproval.

I walk away, and I don't look back.

CHAPTER 4
LENNIX

DEFEAT AND DUST MINGLE IN THE CLEAR MORNING AIR. WE gather on a cliff overlooking the sacred ground we fought so hard to keep and watch helplessly as the bulldozer's sharp, jagged teeth devour the earth. The trucks plow a careless path over our memories and sift through our holy soil like a conquering soldier pillaging the pockets of the fallen.

This battle is over. The field, lost.

Mena clutches my hand, tears streaking her cheeks. She has been there for me since she stood as godmother at my Sunrise Dance. She wiped away the sweat when I thought I'd die from dancing, from kneeling, from running those four days. She reassured me through every grueling hour. And when we realized Mama was gone, was never coming back, she held me, wiped my tears, and shed her own for her best friend. It wasn't always easy for my father raising a teenage girl alone, especially one with a cultural history as complex as mine. I had to navigate his world but also be a part of my mother's. The community embraced me fully even after Mama was gone and I was attending the private school miles away from the reservation. And this woman, her best friend and my auntie, has been my greatest guide.

Mr. Paul bows his head, shoulders slumped and despondent. Dozens from the reservation and many of the Apache who live in town like I do have come to witness one more desecration. One more broken promise.

"Senator Middleton should be ashamed of himself," my father mutters, his gray eyes as pained as if this were his land, too. "We can only hope the voters make him pay at the polls next year."

"They won't," Mr. Paul says. "The politicians, the corporations, the government—they take and take and take. They promise and they lie and they trick and betray, but they never pay for crimes against us. We never get our due."

"How ironic that the pipeline is here," my father says. "So close to Apache Leap."

I imagine those brave Apache warriors, with the U.S. Cavalry and certain defeat before them and certain death behind. They chose death over surrender, leaping over the cliff's edge and into the next life.

"How much has really changed?" I ask, cynicism clogging my throat. "Death, defeat, sickness, poverty. These are the choices they always offer us like they're doing us a favor."

"What gives them the right?" Mena asks. "I danced here. I ran and sang and became a woman here." She turns liquid, dark eyes to me. "So did you, Lenn."

I can't even manage a nod. I'm numb. She's right. If I close my eyes, I can still see the bonfire flames licking bright orange into the darkness, ringed by friends and family, singing, dancing, celebrating. Mama stood by, her face wet with emotion, her eyes bright with pride.

In me.

"My crowns," I whisper, sudden realization bringing fresh tears to my eyes.

"Oh, honey," my father sighs, pulling my head down to his shoulder. "I'm sorry."

At the end of the Sunrise Dance, young women receive the crowns worn by the Mountain Spirit dancers. The elaborate headdresses are decorated beautifully, painted with symbols representing the visions seen by the medicine man. Sacred, they can only be used once and are then hidden. Mine are secreted in the hills surrounding this cursed pipeline slithering through our valley like a serpent, every sound from the heavy machinery below a hiss and a strike.

Injustice never rests, and neither will I.

My mother's words float to me on an arid desert breeze. It feels like we never win, but my mother never gave up. I don't know how she died, but I do know how she *lived.* She would have fought until the end. And so will I. I'll learn to work the very systems set up against us.

Some of the women start singing one of the old songs. The Apache words, the sound—it's mournful like a dirge. Their voices rise and fall, cresting and crumpling with sorrow. We stand by like pallbearers watching the land flattened and hollowed and filled with tubing. I'll never forget this feeling but will call on it when I'm weary in the fight. No, I'll never forget this feeling.

And I'll never forgive Warren Cade.

PART 2

"What you get by achieving your goals is not as important as what you become by achieving your goals."
—Henry David Thoreau

CHAPTER 5
LENNIX

FOUR YEARS LATER

"So have you decided what you'll do after graduation?" Mena asks.

The question may as well be a pebble she tosses into the river we sit beside. It ripples through the doubts puddled in my chest. My time in Arizona State's College of Public Service and Community Solutions has been amazing, but now the real world awaits. And it's broken and hurting and a landscape wrought with so much injustice, I'm not sure where to start.

"I'm still deciding." I stretch my bare legs out in front of me on the riverbank's dry patch of grassy land.

"What are your options?" she asks.

"Hmm, options. Maybe that's the problem. I have too many of them."

"Tell me."

"I've been accepted into Arizona State's master's program." I push the heavy rope of my hair back over my shoulder. I haven't cut it in forever. "I've been offered the Bennett Fellowship, which would be awesome and require me to serve in a designated area of community service for a year. Or I have an offer from this big lobbying firm in DC."

Mena whistles and sends me a wide grin. "Well, look at you. Those are all great options."

"Yeah, but I graduate in a few months, and I'm still figuring out which is the right one. Nothing feels like *it*."

I'm like this river, twisting through Arizona's hills and forking along the way, each tributary leading somewhere different, directing the flow of water in a new direction. You can't take them all at once. Not for the first time, I recall running to the four directions when I was thirteen, gathering the elements into myself. *Which way should I go?*

"Maybe it will become clear while you're away," Mena offers.

"Somehow, I don't think Viv and Kimba have meditative pursuits planned for spring break," I chuckle, plucking at the sun-fried grass.

"Amsterdam, huh? That should be fun."

"Yeah, Vivienne's best friend Aya goes to college over there. She's half Dutch and has promised to show us everything."

"You're so lucky. Make the most of your time there." She gives me a teasing look. "And maybe finally find a man."

"Auntie!" I fake a scandalized tone and expression. Mena has never been shy about her love of a fine man. "Well, I never."

"Exactly. You've never," Mena says, her chuckle knowing and throaty. "And, girl, you have no idea what you're missing."

I'm picky. I know that. My bar is high, and I haven't found a man I wanted to take that final step with, to give my body to. I dated a few guys in college, had a good time, and even experienced real passion. But when it came down to it, I just didn't want to be with any of them that way. I've taken the elements into my body. The first time I take a *man* into my body, I want it to mean something to me.

"I'm not judging you or anyone else," I tell Mena. "Believe me. I know I'm in the virgin minority, but I'm just not that pressed. When it happens, it'll happen, and I think I'll know who that first time should be with."

"I'm not rushing you, honey. I see too many girls down at the reservation clinic pregnant and stuck with a baby before they're ready. I say anything you're not ready for, just wait. That includes sex." She slides me a wicked grin. "But, oh, when you find the man worthy to crack that code."

"I'm not a safe, Auntie," I protest with a short laugh.

"I think you are." Her eyes and mouth sober. "I also think something kind of froze in you when your mama disappeared. I wish you'd kept seeing that therapist. I told Rand one session wasn't nearly enough."

My good humor slips, too, but I force a grin, hoping to restore it. "I have a ten-year plan, and the therapist doesn't happen until around year eight."

"You'll have to let yourself feel again, Lennix. I see it, you know? That reserve you have with everyone. That guard that locks into place when you feel anyone you could care about getting too close."

She's right. Something inside me did flounder, fall when Mama never came home. That hurt is a dull ache I'm not sure will ever go away. Better not tempt fate to do that to me again. My father? Well, it's too late to block him out. And if the Sunrise Dance hadn't tied us together inextricably, the past eight years when Mena has surrogated for my mother time and time again would have. I have my best friends I made at college, Vivienne and Kimba, but that's about it. Anyone beyond them stands outside a closed circle. I think again, as I do unreasonably often, of the man I only knew by his first name, Maxim. Something about him stormed through my defenses right away even though I was too young for anything with him.

"Lennix," Mena says and snaps her fingers in my face. "You hear me talking to you, girl?"

"Sorry, Auntie." I pass a hand over my eyes, blinking away the image of a young, handsome man who'd traveled far to protest with us. With my tribe but, ultimately, with me. He took a dog bite that was intended for me, and as I think of it, I don't know if I ever properly thanked him. "I was daydreaming, I guess. What'd you say?"

"I said let's do what we came here for, to clear your mind and set your heart." She nods to the river.

The sun may be warm, but that river is freezing. It wouldn't be the first time its rushing frigidity set me to rights and cleared my head.

"Let's do it." I stand and strip away my denim cutoff shorts and peel the tank top over my head to reveal my one-piece bathing suit.

Aunt Mena does the same until she wears only a black sports bra and boy-leg underwear. She was a little older than my mother, but they had been friends since they were girls. She's still relatively young, barely over forty, and in great shape from the yoga she does outdoors every day. Makes me wonder what Mama would be like if she were still here.

"Ready?" Mena asks, brows raised.

"Ready."

With careful steps, we make our way down the bank toward the river. We wade in until the water laps at our thighs, shockingly cold. Mena holds a tiny bag, which she tips over her hand until pollen, like powdery sunshine, spills into her palm. I'll never forget the medicine man sprinkling me with sacred pollen from the cattails. I feel just as reverent as Mena dusts it over my face now. I close my eyes, letting it flutter over my cheeks and eyelashes as if each particle holds healing restorative power. And maybe it does.

"It's not science or magic," Mena whispers to me. "It is hope. It is faith that connecting with the land, with *our* land, will tell the universe, tell the Creator, that we have been blessed and are ready for what is ahead. Now, dip to wash it away. Not just the pollen, but all the things that cloud your mind and blur your vision."

She points to the river. I hold a bracing breath against the cold I know waits for me and sink into the water. It closes over my head, insulates me for just a few seconds, and I feel it all. I feel the loneliness, the fear, the uncertainty about my future. The river swallows me whole and then spews me out, making me gasp and swipe hair from my face.

"You feel more clear?" Mena asks, her tone and eyes searching my face, coated with droplets of water.

"I don't know about clear," I say, smiling and letting the sun kiss my face. "But I'm ready."

CHAPTER 6
LENNIX

"So you made it?"

The concern threading my father's voice kicks in my instinct to reassure him. He needs lots of reassuring. Ever since Mama disappeared, he worries constantly.

I get it. He's a professor of Native American Studies. He knows the statistics. Four in five American Indian women have experienced violence, and more than one in two have experienced sexual violence. Even knowing the facts, he never expected them to hit so close to home. He and my mother never married and didn't always see eye to eye on how I should be raised, but I know he never stopped caring for her and was devastated when she disappeared.

"We made it, yeah." I lean against the wall outside our hostel room. "I'm fine. The hostel's great. Amsterdam's beautiful."

"Please be careful, Lenn. Three pretty young girls in a foreign country—you could be snatched off a corner in broad daylight. You know not to drink anything you're not sure of. God, not to mention sex trafficking."

I've heard his concern veer into panic before, so I stop him before it goes there. "Dad, did you watch *Taken* again?"

His guilty silence provides my answer.

"No one is going to snatch me off a corner or traffic me or sell my virginity to the highest bidder."

"Could we not discuss your virginity? I'm not prepared for this."

"I'm twenty-one, and believe me, my father is the last person I want to discuss my sex life with, too." *Nonexistent though it is…*

"Could you also avoid using the word 'sex' in the same sentence as…well, you?" he asks. "Men are pigs. I've told you this, right?"

"Um, on more than one occasion. I believe you once called your species the scourge of the earth and told me they were basically petri dishes with bad intentions."

"I stand by that assessment."

"Yeah, well, you'll be happy to know I'm not even in the lab, so to speak. Maybe I'm asexual? Or broken? I just don't ever meet guys who seem worth my time, ya know?"

"When I asked you not to use the word 'sex' in the same sentence as you, that included 'asexual.' But, baby, you're not broken. You're… discriminating. In the good, picky way, not in the systemic racist way."

"Yeah, I figured."

"All jokes aside," he says, his voice dropping, sobering, "someone will feel more special than the rest."

I want to ask if Mama felt more special to him than the rest. I want to ask if he ever cries for her, like I still do. Does grief hit him in the most unexpected times and hang over the day until he wants to crawl back in bed and sleep so he won't remember she's gone and never coming back? Does she come to him in his dreams?

Or is that just me?

They weren't together for years before she died, and it makes me wonder if I'm the only person on Earth still hurting this way for her. If her memory only lives in my heart like a knife lodged between my ribs. Grief is its own kind of intimacy, a bond of sorts between you and the one you lost. No one else feels it the way you do about that person you loved most. And maybe it helps to know someone reaches that same level of despair. That's what family is for, right?

I wish I could go back to the night of my Sunrise Dance and beg her not to go to that protest. Ask her, just this once, to let someone else fight the world's problems because I needed her more than everyone else did.

"Lenn, you still there?"

I shake off the helplessness of done deals and irreversible things and straighten from the wall. "Yeah, I'm here. Sorry. Time difference has me out of it. I just wanted to let you know I got here safely."

"Thank you for that."

"I'm sure you have a stack of papers waiting to be graded, so I'll let you go. You need a social life, old man."

"You're right," he says, his voice lightening. "So you'll be happy to hear I might be getting one. I have a date tonight."

I frown and blink and lick my lips and tug on my ear. Apparently the thought of my father on a date makes me fidgety. "A-a date? Wow. Good. Good for you."

"Yeah?" he asks with unexpected tentativeness.

I think of my father as I usually see him. Distracted in that way academicians often are, lost in a pile of papers he's grading or books he's reading or something he's researching. His gray eyes always half-hazed with whatever task I interrupted. He deserves more than that.

"Yeah, I'm happy for you, Dad. Do I know her?"

He goes on to tell me her name is Bethany. She's an English professor who started a few months ago. They've had coffee but are grabbing dinner tonight. Hearing him excited about something other than his work lifts my heart a little. I find myself smiling as we disconnect.

"I miss you, too." Vivienne, my best friend number one, is clutching her phone and wiping a tear away when I enter the hostel room we're sharing. "I keep telling myself it's only a week, but my heart won't listen."

I catch the eyes of my best friend number two, Kimba, who gives me her famous *can you believe this shit* look.

Vivienne glances at us a little self-consciously, turns her back, and lowers her voice.

"Sorry, I should have told you. I took the pillowcase," she says in a sad whisper. "Because it smelled like you."

"Jesus, keep me near the cross," Kimba mutters, rolling her eyes and raising her voice. "Bitch, get off that phone. Stephen, she'll be fine. We'll make sure she doesn't screw anyone before the wedding."

I snort, but over her shoulder, Vivienne's eyes are wide and horrified and filled with poison.

"Sorry," Kimba hisses with unrepentant humor.

"I have to go, Stephen," Vivienne says. "The girls need help settling in."

As soon as she hangs up, she grabs a pillow from a nearby couch and puts it over Kimba's face where she lies on the bottom bunk.

"You're smothering me," Kimba's muffled voice, mixed with laughter, comes from under the pillow.

"That's the point." Vivienne chuckles and lifts the pillow. "Were you *trying* to get me un-engaged?"

"It would take a stick of dynamite to blast you and Stephen apart," I tell her, climbing the short ladder to my upper bunk on the opposite side. "I'm not sure he'll make it this one week without you."

"It's gonna be tough," Vivienne says, completely serious, which sets my and Kimba's eyes to rolling again. "What? It's our first time apart since the engagement."

"I get it," Kimba says and then shakes her head and mouths, *I don't get it.*

"I mean, it's a week." I try to keep the exasperation from my voice. "Surely you can last a week without him."

"Just wait'll you meet the one," Vivienne says. "And you'll see how it feels. Maybe even here in Amsterdam. Wouldn't that be romantic?"

"Until I figure out what I want to do with my life," I say dryly, "the great problem of 'the one' will have to wait, and I'm in no hurry."

"While I'm looking for the one of many," Kimba says. "Nothing that lasts beyond an orgasm. Maybe I'll find a big, blond Dutchman to woo me with his foreign tongue."

"Some tongue." Vivienne laughs. "And some abs, chest, arms, dick."

"Oh, for sure some dick." Kimba high-fives Vivienne and peers up at me from the bottom bunk in our tiny but cozy hostel room. "Come on, Lenn. You planning to get you some while we're here?"

"Oh, yeah." I turn over onto my stomach. "Because I'm most likely to rando hook up. I doubt very seriously I'll be surrendering the V-card to some stranger in Amsterdam. I've held on to it this long; that would be a waste."

"Already a waste, if you ask me," Viv says. She climbs the ladder to her top bunk but stops midway, propping her butt against a rung. "I know you've been tempted."

"Of course I have." I shrug. "But it passes, and I always see something I don't like, don't trust, or can't tolerate. I'll know when it's the right time, the right guy. I literally just had this conversation with my father."

"You and your dad," Vivienne says, shaking her head and grinning. "How is the professor?"

"Better now he's heard my voice and knows I haven't been sex trafficked yet."

"Ugh," Kimba groans from the lower bunk. "Did he watch *Taken* again?"

"I know. I told him to stop. Anyway, he assures me that I'm probably not asexual."

"Was that a serious thought?" Vivienne asks. "I mean, it'd be okay if you were, but you've had boyfriends and seemed to like all the pregame activities. I bet you'll like dick once you get some."

"I'm just not a dick-for-the-sake-of-dick girl, I don't think." I bury my head in the cool pillow and breathe in clean linen. "I trust myself to know when and who."

I've never been ashamed of my virginity; I've never avoided discussing it if people asked either. Both my parents taught me to know what I believe, to articulate it first *to myself* and then to others. If it's any of their damn business, that is, which in most cases, it's not. But nothing is off-limits between me and these two girls.

"You're in no hurry," Kimba says from down below, "because you haven't had it. Once you do…whew, child. Hard to go without."

I've never liked the idea of my body making decisions my head and my heart don't cosign. I've seen both of my friends crying, depressed, or dejected after some man disappointed them. No dick is worth that.

"Hmm-mm," Kimba breaks the sound into two syllables and bites her bottom lip. "One taste, one *good* taste, and you'll be hooked."

"God, there's nothing like really good sex," Viv groans, closing her eyes and tipping her head back. "Even going a week without Stephen…ugh."

"A week?" Kimba scoffs. "Try months. I'm in a drought, but I've read the weather forecast, and it's raining in Amsterdam, honey!"

The three of us laugh and shift into planning for tomorrow. We have a week in one of the most beautiful cities in the world, and we want to take full advantage of it.

"So I know we're all a little jet-lagged," Viv says, her voice drowsy, "but will you be refreshed enough after a power nap to go out?"

"Sure." I yawn and tuck my arm under the pillow. "A few winks and we'll be ready."

"Good," Viv mumbles. "Aya says we'll start off nice and slow tonight. Just hit a brown bar, eat, drink. Maybe you'll pick up something nice and blond to bring home, Kimba."

"Fingers crossed," Kimba says. "Legs open."

"Oh, my god," Viv groans. "Hussy. We need to establish mating rules. You better not be fucking some huge Norseman in the bunk below."

Our drowsy chuckles intermingle and fade.

"We'll work out a system," Viv says. "Well, for you, Kimba. Ms. I'm Waiting for Mr. Right Dick over there won't need a system."

I'm used to the teasing, but is it so wrong to wait until it feels right? To wait until you feel like you've met someone you want to share your body with?

My mind wanders back to my Sunrise Dance. The whole ceremony leads to that point when the spirit of Changing Woman supposedly inhabits you, even just briefly. For a slice of time, you take something holy into your body, and it changes you forever. I'm not saying sex will be holy, but the first time I share my body with someone, it will be special.

And I think it might change me forever.

CHAPTER 7
MAXIM

I NEED NEW FRIENDS.

The three with me tonight don't make the best companions.

"Fuck," Hans mutters into his beer. "I'd do all four of those at the bar."

"Oh, yeah." David Barnes, whom I know best of the trio, agrees, assessing the four women in question. "At the same time, if they'd all have me."

"I think you overestimate your stamina," I tell him, sipping my beer. "And your appeal."

David snorts and sends me a sidelong glance tinted with the good-natured humor I've appreciated so much over the past four years. We both just successfully defended our dissertations, and for the first time in what seems like forever, I'm not a student.

"You have to admit, those four are lookers," Oliver says. As British as they come, before starting his master's at Utrecht University where we all met, he attended Oxford. He was Eton educated before that. Parents of the peerage. There's a seat in the House of Lords waiting for him one day. Not that he's interested in politics, but his parents hold the purse strings and, thus, sway over his life.

Not me. I've cut all the familial strings. Apron strings. Purse strings. Heartstrings. I've only seen my mother and brother a handful of times in the past four years and my father not at all. I took for granted what they meant to me—the place they occupied in my life, even though I saw them infrequently.

"The blond is hot," Oliver says. "Wonder if she's actually Dutch? Can you believe I've been in this country for four years and have never fucked someone actually from the Netherlands? I have to before we leave next week."

Next week.

It took some finagling, several glowing letters of recommendation, and a ton of personal training to physically prepare, but I'm leaving next week to winter over in Antarctica. I secured a spot on one of the few wintertime research expeditions. Not what most guys my age are clamoring to do when they finally finish school, but Cades have never been most guys. In this, I'm no exception.

"The black girl is gorgeous," David says, smacking his lips like he's famished. "She stood up a minute ago, and her ass is like an eighth wonder. Dibs on that one."

We all chuckle, and Hans clinks his beer glass to David's.

"What say you, Kingsman?" Hans asks, his Dutch lilt more pronounced with each round of drinks. "Which one are you trying your luck with?"

Sometimes, I still don't answer right away when someone calls me by "Kingsman." It's not a lie. It's at least my middle name. All the men of my family share that middle name. Somehow, one of my ancestors a few generations ago got it in his head that we descended from Welsh princes. They immigrated to America as miners and gravitated to the West with the gold rush. They got lucky. Struck gold in California and then lucky again with "black gold" later in Texas. Texas kings, they started calling themselves, and the middle name was born.

"I'm looking for all the king's men," my mother would yell, her playful voice carrying across the shiny hardwood floors and up the stairs of our Dallas home when she chased Owen and me for hide-and-seek.

A familiar ache settles in my chest. I haven't seen my mother in a year. David invited me to spend Christmas with his family, and the summer before I stayed here in Holland for studies. I'm in a strange land, a sojourner with no home and no family. At least, not one that claims me any longer. That house where my brother and I played is no longer mine. Hell, even the name isn't. No one has called me by Cade in four years. I've made a completely separate life for myself in another world, and if the Atlantic didn't separate me from Warren Cade, our last fight did.

With my back and elbows propped against the lip of the bar, I take a draw of my beer, promising myself Maker's Mark on the next round.

"For God's sake, Kingsman." Oliver laughs. "Stop counting the hairs on your arse and choose your pretty poison. Which girl will it be?"

"I haven't even looked," I admit.

"Aw, come on," Hans says. "We need you to choose the one you want because we all know you'll have your pick. They all go for you. Surprised that dick of yours hasn't fallen off."

Not exactly accurate, but the Dutch women *have* been good to me. I turn on my stool so I can see to the other side of the bar. The four women seem to be having a great time without us, laughing, clinking glasses, and yelling *proost* every few seconds. I see the blond, David's pretty brown-skinned girl, and a cute brunette, but it's the one with hair so dark it's black under the lights that snares my attention. A dramatic slant of cheekbone, thick black brows, straight, bold nose. Her face is a collection of features that dare you to look away.

There's something…familiar about her. I don't know her because I'd never forget a woman who looked like this. But it's more than how familiar she looks to me—it's the way I *feel* when I look at her that is familiar. I scour my memory for anything that would tease it out, and then she laughs at something one of her friends says. She tips her head back so that river of hair falls behind her, and her laughter—warm, rich, throaty—grabs me from across the room.

And I know. Hell, I'd know her anywhere.

She's older. Four years older to be exact, but she looks much the same, and her laugh captivates me exactly as it did in that holding cell. For the first time in years, the thrill of the chase rears. The promise of catching drags me to my feet.

"The one with the black hair," I say, not waiting for my friends but taking the first step toward an old temptation that is no longer off-limits. "That one's mine."

CHAPTER 8
LENNIX

"Oh, dear Lord." Kimba slides the words from the corner of her mouth, her stare fixed over my shoulder. "Don't look now, ladies, but there is a fine pack of wolves headed right for us."

I don't even bother looking up from my glass.

"What did you say this drink is called, Aya?" I ask, inspecting the amber liquid.

"It's *jenever*," Vivienne's friend answers, her blue eyes bright and her skin flushed, pale hair falling around her pretty face. "Like Dutch gin."

I take a cautious sip and grimace. Never a fan of gin, I wonder if I should have just ordered one of the tap beers.

"It's good, no?" Aya asks, her smile hopeful.

No.

I don't say it because I don't want to insult her or any aspect of her country, which really is beautiful, within an hour of us meeting each other.

"I could get used to it," I settle on saying aloud.

"Seriously," Kimba squeals and turns to face me, her eyes wide with excitement. "These hot guys are coming over."

"No one's that hot. Geez." I laugh and take another sip of my drink, which tastes better the second time around. I lift my glass for another sip, but a dark rumble of a voice freezes my glass halfway to my mouth.

"Lennix Moon Hunter."

I glance up and literally almost drop my glass. Like, I have to catch it with my other hand.

If you'd asked who was the very last person I'd expect to see in Amsterdam or ever again, my answer would have been…

"Maxim?" My voice squeaks like it needs WD-40.

"So you do remember," he says, his smile so wide and white I'm dazzled.

"Of-of course. How could I forget?"

To my seventeen-year-old eyes, he was handsome. The most handsome guy I'd ever seen, but now? *Oh, my damn.*

Now, he's devastating. Bigger. Like everything was carefully tended over the past four years—watered and given the perfect amount of sunlight. His dark hair is slightly longer. Dark, but with those russet strands woven throughout. His face is leaner, the bones and angles modeled into something even bolder than before. Those precious-metal eyes gleam green in the dim light of the bar. And his body? Before he was lean and almost rangy, but no more. His biceps stretch a little at the sleeves, and his shirt pulls taut over the muscles of his chest. He's filled out considerably in the past four years.

Beyond his physical appearance, there's something else different about him. Something beneath the skin. A deeper confidence? Self-assurance? I can't put my finger on it, but several women around us are watching him like they want to put *their* fingers all over it.

"Aren't you going to introduce us to your friend, Lennix?" Vivienne asks, pointed and curious.

"Oh, yeah. Sorry. Vivienne, Aya, and Kimba, this is Maxim…" I falter and laugh up at him. "I just realized I never knew your last name."

"Oh, Kingsman," he says, spreading his smile to my friends.

"Maxim Kingsman. Nice to meet you, ladies. And these guys are David, Oliver, and Hans."

We all exchange smiles and pleasantries and move our newly formed party to a large booth at the back. The brown bar lives up to its name. The paneling, the floors, the bar—all brown. The walls are studded with stained glass, and kitschy signs introduce lighthearted-ness into the somber decor. It's warm and perfect for hanging out and laughing with a group of friends. Or in our case, a horny group of people who barely know each other. I'm too focused on the man I've dreamed about since I was seventeen sitting at a table with me in Amsterdam, of all places, to pay the others much mind.

"What are the odds, huh?" Maxim asks after we're all settled and have fresh drinks and bar food.

"I know, right? I can't believe you're here." That sounds so wistful, like I've been some damsel waiting for her prince. "I mean, that we'd run into each other like this."

"Yeah, crazy. We have a lot of catching up to do."

"Well," I say, lowering my eyes to the drink in front of me, "I wish I could say our efforts that day paid off. Not sure if you heard— Cade Energy won and built that pipeline."

"I'm sorry, Lennix." When I glance up, the sad resignation in his eyes feels so sincere, it makes me smile despite the pang in my chest every time I remember those bulldozers scraping up and destroying our land.

"It's okay. Not your fault. It would have taken a miracle, and they're hard to come by with the government, corrupt politicians, and that bastard Warren Cade against you."

"Yeah, I guess so." He clears his throat and shifts in his seat, a frown bending his thick brows.

"Hey, sorry. I don't mean to sound cynical, but it was just tough. We've been lied to and tricked so much. I shouldn't be surprised, but it still hurts."

"I understand." He nods, looking down into his glass, too. "Well,

I guess I can't ever really understand, but I sympathize, and I hate that it has been what it has and that it keeps being that so much."

It was said perfectly, his sincere wish that things had been and could be different. It wasn't condescending or defensive or any of the things people say when they aren't sure what to do about pain they didn't cause but feel connected to.

"Yeah, it all sucks, but what are you gonna do, right?"

"What *are* you going to do?" he asks. "What *have* you been doing?"

We grin at each other like we've won the lottery and are splitting the ticket right down the middle. What fortune. What luck to have found each other again. This time, there's no cell full of protestors. No watchful Mr. Paul. No prostitute.

"Oh my God, remember the lady who offered to blow you with Pop Rocks?" I ask, suddenly transported back to that strange night. Every second burned itself in my memory.

"Jesus." His low-rumbled laughter coats my shoulders and arms with goose bumps. "That was awkward. I was hoping you'd forgotten that part."

"I never forgot any part," I say before I can stop myself.

Like we're tied together, our smiles dissolve simultaneously, and something intense swallows the humor in his eyes. The air turns humid, heavy with possibility. There was energy between us years ago, but it was all potential energy. My age, the circumstances—things could only go so far. This energy, though—it's kinetic. Already in motion. Now things between us can go as far as we want.

"What are you two crazy kids up to in a corner by yourselves?" Vivienne asks.

"We're just catching up," I offer with a small smile.

"Now how did you say you know each other?" Oliver asks.

"I was part of a protest Lennix's tribe organized when a company planned to lay a gas pipeline," Maxim answers.

"What?" Kimba interjects, tearing her attention away from David, who is obviously into her. "When was this?"

"My senior year in high school."

Maxim and I share a loaded look at my words. I'm not in high school anymore. The knowledge sits between us unspoken, but I know for sure he feels it, too. The tight space brims with it.

"Lennix was incredible," Maxim says for everyone to hear, but his eyes are for only me. "I couldn't believe she was just seventeen. She had that crowd eating from her hand."

"You spoke?" Aya asks, her voice laced with disbelief. "I hate public speaking."

"She was brilliant." Maxim chuckles and takes a quick sip of the whiskey he ordered. "And then we got arrested."

"Arrested?" Hans asks, delighted incredulity all over his distinctly Dutch features.

"Yup." I nod and laugh. "We got tossed in the slammer, and you got bitten by a dog."

"You got sprayed with tear gas."

"*You* got propositioned."

"By the wrong girl," Maxim says softly, his eyes resting on me like a flame set to low. "But you were too young for me anyway. *Then*."

All the banked heat and want that we couldn't acknowledge before is unabashed in the look he gives me now. A silence falls on the table, punctuated with a few cleared throats and a giggle or two. We don't care. We don't look away. I have no frame of reference for the fluttering in my belly. For the tightening of my nipples. For the way I'm wet between my legs just because his thigh keeps brushing mine under the table. Just because he smells clean and masculine and fresh. Just because this close, I see the dark starburst at the center of his clear green eyes.

"Yes, well," Vivienne says, tossing back her drink and gulping it all down at once, "it's getting late, and we're all tuckered out from jet lag. What do you say we call it a night, ladies?"

David and Kimba exchange numbers while everyone settles their tab and prepares to leave.

"Are you tired?" Maxim asks.

"No," I answer quickly. "Not at all."

"Where are you staying?"

I give him the name of the hostel, and he nods.

"I know where that is. I could walk you back if you want to stay and talk some more?"

"Hey, I'm gonna stay for a bit," I tell my friends.

"What?" Vivienne and Kimba ask in unison, the same cautious look on both their faces.

"We just want to catch up some more," Maxim offers, his voice pitched to *I promise I'm harmless and won't hurt your friend.* "I'll walk her home as soon as we're done."

"Sounds good," Kimba says, eyeing him closely like she's memorizing his face, which she probably is. "Okay."

She bends to kiss my cheek and whispers in my ear, "Girl, get you some. If you say *this one* isn't right, your ass is mine. That V-card? You better play it!"

We chuckle, and I glance over her shoulder to find Maxim watching me with single-minded intent.

"I'll see you when I get home," I whisper back, not confirming, but I acknowledge at least to myself that meeting Maxim again feels like destiny; like fate set us up. I'd be a fool to ignore it, and for the first time, I think the V-card might actually come into play.

CHAPTER 9
MAXIM

GOD, I THOUGHT THEY'D NEVER LEAVE. OUR FRIENDS SPILL into the street, leaving the faintest echo of their laughter and conversation behind. I can tell David's into Kimba. I wish him luck, but I'm too preoccupied with a second chance I never thought I'd get. Can it be called a second chance when there was never a chance before?

I'm still, on some level, processing that the girl I was so drawn to four years ago is this even-more-beautiful-than-before woman here in Amsterdam, in my favorite brown bar, watching me with the same kind of stunned excitement buzzing through my body.

"Your friends are nice," Lennix says, popping a triangle of gouda into her mouth.

"They're not." I laugh. "But they were on their best behavior tonight. They can fake it when pretty girls are involved."

"The night definitely took a turn when you guys came around." She smiles, pushing a chunk of straight black hair behind her ear. "It's spring break and they're looking for hookups, so your friends might get lucky. Well, not with Viv."

"I hope not with you. I was kind of hoping I'd have you all to myself."

She doesn't laugh. Or smile even. She looks up from the cheese board and levels an intense stare at me.

"Is that what you want?" she asks, her voice more casual than her eyes. "A hookup?"

If she's asking if I want to fuck her, then of course. If she's asking if that's all it would be…who knows? Nothing ever felt typical where this girl was concerned. Not the way we met. Not the things I learned about her. Not the way her image, her voice, that throaty laugh would revisit me in the middle of a lecture or even while I was kissing someone else.

"I want to get to know you," I tell her, answering and not answering as honestly as I can. "Tell me what's been happening with you the past few years."

"Yes, well, let's see. I was, as predicted, grounded until graduation." We share a quick glance and a chuckle.

"I'm not surprised," I say. "I wouldn't want my seventeen-year-old daughter getting bitten by dogs and tear gassed and stuck in a holding cell with a bunch of grown men and prostitutes."

"I didn't get bitten by a dog." She surprises me, reaching out to push up my sleeve and touch the scar on my forearm. "You did."

Her fingers on my skin make my breath shorten and my body harden. Really? One touch and I'm ready to blow?

"So from grounded to graduation." I stroke my fingertip over her thumb where it still rests on my forearm. I don't miss the quick catch of her breath, but I keep talking. "Then college?"

"Uh, yeah." She traces the labyrinthic pattern of my fingerprint. "Arizona State."

"Major?"

"Public service and public policy with a concentration in American Indian studies."

"Cool." I squeeze the hand still resting on my arm. "What do you want to do?"

"That's the million-dollar question. Maybe get my master's. I've been offered a pretty prestigious fellowship, which would require I serve in some field-related area for a year, or I have a great job offer from a firm in DC."

"What kind of firm?"

"A lobbying firm. For some reason, I think I may end up in politics." She eyes me closely. "I remember you went to Berkeley. That was…undergrad?"

"Undergrad and my master's. I just finished my PhD in climate science."

"Wow. So *Doctor* Kingsman. I would never have guessed."

"What would you have guessed?"

She squints one eye and hums, considering. "Business maybe?"

"I double majored in business and energy resources engineering at Berkeley, so you're not far off there."

"Why those fields?"

"Just seemed smart to have a business background." I don't add that my family's company has been a *Forbes* lister for decades.

"And the energy resources?" she asks. "How'd you come to that?"

"I'm fascinated by the climate. How we can reverse all the crap we're doing to ruin this planet. Most importantly, how America can become less dependent on fossil fuels. Our leaders are so damn shortsighted, leaning on oil and gas as much as we do. It's not sustainable."

"Is that why you were there protesting the pipeline?"

"Yeah, something like that." I rush on before she can probe any further. "So still figuring out what you want to do with the degree, huh?"

"I know I want to change the world. I'm just not sure how yet."

I've never heard anyone more confident saying they don't know something. She says it like *she* is the question—like as soon as she determines her plan of action, the world will be putty in her hands to shape and mold into something better. I could laugh in her face, call her naive, but I don't because I feel the same way.

"I get that," I reply, linking my pinky finger with hers on the table. "Sometimes my goals and dreams feel too big. Like you really think you can convince a nation to change its ways? And the answer is always yes. I don't know how either, but yes." I force a chuckle, growing uncomfortable under her unwavering regard. "Is that arrogant? Presumptuous?"

"Yes, but I think revolution requires a certain degree of hubris."

"Who said that?" I ask, racking my brain for a reference for the quote.

"Oh, I did. Just now."

Well, impress the hell out of me.

She lifts her beer with the hand I'm not holding and yawns into the glass. "Sorry. I guess jet lag *is* starting to kick in."

I stand, pulling her to her feet, too. "Let's get you home, or at least your home away from home. Let's get you to your hostel."

When we step outside, crisp, cold air greets us on the street.

"It's much cooler than I thought it would be," Lennix says, chafing her bare arms. "Glad it's a short walk."

"Yeah, the weather here can be unpredictable and cool until it's not." I tug my leather jacket off and drape it around her shoulders.

"Oh, no." She starts to slide the jacket off, but I stop her.

"Look." I point to the long sleeve of my T-shirt. "I'll be fine for a few minutes."

She nods, reluctance and gratitude in her smile.

It's a straight shot to her hostel, but I take us down a side street to stretch out our time. That and it puts us along the Amstel River, a romantic promenade if ever there was one.

Moonlight refracts from the glassy water. The slightest breeze, the breath of night, lifts Lennix's hair, and I'm reminded how it seemed she commanded the very elements that day in the desert.

"You really were remarkable at that protest," I say, breaking the companionable silence we've been walking in.

"Huh?" She looks up at me, her leisurely stride never breaking. "What?"

"At the protest that day. You spoke with such conviction and passion."

"So many things were taken from us," she says, her voice hushed but strong. "They tried to strip our language, our land, our home, our family. Even our traditions."

I listen, wanting to hear her much more than I want to hear myself.

"To me, to many of us, activism is as holy as the ceremonies we almost lost because it connects us to the land and to our ancestors. It's how we join their fight. We take our place in the line of generations who will resist." A snort of cynical laughter escapes her. "Even when it seems like a lost cause."

"It's not." I grab her hand and tuck it into the crook of my elbow, shorten my steps to match hers. "Don't ever think that."

She glances up at me, searching my face before nodding, smiling.

"Why Amsterdam?" she asks, shifting the focus to me.

"Well, Europe is far ahead of us in clean energy. For whatever reason, Europeans are less resistant to the energy shifts we need. I came here to study the progress they're making. How the governments educate the populace and persuade them the changes are necessary. The Dutch are really forward-thinking, especially when it comes to wind."

"You're kinda smart, aren't you?" She grins and tightens her fingers on my arm. "PhD and all."

"I promise not to make you call me Doctor."

"I think I will, *Doc*." Her grin widens, and the humor is like a candle lit inside her, illuminating all the things I like most about her face. The pride in the jut of her chin. The strength to the set of her jaw. The kindness, intelligence, and curiosity in the metal/mettle silver eyes.

I break our stride, look down at her, and cup one side of her face in my hand. It's cool against the dry warmth of my palm.

"Ask me how many times I've thought about you since that protest." My voice scratches gruffly against the cool silk of the quiet night.

She stares up at me, and at first I think she'll wave off my question, pretend this is normal, what's happening between us. But she doesn't do that. She doesn't pretend or wave it off. She meets it head-on and answers with unflinching honesty.

"Maybe as many times as I've thought of you."

CHAPTER 10
LENNIX

MY FATHER WOULD LECTURE ME UNTIL HIS FACE TURNED BLUE.

He'd send the authorities searching for me.

A man I met only once before tonight, a stranger whose last name I just discovered an hour ago, has me alone on a nearly deserted street in a foreign country at three a.m.

It may not be wise, but I'll be damned if I would be anywhere else right now. Not safely tucked into my top bunk at the hostel knowing Maxim was out there wanting my company. We've been wooing each other with tiny touches and furtive brushes and lingering glances. I'm not sure how much longer I can stand it.

"So you thought of me, too, huh?" His grin is rakish on the handsome "somebody" face. There's a Kennedy vibe about him. Not just the dark, dappled hair or the tall, fit body or the confidence in his shoulders. It's his ideals and the iron will barely hidden beneath the casual manner. I'm not fooled. This man is not casual. He bleeds ambition. I wonder if he tries to hide it—to blend in with everyone else. It's laughable to think he could camouflage his driven nature and be something that he's not. Be domesticated when he is indeed, like Kimba said, a wolf.

"You're probably already too conceited for me to answer that." I grin back and start walking again.

"Tell me." He says it like he means it, grasping my arm gently and halting our steps again. "You thought of me?"

Words rise and fall in my throat. I could tell him that I didn't realize it until right now, but he was a bar no other guy ever cleared. That it had nothing to do with how handsome he was or his formidable body or dazzling smile. That the moment he stepped between me and that dog, something inside me recognized him as more than the rest.

I can't say any of that, so I answer with only a solemn nod. There's a wild flare in his eyes, like that ambition, that will I see tucked beneath his easy demeanor, roaring to life. He places a hand on either side of my face, his palms to my cheeks, and caresses the sides of my neck.

"Can I kiss you, Lennix?"

The question lights a fiery thread that binds us to one another, and it burns so strong, so hot, that words seem superfluous. How could he not know I want that, too? He has to know I hunger for this kiss, but I nod again.

He slowly backs us up a few feet to where the cobblestone street meets a wall. We're partially hidden in the shadow this building casts. There's stone at my back, the Amstel River glitters ahead, and Maxim's body is flush against mine. I feel every hardened ridge of him perfectly fitting to my body. His fingers slide into my hair. He looks down at me, and though his face is painted in shades of night, I see those gem eyes, gleaming bright and green, staring at my mouth.

He doesn't ask again if he can kiss me. He just does, bending to test the texture of my lips with one swipe of his tongue and then another, like I'm a lollipop he wants to know how many licks it takes to get to the center of. He probes at me, seeking something I want to give. I open and take him in completely, tasting that last glass of whiskey and him. God, *him.* I want to crawl down his throat. My hands climb his shoulders and rove into the thick hair falling around his nape, all while I tilt my head to get and give as much as possible.

If a kiss has a color, this one is the muted shades of the sky overhead, a ménage à trois of midnight and indigo and moonshine silver. If a kiss has a sound, this one is the concert of our breaths and sighs and moans. If a kiss has a taste, it tastes like this. Hunger flavored with yearning and spiced with desperation. With bites and growls and tender licks and soothing whimpers. Perfectly served portions of sweet and scorching.

One powerful thigh presses between mine, and I'm riding it before I realize my hips have taken up a rhythm of their own. He holds my head still as he plunders my mouth. He cups my breast, teasing the tip into a tight bud. I break the kiss to cry out, my back arching away from the wall to press deeper into his hand. My thighs straddle his as I rub myself against him over and over, seeking the abrasion of denim through the layers of my dress and panties.

"Shit, Nix." He rests his forehead against mine. "My place is just a few streets over. Come home with me."

Is this how it happens? My first time with a man? In a mad dash through cobblestone streets and a frantic push and pull of clothes and a head half-fogged by Dutch gin and jet lag?

I pant into his mouth, brushing my lips against his but pulling back when he would dive inside again to muddy my thoughts and steal my reason. I give him one last kiss, brief and hot, before disentangling myself from him. I leave him at the wall, his broad shoulders heaving with the force of his breath, of his passion. His face is shadowed by the moon hiding behind a cloud.

"Not, um…" I pull his jacket tighter around me. "Not tonight. Is that okay?"

"Yes." He pushes from the wall and is close in two strides. His hands are back on me in seconds, one at my hip and the other cupping my face. "Of course it's all right. I'm sorry. That was fast. Damn, I'm sorry."

"No, I wanted it, too. I… I want it, too."

He leans into a beam of moonlight, revealing his pleased smile.

Not smug or cocky. Just pleased that I want him, too. He kisses me again, but without the madness. With a sweet brush of lips and a gentle touch at the side of my mouth before pulling back to peer down at me.

"Let's get you home…or rather let's get you hostel."

We both grin at that, but there is still this niggling fear that maybe I've ruined something. Maybe I should have gone home with him.

"I'm glad you stopped," he says, and I wonder if I've worried aloud.

"You are?"

"I want us both clear-headed and alert and certain when it happens. I can't pretend I don't want it to happen, though. I do."

"I do, too." I huddle deeper into the *him* smell of his leather jacket and into the warmth of his body it still wraps me in. He shoots me a hot look, one that transports me back to the wall in the shadows with his hand teasing my nipple. Wordlessly, he takes my hand. It feels natural to twine our fingers and swing our joined hands between us just the slightest bit, making our own breeze in an otherwise still night.

We complete the short walk in silence and far too soon stand outside the hostel. I start sliding his jacket off, but he stops me again, clutching the lapels to pull me in for one final kiss.

"Tomorrow," he murmurs against my lips, licking into the corners and nipping at the center. "I'll get it back tomorrow."

It's all the promise I need.

CHAPTER 11
MAXIM

MY BROTHER'S NAME ON MY CELL ALWAYS TAKES ME BY SURPRISE. He calls so rarely that it jolts me, mostly because I always assume something must be catastrophically wrong for him to cross the picket line my father has drawn between us. Or maybe I drew it. After four years, it seems to matter less who drew the line. All that really matters is that I stand on this side of it alone.

"Owen," I answer on the third ring. "Hey."

"I wasn't sure you'd pick up." My brother's deep voice comes across the phone.

"Is Mom okay? Are you?" *Is Dad?*

I leave that last question unasked, but I dread the day when Owen calls to say our father is gone.

"Damn, Max, why does it have to be doom or gloom before I can talk to my little brother? Maybe I'm just calling to say hi."

"Okay, hi. What do you want?" The small pause after my words makes me feel ashamed.

Owen is a good man. He may be on the path our father set for him, but he's not like him. Not like us. He may have balls of steel or whatever my father thinks you need to survive politics, but he also has iron integrity.

"That's not fair," he replies with low, firm reproach. "This fight is between you and Dad. Mom and I don't want to choose sides. You barely answer when we call. You never come home. Mom misses you."

"Bullshit. You've chosen a side, O. Is your precious Senate seat courtesy of Dad's deep pockets?"

"You don't know a damn thing, Max. I worked my ass off for this, and it's what *I've* always wanted to do. You know that."

It's true. You have two options in our family: Cade Energy or politics. Owen paid his dues with the company, but he's always kept his eye on the Oval.

"So are you calling to invite me to the inauguration?" I ask, relaxing into the teasing tone that used to come so easily. "I know I haven't lived in America in a long time, but did I miss an entire election?"

"Very funny," Owen returns, a smile in his voice. "That's not in the plan for another ten years. Maybe by then you'll have something to show for yourself and can help me win."

"Oh, I'll have something to show for myself all right. Whether I help you depends entirely on who's pulling your strings."

"The people pull my strings, Max."

A bark of laughter erupts from me immediately. "Damn, O, there are no cameras rolling. Save the poll-tested lines for your next speech."

"It's not a line. I want to do what's in the best interest of my constituents."

"So where do you stand on fossil fuels? I mean, given that you used to work for an oil company, I think I know."

"Let's just say my views are evolving. I represent California, so there's a demand for more clean energy legislation."

"Good luck convincing the public you aren't in our father's pocket on oil when you can't even convince your own brother."

"I've got time to figure it out. In the meantime, back to our mother."

"She's okay?" I ask, tensed for his answer.

"Her birthday's next week."

"I know." I clear my throat. "I'll be…away."

"You mean in Antarctica?"

"How do you know that?"

"Do you really think our father doesn't know where you are and what you're doing?" Owen asks softly. "At all times?"

"Why does he care what I'm doing with my life? All he needs to know is I'll never work for Cade Energy as long as it's built on antiquated ideas and fossil fuels. I mean, *fossil* fuels? Even the name says old."

Owen's low laughter at my joke makes me smile. "I have no idea how you were raised by Warren Cade and grew up to be a tree hugger."

I roll my eyes at the phrase but don't deny it. "If you really love your country," I say instead, "you'll start hugging some trees, too. And if you do plan to lead the free world, you should get a wife. Americans want bachelor reality shows, not bachelor presidents."

"I've got someone in mind, but I'm still sowing a few wild oats like you are."

"A future president is only allowed so many wild oats, and I'm not sowing wild oats."

"You're in Amsterdam, Max," Owen says wryly. "The red-light district holds some fond memories. I know how wild it gets. You've probably got a new girl every night."

"There's only one girl who interests me right now."

The silence following my statement holds so much shock, I'm immediately kicking myself for saying anything. I don't know why I did. Maybe it's a longing for the camaraderie we lost—the easy fraternalism we used to share.

"Wait. There's a girl?" Owen asks. "I'm sure Dad doesn't know that. If there's one thing he wants to control almost as much as our careers, it's who we marry."

"First of all, that's your life he's controlling, not mine. Second of all, who said anything about marry? I just said there's a girl who interests me. I'm not settling down until certain benchmarks are met."

"There are things a girl has to do before you'll settle down?"

"No, there's certain things *I* have to do before I settle down. I can't afford distractions. I've got too much shit to do."

"But this girl is an exception?" The interest in his voice irritates me.

"She's exceptional." I pause a moment before going on. "Did Dad ever tell you about that day we fought? The protest in Arizona?"

"Just that you tried to manipulate him to get the pipeline rerouted." If I didn't know better, I'd think that was admiration in Owen's voice.

"Manipulate." I huff a harsh laugh. "I tried to get him to do what was right, but of course, principles are negotiable with him. It's an old argument that I don't want to have with you. There was a girl there. One of the protesters."

"You fucked her?"

The bald question pinches a frown between my eyebrows. "She was seventeen, and I was a graduate student, Owen. No, I did not fuck her. Jesus."

"But you wanted to," Owen says with wicked insight.

"Anyway," I bulldoze over the innuendo in his voice, "she's here. It's been like four years, and by some crazy coincidence, she's here in Amsterdam."

"So now you want to fuck her."

God, so badly.

I forbid the words from leaving my mouth.

"I want to get to know her. I'm not doing relationships or anything like that. After Antarctica, it's the Amazon. Then after that, we'll see, but I can't do the strain of a long-distance relationship."

"I can't say that anyone has left the kind of impression on me that this girl has left on you."

"I didn't say she left an impression."

"This is me, Max. I've known you since before you knew yourself. I hear *impression* all in your voice."

"Whatever."

"I'm saying maybe she's not a wild oat," Owen offers. "Maybe she's a wild dream."

CHAPTER 12
LENNIX

"THIS," KIMBA SAYS, TIPPING HER HEAD BACK AS OUR TOUR BOAT cuts through the canal and under the arch of a bridge, "is the life."

Kimba, Viv, and I sit at the far end of the sloop. The guide, or skipper as he suggested we call him, stands at the other. A hostess checks on us, ensuring we're still plied with Moët, gin, Perrier, heavy hors d'oeuvres, and sandwiches I can barely get my hand around.

"Agreed," Viv slurs, half-drowsy, half-drunk on cocktails and sunshine, "I'm so glad we chose Amsterdam for our last hurrah."

Last hurrah because when we get back to Arizona, we finish the little that's left of our final semester and real life begins.

I push away all thoughts of the decisions I still have to make about my next steps. I don't want to think any further into the future than tonight. A slow, secret smile pushes the corners of my mouth. Why think of the future when the present holds Maxim Kingsman? A literal sigh slips past my lips at the thought of him. What's next? A dead swoon?

"All that sighing and grinning happening over there"—Kimba waves a finger at me like it's a wand—"means it must have been good last night with the doctor."

I try to control my smile, but it just keeps getting bigger. I cover it as much as I can by taking a long sip of my *jenever*, which really is quite growing on me. Kimba and Viv have been asking about last night, and I've only given them crumbs so far, holding the details close.

"Yeah, he's great," I downplay because I could stand up in this boat and fire off about thirty superlatives for that man and his hands and his lips and those kisses from last night.

But *restraint*.

"What are you wearing on your date tonight?" Vivienne singsongs teasingly.

"I don't know." I look from one to the other, not wanting to abandon my friends but wanting to see Maxim. "You guys sure you're okay with me going?"

"Oh, honey, we've spent the whole day together," Kimba says. "Besides, David buzzed ya girl. I was going to ask if I might be excused anyway for some one-on-one with him."

"Nice. You got my *go for it* vote." I turn to Vivienne. "And you, Viv? I don't want to leave you on your own."

"I'll be fine," Vivienne says. "Aya and I are having dinner with her family tonight."

"So is tonight the night?" Kimba eyes me over the rim of her glass. "Do we need to have the talk before it goes down?"

My uninhibited peal of laugher takes me by surprise. God, where'd this happiness come from? It feels good to be happy about something. Truly giddy, which is how Maxim's kisses and his touch and his words, his *company* make me feel. And to feel certain about something. For weeks I've circled my future warily, unsure of what I'll do next. I'm pretty sure tonight, I'll *do* Maxim.

"I think it's tonight, yeah," I admit. "But I'm good on the talk. Just because I haven't used the equipment doesn't mean I haven't read the manual or played with the knobs."

Kimba cackles and runs a hand over her closely cropped golden-brown hair. "Yes, those knobs have gotten me through this drought, but I think I may give David the controls tonight."

"What time are you meeting Maxim?" Vivienne asks, still grinning over Kimba's comment.

"Uh, I'm not sure. He said he would text me, but of course…" I roll my eyes. "I left my phone in the room."

"I know. Sorry, girl. We'll be back soon," Kimba assures me and bites into a lime wedge.

"I was listening to yet another voice mail from my dad when I was brushing my teeth. I think I left it at the sink."

When we dock and deboard, I force a leisurely pace to match Viv and Kimba's, but I want to run, find my phone, and see if Maxim tried to call or text. We're still talking about the art we saw at the Van Gogh Museum and the gorgeous country hillside from the bike tour when we reach our hostel. Maxim sits on a low stone wall across from the building, reading a book and looking delectable in aviator sunglasses.

God, save me from this man in aviators.

"Well, so much for thinking he'd be deterred by a lost phone," Vivienne murmurs with a smile. "Right here waiting for you."

I send them a gleeful look before walking a little ahead to approach him. He seems completely absorbed in whatever he's reading.

"Hi," I say once I'm standing right in front of him.

His smile packs a rush of adrenaline, a needle plunged right through my heart, deploying blood and endorphins and electricity to all my vital parts. "Hi. Hope it's okay that I just showed up. I called, but—"

"Sorry. I left my phone. And of course it's okay."

He glances past me and offers another smile, this one more polite, less familiar. "Hey, Kimba, Vivienne. You guys have fun today?"

"Yup, so much fun," Kimba says, already turning toward the hostel's entrance. "See you upstairs, Lenn."

"It was great," Vivienne replies, right behind Kimba, both rushing to leave us alone. "We went to the Van Gogh and rode bikes and took a canal ride."

"Oh, I was hoping we could take a canal ride, Nix," he says to me, his eyes and voice private, intimate even though we don't know each other's bodies yet. The abbreviation of my name, for some reason, is so damn sexy. My father and all my friends shorten my name to Lenn. Nix is just… Yeah. I want to be Nix this week. Tonight, I want to be Nix for him.

"We still can," I assure him, my voice softening so only he will hear me. "There were lots of people. Maybe there's one for just two?"

He folds the book facedown on the wall and clasps my hips, pulling me to stand between his legs. He reaches up to roll his closed fist around and down the length of my ponytail. "Exactly what I had in mind."

He's seated on the wall but so tall we're almost eye level. We met four years ago for a couple of hours. We clocked some time last night and even shared kisses. How can we be here already? How can I want this with him after never wanting it with anyone else before?

But then he tugs on my ponytail and pulls me close enough to kiss. Every doubt and question follows common sense out the window. I cup his face and press deeper into the *V* of his thighs. I open to him, take him in, taste his groan, and relish how he tautens under my hands.

"Jesus," he breathes, palming my ass. "I've been thinking about this all day. About how you tasted last night."

"You have?" I smile against his lips.

"Could you please ignore the eighty-four text messages and thirty-six missed calls on your phone when you get upstairs?" His husky laugh behind my ear makes me shudder. "Let's just pretend those didn't happen."

"Do they escalate in desperation?" I ask hopefully.

"They do a little, yeah."

"Then I'm saving them."

He narrows his eyes and drops his hands from me, but the corners of his mouth twitch. How can lips be firm and so lush?

"I'm as bad as your dad. I kept thinking maybe something happened to you or…" His shoulders lift and fall, and he looks away.

"Or?"

"Maybe you changed your mind about getting to know each other." He looks back to me, and there's an unexpected flash of uncertainty. Maxim doesn't strike me as an uncertain man.

"I have the feeling you're the kind of guy people like to get to know. I'm no exception. Sorry if I worried you."

"You can make it up to me over dinner."

"I'd like that."

"Great." He stands and picks up his book. "I'll let you get inside to relax a little, get changed. Eight o'clock okay to come back for you?"

"Sure," I reply distractedly, my attention caught by the cover of his book. "*Shackleton's Way: Leadership Lessons from the Great Antarctic Explorer.*" I turn down the corners of my mouth, simultaneously intrigued and already half dozing. "The Antarctic, huh?"

"I know Ernest Shackleton isn't exactly a household name." He laughs, picking up the book and closing it, holding it. "But he's kind of a big deal as far as expeditions go."

"Are expeditions your thing then? Is there even anyplace left to expedition to?"

"Oh, yeah." He lifts his brows and studies the cover. "On both counts. There's a ton left to explore, and most of it interests me very much. I'm actually leaving for Antarctica next week."

My heart wobbles, and my whole body goes still. If I counted up every minute I've ever spent with this man, it wouldn't even equal a day, but hearing he's leaving next week… Hell, *I'm* leaving next week. Whatever this is or could be, it's most likely short-lived. I need to remember that.

"Wow, Antarctica. A trip to the most remote place on the planet. Were you drafted? Is it a condition for your degree or something?"

"I applied, and it's actually a pretty competitive process. I'll be there all winter and staying through November, which is Antarctic summer. The research you can get in the two seasons is completely different, and I want exposure to both. I'll be inland until around September and then will study along the peninsula on an ice-capable ship for the summer. Some of the best clues we have, some of the best predictors of how the planet is changing and what the implications of it will be, are in the Antarctic."

"When I say I want to save the world, I mean people, but you mean—"

"The actual planet, yeah, but that *is* people. The rapid changes in our planet—that's one of the most urgent crises we face, and the people who can actually do the most about it aren't paying attention or don't seem to care."

I was mistaken. That flare, that spark in his eyes I mistook for ambition? It's passion. It's zeal. It's an important distinction, and I recognize it because it burns through me, too.

"If you ask me, there are plenty of things more urgent than melting ice caps," I say, watching for his response to my words. "Like the fact that an astounding number of Native American women are sexually assaulted and there's barely any data or concern when we go missing. Or the fact that children in certain parts of the world, in *America*, don't have enough food."

"Agreed, those things are urgent, but to put it in perspective, the Antarctic holds 90 percent of the planet's ice and 70 percent of our freshwater. Do you know what that means?"

"It's really cold and wet there?" I ask with a self-mocking grin.

He smiles back, but there is a graveness to the set of his mouth. "It means that if all the ice in Antarctica melted, global sea levels would increase so much that London, New York, Sydney—major cities would be underwater."

"Holy crap."

"It's unlikely that it would all melt, but things are changing rapidly. We could wait until it's too late to do a damn thing, which is why we should be doing those things now. While we can." He caresses my cheekbone. "And you wouldn't have to worry about all those people you want to help, Nix, because they'd all be dead. So, yes. I want to save the world, too."

I feel chagrined and incredibly turned on and concerned about the planet all of a sudden. I want to recycle *and* dry hump him in the middle of the square. These feelings, seemingly at odds with one another, confuse me. Or maybe it's him being so much more than I bargained for and exactly what I was hoping.

CHAPTER 13
MAXIM

THIS WAS A GOOD IDEA. VUURTORENEILAND IS A GREAT FIRST DATE if you can swing it because it's a full experience, not just dinner. Five hours. You usually need reservations, but I know a guy who knows a guy.

"This is gorgeous," Lennix says, her eyes scanning the horizon as we cross the IJ to reach the island where we'll have dinner. "Now explain to me what this is we're doing."

"It's called Vuurtoreneiland, which translates to 'lighthouse island.' You can only really reach it by boat. It used to be a functioning lighthouse, but now there's a restaurant. In the summer, dinner is in a greenhouse. In the winter, which is anything before July for all intents and purposes, you dine underground in a bunker. I'm not sure exactly what to expect, but I hear great things."

"A new adventure. You seem to enjoy those."

"Yeah, I guess I do. Always something new to learn, but I have a lot I want to accomplish, so there's always more I need to know."

"Ahhh." She nods like I've confirmed something I didn't even realize was in question.

"What's that 'ahhhh' for?"

"I pegged you for ambitious at first."

"You were right. Ambitious would be an understatement. Are you one of those people who thinks ambition's a bad thing?"

"No, not necessarily. I'm ambitious, too. My ambition is to serve and help, but I take it very seriously. I want to be the best I can possibly be at it."

"You said at *first* you pegged me as ambitious. What was your second impression?"

"Crusader, I guess. Zealot."

My laughter hides in the chatter of other conversations taking place around us on the small boat. "Like a planet crusader or something?"

"I guess, yeah."

"That's fair. Everything I told you about wanting to know how we can reverse the damage we've already done and figure out how to do less? It's all true, but I don't think I'm pure enough in my intentions to be a true crusader."

"What are you then?"

"A capitalist," I reply, looking her directly in the eye. "Please don't mistake me for someone who doesn't care about making money. Who just wants what's best for the planet. I do want that. I'm dedicating part of my life to it."

"But the other part?"

"Oh, the other part is for me. Once we finally convince our government that fossil fuels aren't sustainable, I'll be right there with wind-, solar-, and water-power solutions. I'll do as much good as I can, but I'll also monetize it however possible." I don't add that it's in my blood, but I know that to be true. Blood will tell.

You won't last a year without the Cade name.

We'll see about that. I don't feel like I have anything to prove to the world. But something to prove to my father? That's another story.

"A capitalist crusader?" She chuckles and casts a wry look my way. "So you want to save the world and make lots of money."

I can't tell if she approves or disapproves, but that doesn't change my answer. "Absolutely. Someone has to write big checks to all your causes."

Her long, thick lashes shield her thoughts, but she doesn't hide the smile teasing her lips. "I haven't thought much about money, I guess. I mean, as part of my future and what I'll do with my life. That must seem ridiculous to you, huh?"

The boat kisses the shore, and the fifty or so guests get off and start for the beacon of light marking where we'll eat.

"Not really," I answer, taking her hand when we reach some uneven terrain and conveniently forgetting to let go. "I'm not surprised."

"No?"

"Think about how we first met, Nix. How many seventeen-year-olds do you know organizing water runs, getting arrested for protesting, and giving speeches that make people want to do whatever you ask of them?"

"A few actually," she says with a small laugh constructed from scraps of modesty and pride.

"When you told me last night about the opportunities you have, the one you seemed the least enthusiastic about was the one with the most potential to make money."

"The lobbying firm."

"Right. Your priorities, your values have been clear to me in every interaction we've ever had."

We pause to be shown into the belly of the restaurant, the bunker downstairs where winter meals take place. The server takes our drinks order, and we're left to pick up the threads of our conversation.

"So you think you've peeped my values, do you?" she asks, some mischief in her eyes.

"You're not hard to read."

"We'll see. I may have a surprise up my sleeve yet."

With that bit of cryptic information, our evening takes a turn that blessedly involves lots of food in the form of a four-course meal.

"Wow," she says over the homemade flaky brown bread. "Everything is so delicious. You're spoiling me. If this is the first date, what's your follow-up?"

I sip the excellent Bordeaux that accompanies the meal. "Well, I've pulled out all the stops so I *can* secure a second date."

"Trying to get lucky, huh?" she asks, bold humor darkening her nimbus-gray eyes.

"Uh, not sure what that means exactly." *Lies.*

I know exactly what that means. And, yes, I'm trying to impress her. And, yes, I hope I get to do all the things I fantasized about. She's no longer off-limits.

"Hmm. You were seventeen four years ago. So now that makes you…" I pretend to calculate in the air. "Carry the one—"

"Old enough."

"Old enough for what exactly?"

"For whatever you're thinking when you look at me like that."

The sexual tension between us is as sharp and bright as crystals, suspended, reflecting her desire for me and mine to her. I'm mesmerized by the color and the light of it. It burns bright. *It burns.*

"When I look at you like what?"

"I think you know, but don't worry," she whispers, leaning forward. "I want it, too. I'm a girl who knows what she wants."

"I thought you were the girl who chases stars."

"What do you think I'm doing right now?"

She wants me, too. I knew that, but to hear her boldly assert it? To not beat around it, no games or pretense, it feels good. It actually feels special, which is dangerous because I'm not sure I can afford special. For the past four years, I've been what my father said I could not be—ruthless. I haven't been ruthless in my treatment of people or the way my father is in business. I've been and will continue to be ruthless with *myself*. The things I want to accomplish are bigger than I am. Bigger than I can even wrap my imagination around. The truths I want to uncover are buried in faraway places. The things I want to sell, some of them don't even exist yet. The world I want to create for myself, the life I want requires me to be an explorer, philanthropist, inventor, businessman, every man and any man. I'm doing what four generations of Cades did, but on my own. Making something out of thin air. I know I'm capable of it, but it requires *everything*. I can't afford distractions or attachments. I don't do relationships. I don't do…special.

Which is a problem, since I suspect Lennix is the kind of woman I'd want all those things with one day but right now can't allow myself to have.

We're on the boat headed back to the city, and it's the same as last night. We touch and stare until it feels like I'm coming out of my skin. I want her in ways I've never wanted anyone else. Not just under me or on top riding me or in front of me when I pound into her from behind but with her hair splayed on my pillow. Talking. Laughing. I want to see her in morning-after sunlight. How does she take her coffee? How does she like her eggs? Does she floss at night?

Really, Cade? Floss?

When we exit the boat and reach the street, I keep her hand and turn her so we face each other.

"I'm fully prepared to take you back to the hostel, but I'd rather take you home. Well, to the place I'm renting because—"

"Yes." Her assent, though softly spoken, is sure. Not colored by even a shade of doubt.

"Okay." I stroke her palm. "Then I guess we can—"

"But first I need to tell you something." She looks away and then back, defiance and uncertainty mingling in her eyes. "I hope it won't change your mind, but some guys are weird about this kind of thing."

"I'm not some guys, and I can't imagine there's anything you could say that will change my mind about spending tonight with you."

We share a moment, a look before she drops her eyes again.

"It's cold out here," I tell her. "Should we go back to my place and discuss this there? I'm not saying this to get you in bed faster. It's just cold."

"For the record, I don't have a problem with getting to your bed faster."

There's no stopping the grin that spreads over my face.

"But," she interjects with one of my least favorite words, "I want you to know something before I come with you."

She looks up through a tangled web of long lashes, and it's a stomach punch, how beautiful this girl is. It makes me really glad she's not seventeen anymore.

"I've never done this before."

What's she saying? Never slept with someone after a day? On the first date? Will this be her first time four years after a protest?

"Done what, Nix?" I cup one side of her face. "I know it's fast, but I don't think of this as some one-night stand. I want..." I press my forehead to hers and sift my fingers into her hair. God, I'm going to sound like some besotted beggar, but I don't give a fuck. "I want as much time as I can have with you. As long as we're here. Until I leave for Antarctica or you go home. I just—"

"No, you don't under—" She stops and smiles, and it's a little self-conscious. "You said at dinner that you could clearly see my values, but I think you overlooked one."

"Okay. Help me out here. What am I missing?"

"I'm a virgin, Doc."

CHAPTER 14
LENNIX

THE PIN-DROP SILENCE FOLLOWING MY WORDS STRETCHES SO LONG I start fidgeting. Maxim just stares at me, mouth slightly open.

"I said virgin, not alien." I run a hand through my hair. "If that's a problem—"

"It's not."

When he takes my wrist between his strong fingers, it feels frail and small. Or maybe that's how I feel, sharing something so personal and…*mine* with him. It reminds me how very little we know about each other.

"My favorite color is blue–green," I blurt. "Not one or the other because they're just better blended together."

He blinks a few times, frowns, and then chuckles, a low, sensual sound that goes straight for my panties. If we actually make it to his place tonight, he'll have the horniest virgin *ever* on his hands.

"Okaaaay. I'll remember that the next time I'm, oh, I don't know, buying you a pair of shoes, but tonight I feel like maybe there are other things we should discuss." He starts walking, semi-dragging me along. "Let's walk and talk."

It's not that late, and the streets still brim with conversations and laughter and people. Amsterdam is distinct and charming and wild and beguiling. It's this amalgamation of medieval and modern that feels distinctly European to my American eyes.

"We're going to your place?" I ask after a few moments of walking in silence.

"Yeah, unless you want your first time to be in a hostel with your two roommates listening and watching? I mean, if you're into that kind of thing, I'm down. I just assumed you'd want some privacy."

"Privacy would be better probably, yeah. Do you, um, want to know why I'm still a virgin?"

"If you want to tell me. It's not like a disease or a contagious condition or something you have to confess to a partner for their personal health or safety. 'Beware of virgin.'"

"Well, a lot of people seem to treat it that way. I mean, guys *do* sometimes get weird about the whole deflowering thing."

"You know, I actually *have* had quite a bit of sex, occasionally with virgins, and I've never found a flower down there."

I punch his arm lightly, and he laughs, draws me into his side, into the warmth of his body, and kisses the top of my head.

"Also, I'm hurt," he says. "Here I was thinking I'm the first guy you've offered your virginity to only to find out you've been trying to get rid of it forever and all these idiots have been so freaked out by an imaginary flower between your legs that they wouldn't take it. Now I just feel like sloppy seconds."

I laugh-growl and turn my head to playfully bite the inside of his arm. Even through his sweater, the muscle is dense and unyielding.

"I haven't, you know," I tell him. "Haven't offered it…myself to anyone else, I mean."

I sneak a sideways glance at him only to find him assessing me from the side, too. He still doesn't voice the question, but I want him to know.

"When I was thirteen years old, I became a woman. I know it sounds early, but we have a tradition, a rite of passage for young girls, called the Sunrise Dance. It's extremely important. For years, the government actually outlawed it, and we had to perform it in secret."

"Damn colonizers," he mutters.

"Um, your ancestors were probably some of those damn colonizers," I say, but give him the slightest smile to remove some sting from the truth.

"My ancestors were Welshmen who didn't come over until the late 1800s."

"And what did they do when they came over?" Before he can answer, I answer for him. "Settled. And I bet they settled on land that was stolen from Natives. And they instantly assumed their position higher on the American totem pole because, believe me, we're always at the bottom."

"Touché. I'm sorry. Am I being terribly white and ignorant?"

"No, it's not that. And as much as I typically enjoy a good lecture on colonialism and its disastrous effects on…well, everything, not tonight."

I take a deep breath and gather my thoughts and spill them into the quiet and the time we have left before reaching his place.

"The Sunrise Dance is four grueling days of stages that are part of the journey from being a girl to being a woman. It's complicated, and maybe one day I'll tell you everything if you want to know—"

"I'd love to know."

I pause, glance up at him, and smile. "Another time then, yeah. I'll tell you everything, but tonight I'll just say that near the end, we believe something remarkable, maybe even miraculous occurs. Everybody has some way of explaining how things happen to make the world make sense. Adam and Eve. Roman gods. Greek mythology. Whatever. Well, for us we have origin stories, and a pivotal figure is the first woman, the Changing Woman. Near the end of the Sunrise Dance, we believe her spirit inhabits the girl. Like is inside of her for just a little sacred while. And when that's happening, the girl becoming a woman is a blessing."

"How is she a blessing?"

"She's empowered. Sick people come to be touched by her. Parents ask her to bless their babies. The whole community is part of the preparation for the ceremony and all it entails, and then the whole community is also blessed."

"Did you feel any of this during your ceremony?"

I love that he isn't looking at me like I'm crazy or disparaging it as some weird tradition but taking it seriously. Like he'll believe whatever I tell him.

"I did," I answer, trusting him with the truth. "I felt like I could do anything, and I decided I didn't ever want to take anything, anyone inside my body that made me feel less than that. I wouldn't waste it. And I don't have any prudish expectations I impose on anyone. It's not like that at all."

"I get that."

"Do you?" I stop, turning to face him in the middle of the cobbled street, searching the stark planes of his face in the lamplight. "I don't think I'm some goddess who no man has been worthy of. I don't think my vagina is a holy prize. I just…felt something in those moments, felt like my body was part of something great. All my friends talked about losing their virginity. The word 'lose' felt careless to me. And I think that was what I felt that day. Not just about sex, but about everything. I felt *intentional*. Like every second, every decision, every person I share myself with—counts. And to be honest, I just haven't met anyone I trusted with that."

"Wow." A white puff of breath swells in the chilly night air when he chuckles. "That should probably feel like a lot to live up to. Like a lot of pressure."

"Does it?"

His brows bend, like he's concentrating, checking. "It doesn't. I've been drawn to you since I first saw you on that hill with stars and stripes on your face. You cried, and there was such conviction in every word you spoke. I didn't know you were seventeen, but I knew you were young. And I wondered, what made her this way? What shaped her into this remarkable person *already*? Now I know. That girl, the girl who drew me in that day, I would never expect things to be simple or typical with her."

For a moment, I'm stunned by his vision of me—of how he saw me so clearly. There are few things more affirming than someone seeing you exactly as you aspire to be—for them to say *I see that in you*.

"I thought you were so hot." I laugh and shake my head. "In the midst of tear gas and Dobermans, I was like, oh my gosh, he's really cute. So I think there was more of the typical teenager in me than you might have guessed."

"Well, I *wasn't* a teenager. I was in graduate school. When I found out you were only seventeen, I felt like a lecher."

"I could tell. And Mr. Paul made sure you knew. He was my elementary school teacher, by the way, and I'm pretty sure he mentioned *my daddy* on purpose."

"And my balls shriveled in statutory terror." We both laugh and start walking again.

"I can't believe we found each other again like this after four years," I say.

"I knew as soon as I saw you in that brown bar last night that I wanted us to end up right here." He stops in front of one of the narrow canal houses along the Amstel. It's red, tall, imposing, and, even to my untrained eye, not cheap.

"Um, you live here?"

"Yeah, this one's mine." He bounds up the short flight of stairs and turns to find me still at the bottom, staring at the row of canal houses his is neatly tucked into. "You coming?"

"Sure."

I take the steps more slowly. I really don't know very much about the man I'm about to share my body with. We step inside a spacious foyer, flanked by a beautifully decorated dining room and an equally gorgeous sitting room. He watches me taking all this luxury in, sliding his hands into the pockets of his pants, which I now notice are very well tailored. His shoes look…expensive. *He* looks expensive. How did I miss that he looks not only devastatingly handsome but expensive? In that way that is so subtle and unattainable you can't quite pinpoint how you know the clothes on his back could pay your rent for a month.

"Nice clothes, fancy place," I say. "Are you rich, Doc?"

Something skitters across his face before he tucks it neatly away.

"Not much has changed in my wardrobe the last few years," he offers wryly. "And this place looks fancier than it costs. I don't have a ton of cash, but my family does, yeah."

Why am I surprised? I knew he had an expensive education. It just never occurred to me that there was as much distance between our backgrounds as there apparently is.

"My father disowned me." His voice and eyes grow sober, and I want to hug him. "I know that sounds like an old-fashioned word, but fathers cutting their sons out of wills apparently never goes out of style. I'm not just cut off from what he would leave when he dies but from who he is his while he's alive. Cut off from him."

I take a few steps closer, reach up to push back the hair that has fallen into his eyes. "I'm sorry."

"Don't be. I don't need his money," Maxim says sharply. "I had a little of my own. I get by."

It's glaringly obvious to me that his father's money is the least of what Maxim misses. I suspect he misses the man himself, though he may not want to admit it.

"If this is what you call getting by," I say teasingly and with an admiring look around the foyer and up the stairs, "I'd hate to see balling."

We both laugh, and some of the tension tightening his shoulders dissipates.

"It's just a rental for the month between finishing my doctorate and leaving for Antarctica next week."

The reminder drains my laughter. I'm leaving soon, too.

"We should make this week count," I say.

"We should." He steps close, linking our fingers at our sides and bending to take my lips in a leisurely kiss, languid and at odds with the energy humming around him. One could be fooled into thinking he was domesticated. Am I the only one who sees the wild wolf?

"My room's upstairs," he says, walking us backward toward the steps.

I nod and follow him up, holding his hand loosely. In his bedroom, the ceilings soar high, and the hardwood floors gleam beneath my bare feet when I slip off my shoes. Gilded threads run through the wallpaper, and the bed is huge and covered with fine linen.

"This room is beautiful, Maxim."

"I can't take much credit for it. Rental came fully furnished. Are we going to talk interior decoration all night, or are we ready to pluck this flower you keep telling me about?"

I chuckle, as I know he meant me to. He's being charming, deliberately relaxing me. It only makes me want him more. I want his hands and mouth on me, but I can't bring myself to say the words. So I show him.

Not releasing his gaze, I tug at the thin row of buttons descending the green silk blouse tucked into my slacks. His nostrils flare in an otherwise unmoved face. I shrug one shoulder, liberating the sleeve to fall down my arm. I reach for the delicate front clasp holding the cups of my bra together, but he stops me. I glance from the long, tanned fingers against my skin up to his face.

"I thought virgins were supposed to be all scared and trembly." His laugh is rough, but his hands are tender, and his eyes scorch me everywhere.

"Not this one. There's power in choosing your own path, and I've waited until I found someone I was sure I wanted to be with my first time. This is what I want, Doc. I've never felt more in control."

What looks like doubt marks the handsome face. "You've been honest with me, Nix. So open, and everything you've shared makes me respect you even more." He brushes a thumb over my mouth. "Makes me want you even more. You're exactly who I thought you were."

A chuckle rasps between our lips when he kisses me.

"Even better than I thought you were, actually. I don't take any of it for granted, so I need to say something, and I hope it doesn't ruin this."

"Okay."

"I can't afford attachments. Next week, I'm off to Antarctica. Then to South America. I have no plans of settling down or committing and—"

"I get it." I steel my heart and suffocate anything soft and vulnerable. I keep my voice steady. "You're saying this is just sex."

He melds our glances together, brings my knuckle up to his lips, and shakes his head. "No, it'll be more than that. I already know with you, it will feel like more." That same bright ambition, hot as passion, or maybe merely a trick of the light, flashes through his eyes. "That's what will make it so hard to walk away at the end of the week, but what I'm saying is that I will. I'll walk away, and I won't look back."

He passes his big hand in the air, sketching an imaginary line between our bodies. "I can't do this right now."

My laugh comes like forced air through a vent, quick and hard and cool. "I'm not expecting a proposal. You think because I haven't had sex before I'll be an emotional wreck next week when we go our separate ways?"

"No, I'm not that arrogant." His lips twist in a show of self-mockery. "Okay, I am actually pretty arrogant, but no. I just want you to know this will mean something to me, but I can't allow it to be—"

"Neither can I." I reach up and sink my fingers into the thick hair at his neck. "I get a week with someone I'm crazy attracted to, respect very much, and will remember fondly as the first man I ever fucked."

I keep my voice deliberately even and neutral and strip away all the emotion. I stomp on all the possibilities that feel like unopened buds ready to sprout. I show him only my desire and willingness to have him as he comes.

"And that's enough?" He scans my face, searching for a lie, the truth, weakness—I don't know what. "A week, our time together, going our separate ways at the end—it's enough?"

I honestly don't know. What do I say? That after only a taste, I already crave him? That I have no idea how my body, my heart will respond to the kind of connection even just conversation and a few kisses have evoked? I don't know what I will feel at the end of the week, but I know I want this, so I tell him exactly what he needs to hear.

"It's enough."

He doesn't move, so I do, tipping up to press my mouth to his. At first he just watches me kiss him, eyelids lowered, lips closed, like he's still not sure we should. I lick into the seam of his mouth, and he groans my name, his eyes closing. That sound vibrates through my lips and to my core—to the seat of my need and want and curiosity. I want to understand this physical mystery I've eschewed all my life, and I want it with him. If the price is ultimately heartbreak, my eyes are wide open.

I cover his hand with mine and coax it up to my breast, press myself deeper into his palm. He squeezes and slides a thumb under the bra to tease my nipple. My breath stutters, and my eyes close. He runs his hand up my shoulder and under the silk bra strap, persuading it down my arm. Under his touch, the bra's clasp snaps free, baring me to him. I'm proud of my body, not because it's a certain size or because I'm fit but because it's what I have to offer him. I chose this man, chose this time. In a world where so many of us don't get to choose, I cherish that. It's my right, but that doesn't mean I take it for granted. Not when I've seen so many stripped of that choice. Not when I've seen so many who regretted their first time.

I can already tell that won't be the case. Not with Maxim.

He bends and takes one nipple into the heat of his mouth. I gasp and shove my fingers into his hair that has half a mind to wave and half a mind to curl. One of his hands cups my butt, and with the other, he kneads my breast. He slips open the button and zipper of my pants, coaxing them down and over my legs until I stand only in the panties to match the bra Kimba and Vivienne insisted I wear "just in case." With his thumbs hooked under the silk bands at my hips, he slides those down until I'm completely naked.

"Damn, you're beautiful, Nix." He breathes the husky praise against my neck, inciting a trail of goosebumps along my arms. He sinks to his knees, scattering gentle kisses on my stomach, the underside of my breast, my hip, the tops of my thighs. Finally, he kisses lower, between my legs. He spreads me with gentle fingers and swipes once with his tongue.

"Jesus," I moan.

He glances up through impossibly, enviably long lashes, his mouth a roguish slash of a smile. With the gentlest of nudges from him, my legs give way, surrendering to gravity and the sensations licking over my body, and I fall back. The bed beneath me is cool and downy. His palms are the perfect kind of rough on the sensitive skin of my inner thighs as he spreads my legs and bends his head again, running his nose along the crevice of my pussy.

"I want this so bad," he rasps, his breath a caress. He lifts my legs onto his shoulders, the breadth of him widening me, exposing me. I expected to feel embarrassed or self-conscious, but I don't. Some wild, wanton thing longs to grab him by the hair and force his head down into the wet, throbbing place where his mouth hovers. Anticipation is the match to a line of gasoline, and I'm already on fire. He doesn't move.

"Dammit, Doc," I whisper hoarsely. "Do it."

With a growl, he does. He licks into my secrets and eats away my inhibitions, his mouth and tongue and teeth consuming me like it's his first time and I'm his last supper.

"God, you're perfect down here," he says roughly. "You've done this before? Someone's gone down on you before?"

I can barely breathe, can barely form words through the haze and havoc he's wreaking on my body. "Yeah."

His fingers tighten around my thighs, and he pushes his face deeper into me. "I hate everyone who's ever tasted you."

The possessive words slide into the hungry places lurking under my defenses. I want to tell him not to say things that contradict our agreement, but his fingers inside me steal all thought. He sets a rhythm of advance and retreat, his middle finger thick and satisfying when he's in, and denying me when he's out. He adds another finger, stretching me. My muscles clench. My head thrashes on the bed. I claw his hair while his thumb works the sensitive bud where all my concentration and thoughts have convened. I can't think beyond his hands and mouth. Guys have touched me there, have kissed me there, but it never felt like this. He's tearing me up and tossing me in the air like confetti until finally I'm fluttering, floating, falling, little bits of myself swept into a storm.

"Oh, my God," I mumble through numb lips. I've had a few orgasms before, mostly at my own hand, but this one made my lips go numb. My entire body is limp and boneless.

"Good?" he asks.

"Um, yeah," I say on a startled, laughing breath. "You could say that."

He licks greedily at the wetness kissing my thighs. "I want to make you come again just to have more of this. I'll never forget this, Nix. I'll smell you, taste you, in my dreams."

Head bent, he worships at the very center, where little after-shocks still roll through me. His mouth is avid, sucking, growling, making the wild wolf noises, all pretense of civility left behind. My hips roll into him in a deep, back-cracking wave. My body is an empty chamber, and my own cries of pleasure echo, hollow and desperate.

"I need you inside me, Maxim. I'm ready."

"I'm not," he mumbles against my pussy, still loving and laving it. His hand wanders over my belly and ribs until he reaches my breast to squeeze and plump the nipple even while he keeps eating. The tandem of his hands and mouth sends me spiraling, flying again.

"Maxim." I grip the sheets at my side, desperate for an anchor. "Now. Please."

He finally stands at the foot of the bed between my knees and pulls the ribbed sweater over his head.

Every inch of him is finely constructed. The copper-coin nipples. The masonry of his chest and abs, like bricks laid with mortared muscle. When he drops his pants and briefs, the sinewy slashes at his lean hips point south, directing me to where he is fully erect, long and topped with a crown, his balls hanging low. I've seen men before, but I realize my inspection until now was a clinical thing, marked by indifference or even simple appreciation. My first sight of Maxim naked is anything but. His body, so beautiful and strong, sets off an impossible, primordial chant inside of me.

Mine. Mine. Mine. Mine.

Like the drums from my dance into womanhood, the beat possesses my blood and gallops through my veins as I approach another rite of passage. The drumbeat, my heartbeat—one.

Mine. Mine. Mine. Mine.

I want to ignore the insistent rhythm demanding I claim him, but it's impossible. He's stroking himself, biting his lip, his eyes roving over my body as I scoot back farther on the bed, propped against his pillows.

"Now." It's not a virgin voice—there's no uncertainty of the unknown. It's a command, a mandate for my pleasure. "Right fucking now, Doc."

"You're ready?" He crawls onto the bed, slips his hands between my legs, and drops his forehead to mine with a groan. "You are."

"I'm ready."

"We should go slow, Nix." He reaches into the dresser and puts on a condom, scanning my face, concern filtered into the desire. It only makes me want him more.

"I don't care if it hurts," I tell him, my voice husky and pleasure-strained. "I want it. I want you."

His nod is terse. His lips, set. His hands are so gentle but firm and demanding when he presses my legs wider. He props himself on his elbows, looking down at me for a moment and scattering kisses across my cheeks and then my lips. He licks into me, a tender, open-mouthed exploration that twists our tongues and heartbeats. Slowly, he eases between my legs and inside, thick and rigid and hot. An invasion by inches. A surrender by sighs. I give one pained gasp, and then he's in so deep, for a moment I can't breathe.

"I'm sorry," he whispers, sounding tortured. "Nix, baby, are you okay?"

"Yes." I swallow a moan, struggling to adjust, lifting my hips.

"Fuck." He breathes shakily into my hair. "You feel incredible."

I move my hips again, an experiment, a line I cast into the water. *He bites.*

He moves, at first a slow push and pull and then more driving. Pounding. A freight train between my legs. Grunting and heaving and panting. It hurts so much, and it feels so perfect. I must be bleeding, and I couldn't care less. With each twist of his body deeper into mine, he's carving himself inside me, slice after blissful slice.

"You still okay?" he asks, his eyes glazed and his body mercilessly, beautifully, wonderfully taking mine.

"Stop talking," I reply. He hits a spot that couldn't have been there all this time dormant inside me. That spot waiting for the just-right caress of him buried inside me to erupt. The *feel so good* obliterates the pain. "Just fuck me."

The sound he makes is unintelligible. We are wound together so tight, a tangled tempo of limbs and hands and lips and sweat and tears.

Tears trickle from the corners of my eyes when he roars and shakes over me. I clamp my legs, my arms around him, holding him so close even the rhythm of his heart belongs to me. The sweat slicking his chest is *mine*.

Through a rain of adoring kisses he leaves on my face, my shoulders, and my breasts, I try to remember he is *not* mine. He told me it would be more—that it would feel like this. Like more than sex, and it does. It already does. If I plan to make it out of this week whole, I have to cling to the only promise Maxim made.

That when it's time to walk away, he will.

CHAPTER 15
MAXIM

TEA.

I wondered how she takes her coffee, but she doesn't. Lennix likes tea.

And her eggs? Scrambled hard.

And how she looks in the morning-after light? Thick, still-damp hair hangs over one shoulder, an unrelieved fall of inky black. Her skin, smooth dark gold, glows from her shower. I'll never forget how she looks right now. I'll never forget how she looked last night.

"You're staring," she says, not glancing up from the newspaper someone delivers to my door every morning, I assume courtesy of the last tenant.

"No, I'm not." I turn my attention to the toast and away from her wearing some robe she found at the back of my closet. I don't have the heart to tell her I have no idea whose it is.

"You weren't?" She shifts so the robe falls open, gifting me shadowy glimpses of her breasts and long, firm thighs. "My bad."

I eat up the sight, licking my lips, searching for traces of her taste.

"I said I like my eggs scrambled hard," she says with a sweet smile. "Not scrambled burnt."

"Shit." I shift the pan from the bright-red eye of the stove onto a cool burner. I'm still pulling toast from the toaster and scraping at burnt eggs when she walks up behind me and circles me with her arms.

"Made ya look," she whispers, tipping up to kiss the nape of my neck. I turn off the stove and face her, linking my fingers at the small of her back.

"You were staring, too," I mumble into our first kiss of the day.

"Was not." Her smile against my lips calls her a liar. "I was minding my own business, reading that newspaper."

"Oh, did you learn Dutch overnight then?" I ask, eyeing her abandoned copy of *de Volkskrant* with its distinctly non-English headlines.

Laughter shakes her shoulders beneath the robe, and I slide my hands over the slick fabric clinging to her body. She's healthy. Fit. Tight bends and lush curves. I caress one of my favorite curves, her ass, and kiss down her neck, breathing in my shampoo in her soft hair. *Me* on *her*.

We may part ways next week—no, we *will* part ways next week. We have to—but I'll remember this night and any more she gives me for the rest of my life. She's that special. My body knows it. My heart, which I don't consult in any of my decisions, won't be far behind if I'm not careful.

"Spend the day with me," I say.

I don't want to sound needy, clingy, pathetic, but it only took one night for me to know I won't be able to get enough of this woman.

"I'm here with my friends, remember?"

"They have you all the time. I only get a few days with you before you go back to the States."

I lower until my mouth is level with her breast and suck the curve and nipple through the silk robe. She groans and plunges her fingers into my hair, scraping my scalp.

"Please." I nudge the lapel aside to find clean-scented, soft flesh beneath the robe. I slide the sleeves down her arms until the belt loses its fragile hold on her waist and falls open, catching at her elbows. She's nearly naked in my kitchen, and I want to bend her over the table and take her from the back. *Hard.*

"I can't just forget about them," she says, sounding husky and unconvinced.

"Tell them good dick is hard to find. Surely they'll understand."

My fingers delve between her legs, searching for the nirvana I found last night.

"Are you sore?" I hope I don't sound as desperate as touching her makes me feel.

"A little." Her fingers tighten at my neck. "But I'll be ready by tonight if you want me again."

Tonight. Damn. Not as persuasive as I thought I was. "So you won't spend the day with me?"

"I have plans with Kimba and Viv," she says, apology and regret in her eyes. "I promise tonight is yours."

"Will you spend the night again?" I'm asking too much too soon. I know that, but everything feels compacted. Seeing her again randomly after four years, making love our second night together, whatever we get this week—it's all shoved through a tiny window I want to toss a rock at and shatter.

"I'll spend the night, yeah." She draws the robe back and up and around her, tying it at the waist. She reaches past me to grab a slice of burnt toast. "But I have to go now."

My arms and my kitchen are empty. She starts up the steps, and I take off after her. Her eyes widen over her shoulder when she sees me on her heels.

"No!" She laughs and speeds up, zigzagging down the hall like that will deter me. She makes the amateur mistake of running into my bedroom and trying to close the door. I push until it opens and stumble into the room. She's giggling and spread out on my bed, the robe gaping to show me her supple curves and lean lines and pretty pussy.

"Come catch me," she says, her arms extended to me.

I fall into the disarray of sheets scented with last night's sex and pin her beneath me.

"Are you sure you can't stay?" I ask, one last plea.

"No, my friends are waiting for me." She reaches down between us to grip my cock, squeezing. "But I'm not *that* sore, and they *can* wait."

CHAPTER 16
LENNIX

"Your dad or your boyfriend?" Kimba asks, dipping a trio of French fries into a dollop of mayo nestled in the red-and-white-checkered paper cone.

I glance at my phone.

"Maxim's not my boyfriend," I answer, giving her half my attention and the remainder to the call. "And it's not him or Daddy. It's Mena. Better see what she needs."

"If you say so, Miss I Popped My Cherry by Spending the Night with a Stranger." Vivienne laughs and takes a sip of her ginger beer. "We'll just be here eating our weight in fries and rubbing our feet."

We visited the Anne Frank House today and did a walking tour of the major sites. We're sucking this city dry of every experience possible.

I leave them and their ribbing at the sidewalk café and walk toward a low wall a few yards away.

"Hey, Auntie," I greet Mena. "How goes it?"

"Fine," she returns, a smile in her voice. "Enjoying Amsterdam?"

"Very much." An unrepentant grin spreads across my face. I'll share all the details with her when I get back. "Everything okay? Did my father put you up to this? I've got him down to one call a day, but if he—"

"No, I haven't spoken to Rand, but it doesn't surprise me he's calling so much. You know how hard it is for him when you're away."

"I know. I get it, but what happened to Mama…" Mama's disappearance and presumed death form a broken circle that never closes, and I know those question marks are like scythes chopping into my dad's sanity some days. The least I can do is take his calls and reassure him I'm okay.

"I get it," I finish lamely after a moment. "So if you aren't calling for Dad, what's up?"

"Remember when we talked by the river right before you left?"

"Of course."

"Has your path been made clear yet?"

I hesitate before answering. I want to tell her yes, but the three options I have still sit there, none of them compelling me to take a step. "Not really."

"Okay. I have something that may interest you while you decide. Maybe. No pressure. I don't want to influence your choices, but this just seemed—"

"Spit it out, Auntie."

"I have a friend from college in Oklahoma, Jim Nighthorse," she says, an eager note entering her voice. "Cherokee Nation on his mother's side. He's running for Congress."

My mental antennae peak, and I go still. My fingertips tingle.

"Okay," I say slowly. "Tell me more."

"He's amazing, Lenn. He's a lawyer and has represented several cases on behalf of the Cherokee Nation the last few years."

"That all sounds incredible. What do you want? How could I help?"

"You could work on his campaign. I can email you his file, but don't take a long time to decide. He's setting up interviews now to outfit his staff. It's gonna be a tough race. His opponent, the incumbent, supported a company's bid for a pipeline in Oklahoma a few years ago."

As soon as she says the words, something clicks and settles inside me like I was waiting to hear them. I've heard so little about this man and this opportunity, but already it feels right. That's been happening to me a lot lately. I felt certain about last night, about Maxim, and for some reason, I feel certain about this.

"And you think I can help?" I ask, even though I already believe I can.

"Yes. He needs someone bold and young but wise and wily."

"And you think that's me?" I ask with a huff of humor.

"Oh, I know it is."

I straighten from the wall and start back toward the table where my best friends wait, still dipping fries in mayo.

"Send me the file."

CHAPTER 17
MAXIM

"My mouth is on fire, Doc." Lennix waves her hand in front of her pouty lips, her eyes watering. I laugh and lift my glass of water for her to drink. Between greedy sips and gasps, she grins.

"I told you to slow down." I fork through the portion of *daging blado* on my plate, the spicy, tender braised beef singeing my tongue and setting my taste buds on fire.

"Well, I, for one," says Kimba, "am loving the hell out of this fish. It's spicy, too, but so good. What'd you call it, Max?"

"It's *sate lilit*," I reply. "Glad you like it. How's yours, Viv?"

The pretty brunette's glasses are practically fogged from the heat piled on her plate. "Everything is delicious. Thank you for bringing us here."

"Best *rijsttafel* in the city." I glance around the table, loaded with more than a dozen dishes of meat and vegetables and rice. Lots of rice, which is kind of the point. "You can't come to Amsterdam and not have *rijsttafel*."

"It's a lot of food," Lennix murmurs, scooping up rice and *sate kambing*, the savory goat she agreed to try.

"This is one of my favorite places in the city for it," I tell them. "We had some in Utrecht, but this one's better."

"So you studied climate change there?" Kimba asks, chewing goat meat carefully as if considering whether she likes it.

"Climate science is my degree, but climate change is certainly a part of it, yeah."

"What will you do with it?" Kimba asks.

"Everything," I answer simply.

Kimba and Vivienne laugh, but Lennix watches me, her eyes and mine locked in recognition. She's glimpsed my ambition in flashes, in the few things I've shared. She knows I won't be deterred by anything when pursuing my goals.

"I also have a degree in business," I clarify, answering the questioning looks the other two women give me. "I'm interested in the intersection of clean energy and commerce."

"In other words," Lennix drawls, her smile affectionate and cynical, "he wants to make lots of money off the planet."

We all laugh, but I feel the need to reassure them I'm not some heartless capitalist asshole who would compromise greater good for greater gain. I'm not my father.

"It's true I want to monetize green energy innovation," I tell them, sipping the last of my Bir Bintang. "But I also refuse to let this planet go to crap without at least trying to convince people we should stop treating it like a bottomless trash can."

"That's why you're going to Antarctica next week?" Lennix asks.

"There's a lot to learn there, yeah."

"Is it dangerous?" Vivienne loads a little more beef and rice onto the small plate in front of her.

"It's the most remote place on Earth," I reply wryly. "And basically, an ice-covered desert. Civilization is literally thousands of miles away, and you're surrounded by icebergs. Not to mention the weather changes faster than you can say blizzard, so yeah. There's some risk."

Lennix's brows knit into a frown over concerned eyes.

"I mean, not that much," I rush to tell her. "We'll have some limited phone and internet access for the most part."

Not always frequent or reliable, but I've already made it sound bad enough.

"How long will you be there?" Vivienne asks.

"We fly out next week and will be there until November," I reply. "So about eight months. One of the major hazards, beyond the weather and unpredictable conditions, is depression. Most of that time, there will be no sun. It's dark for months in the winter, and a lot of people deal with seasonal affective disorder, some depression."

"It sounds intense," Lennix says.

"It can be. We have to adjust to chronic hypobaric hypoxia."

"Um…what?" Kimba asks.

"Sorry," I say, laughing. "We'll be living for a long time with a third less oxygen than is available at sea level, but we've been training for these conditions. There's a former Navy SEAL in our group, and I worked with him for weeks and have been maintaining the regimen he suggested."

"So that's why you're so much bigger," Lennix says. She grimaces a little when her friends giggle and snort. "I mean… You've just… It was four years ago. Just more muscle or whatever."

Under the table, I slide my hand across her lap and find her hand, a courtship between our fingers. I chuckle and kiss her temple. She shifts to catch my lips, opening to briefly brush my tongue with hers. My unoccupied hand knots into a fist, and I fight the urge to haul her onto my lap.

"Ahem." Kimba clears her throat and then stretches into an elaborate yawn. "I'm beat. Aren't you beat, Viv?"

"Huh?" Vivienne looks up, her jaws stuffed with rice and beef. "No, I actually wanted to order another beer. Do we have this stuff back in the States?"

"But aren't you ready to *go*?" Kimba widens her eyes and ticks her head subtly in our direction.

"Go?" Vivienne shoves an errant grain of rice back into her mouth. "I haven't even tried the goat yet."

"Well, *I'm* beat," I say, letting Kimba off the hook and deciding we'll be the ones to leave. "And stuffed and ready to go. My treat, ladies. You two stay as long as you like, and I'll take care of the bill on my way out."

I brush the hair back from Lennix's face and whisper in her ear, "You still staying with me tonight?"

She turns her head, and the need and desire in her eyes match everything I've wanted since she left my house this morning.

"Hey, guys." She drags her gaze back to her friends. "I'm going with Maxim, okay?"

Their knowing grins and nods answer. I fully embraced the idea of eating dinner with Vivienne and Kimba. It gave me time with Lennix but also assuaged her guilt for spending less time with her friends on holiday.

"We'll see you in the morning," Kimba says. "Thanks for tonight, Maxim. It's been great."

"And I don't think you've checked your phone once to see if Stephen called, Viv," Lennix teases.

Vivienne instantly digs into her purse and retrieves her phone.

"He did!" She holds the screen for us to see, her face triumphant. "Two missed calls. God, that man loves me."

They continue chatting while I settle the bill. Vivienne and Kimba are still nibbling from half-empty dishes and sipping their beers when Lennix and I slip out the door, rich aromas following us into the street.

"That was really sweet of you." Lennix grabs my hand and pulls me closer until she's pressed into my side. "Dinner for them, I mean."

"Small price to pay for time with you. I was more than willing. Besides they're great."

"They're the best. Kimba and I met at a voter registration drive on campus." She chuckles against my shoulder. "We registered Viv to vote. We're both public policy majors. Vivienne is journalism."

"Nice. She and her boyfriend seem really serious."

"Fiancé, and I can't believe he let her out of the country. He's as bad as my father. Stephen and Viv are joined at the hip."

"That's great, that they've found each other so young."

"I guess. I do worry sometimes that it's a lot. I mean, he's out of school already. Living in New York. He's in finance. She'll move there when she graduates for sure."

"What's wrong with that?"

"She's turning down the *LA Times* to be with him."

"And you don't think that's wise?"

"I wouldn't do it. I mean, it's New York, so she'll probably find something else, but there's no guarantee. Would I set aside my ambitions and goals to follow some man?" Her scoffing breath clouds in the cool air. "No way."

"Good for you. You already know how I feel."

"Yep." She turns her head from my shoulder to consider the glimmering canal bordering the street. "No attachments."

"Right." I thread our fingers together and pull her closer. "No attachments."

The silence deepens between us while we walk, and I wonder if I said the wrong thing somewhere along the way—if I've been too honest about how things need to be between us.

"So what about you?" I ask after a few moments. "Thought any more about which of the three opportunities you'll take?"

"There's actually a fourth on the table now. My godmother called today. Her friend is running for Congress, and she thinks I should be on his team. He's Native and smart and has been doing great work for the Cherokee Nation in Oklahoma."

"Wow. That sounds like it could be amazing. You gonna do it?"

Her shrug is quick. "Mena, my godmother, is sending some stuff for me to look at so I can see what he's all about. This could be it, though."

"It?"

"I feel like a missile ready to go but waiting for launch codes and a destination. Poised, powerful, but not sure where to aim. Today when Mena was telling me about this campaign, I wondered if this is my target. Something seemed to…I don't know, make sense. You ever thought about going into politics?"

"Hell, no." I fake a shudder. "Dirty business, politics. You can't have a soul and be a politician. Believe me, I have a family full of them."

"Really?"

"Yeah, my uncle was a mayor. We've got a few congressmen in our illustrious family tree. And my older brother's a senator. He's gonna be your president in about ten years, by the way."

"You say it like it's only a matter of time."

"You haven't met my brother," I say dryly. "When he sets out to do something, it's a foregone conclusion."

"Sounds like it runs in the family."

I pause, considering. I'm a Cade. Ambition, achieving was never a choice for me. It was just a question of if my ambitions would take me down a path that satisfied my father. But I've removed that factor. I may have shunned the Cade name, but the Cade nature is not so easily shed.

"You didn't want to get into the family business, so to speak?" she follows up.

"Let's just say the family business is not for me." *Neither of them*, I add to myself.

"Besides, it's the dreamers, the inventors and entrepreneurs who change the world the most. Gutenberg, Edison, Stephenson, Jobs— something about the present wasn't good enough, so they made the future." I almost choke on a jaded chuckle. "What do politicians make? They make war. They make profit off the misfortune of others. They make mistakes they won't take responsibility for and decisions they never have to feel the impact of. No, thank you. Not for me."

"Well, when you put it like that, I guess you think I should turn down the campaign job."

"Not at all. If anyone can make that rotten system work, it's you."

A fat raindrop plops on my nose, sliding down the bridge, followed by another and then a wet succession.

"Aw, hell." I pull my jacket up on my elbows to provide some shelter for the two of us, but the rain trebles, more coming down and faster.

"We still have four blocks before my place," I say. "Sorry, but the weather is unpredictable this time of year."

Rain has already started molding the thin dress to her body, faithfully hugging every swell and curve. A hard shiver runs through her, and her teeth chatter.

"Come on." I grab her hand and duck into an alleyway. An overhang provides a tiny patch of dry ground and shelter. "We may be able to wait it out. These showers sprout up and pass over like they never happened."

We're sandwiched between two buildings, and there is barely any light, but the moonlight finds her, sculpting shadows beneath her cheekbones and etching dark crescents of her lowered lashes. The rain has smeared her mascara, and water-slicked hair flattens to her head. She should look bedraggled, but she manages to be the prettiest girl I've ever seen.

I bend, tentative at first, even after last night. Even after making love to her again this morning when I chased her up the stairs. I approach slowly, giving her the chance to refuse, but she doesn't. She meets me, eyes open, lips eager, hands bunched in my wet hair. It's a freshwater kiss, made of rain and passion. Slow touches pick up steam until we're frantic against the wall, hands searching, desperate to find the flesh under our soaked clothes. The inside of her thigh is slick with rain, and I trace the droplets with my finger before inching higher and burrowing beneath her panties, inside.

"Do that, Doc," she says, a breath-starved command. "Yes."

I lean into the damp, scented curve of her neck, leaving kisses there while my finger is knuckle-deep in paradise. Every sound she makes gets me harder, ready. She kisses my jaw, my cheekbone, pulls my bottom lip between hers.

"We should stop," I pant across her mouth. "I can't… Let's stop before…" How do I tell her that if we don't, I'll be fucking her in an alley with no regard for who might see? How do I say that without sounding disrespectful and selfish?

"Don't stop." She fumbles at my waist, tugging the belt from its buckle and pulling the button loose, the zipper down. "Do it."

"Baby." I drop my head back and groan. So tempting. I want to so badly. "The rain should let up soon. We can make a dash for my house."

"Or," she says, working her hand into my pants, finding me. Squeezing me.

"Dammit, Nix," I groan. "Don't make me want you any more than I already do."

"Or," she says again, "you can do what we both want. Take what I want to give. Right here. Right now."

Is it surrender when you both want it? I'm not sure if it's her will or mine that wins out, but I hitch her up, my hands full of her ass, and lock her legs at my back. I reach between us to push her panties aside and plunge in.

I feel like a god.

Yet every time she gasps and groans and tightens around my body, *she* conquerors *me*. She's indelible. I may end up with someone else, may even love someone someday, but there is a place Lennix Moon has carved out inside me in a matter of a few days where only she will ever fit. It's irrational and goes against all the rules I've set for myself, but she feels like mine. For the next two days, she *is* mine.

And then we'll walk away.

That rule has always worked for me. It kept me focused through undergrad, my master's, and my PhD. It has me headed to Antarctica and other far reaches of the Earth to unlock the mysteries that could shape a generation. Tonight, though, my body has found a slick, sweet home inside her, and when she comes, when I do, the words, the rules, sound like foolishness.

Her legs are still wrapped around my waist. Her elbows rest on my shoulders, and she's pinned between me and a brick wall. Harsh breaths bounce between our mouths and steam the cool air around us.

"Can I ask you something?" she asks.

Still slightly breathless, I simply nod.

She lets her head fall against the brick wall so she can peer into my eyes, search them before asking her question. "Is it always like this?"

I know what she means.

Volatile. Wild. Passionate. Satisfying. Perfect.

What do I say? That in my vast experience it's never been like this? Never been a conflagration of savory smoke and white-hot flame? That I've never wanted to break my rules for anyone, no matter how good the sex? That when I saw her on that hill four years ago, I knew I'd never forget her and that when I saw her again I knew I had to have her? And that being with her, being *inside* her surpasses anything I've ever had with anyone else?

If I tell her the truth, it might lead her to believe I can break my rule.

Worse, *I* might believe it.

So I lie.

"Sometimes."

She watches me for an extra second before nodding and shifting her hips.

"Shit," I hiss. That simple movement feels so good, my dick stirs, and I want to start all over again, surge into her and lose all sense of the world except Lennix Moon Hunter as my one point of light.

"Dammit." I shake my head, disgusted with sudden realization. "Forgot the condom. I'm so sorry, Nix."

Her eyes widen. She bites her lip, her long lashes dropping.

"My godmother works at a clinic," she says, her voice husky and her breath still short. "She's had me on the pill since I was sixteen, and I'm clean. I mean, you know I've never been with anyone else."

She meets my eyes, silently asking for my reply.

"I'm clean," I rush to assure her. "Yeah, no. I always use protection and get tested regularly just to be... I'm clean, but I'm still sorry I got caught up that way. I would never want to make you feel unsafe."

"*Geeft het als ik meedoe?*" a gruff male voice asks a few feet deeper into the alleyway, just beyond the edge of light.

"Fuck off," I snap, turning Lennix's head into my neck so he can't see her face.

"What'd he say?" she mumbles, her breath warm against my skin.

"Um, he asked if he could join us," I grit out, mortified that I put her in this position.

A muffled giggle rasps into my hair. I pull back, staring down at her in the faint light from the street. "Are you...laughing?" I ask, the grin on my own face surprising me.

Her legs drop from my waist, and her feet hit the ground. She presses her palms to my chest, leaning forward and looking up at me with a wide smile. "You have to admit it's kind of funny."

"No, I don't." I slide my hands down to frame her hips. "The rain has let up some. Let's get out of here before he presses the issue. I'd prefer not to end up in a Dutch prison."

I take her hand, and we venture back out into the street. Now there's only the faintest drizzle, a steady light shower. She lifts her arms, spreading her fingers like some young goddess receiving an offering poured from the sky. The rivulets bathe her face, crystalline drops clinging to the curled tips of her lashes. Something clenches in my chest at the sight of her. Some part of me moves that I didn't know existed. I take her arm and stop us in the middle of the street, in the middle of the rain, in the middle of one of the most beautiful cities in the world, and I kiss her.

Even drenched by a downpour, we're thirsty for each other. Her mouth goes wide and searches under mine. I feel every line and curve of her body through the wet dress clinging to her. *I* cling to her. My shoes are slogged, droplets run down my back, but lightning would have to strike us before I'd let her go.

Finally, she pulls away, her eyes as dazed as I feel. Her mouth, swollen and wet with raindrops and kisses, curves into a secret smile. She walks ahead, turning to face me, and keeps stepping backward. She flicks her head in the direction of my house, which is in view but still over a hundred feet away.

"Race?" she asks.

Before I can answer, she takes off, slipping on the cobblestones, pumping her arms and legs. Her siren laughter drifts back to me, and I shake myself, running to catch her. She's halfway up the steps of my rented house when I zip past her to reach the door a second before she does.

"No fair," she breathes, exerted, gorgeous.

"You even had a head start." I laugh, unlocking and opening the door and then dragging her in with me by the hand. "To the victor go the spoils."

I haul her over my shoulder and charge up the steps.

"Doc!" She bangs half-heartedly on my back, her giggles bouncing off the high ceilings. "Put me down!"

I take her through my bedroom and keep going to the bathroom.

"Gladly." I set her on her feet, grab a towel, and start drying her hair. We grin at each other, and I think she's as happy with me as I am with her. She reaches for a towel and starts drying my hair, too. Our smiles fade. We drop the towels and start undressing each other, peeling away sodden clothes and kicking off shoes. I hastily discard her bra and panties and gently drag the towel over her nipples, like berries in the dark golden brown of her skin.

Her head drops back, and she leans into my hand, her moan acoustic in the large, empty bathroom. I sit her on the counter so her legs dangle. I lower to the floor and kiss the high, delicate arch of each foot and then behind her knees. I press my lips in a straight line of kisses up her inner thighs to her pussy, lured by the heavy, intimate scent of her. I'm starved for it, biting the plump lips and sucking the bud tucked inside.

"Good grief, Nix," I breathe against her thigh. "Your pussy is spoiling me for all others."

She laughs, holding my head between her hands and running her fingers through my hair. When I glance up, deep affection floods her eyes. She puts her foot on my shoulder and gives me a shove, knocking me on my ass. She hops off the counter and sprints back into my bedroom, flopping onto the mattress and opening her legs. The laughter melts from her face leaving only brazen invitation. An invitation impossible for me to resist.

When I reach the bed, she rises to her knees and tugs my belt, the glance she gives me penetrative, starved, and digging deep.

"I want you in my mouth, Doc."

Not looking away or saying a word, I pull my pants and briefs down, freeing my cock. I guide her to the edge of the bed and over the side, pushing her onto her knees. I don't know how long I've envisioned her this way, but it's a fantasy I plan to fully indulge. I nod to the tiny space separating her lips from my dick. "Do it then."

She lowers her head, and those full lips wrap around me, taking as much down her throat as she can. I wrap her hair around my fist and press deeper until she gags just a little.

"Too much?" I rasp, not sure I'll survive it if she takes even another inch.

She doesn't look away, those nimbus-cloud eyes dark, and eases more of me in.

"Fuck." I cup her jaw and caress the muscles in her throat as she starts working her mouth around me, a suction so perfect my vision goes blurry for a second. If I look at the way I disappear in her mouth, I'll lose it down her throat, and I want this to last as long as humanly possible.

With my eyes closed, every other sense awakens. The mewling little sounds she makes, like a thirsty cat at a trough of cream. The way her nails dig into my thighs, little claws holding me still so she can get it just how she wants. The warm, wet brush of her tongue and the lining of her cheeks caressing my cock. It feels so good, like she peeled back the skin and is sucking my nerves.

"Nix, I'm gonna…"

I open my eyes and know it's a lost cause. Her eyes are squeezed shut, and I'm so far down her throat, choking her just enough for tears to slip over her cheeks. The sight of her like that… I try to pull her mouth away in time, but she opens her eyes, stares at me, and deliberately moves my hand, linking our fingers while she sucks and swallows. With my other hand, I press the back of her head, pushing in deeper and letting myself go, shedding all thought and giving in to an unbridled fucking of her mouth.

"Shit." I can barely speak, and I come so hard, spilling down her throat, overflowing the sides, running down her neck. It's the most erotic thing I've ever seen. She licks from base to crown, torturing me even more.

When she's done, we crawl onto the bed. She hovers over me, kissing me, feeding me the salty taste lingering on her lips and coating the sweet interior of her mouth. Never breaking the tender kiss, she lies down beside me. Exhausted, we lay our heads on one pillow, twist our hands together between our chests, and in the tumble of sheets and rain-damp bodies, we fall asleep. And in my dreams, we make love all night.

CHAPTER 18
LENNIX

I'M THERE AGAIN, STANDING ON A RISE OF ROCK OVERLOOKING THE sacred grounds where my tribe has wed and danced and sung and mourned. We cluster at the edge of the cliff, watching the clearing. Mena, my father, Mr. Paul—everyone from my Sunrise Dance all stands with me. A gentle touch pushes my hair away from my face.

"Mama," I whisper. My throat burns, and she blurs in front of me through a scrim of tears. "I thought you were gone. They said you were gone."

"No." Mama's eyes shimmer with tears, too. "Never. I'm always here, Lenn. Always with you."

I reach for her, needing to hold her, to feel her solid and soft against me, but she disappears.

A sound forces my attention to the plains below. The trees, there moments before, are gone now, and the land has been invaded by monstrous machines. They claw through the dirt, overturning clumps of it and shoving it aside. The bulldozer's massive jaw scoops up the earth, and an arm dangles over its row of steel teeth. The truck turns and drops its burden of soil and limbs to the ground. The body falls and rolls over, revealing the face. Lifeless eyes stare back at me through a veil of dark hair.

A low, keening scream builds from my belly and scrambles up my throat. "Mama!"

CHAPTER 19
MAXIM

I wake to the sound of Lennix's terror and reach to turn on the bedside lamp. She kicks and strikes out. I put my arms around her and press her back to my chest.

"Nix," I say, my voice sharpening as I force my way to full consciousness. "Nix, baby, stop."

"Mama," she mutters, tossing her head back so hard she nails my chin.

I work my jaw and flip her onto her back. "Lennix, wake up."

"Mama, oh God," she says fretfully, her eyes still closed. "Come back. Mama, don't go. Don't go."

The words jumble, dissolving into sobs that shake her shoulders and crumple her pretty face.

"Shhhh." I bend my lips to her ear. "I'm here. Hey, I'm right here."

When I push her hair back, she stills, grabbing my hand and bringing it to her face. She kisses my hand, and her tears wet my fingers.

"Mama," she says, her eyes squeezed tightly shut. "I thought… I thought…"

"I'm here," I whisper to her. I'm not sure if I'm telling her that I'm her mother to keep her calm, or if I'm telling her that I'm here, but it doesn't matter. I am here, and I want to do whatever I can to ease this pain.

In slow blinks, she comes awake. She looks up at me and then around the room.

"Was I dreaming?" The words emerge hoarse and hesitant.

"Yeah." I brush tears from her cheeks, that same spot in my chest going tight seeing her pain as when I witnessed her simple joy in the rain.

"I woke you up," she says. "I'm sorry."

"It's fine."

I lie down beside her. She's shaking, and I can't tell if it's a reaction from the dream or the coolness of the room.

"Are you cold?" I pull away to get out of bed and adjust the temperature.

"No." She grabs my arm under the sheet and huddles into me, her bare skin cool against mine. "Please just…hold me." Her laugh comes shaky and thin. "You said no attachments, and here I am in your bed, clinging and crying and—"

"You know that's not what I meant." I tuck her into my side and kiss her hair.

I hesitate when she doesn't respond but just shivers against me.

"You remember your dream? You want to talk about it?"

An anxious breath is her only response. I'm about to move on, make sure she knows she doesn't have to talk about it, but then she nods. I wait a few more beats while she grips my arm a little tighter.

"I've had the dream before. I'm always at the cliffs overlooking the valley where Cade laid the pipeline."

When she mentions Cade, I'm not sure if she means my father or the company, but I know to her they're one and the same.

"We're all there." Her short chuckle breezes over my skin. "Even your friend and mine, Mr. Paul."

I chuckle a little, too, but I still hear her crying in her sleep, frantic and trapped in her unconsciousness, still feel her shivering against me, so her comment only goes so far to lighten the moment.

"My mom is there." Her voice cracks and she pulls in a wispy breath. "She's so beautiful. So alive. And then she's not."

"What happens?"

"When I look down again, the construction trucks are there, and they dig up my mom's body."

I pull her closer, unable to wrap my arms around her tightly enough. "I'm so sorry."

"It… There's just no closure, you know? The cops were a joke when she disappeared. I mean, it's so tough getting justice when our women go missing."

"Why is that?"

"Sometimes it's complicated because of where it happens. If it's on a reservation, most Indian nations are so limited in criminal authority over non-Indians. Communication between local police and tribal government sucks, and there's bureaucratic breakdown. Mostly they simply don't care as much, if you ask me. Whatever the reason, it's tougher to protect Native women and to prosecute for them. The trail grew so cold with my mom's case, we found nothing."

"No one was ever arrested or even questioned?"

"No. They found her phone beside her car and traces of her…" She pauses to clear her throat. "Traces of her blood like maybe there had been a struggle, but nothing that could lead us anywhere."

"I'm so sorry."

"It's like when someone you love disappears like that, you don't want to stop hoping. There's no body. No certainty, so there's this stubborn part of you that refuses to believe they're gone. There will be some miracle. They've been abducted. They've been in someone's basement for years, and just when you're about to give up hope, they'll escape." Her laugh is humorless and pained.

"But that is one in a million," she continues. "In most cases, some monster just got away with it, and you'll never have answers."

I have no idea how to comfort her beyond holding her close, rubbing her arms, and shutting the hell up so she can say what she needs to say, letting her know I'm here and I'm listening. I want to know.

"My only solace—and this won't make sense, I warn you of that now—was that at Christmas, we went to that clearing where I had my Sunrise Dance, where so many of our sacred ceremonies happened, where some of our heroes are buried. I laid her to rest there in the only way I knew how. I still go there every Christmas, even for just a few minutes. It's like spending part of the holiday with her."

She shakes her head, tucks a wild chunk of hair behind her ear.

"I know it seems morbid. It was a false peace, but it was the most I ever got. And then Warren Cade and that senator came in with their damn pipeline."

Bitterness and hatred drip from her words, and it almost doesn't even sound like my Nix—like the funny, brave, brilliant woman I've known for the past few days.

"One thing I can say is that protest, that pipeline gave me focus," she says. "It's shaped me. I know I'll fight men like Warren Cade for the rest of my life, and I know I have to work the system to help people it doesn't care about. That's why I've been so careful about my next steps."

"It's too important to get it wrong," I say, understanding for the first time the pivotal role the pipeline and my father have played in shaping the girl I've come to care so much about in such a short time.

"Exactly." She tilts her head back and sets her eyes on my face. "I have to be intentional about everything. I can't afford wrong steps, bad moves. It's not for me. It's for the people I want to help."

I should have told her that first night who my father was. Who I am. Hell, I should have told them in the cell that day four years ago, but I didn't see it serving any purpose. I know most people would love to be a Cade, but I can't say I've been proud of that name or of my father in a long time. I've lived the past four years out from under the shadow of my family and all that comes with them. Hearing my father's role in the dreams that torture Lennix, I can't ruin this connection by telling her the truth yet. It's all tangled up in her mind and heart—her mother's disappearance and death and the pipeline that ruined the sacred grounds where she laid her mother to rest. It's a sticky, convoluted web, and my father? He's the spider.

"Let's not talk about it anymore." She snuggles closer, pressing her naked body into mine. "I'm better now."

I'll deal with the issue of my name later. Now I just want to fully embrace our past few days. We said at the end of the week we'd walk away, but I refuse to wreck the little time I have left with the truth.

I roll her onto her back and prop myself up on my elbows so I'm looking down at her. "The day after tomorrow, I have to go to London."

"What?" Dismay and disappointment tint her voice and her face. "Why?"

"It's a meeting for the Antarctica expedition. We have people on the team from all over the world. Those of us in easy traveling distance of London, like David and me, will go in person. Others will Skype in."

"So we lose a day."

"Yeah. When I come back, we'll only have one day before you fly home."

"Then I guess," she says, kissing my neck and sliding her hand down my back to squeeze my ass, "we should make the most of it."

My laugh is an aroused exhalation. "My sentiments exactly, which is why I want you to ditch your friends and spend the entire day with me tomorrow. They can have you back when I go to London."

"What do you have in mind?"

"You have to trust me." I trace the contours of her face with my index finger.

"Okay. I trust you."

I feel like an ass because I know how precious and hard-won her trust is. Her hatred for my father still burns bright and fresh. I have to tell her the truth, but I'm selfish enough, I *want* her too much just like this for as long as I can have this, to even tell her my real name.

CHAPTER 20
LENNIX

MAXIM'S SMILE STEALS HEARTS FOR A LIVING. THE MAGNETISM OF it draws me to him sitting on that wall across from the hostel.

It's only been a few hours since we parted ways. Maxim brought me home long enough for us to both change and prepare for our day together. He slides his aviators into his hair, and strands of it curl around and cling to the lenses. I'll miss the way his hair feels threading through my fingers when he's inside me. I'll miss the way he kisses me like he can't believe it's real—a startling sense of wonder from someone so pragmatic, cynical even. I'll miss the way he tangles our fingers under tables and touches me every chance he gets. There are a dozen things I'll miss about him. I'm already cataloguing them with only two days left of whatever this is, has been.

"Hey." He stands from the wall, laying that same book about Antarctic expeditions down, spine up. He grabs my hand and pulls me into a hug. I don't wait for him to bend and kiss me but tip up on my toes to take his mouth with mine. My hands slide over his shoulders and into his hair. I press him close and keep my eyes sealed tightly over sudden tears.

I'm going to lose him.

I've only had a few days with him, but just the thought of not having this every day brings tears to my eyes.

He pulls back and links our hands at our sides.

"Well, good morning to you, too," he says with a chuckle.

I force a laugh and keep my lashes lowered a second longer, composing myself. *Get your shit together, girl.*

My little pep talk goes to hell when I glance up to find his stare fixed intently on my face. I fear my shit is beyond getting together. Can you feel so deeply for someone after just a few days? But Maxim has been inside me. It's not just sex; he's entertained my impossible dreams. Witnessed my nightmares. Maybe I waited so long to make love because I knew I'd be bad at this—at taking someone into my body but checking them at the door to my soul. I rolled out a welcome mat for Maxim, and it's no one's fault but mine. He said no attachments from the beginning.

I don't care if it hurts.

I said that the first night we made love. Naive, silly girl. Myopic child, thinking only to have him with no notion how hard it would be to let him go.

"You okay?" he asks, a frown pleating his thick brows.

"Yeah." I brighten my smile for him. "I'm fine."

"Kimba and Viv didn't mind me kidnapping you for the day?"

My smile becomes more natural. "They're actually relishing sleeping in. After dinner last night, Aya took them drinking. They're pretty hungover."

"Good. Then they won't miss you too badly."

We walk to the train station and board. Anticipation overtakes the sadness the thought of our pending separation brought on.

"Where are we going?" I lean onto his shoulder where he's seated beside me.

"West," he says, deliberately cryptic.

I pinch his side, though it's just lean muscle, not much to get hold of.

"Ow!" He laughs so loudly several heads on the train turn. "You little… I'm punishing you for that later."

"Spank me?" I give him an eager look. "Tie me up? Gag me?"

"Are you sure you were a virgin just days ago?" he whispers. "I'm not sure I can keep up with you."

"You seemed to be doing fine this morning."

"And last night." He licks at the seam of my lips, teasing them open for a deepening kiss. "God, I want to fuck you all the time."

"We have that in common then. Now tell me where we're going."

"Sassenheim. Keukenhof Gardens is a little more curated. Like a tulip museum. I thought we'd go a little off the beaten path."

"Says the man leaving for Antarctica in a week. I'm pretty sure you're king of 'off the beaten path.'"

"You may be right about that." He laughs. "I think we can access tulips better on our own, finding the fields, seeing windmills along the way. Maybe have a picnic. Sound okay?"

"Seriously? It sounds like the best day ever." As soon as he said "we," it sounded perfect. I want to see tulips and the coastline and anything of this country he wants to show me, but I mostly just want more time with him.

"Good. The season for tulips is just beginning, so they won't be in full bloom but still beautiful. The weather has been favorable this year. Mid-April is best, so we're about a month early. I just wanted some time out of the city," he says. "Some quiet with you. A slower pace with fewer distractions where we can just enjoy each other."

"It's working already."

The train ride lasts about a half an hour, and as soon as we step off, I'm in love. A canal runs through the village, bordered by narrow houses. Small boats line the canal walls, and stone bridges crisscross the water. It reminds me of Amsterdam but emits a different energy, like the city's restive cousin. It's so vivid, and the air is crisp. It only takes a few minutes to rent bikes, find a bike path, and start off. It's cool, and the wind whips at my face and hair. *Exhilarating.*

"You okay?" Maxim asks over his shoulder, pedaling slightly ahead of me on the bike path.

I increase my speed to pull up beside him. "Yes. I'm loving this."

"I thought you would."

As we ride, the landscape changes, signs of the village falling away and replaced by lush countryside, by fields and horses leisurely grazing, not bothering to look up when we ride past. Stout windmills, their thick, wooden arms lazily whirring, dot the scenic route along the highway hugging the coastline.

He pulls over and stops at a railing bordering the bike path. I pull up beside him.

"See those?" He points out to the water.

"The windmills?"

He slants me a grin. "Those are wind turbines, not windmills. There's a difference."

"Yeah, well, what about them?"

"They're mine," he says, a possessive glint to his eyes.

My mouth falls open, and I scoot closer to the rail like that will somehow bring me much closer to the objects floating on the water, starkly white and elegant.

"What do you mean they're yours?"

"I bought them. Just those few, but it's a start. I used the last of my money."

"You *own* them? Oh, my God. What are you gonna do with them?"

"The Netherlands is making real headway with wind energy. It's a viable substitute for fossil fuels and the dirtier ways we get power."

"Wow. You own windmills."

"Wind *turbines*, Nix."

"You're a regular old Don Quixote," I go on, warming to my analogy. "A knight errant, determined to save the world. Comes fully equipped with windmills."

"So I'm a joke now, huh?" He reaches for me with a playful growl.

"Ahhh!" I jump on my bike and take off, pedaling furiously, yelling over my shoulder when I see him coming after me, "It's Doc Quixote!"

We ride and laugh until we reach the tulip fields, rolled out like vibrant carpets displayed in an open-air bazaar. Great swaths of purple, yellow, red, and pink.

"Most of these fields are owned by farmers who sell the tulips. Some won't even let you take photos, much less pick the flowers," Maxim tells me, bringing his bike to a stop. "Fortunately for you, your guide knows where to pick 'em."

We ride a bit farther, alternating between moments of easy silence, conversation passed between us as we ride beside each other and, at one point, a rousing chorus of Billy Joel's greatest hits. Maxim makes up his own ridiculous lyrics for "We Didn't Start the Fire."

"Rabbit ears, Britney Spears, iPhone, *Home Alone*."

"I'm pretty sure the iPhone hadn't been invented when Billy Joel wrote that song." I laugh after his last chorus, which included such anachronisms as *The West Wing* and DVRs.

"You have to go ruin it with technicalities," he says.

"Also known as truth."

"Truth is relative."

"If you think that, maybe you *should* go into politics," I say. We've reached the flower-picking garden and walk our bikes through wide aisles between the rows of tulips. "Do you have a general disdain for all politicians, or have there been any good ones, in your expert opinion?"

"There's just always an agenda. Their own glory usually, but a few of them have inspired me."

"Like who?"

"I liked the Kennedys."

"Figures," I say with a snort.

"Excuse me?" He sends me a lifted brow and a half grin.

"Don't tell me no one's ever compared you to JFK Jr."

"What the hell?" His surprised laughter rings loud in the relative stillness of the field. We've come on a weekday at the very beginning of tulip season. There aren't many tourists today, and we have a private patch of this colorful quilt to ourselves.

"Oh, come on." I smile and tip my bicycle's kickstand, leaving it and walking down a row of flowers. "The height, the dark hair, the dreamy smile and bedroom eyes."

"You think I have bedroom eyes and a dreamy smile?"

"Like I would have given my V-card after a day to some slouch with a non-dreamy smile."

"Don't forget my bedroom eyes." He bats his long eyelashes rapidly and laughs when I flip him off. He settles his bike between two rows of tulips and joins me.

"The Kennedys were far from perfect, you know," I tell him.

"Well documented, but why do we expect our politicians to be perfect? I'd rather have someone say, 'Hey. I cheat on my wife, but what does that have to do with me keeping us out of stupid wars? Or raising taxes on the people who can least afford it?'"

He takes my hand and pulls me into his side as we walk farther away from the bikes.

"When you think about it, we had so little time with JFK," he continues. "But he's the one everyone talks about. He understood the importance of vision—of inspiring people. He literally said we're going to the moon. And we did. He told us to ask not what the country could do for us but, dammit, what can we do for this country. Responsibility, balanced with compassion. That's the problem with most Democrats. So much compassion, but they never show me how they'll pay for it or who's going to take responsibility for it, and they need to be ruthless from time to time. Show me some killer instinct. If you care so much about people, fight for them. If your opponent fights grimy, maybe you'll have to, but get it done for the people you say need it."

"And what's the problem with Republicans?"

"*They* have a compassion problem." He kicks a rock, sending it skipping ahead of us. "They're medieval in their views on just about everything, including climate change."

"And you are which?"

"I'm myself. I hate the two-party system. It asks people to set aside their individual principles for a platform. Give me a guy who says, 'I believe like four of their things and maybe three of theirs, and they both get it wrong on this shit, but don't worry. I got my own plan for that. Follow me.'"

"Wow. A campaign slogan if I ever heard one."

"Now you see why I'll never do politics. It's all power games and manipulation, not actually giving a shit. If they cut a deal that's advantageous to them and their constituents happen to benefit, that's fine, but they are first."

"So there's a very short list of politicians you've approved of."

He shrugs. "Some exceptions. I actually liked Bobby even more than President Kennedy. He said, 'The future is not a gift. It is an achievement.'"

"I love that."

"I'm gonna *do* that," Maxim says. The force of his will and ambition is like a wall. "You don't have to be a politician to change the world. Matter of fact, I think your chances are better if you're not one. Power blurs everything and can rob you of perspective."

It's a shame he doesn't want to run because I'm here for everything he just said. And the man is fine, which goes a long way with American voters. They love a pretty POTUS.

"I honestly don't care about left or right," I tell him. "I just want things to change, and I don't care which side does it."

"Agreed."

We walk through rows of tulips with color so rich each bulb looks hand-painted. I pick them and drop them in my basket along the way, taking a few photos of the flowers and sneaking a few of Maxim, who looks incongruously big beside the delicate blooms.

"Getting enough?" he asks idly. "Pictures, I mean."

"I need one of us here together."

He lifts his head at that, his eyes meeting mine, and a smile fully blooms on his handsome face.

"Miss," he calls to an older woman a few rows over and down. When she looks back, he turns that dazzling smile on her, and of course in a few seconds she's headed our way.

"Would you take a picture of me and my…" His words falter, and he looks as unsure how to fill in that blank as I am. "Would you take a picture of us?"

"Certainly." She takes his phone and smiles indulgently.

He pulls me in front of him and rests his chin on my head. She snaps the first picture. When I glance up at him, the look in his eyes warms me and melts any reserve I had left. He bends to cup my chin and kisses me tenderly. I hear her snapping the photo but couldn't care less. I lean up into that kiss, deepen it, drag it out until she clears her throat.

"Sorry," he says, offering her an apologetic grin. "Thank you."

"Anything for young love," she says wistfully and returns to her basket a few rows away.

Young love. That's not what we have. It must be too soon for that, but we have something, and it's making itself at home in my heart more every day, as much as I try to fight it. I try to hold myself back, remind myself that this isn't permanent, but my heart gives me the finger and goes its own way.

"Hungry?" Maxim asks. "Food?"

"Yes, please."

After we buy a picnic basket stuffed with wine and cheese and fruit and sandwiches, we walk our bikes down to a riverbank. He spreads the blanket, and I lay out our lunch. The sun is high, the weather mild, the air fresh, and the company? Maxim is the only person I want to be here with right now.

"Any more on your politician back home?" he asks, the strong length of him stretched out. He's propped on one elbow, popping grapes into his mouth.

"When I got back to the hostel this morning, Mena had emailed me some things to look over." I take a sip of wine from a disposable cup. "The pay is almost nonexistent, of course, but it would be great experience. Nighthorse is the real deal. The things he wants to do for Natives in Oklahoma are exactly what I would love to see happen everywhere. I'm impressed."

"Think you'll do it?"

"I told her I want to if he's interested."

"Oh, he will be. How could he not be?"

"We'll see." I shrug. "I'm with you. I can't stand most politicians. They're the main ones who lied to Natives. Tricked us. Betrayed us. Our own senator slipped that pipeline in at the eleventh hour for Warren Cade."

Maxim makes a strangled sound, and when I look over at him, he's coughing.

"You okay? Wine go down the wrong way?"

"Uh, something like that." He stares into his cup. "Sorry. You were saying something about—"

"Warren Cade, yeah. He's such an asshole." I take a deep breath to counter the fury that rises every time I think about that heartless man. "But of course he'd look after his own interests. Senator Middleton was supposed to be looking after ours. I'm going to learn this system inside and out and put leaders in place who will look after what's best for the people."

"Who determines best, though?" Maxim crumbles a crust of bread on his napkin. "Some would argue what Middleton did created new jobs for his constituents, and that was right."

He holds up his hands defensively when I aim a baleful look at him. "Hey, just playing devil's advocate. Don't shoot me."

"I know that pipeline created jobs, but it also broke promises the government made to my people. *Again.* It endangers the water supply for an entire community. And you know what? They declare buildings historically protected so businesses can't destroy them with new offices or whatever they determine means progress. That's because someone says the value of that thing is worth more than the revenue destroying it would create. Yet every time something of *ours* has been declared sacred, it's desecrated as soon as protecting it inconveniences someone in power."

"So you want the power."

"I want to spread it. Create it. Put it where it will be used better," I say, indignation riding the blood in my veins. "Yes, there's usually more than one 'right.' Right is relative sometimes. Not life or death or cruelty or those absolutes. All you can do is fight for the right you believe in. There aren't enough people fighting for my people's 'rights.' What is right for us *and* the basic rights it seems are so quickly afforded to everyone but us. That's what I plan to spend my life fighting for."

He smiles, and it's almost sad.

"What?" I ask. "What are you thinking?"

"I'm thinking," he says, pushing my shoulder gently until I fall back on the blanket and he hovers over me, "that you are going to be so damn incredible." Our eyes catch, and his smile fades. "And I wish I could be around to see it."

He told me. I knew this wasn't permanent. He said no attachments and that he would walk away, but the finality in his words hurts so much.

"You'll be off on your expeditions, huh?" I ask, reaching up to push back the dark hair falling in his eyes. "Saving Mother Earth?"

"Something like that." He runs his thumb over my bottom lip. "Antarctica. Then I'm going to the Amazon. You know 20 percent of the world's oxygen comes from the Amazon?"

"No shit. You learn something new every day."

"You can if you wanna." He laughs. "Then possibly the Maldives, which within just a few decades may be uninhabitable."

"Wait, like the islands? Like great vacay Maldives?"

"They're only six feet above sea level. By the middle of this century, parts of the Maldives and even parts of Hawaii may be underwater."

"You're serious?"

"Of course I'm serious. The shame is that by the time people start believing how serious this really is, it'll be too late."

"How did you get into this? Why is it so important to you?"

"Let's just say I grew up thinking a lot about our natural resources," he says with an ironic smile that tells me absolutely nothing. "And didn't always like what I found."

"So you're off to save the planet."

"And don't forget I want to make a lot of money."

"Capitalist," I whisper, straining up to kiss his neck.

"Crusader," he whispers his retort over my shoulder, licking and sucking my collarbone.

"We're going in completely different directions, aren't we?" I hate the pathetic sound of my own voice—the way my heart constricts at the thought of him in the wilds of Antarctica and the Amazon while I toil on behalf of the future Senator Nighthorse in Oklahoma.

"Yeah, we are." He tugs on my hand and pulls us to a sitting position on the blanket, seating me between his knees with my back to his chest. "Let me show you where I'll be."

"What?" I peer at him over my shoulder. "What do you mean?"

"Gimme your hands," he says, his voice resonating in my back. His arms bracket me as he reaches for my hands, holding them out in front of us.

"Let's go back to the days when the world was flat for a second." He places my hands side by side, palm up. "I don't have a globe, so we'll make a map. Here's the good old US of A." With his index finger, he sketches what roughly looks like the shape of the United States at the far edge of my left palm. "You'll be there in Oklahoma."

He draws a line down and across to the far lower quadrant of my right palm and stops at my wrist. "I'll be all the way down here in Antarctica."

He moves up a little, leaving tiny needles of sensation across my skin with every touch. "The team will leave from here to get there."

"Where is that?" I ask, my throat closing up and my eyes stinging.

"New Zealand. It's closest."

"I always think of New Zealand as hot, not that close to the coldest place in the world."

"That's one of the fascinating things about it," he says, the excitement piquing in his voice. "There's this point where tropical and arctic merge. Antarctica is this study of paradoxes. An icy desert. Two things that never should have been together." He kisses my neck, his breath feathering my hair with the words. "But they fit. Make sense. Belong."

Like us.

I don't say it, but I feel it.

He closes my hands on the map he sketched into my palms, holding them together and pulling me tighter to his chest.

"Now you've got the whole world in your hands." He laughs into my hair. "I know. Corny, right?"

"No. Not corny."

Sweet.

I open my hands again, studying the path he drew from the upper corner of my left palm to the lowest corner of my right. We'll be at extreme points on the Earth. As far apart as two people could be.

If I was smart, I'd begin putting distance between us now, preparing my heart for his absence. For his ultimate, inevitable departure. But I'm not as smart as I thought I was. I turn to face him, wrap my arms around his neck, and push until he's on his back and I'm straddling his hips with my thighs. I slide my hands into the luxury of his hair. With every kiss, I brush my palms over it, erasing every mile that soon will separate us. We don't have long, but right now, I have this.

CHAPTER 21
MAXIM

I miss Lennix already.

I should be reviewing my notes for the team meeting in London, but what am I doing? Looking through pictures of us...of her at the tulip fields yesterday.

This is why. This is why the *fuck* I don't do relationships. I have goals. All the things my father thinks I can't do without him and the Cade name, I'll do. Yet here I am, embarking on the most treacherous and important trip of my life, and I'm grinning like an idiot at pictures of Lennix in a tulip field. The wind whips through her hair like it did the first day I met her, but her eyes aren't stormy or teary like they were at the protest. They smile at me, that indefinable gray. There's a sea of color behind her, countless beautiful flowers, and she puts them all to shame.

"She really is gorgeous," David murmurs from the seat next to me.

I darken my phone screen and snap my head around to glare at him. "Don't even think about it."

"Dude, I'm screwing her best friend. Seriously?"

"I don't care if you...wait. What? You and Kimba?"

"Where have you been all week? Yeah, I tapped that on day two. You didn't notice because you were too busy falling in love."

"Am not." I frown down at the dark screen.

"Oh, so you're just tapping that ass, too?"

My fingers curl reflexively with the urge to strangle him for talking about Lennix and what we've shared like that. "You don't know shit," I say as casually as I can manage. "We're all on vacation. Whatever."

"Yeah, Kimba and I were totally up front. Just a holiday lay. I mean, a damn good one. Did I mention her ass?"

"You don't have to, thanks."

"But when she leaves in a couple of days, I'm cool. That's it. Can you say the same about Lennix?"

It feels like there's an uprising at the cellular level in my body at the thought of leaving her forever. At the thought of reducing what we've shared to a holiday lay. I'm a learner, a researcher, a student. I don't ignore facts because I don't like what I find. Maybe that's why I haven't allowed myself to examine my visceral reaction to Lennix from the first moment I saw her. Seeing her again felt like a miracle. Am I really going to let her go for good?

"It's probably good you do stay focused, though," David says. "About a dozen things could go really wrong on this trip, man. And every one of them could kill us."

"That's pretty bleak. We'll be fine. We've prepared as much as we possibly can."

Hadn't Shackleton prepared? And Douglas Mawson? They were not only both brilliant scientists but also exceptional tacticians. Sheer will and the force of their leadership got them out of the worst conditions when things went wrong on their Antarctic expeditions. Both ended up stranded. Men died.

"We're lucky to have Grim," David continues, scanning the manual Brock Grimsby assembled for us. The guy is a former Navy SEAL. He devised the fitness regimen we've followed the last six months of preparation.

"Damn lucky," I agree.

"He's good, but even he can't beat a blizzard alone. Every one of us needs to know this shit inside and out."

He's right. Shackleton lost his ship *The Endurance*. He stood on the Arctic's icy banks with the men he had left and watched it sink. I can't afford distractions. As much as I would enjoy losing myself in that spill of black hair and that angel's body, we leave for the Antarctic next week. I have to be ready to pull my weight.

When I get back to Amsterdam, I'll have one more day with Lennix. Then I'll walk away like I said I would. After that, who knows what will happen? All I know is it can't happen now.

Determinedly, I take out my notes to review our emergency plan and put my phone away.

CHAPTER 22
LENNIX

One. More. Day.

That's all we have left. Once Maxim returns from London tomorrow afternoon, we'll actually have less than a day before I fly back to the States.

"These are nice," Vivienne says. "What do you think?"

I crawl out of my own head to see what Vivienne is considering. We've been exploring Amsterdam's famous floating flower market, bursting with narcissus, carnations, violets, orchids, and any number of buds that saturate every inch of this morning with color.

And tulips. Like the ones Maxim and I picked yesterday. What a perfect day that was with him. For how long after I leave will everything come back to him?

"That bad?" Vivienne frowns at the flowers bundled by their necks in her hand. "I thought they were—"

"They're beautiful," I say. "Sorry. Really so pretty."

"Agreed," Kimba says. "Get seeds for those. Make sure they're packaged and okay for export before you buy them."

"Right," Vivienne says, nodding at the advice. "Forgot about that."

"You didn't tell us much about your day in the tulips," Kimba says while Vivienne completes the transaction for the flowers and seeds.

"Oh." I adjust the oversized bag on my shoulder and smile, I'm sure unnaturally. "It was great. Fine. Fun."

Kimba and Vivienne exchange a meaningful glance before looking back to me.

"Okay, Lenn," Kimba says. "We need to talk."

We exit the greenhouse suspended on water and step back onto the street. Glimpses of the Singel canal brighten our view, and the plethora of flowers makes the air heavy with fragrance.

"We really like Maxim," Vivienne says.

"He's great," Kimba adds. "And fine as hell. That goes without saying, but I just said it."

We share a laugh, and I hold my breath for the lecture I feel coming on.

"But," Kimba continues, "we all know he said it was just this week."

"And it was no strings," Vivienne says. "No attachments."

"I'm well aware," I reply stiffly. "This is under control."

"Oh, honey, if you actually believe you have this under control," Kimba says wryly, "it's even worse than we thought."

"Guys, my eyes are wide open."

"So is your heart." Vivienne grabs my elbow so we stop in the street. "He's your first, Lenn. And he's gorgeous and fantastic in bed and a freaking PhD."

"And he looks at you like the sun rises and sets on your vagina," Kimba mutters, stopped on the other side of me. "A man looks at you like that, fucks you like that, it's hard not to get ideas, even when they tell you straight up, 'Don't get ideas.' You hit the V-card lottery, boo."

"I'm not a child. Just because I was a virgin—"

"Four days ago," Vivienne interjects drolly.

"Doesn't mean I'm some pitiful little girl who'll be all clingy when Maxim and I go our separate ways." I say it even though my heart mocks me that I might be exactly that when I lose him. God, *lose* him? I don't *have* him. He's not mine. *We're nothing.* I feed myself the mantra that was supposed to protect my heart, to keep it safe and separate from the way Maxim makes my body feel. I can barely admit to myself, much less to my friends, that it's not working.

"We'll be the ones mopping up the tears," Vivienne says, taking my hand. "And we won't mind 'cause you've done it for both of us more than once."

"A lot more than once." Kimba takes my other hand. "So we know how bad it hurts, and we just don't want to see you go through that."

"Especially with this amazing opportunity on the horizon," Vivienne says. "I mean, working for a Native American candidate running for the Senate? Could it be any more tailor-made for you? You need your head screwed on right to make the most of it."

"I know." I squeeze their hands, drawing strength and sensibility from the contact. "You're right. Maybe I'm feeling…more than I should for Maxim. And he did tell me it was just this week and that he would walk away."

But every look, every touch, every time I'm with him, I see *stay* in his eyes. We agreed it was only for this week, but when he kisses me, it feels like it could be *forever*. Like we could make a world for ourselves, even though our paths are taking us to different corners of the globe.

I don't tell my friends that because they're already worried something might happen to my heart. I can't tell them something probably already has.

"You've been heard," I say, turning a grateful grin on them both. "Duly noted. I get it. This week. No more. No heartbreak. Now didn't we say we'd do some damage at Leidsestraat? I got euros burning a hole in my pocket. Let's shop!"

We're obsessing over a pair of earrings when my phone rings.

"Auntie, hey!" I answer Mena.

"Lennix, I have some news."

I step away from the counter where Vivienne and Kimba sort through the array of jewelry. My heartbeat picks up.

The job?

"Okay. What gives?" I ask, not even trying to keep the excitement from my voice.

"You got it!"

"Oh, my gosh." I press my hand to my chest, but it's no use trying to calm down. My heart is banging at my ribs like a drumline. "Seriously?"

"Seriously!" Mena laughs. "One catch."

"A catch? What is it?"

"Well, he wants you to come right away."

"Yeah, I fly back home Friday."

"He'd like you *here* on Friday. Can you fly back tonight?"

"Wow. Why so quickly?"

"He'd, um, like to tell you himself," Mena says, her voice pitched lower. "He's here with me. Would you speak to him?"

"Now?" I squeak. "He's there with you now?"

"It's a special situation, Lenn," she says, her voice sobering. "Or he wouldn't ask. Talk to him."

"Okay," I say after a brief pause. "Put him on."

"Lennix?" A smooth, deep voice comes over the line.

"Uh, yes, Mr. Nighthorse?"

"Please call me Jim."

"All right. Jim."

"Thanks for talking with me. I understand you're on spring break in Europe."

"Of course." I allow a beat before going on. "Mena has told me a lot about your campaign, and I'd be honored to work with you."

"I'm the one who would be honored. I remember the Cade Energy pipeline protests, and I've read about the sacred runs you organized throughout college on other projects. Your transcript and résumé are outstanding. You're an impressive young lady."

A smile spreads over my face, and I lean against a nearby glass showcase counter. "Thank you, sir. That means a lot to me."

"Just the truth."

"Mena said you need me to come there Friday? Like—"

"Tonight if you can," he interrupts. "We have a situation down here I think you're uniquely equipped to help us with. A young girl is missing."

That was how the police described my mother at first.

Missing.

We've lived in the agonizing limbo between *missing* and *murdered* ever since.

"She went missing two days ago," Jim continues. "Her family is Cherokee, and they live not too far from one of those pipeline construction sites. Third girl to go missing this year from this community. I don't have to tell you what this could be."

No. Tales of young girls missing, held hostage, raped by horny men far from home for long stretches of time, certain if they could hurt any woman with impunity, it would be one of ours.

"Time and visibility are of the essence," Jim says. "We need as many people to hear about this as fast as possible. The longer this goes, the less chance we find her."

"Yes, for sure."

"This is happening all the time to our women. Underreported. Undervalued. We want to make some noise and get her face everywhere. Any leads we can find. Anyone who can help. At the town meeting, I'll talk about her, but I'll also talk about how she's one of too many."

"What do you want me to do?" I ask, keeping my voice level even as panic rises on the young girl's behalf.

"Speak. I want you to tell your story, Lennix. I want you to tell your mother's story."

My mother's story has no end. Her life was interrupted mid-sentence—a dangling participle. An infinite etcetera of dots but no period. I know what this girl's family is feeling right now, and I can only pray they won't have to live with the unending mystery of what has happened.

"I don't want to seem like I'm exploiting this situation," Jim goes on, "but I do believe gaining visibility for this case may help us find her and also raise the issue of why this *keeps* happening. With the election coming up, I want people to know I care about this—that if they elect me, I'll work hard for our women. I want them to know that I see them. I hear them."

Can you see me? I don't think you can.

My own words from the pipeline protest four years ago drift into my memory. That moment and this one feel like two ends of a cord finally tying together. And at that point, in that knot, my passion and my purpose meet.

"Jim, I'm on my way."

CHAPTER 23
MAXIM

"You're distracted."

The words come from one of the most formidable men I've ever met. Brock Grimsby stands about six inches over six feet and as wide as a billboard. Think the Rock but without a comic eyebrow. Without a comic *anything*. I'd hate to meet him in a dark alley, but I'm happy as hell he's coming with us to Antarctica.

"Excuse me?" I fake imperiousness and obliviousness.

"You're distracted," Brock repeats. "I can't afford it now, and I for damn sure can't afford it in the middle of Antarctica. I know what you look like focused, and you ain't focused, brother. I need to know your head's gonna be in the game."

"My head's in the game." I glance at my phone to see if I've missed a call from Lennix. "Don't worry."

"Oh, I do worry. That egghead may be the leader, but you're the smartest man in the room."

I glance over to Dr. Larnyard, the professor who funded this expedition with a hodgepodge of grants from the British government, endowments from a climate change research foundation, and donations from select private benefactors. He's a brilliant scholar, but he's no Shackleton. I've read Shackleton's journals. He combined the physical prowess, innovative brilliance and unassailable will it took to lead his team through the worst conditions. Convincing his men they would not die in the frozen wasteland of the Antarctic when there was every indication they would stretched his leadership to its limits, but he was up to the task.

No, Dr. Larnyard is not Shackleton.

"He'll be fine, Grim," I say, using the shortened version of his last name that also describes his general demeanor.

"I know he will because you and I will make sure, but I need your complete focus. This isn't something you do lightly. Make no mistake about it. We're on the last flight in until November. Anything happens once we're there. We're on our own. Men have died in the Antarctic, and if you aren't prepared for the worst, you could, too."

He doesn't have to remind me of the risks involved with this expedition. I've taken every physical, emotional and psychological test they could come up with to ensure I'm prepared and suited for the isolation of wintering over. I've signed every waiver ensuring that if I die, no one is to be held responsible but me.

Our team consists mostly of scientists and doctoral students like me. There are a few unexpected additions. Kind of like when we send teachers up into space. An everyman's perspective on something extraordinary. This will be our rocket ship. Because of the extreme isolation, psychologists actually do study these conditions to analyze how astronauts are affected in space.

There's a congresswoman from Kansas who has been a proponent of climate change legislation. I'm looking forward to talking with her. A schoolteacher from Iowa is joining us. And then there's Grim, who I can only assume, as former special ops, could survive on Mars if he had to. Antarctica isn't space, but there is more of it that has never been seen by human eyes than any other place on Earth. Close enough.

"Gentlemen," Dr. Larnyard says in his clipped British accent. "Shall we proceed?"

I nod, tossing a cup of long-gone-cold coffee in the trash, when my phone rings. It's on silent, but it's Lennix. I assigned a picture of us from the tulip field to her contact. She's looking into the camera, standing in front of me with my arms wrapped around her. I'm looking down at her like none of the glorious flowers around us is worth a glance when she's with me. That's how I felt. I've wanted to talk to her all day.

"Kingsman," Grim says sharply, glancing at my phone. "It's time. Let's get back to it."

I look from my phone to the map of Antarctica on the wall, tiny red flags marking the spots where we'll collect data and samples for our research. Gritting my teeth, I send the call to voice mail.

"Hey, there's been a change of plans," Lennix says on her voice mail when I finally get to listen. "I'm leaving, um, today. I'm trying to get an earlier flight out. Mr. Nighthorse needs me there by Friday. There's this special town hall meeting he's called, and he wants me to speak. I was hoping to see you before my flight leaves. Maybe I still can. I may not be able to get a flight out until tomorrow anyway."

She pauses, and I hear the shaky breath she draws. "Look, I haven't forgotten what you said. You know. About not getting attached. About walking away, even if it feels like more. I just wanted to tell you that it, well, it does feel like more. It feels like…"

Everything. It feels like everything.

The whisper comes from a subterranean place inside me.

"Anyway," she continues, "I wanted you to know that this week with you was really special to me. I don't regret one minute of it."

Her broken laugh comes over the phone. "Guess we never got that canal ride, huh?" she says softly. "If we never see each other again, I'm glad it was you. I'm glad you were my first, and I'll never forget you, Doc. Goodbye."

I've listened to Lennix's message a dozen times since the meeting broke. Since I rushed to Heathrow for an earlier flight back to Amsterdam. Since I landed, caught a cab, and generally bent and broke every rule to get here in record time.

"Here" is the hostel where Lennix has been staying. I've called her several times and kept getting voice mail. She said she was trying to get an earlier flight out. Maybe she didn't. Maybe she's still here. *Maybe...*

"Maxim?" Kimba asks the question from the top of the steps leading from their hostel. She and Vivienne meet me at the street, their glances as curious as they are cautious.

"Is she gone?" I ask. No need for pleasantries. They know why I'm here.

"Yeah," Vivienne answers first. "She found a flight. She's on her way to Oklahoma."

"Dammit." I punch my fist into my palm. "I've been calling her and keep getting voice mail."

"Phone probably turned off for the flight," Kimba says. She glances up the street and then, after a brief hesitation, back to me. "Look, we like you, Maxim."

"Thank you," I reply, braced for their "but."

"But," Kimba continues, "we don't want to see our girl hurt. You know?"

"I won't hurt her."

Won't it hurt when she finds out who you are? a little sanctimonious voice asks.

She does know who I am.

Kimba and Vivienne make me feel as bad as my guilty conscience with their pointed stares and sighs.

"You won't mean to hurt her," Kimba says. "But when a guy says this doesn't mean anything—"

"I never said that." I suck my teeth, exasperated. "We both have huge things going on that require our complete focus."

"Hey, I get it," Vivienne says with a shrug. "But she's a special girl."

"I know that."

"So don't expect her to stay *un*attached," Kimba picks up, "while you roam the globe hunting for icebergs."

I don't reply, but the thought of someone else touching Lennix, of her hair on someone else's pillow, of someone else making her tea the morning after—it makes me want to break something. It makes me want to abandon the trip that has been in the works for a year and fly to Oklahoma.

But I can't. I won't.

"We gotta go," Vivienne says. "A few souvenirs to get before we leave."

"Oh," Kimba says over her shoulder as they start down the street. "Tell David I had a great time and goodbye."

"You don't want to tell him yourself?" I ask, following for a few steps so I can hear her response.

"Oh, no." Kimba laughs, lobbing an ironic look at me over her shoulder. "When *we* said just for fun, we actually meant it."

For an hour after they walk away, I sit on the wall outside their hostel. I almost fool myself into believing the door will open any minute and Lennix will come running out. I picture her the way she looked the night we went to Vuurtoreneiland. The first night we made love.

My mind wanders to a few last-minute items on the supply list Grim tasked me with securing. I haven't tracked down one yet, and we leave for New Zealand, our ship's departure point, in two days.

You're distracted.

Grim said it, and he's right. I can't afford this right now. My life, the safety of our team, the success of our efforts all require my absolute attention. I'll go see Lennix after Antarctica and before the Amazon expedition to see what we should do about this *attachment* we've formed.

I dial her number. I don't know when she'll get this message. Whatever is between us is not for now, but it's not over.

"Nix, hey," I say to her voice mail. "Viv and Kimba said I missed you. I flew back early because I wanted to see you. Look, I, uh, know we said we'd walk away, but I want you to know this week meant so much to me, too. Guess I broke my own rule, huh? I need to focus on this trip. It's not fun and games, and there's still a lot I need to do before we leave. And I know you have some serious shit you're handling there in Oklahoma. Internet access and cell phone will be pretty spotty for me, but when I get back, I'd love to talk about…I don't know. What else this might be. Take care."

Yeah, I'll go to her after the trip.

There will be time then.

CHAPTER 24
LENNIX

"That went well." A grimace skims Jim Nighthorse's distinguished features. "Or as well as something like this can go."

"No, it *did* go well," I agree, glancing around the table at the team he has assembled for his campaign. "There were TV cameras everywhere. This community definitely knows Tammara's missing."

"Her family," Mena says, brushing at her tears. "My heart breaks for them."

They wept openly, begged for any information that might lead to finding their daughter. The helplessness I saw in their faces was so familiar. I know that pain and that plea.

"You were brilliant, Lennix," Jim says.

"It never seems to get any easier," I say with a sad smile. "Talking about my mother. It just reminds me I'll never see her again."

Jim grips my shoulder, firm but gentle. "Thank you for doing it. I know you helped Tammara's cause today."

"I just pray we find her," I whisper.

My phone rings, and I glance at the screen.

"Excuse me," I tell Jim and Mena. "I need to take this."

I step outside, closing the door of Jim's campaign headquarters behind me.

"Hey, Viv," I say with one of the few smiles I've managed over the past two days. "What's up?"

"Just checking on you," she says. "I know you got tossed into the campaign all 'sink or swim.'"

"Yeah, but I'm swimming. At least, so far. It'll be hard to come back to campus next week and finish the semester."

"I know, but you'll be done and back on the trail in just a few months. Did you, uh, talk with Maxim?"

I stiffen and draw a quick breath. "He left a voice mail and said we'd talk when he comes home after Antarctica."

"He seemed pretty desperate when he came back and you were gone."

My heart lifts the slightest bit, but I caution myself. "His voice mail was sweet, but not a commitment or anything. I don't expect to hear from him until he's back in the States," I say, not giving away the signs of heartbreak I know Vivienne is looking for. "You don't have to check on me, Viv. I'm all right."

"I know. I just love you."

"I love you, too, Lennix!" a guy screams from the background.

"Oh, my God." I laugh and lean against the wall. "Is that Wallace?"

"Yes, you know he has the biggest crush on you ever."

"Is he still a brainiac?"

"Total dweeb patrol."

"Shut up, Viv!" Vivienne's older brother, Wallace, says. "And give me the phone."

There's a scuffle as they apparently wrestle. Brain must win over brawn because Wallace's is the next voice I hear.

"My darling," he purrs. "How I've missed thee. Run away with me."

"Oh, my God, Wall." I giggle as only he can make me. "I don't have time to run away with you. Didn't they tell you? I'm that rare entity, someone who has a job all lined up before I've even graduated from college."

"Not so rare, Lenny," he says, pride and amusement mixing in his voice. "I just got a job at the CDC."

"That's amazing! I'm so happy for you."

"Yeah. You know what that means, right?"

"Tell me, please."

"It means I'll have just enough money to keep you in the lifestyle to which you've become accustomed."

"Oh, you mean cup noodles and thrift stores? So glad that MIT education didn't go to waste."

"MIT was two degrees ago," he says with false haughtiness. "Duke, my darling. Duke."

"Well, excuse me, Mr. Microbiologist."

"I promise it's not as fun as it sounds."

"It actually doesn't sound fun at all."

"Seriously? How many men could recite the periodic table to you while making love?"

"Not enough."

The door opens behind me, and Mena points over her shoulder. "Team meeting in two minutes."

I nod and turn my attention back to Wallace and Vivienne. "Hey, Wall, tell Viv we'll talk later. I have to get into this meeting."

"Okay. Just save me a corner of your heart, okay?"

I laugh, but the heart in question flinches. After only a week with Maxim, I'm not sure there's anything left.

CHAPTER 25
MAXIM

"It's cold as a witch's tit."

The observation comes from Peggy Newcombe, the Kansas congresswoman who's one of the smartest people I've ever met in that highly practical way that makes you realize what utter bullshit most people spout. She's a get-things-done kind of person, and I'm glad she's with us.

"And apparently this is just the start," I say. From our base's rooftop, I take in the tarrying sun, its multicolored brilliance washing the sky in shades of twilight. "Winter's here to stay for a while."

"Yup." She squints into the radiant horizon. "This may be our last sunset for the next four months. Now the fun really begins."

The space between sunrise and sunset has shortened more every day during the three months since we've arrived. Now there's barely light at all. We'll live in darkness for the rest of the winter until around September and have very few outlets beyond the walls of the base where we're conducting research. Our winter work focuses on greenhouse gases like carbon dioxide and methane, measuring these particles in the atmosphere. We also study the fossilized particles found in ice cores.

Winter will be setting in, and the long Antarctic night is coming.

There will be times when it's so cold, breathing outside for any amount of time would make the lungs hemorrhage. We're relatively safe as long as nothing goes wrong. That sounds self-evident, but we're on our own until summer. No one can get to us, and we can't get out. We have a doctor in our group, but his medical reach is relatively limited. We are past the PSR—*point of safe return.*

Grim walks up to join us, wrapped in the extreme cold-weather-wear uniform we all sport. He has one of those faces that never tells you anything until he's royally pissed over something stupid you've done. His face is like the rest of him—stern and austere. He doesn't say much, but there's no one I'd rather have at my back if things ever go to hell.

"Men shut their doors against a setting sun," he mutters, gazing unflinchingly at the last rays illuminating the sky.

"Shakespeare?" Peggy asks, brows lifting. "You're a hard man to figure out, Grim."

"Don't try," I advise her. "It's like banging your head against a brick wall."

Grim grunts and takes the lid off the thermos he's holding. He flings his arm out, tossing water over the side. The liquid literally crystallizes in the frigid air, turning to ice and falling to the ground in frozen spikes.

"This is the most amazing place on Earth," Grim says, the closest thing to wonder I've ever seen on his face as he watches the sun's swan dance. "Like living on another planet."

He's right. The perfectly flat, lifeless plateau appears so starkly white you forget color. The quiet rests in a well so deep you don't remember sound. And the loneliness some days grows so thick, it's impenetrable and you forget how it feels to be touched.

Those are the times I think of Lennix most. Of how she's moving on with her life. It's May. She's graduated and is probably on the campaign trail for Mr. Nighthorse. She's a launched missile now, deployed and doing what she was created to do. Maybe she's met someone. Kissed someone else since me. Slept in someone else's bed. I cage a growl behind the bars of my teeth. The thought of someone else touching, having Nix…

"Doctor Larnyard was looking for you, Kingsman," Grim says, slanting me a wry look. "Man doesn't take two steps without consulting you."

I nod and start toward the stairs that will take me back inside. I allow myself one last glimpse at the final sunset.

It's spring in the States. Flowers and sunshine and lengthening days. For some reason, I think of the map I sketched in Lennix's hands. In the span of her palms, we were separated by only inches. On the scale of real life, we're separated by thousands of miles, by epochs. And with the austral winter swallowing up all the light, I'm not sure how or if I can find my way back to her.

CHAPTER 26
LENNIX

"THESE NUMBERS LOOK GOOD," JIM SAYS, TRACKING THE COLUMNS of data with one finger. "Your plan's working, Lennix."

"Well, instead of trying to get all the people we can't convince to vote for you," I say with a broad smile, "we're building a coalition of all the people who have every reason *to* vote for you. We need every black and brown vote, the woman vote, the gay vote. If they're marginalized in any way, they need to know you'll be their voice, but they have to put you in power before you can speak for them. That's our message, and we just keep saying it."

"Nice," Mena says from the couch, her long legs folded under her. "Are you the speechwriter now, too?"

I shake my head, smiling and poking at the cold pizza boxed on Jim's desk. The team often teases me about all the hats I wear on the campaign team. Truth is, turns out I'm damn good at politics. I feel like one of those infants people toss in the water and they just start swimming. It all feels intuitive; people and their needs make sense to me, and politics *should* be about meeting the needs of people.

"Hey," Portia, the campaign finance director, says from the doorway to Jim's office. "The sheriff's out here and needs to speak with you, Jim."

"Maybe he's interested in that town hall on the MMIW issue we proposed," Mena says, eyes alert.

"You may be right." Jim re-knots the tie he loosened hours ago and drops a tender kiss on top of Mena's head when he passes on his way out of the office.

Well, all right now!

I wait until the door closes behind him before springing into squealing action.

"Oh, my God!" I throw myself onto the sofa beside her. "What was *that* all about?"

She presses her lips together, fighting a smile. She's not fooling me.

"Auntie, out with it. You and Jim? Tell me everything."

"Lenn, don't be silly. We're just friends."

"Yeah, he and I are 'friends,' too, but he's never kissed my head like that. I haven't seen him kiss *anyone's* head like that."

An irrepressible light enters Mena's eyes, and her smile isn't far behind. "Okay. We've gone out a few times."

"How have you managed to keep it a secret? This campaign is so tightly knit, I gain five pounds when anybody eats ice cream."

"We've been discreet, but I think it could lead to something serious." She pauses, giving me a speculative look. "Speaking of something serious, have you heard from that guy you met in Amsterdam?"

I swallow the knot thickening in my throat. "Who? Maxim?"

"Right, him." Mena studies my face. "He seemed like a great guy from what Kimba said."

I make a mental note to keep my auntie and best friend apart in the future. "You can't believe a word she says."

"So he isn't handsome, thoughtful, sexy, and a PhD?"

"Oh, yeah. He actually *is* all those things." *And more.*

"And?" she persists.

"And…he's in the wilds of Antarctica and I'm here." I shrug and stretch out on the couch, laying my head in my godmother's lap. "He told me from the beginning it would be just that week."

"But he left you a voice mail that kind of propped the door open, right?" she asks, brushing through my hair with her fingers.

"Wow. Kimba is more thorough than I thought. Yeah. He said when he gets back, he'd like to talk and see where things could go. I'm not getting my hopes up."

"We need to talk about you and hope, young lady."

"Hope is hard." I close my eyes to block out her persistent concern. "Hope hurts when it doesn't deliver."

"I know you're thinking about your mother, but—"

"Don't." I sit up and push my hair back. "I don't want to hear about how I'm still holding on to that. How I can't open myself up to anyone because I'm afraid to fully feel."

I just fully felt with Maxim, and look where that got me. Probably nowhere but "deflowered" and with my heart cracked.

"Sounds like I don't have to tell you," she says softly, "because you already know. You should see a counselor, honey. I told Rand when it happened years ago."

"I talked to someone…once." I twist the hem of my shirt between my fingers and eye the door. As much as I love Mena, I want out of this conversation.

"You were so young, and a situation like that—"

"Auntie, please," I groan. "Can we drop it?"

She sighs, resignation on her pretty face, and nods. Jim comes back into the office, and his face is ashen, his mouth grim. As soon as he's close enough, he reaches for Mena's hand. She stands and presses into him, her anxious eyes fixed on his face. There is obviously more than just a "few dates" between them.

"What's wrong?" she asks.

"The sheriff," Jim says, shaking his head and closing his eyes briefly before opening them, meeting mine. "He had bad news."

"What kind of bad news?" I ask, but somehow I already know. Before he even says it, I know that hope has let me down again.

"It's Tammara," he says hoarsely, sorrow etched into the lines of his distinguished features. "They found her."

CHAPTER 27
MAXIM

I'LL NEVER TAKE THE SUN FOR GRANTED AGAIN. WE SPENT FOUR months cloaked in darkness. Every day without the sun, it's harder to lift your spirits. Depression, seasonal affective disorder, vitamin C deficiency—whatever you want to blame for it or call it, it's real. We ate the dark like nightshade, and it was poisonous. Melancholy with every meal. The weight of the endless night can suffocate you if you're not careful. I know now why men have gone mad in the Antarctic. I understand the rigorous psychological testing for those who winter over. We aren't built to live this way.

Just as I'm sure I'll lose my mind, one day, the faintest glow illuminates the horizon, and we at least don't need head torches to see and move around.

"I'm counting the days to the peninsula," Grim says over a hand of poker one night in September. "After all this snow, I'll take the water for a few months."

"Not sure how open the waters will be," Peggy says, chewing on a cigar she never actually smokes. "We'll be contending with ice floes and another set of challenges."

"I need another set of challenges." I fold my hand. "I'm kind of ready to go home."

"Tulip girl's waiting for you?" Grim asks, his eyes briefly flashing the humor his mouth doesn't allow.

"Shut up, man." I shake my head and slide my seat back, not in the mood to be teased about Lennix.

"I've seen you looking at the pictures of her in the tulip garden," he says, his voice serious. "She's pretty."

"Pretty is the least of what she is, but she is that, too."

I miss my mother, my brother. Hell, as strained as our relationship is, I even miss my father. But what I'm missing with Nix is more somehow. Even after only having a week with her, it's more. For every time Grim has caught me looking at that photo on my phone, there's a dozen times I've pulled it out he hasn't seen.

I'll never regret this trip. It's been good experience, and our research is valuable, but even with the part I'm most excited about still ahead, getting outside this summer and exploring the peninsula, I'm ready to go home. The quiet and the scope of this place change your perspective on life. And if there's one thing I know about my life after this trip, it's that I want Lennix Moon Hunter, however I can get her, in it.

Being on the water breathes new life into my passion for this Antarctic voyage. Living confined and in the dark with limited human contact for so long felt like my hope was packed under ice as tightly and surely as the prehistoric snow we collect.

We worked ashore the past few days, which took an enormous amount of preparation. Bureaucratically, because the area is so closely guarded and managed that it takes a machete to cut through all the red tape. We received our approval to gather data mere days before reaching shore. Now that we're off the peninsula and our ship *The Chrysalis* is floating alongside an armada of glaciers, I feel as buoyant as the ice floes bobbing around us.

"The landscape looks different every day," David says from beside me, his forearms leaned on the ship's railing.

"That's part of what makes it so unpredictable," Grim adds. "Glad we got some good work in before conditions changed."

"The birds were my favorite part," Peggy inserts with a laugh, chewing on her ever-present unlit cigar.

She worked with our seabird specialist to get population counts for various species, which will be compared with previous data, helping identify any potentially endangered populations. They've been able to perform a thorough penguin census and collect blubber from the seals in the area. We also gathered several mud samples that will be analyzed and hopefully give us information on how carbon may be trapped under ice.

"I think Larnyard may wish he'd listened to you," Grim says, hitching his chin toward the sky. "Look at those clouds."

I recommended we make camp on shore for a few days and spend some extra time collecting much-needed data since it had taken so much time and effort to even access the area. Dr. Larnyard had disagreed and wanted to get back on the water for the next leg of our expedition.

Sailing through ice is a treacherous, exhilarating prospect. *The Chrysalis* is ice-capable, but no vessel guarantees safety if you clip a 'berg the wrong way or get trapped out on the water in one of the Antarctic's volatile storms. The clouds looming over our ship promise storms. We're hundreds of miles from shore, thousands of miles from civilization, and a hairbreadth from catastrophe.

"I don't like what the sky's telling us," David says, his brows rouching over concerned eyes. "Iceblink."

There are only a few places in the world where the phenomenon of iceblink, glaring white near the horizon reflecting light from ice, is even possible. Antarctica is one of them. Polar explorers and sailors have been using iceblink to navigate arctic seas for centuries. In contrast, water sky projects open lanes of water onto the clouds, showing how to avoid hazardous ice floes that could lock up a ship for days or even weeks. Hell, for months.

When I saw water sky, it was the first time I could articulate the exact color of Lennix's eyes. Dark, stormy gray and seeing far. Seeing things no one else did.

"What I wouldn't give for a water sky," I say softly, only giving the situation half my focus. What I wouldn't give to see her. To tell her I was a fool to think I could walk away from eyes like that.

"Right," Grim says, frowning at the gathering clouds. "We need open water. You see all this ice crowding around the ship?"

He's right. Even just an hour ago, our path was clear, but now tessellations of ice have interlocked around the ship, a tundra jigsaw puzzle that, if not navigated skillfully, could strand or even sink our ship. Beyond skill, we'll need a lot of luck.

That night, I fall into a dead slumber after all the work we've done over the past few days. It's not a loud boom or crash that jolts me out of my sleep. It's another sound that sends a shiver down my spine.

Absolute silence.

The engine of *The Chrysalis* is quiet. The steady throb that's become so much a part of the ship's environment is gone.

David and Grim jerk up in their bunks, too, and we stare at each other for a few seconds, absorbing the quiet together before leaping out of bed and dragging on our sweats and down jackets.

On the bridge, there's a forced calm to the energy as the captain and crew study satellite feeds and maps. They say for every iceberg, the visible ice comprises only 10 percent of the whole. The other 90 percent lies below the surface. That's what this is. The 10 percent the captain shows us is controlled, but an icy panic rules the atmosphere from beneath. Dr. Larnyard sits on a bench with his head buried in his hands.

"What's happening?" I ask Captain Rosteen, a former Australian naval officer who has negotiated this planet's roughest seas for decades.

"We're locked in," he answers, deep lines around his mouth and eyes showing distress from the typically unruffled Aussie. "Rudder's blocked by ice."

"What's that mean?" David asks.

"Means we aren't in control of this ship," Grim says with a dark frown. "We got no steerage, right, Cap? The ice is steering us."

"Right." Captain Rosteen gives a terse nod. "According to our satellite projections, a powerful storm's coming, blowing westerly winds." He pulls up an image on one of the radar screens.

"What's that big blue thing?" David asks.

"An iceberg," Dr. Larnyard answers, his voice muffled behind his hands. "It's on the move and headed for us."

"Dammit!" I link my hands over the tensed muscles behind my neck. An iceberg of eighty thousand tons will easily break through the ice floes that have us trapped and crush our ship.

"Should we evacuate?" Peggy asks. "We have enough lifeboats to get off before the 'berg hits."

"That storm that's coming," Captain Rosteen says, shaking his head. "Being caught in a lifeboat in the middle of that with no land for miles could be as much a death sentence as a sinking ship."

"We'll call for help," I say quickly. "Planes should be able to get in now that winter's over."

"Already called," the captain says. "They'll try."

"They'll try?" Grim asks, anger showing through on his usually impassive features. "What the hell do you mean *they'll try*? We have sixty-five people on this ship in addition to your crew. Students. Teachers. *Women.* They need to do more than fucking try, Cap."

"The closest team that could help is a Japanese ship that can only break through ice that's three to four feet thick," Captain Rosteen explains. "It's impossible. Everything around us is at least twice that now."

"And the storm that's closing in on us," Dr. Larnyard says wearily. "It's already all around. The visibility in the surrounding areas is too low for anyone to fly in safely."

Even as he says it, wind whistles violently beyond the porthole, rocking the ship. The Antarctic shows us what a capricious bitch she can be—placid one moment and vengeful the next. A thump jerks the ship dramatically.

"Shit," Captain Rosteen says, moving over to check the tilt meter. "Ship just went three degrees to the right."

He runs from the cabin, and we follow. Dread sinks in my belly like an anchor dropped overboard. The wind, silent just hours before, wails high-pitched screams all around. Up on deck, the three degrees on the tilt meter is more obvious, setting the ship slightly askew. A cluster of ice floes jostling for position have formed a pointy steeple and pierced the side of the boat.

The captain searches the sky crowded with ominous clouds and looks up at the stars imploringly, like they might pose a solution where there apparently is none. He says the words we all hoped we'd never have to hear.

"We've been hit."

CHAPTER 28
LENNIX

"Don't leave a street unturned," I tell the volunteers sitting around the cheap wooden table in Nighthorse campaign headquarters. "We need to get as many eligible voters to vote early as possible. Inclement weather, long lines, voter suppression tricks onsite the day of—all well-documented barriers for our demographic on voting day. Let's get as many of them to vote in advance as possible." I pause to smile. "Vote for us, of course."

The small team composed mostly of student and elderly volunteers laughs at my tiny joke. I try to keep morale high. Have to. We are in the fight of our lives with a strong incumbent still in the lead, according to every poll.

Last week, Mr. Nighthorse asked me to help with our voter drive. We're about six weeks away from the election, and we may be behind, but we gain ground every week. By Election Day, I believe we can not only eliminate the sitting congressman's lead but overtake him.

"Okay," I say once the laughter and chatter die down. "Let's get out there."

Everyone has their assignments and grabs clipboards already loaded with absentee ballot forms if people want to complete them onsite.

I'm grabbing a clipboard, too, ready to hit my assigned streets when Kimba walks in. She started working with the campaign a few weeks ago. I know she believes in Jim, but I think more than anything she didn't want to be apart from me. After four years of college and inseparable friendship, I don't want to be away from her either.

"Have you seen the news?" she asks, her face troubled.

"News about what?" I ask distractedly, checking to make sure I have my forms, buttons, and campaign signs to give to anyone who wants them.

"It's Maxim."

A droplet of ice water cuts down my back. I haven't heard from him. That was fine. We agreed to that. I knew that, though a tiny part of me has been marking off the days until his expedition is over and, according to his voice mail, we can talk. I haven't let myself consider the dangers he was potentially facing. No news has been good news.

Until now.

"What about him?" I ask, trying to keep the panic from my voice.

Kimba picks up the remote, turns the TV on, and flips through a few channels until she reaches CNN.

Antarctic expedition team trapped in deadly storm

Deadly?

Trapped?

The headline appears above a line of photos, and I recognize David and Maxim immediately. The words and images are a one-two punch to my solar plexus. I can't breathe, and I'm choking.

"A dangerous situation is unfolding in Antarctica," the reporter says with the appropriate amount of professional graveness. "A team researching climate change in the southern hemisphere finds themselves caught in a storm of imperfect conditions. Their ship has been hit and is sinking. They're thousands of miles from civilization and hundreds of miles from shore. Extreme winds have assaulted the area, and low visibility makes flying in to rescue them nearly impossible."

I collapse into a rolling chair and fold shaking hands in my lap. I'm not sure I can do this again. When they found Tammara's body, there was barely time to cry, to attend the funeral and console her family. If I think too long about how she died, I'll wonder if Mama died that way, too. If her body was so carelessly used and then discarded but, unlike Tammara's, never found. I pushed grief aside, old and new, the demands of the campaign as much a distraction as a necessity.

Now this. I feel trapped here with my frigid grief and icicle fear and the thing I don't often allow myself anymore but, for Maxim, I must find.

Hope.

CHAPTER 29
MAXIM

"IT'S TOO DANGEROUS."

I say the words to the entire group, but Dr. Larnyard is the one I pin my hard stare to.

"What do you suggest, Kingsman?" he snaps. "We stay on a sinking ship and die in the ocean?"

A few of the university students gasp at the word "die."

This motherfucking idiot.

"We're not going to die," I reassure them, taking a moment to look directly at the youngest students. "I won't let that happen."

Grim meets my eyes with raised brows. His message is clear. How you gonna keep *that* promise?

"We've been hit," Dr. Larnyard reminds us unnecessarily. "We were three degrees to the right yesterday, and now we're how many, Captain?"

Captain Rosteen glances from his tilt meter to me. "Five degrees now."

"Two degrees in a day is significant," Dr. Larnyard says. "We need to get off this ship. Some of those ice floes are a full acre. We can take rafts to those and wait there to be rescued."

"Except no one can make it to us right now," I say. "And we don't know when they'll be able to. You'd have us in tents on an acre of ice in the middle of a blizzard?"

"It's the best of two evils."

"The best would have been if we'd listened to Kingsman in the first place," Grim snaps. "And stayed ashore where our chances would have been better."

"There's nothing we can do about that now," I cut in. We have enough we're fighting without fighting each other, but I have to talk some sense into Dr. Larnyard before he actually convinces anyone to follow him into a deadly storm. "We need to find the best way out of our *current* circumstance, and I cannot endorse leaving this ship in a storm this bad."

"And I cannot endorse staying on a ship sinking into the Southern Ocean," Dr. Larnyard fires back. "This is your first Antarctic expedition, Kingsman, yes?"

"Yes," I grit out. "You know it is."

"Well, it's my fifth," he says. "And I'll be damned if I let some amateur with a superhero complex lead our team into a death trap."

"*Him* lead us into a death trap?" Grim asks, anger imprinted on his usually stoic features. "You were the one who—"

"Grim," I snap. "Shut the hell up. That's not helping."

There's a brief silence while our angry eyes clash in the tension filling the ship's meeting room.

"I'm leading this expedition," Dr. Larnyard says. "It's my call to make, and I say we take our chances while we can. If the storm worsens, it'll only make it harder for us to leave later and get to safety on one of the nearby ice floes. It's now or maybe never."

His dire words spark a flurry of concerned murmurs from the team, just shy of panic.

"I'm staying with my ship," Captain Rosteen says. "I'm not saying it's the safest option. I'm saying this is my ship and I won't abandon it until there is no choice left to me."

"I'll go with them," one of his crew members offers, his dark eyes anxious when he glances out the porthole to the howling storm beyond.

"I'm not leaving either," Grim states firmly. "It's not the smartest option."

"I'm staying," I add, hoping reason will prevail if enough of us push for it.

In the end, most of the group decides to stay aboard the ship. Even as Dr. Larnyard and about a third of our team prepare to take a few rafts to the nearest ice floe, I keep watching the radio, willing someone to call and say conditions have improved enough for them to fly in and rescue us. It's not safe on this ship. I know that, but it's our best hope.

I watch through the porthole when Dr. Larnyard and his contingency load into a few rafts, insulated in their extreme-weather gear and pressing into the howling winds.

"Fool," David mutters from my left.

"Asshole," Grim adds from my right.

"I hope they don't regret leaving." I blow out a worried breath. "Hell, I hope we don't regret staying. Any word from anyone?"

"Nope," Grim says. "Visibility is shit, and no one with half a brain would risk trying to fly into this storm right now. It'd be signing their own death warrant."

I hope we haven't signed ours.

It's only been a few hours when we hear a shout from outside. Grim, David and I run to the porthole.

"Shit," I say through clenched teeth. "I told that stupid bastard."

If it wasn't for the bright-red jacket, I wouldn't be able to make out the figure bobbing in the icy water through the sleet and snow. A tent floats not too far from him, picked up and tossed carelessly by the screeching winds.

"Larnyard," Grim mutters.

"Is he dead?" David asks.

The frantic movement of Larnyard's arms answers his question.

"We have to help him," I say, crossing our room to grab my puffy jacket and slip on my extreme-weather gear.

"Motherfucker," Grim says. "I'm not risking my life for that buffoon."

"Well, I am. If you can live with yourself knowing a man drowned not even a hundred feet away and you did nothing, go right ahead. Not me."

"King, you can't," David says, grabbing me by the arm. "You gonna die for that idiot?"

"We have to try. At least let's talk to the captain to see what he says."

Captain Rosteen already stands at the railing, his grip white-knuckled as he holds on against the wind.

"What can we do, Cap?" I ask, tugging the woolen toboggan lower over my ears.

He shakes his head, resignation in his eyes. "Someone would have to go out in that to get him." He tilts his head toward the roiling waves, rising walls of water surrounded by icebergs. "I won't. We all heard you urge him to stay."

"So lesson learned?" I ask, anger and disbelief warring inside me. "Yeah, he made a dumb call."

"The last of many," Grim interjects.

"But we have to try." I swallow my own dread. "I have to try. I'm not asking you to go. Just help me."

Captain Rosteen looks doubtful but then nods. "We could tie a rope around you, put a life jacket on you, and send you out in a raft."

The wind whips so hard against the glass of the bridge's windows, it's almost like the storm is daring me to take up such a foolhardy mission.

"Let's do it."

"King," Grim snaps, grabbing my elbow. "You idiot. I'm not letting you do this."

"You think you can stop me?" I step closer to him. "I don't have time for this, Grim. Either help me or get out of my way."

He releases a frustrated breath, his brows dipping so low they shadow his eyes. "Cap, make it two ropes."

I nod grimly and slip on the life jacket. The rope is tight but only so long. It's been a matter of a few minutes, but Larnyard's red jacket seems farther away. Grim and I grab a lifesaver for Larnyard, climb into the raft, and start paddling toward him. He's still bobbing up and down wildly, screaming over the storm, but the rope between us and the ship catches. We've gone as far as we can, but we're a few feet shy of Larnyard's struggling figure.

Shit.

It's in that moment I realize how truly vulnerable we are. We strive for control, for power, to rule our small domains. But in the end, one wave, one storm could toss us beyond saving. I don't know where the winds and water will take me, but I untie the rope from my waist.

"No way!" Grim screams over the wind. "King, no."

"I have a life jacket," I yell back at him. "His chances are better if he has one, too. We're too close not to try, Grim."

"You keep saying that shit."

I grab the lifesaver and dive into the icy water. I press through the water toward him, my arms fresher than his but still struggling against such powerful waves. I'm grateful for even a few seconds of the wind lessening enough for him to hear me.

"Larnyard!" I shout. His wide, frightened eyes meet mine, and he starts frantically swimming against the heaving waves toward me.

I toss the lifesaver, keeping the rope end in my tight grip. He grabs hold of it and manages to slip it over his head. I tug on the rope, pulling him closer, even as the winds and waves pull harder. I start swimming toward the boat, feeling his heavy but reassuring weight as I cut through the water toward the raft and Grim's outstretched hand.

"Damn idiot," Grim mutters, pulling me into the raft and adding his strength to drag Larnyard by the lifesaver's rope toward us. We immediately start paddling to the ship and the ladder lowered on its side, waiting for us. Grim scrambles up and Larnyard follows, dripping and shivering. Icicles are forming on my life jacket, and I know the frigid water only adds to the dangerous cold. I'm probably mere minutes from hypothermia despite the extreme-weather gear. My teeth chatter, and my bones rattle. They have to pull me the last few feet when my exhausted arms and legs finally give out. I'm drawing a huge sigh of relief when one last gust of wind tosses me as I'm climbing back onto the ship, slamming my head into the railing, and everything goes as dark as the Antarctic sunless winter.

CHAPTER 30
MAXIM

"This ship cannot sink," I say, my words slurred with fatigue and whatever the team doctor gave me for pain. I wince when he pulls the thread through a small wound at my hairline.

My words cut into the shouts of jubilation and fill the ship's meeting room where everyone's gathered. It's only been an hour since I regained consciousness. I wasn't out long, but I have one hell of a headache. It's hard to concentrate, to follow the developments, but I do know we cannot allow the ship to sink.

"We're getting off, Kingsman," Dr. Larnyard says, brows drawn together. "The winds have let up just enough, maybe only long enough for us to get out of here."

He's nursing a mug of cocoa, no worse for wear from our little swim in the icy ocean.

"Yeah, King," Captain Rosteen says. "Neither the Japanese nor the Russians could risk a helicopter to reach us. Your Americans are coming through."

The team gives another shout of relief and round of high-fiving.

"I get that," I say, my teeth still chattering despite the warmth from the heater. "And I'm grateful, of course, but we can't abandon this ship."

"The hell we can't," David snaps. "Maxim, we have to jump through this window before it closes. What the hell, man?"

"Of course we'll leave," I agree, keeping my tone reasonable. "But it's not enough that we're saved. *The Chrysalis* has to be saved, too. Or else we may create the worst Antarctic disaster since—"

"*Bahía Paraíso*," Grim says, running a hand over his military-cut pelt of hair.

"Right." I look to Dr. Larnyard. "Do you want to go down in history beside the largest oil spill and possibly man-made ecosystemic disruption ever in this hemisphere?"

The professor gulps, and I can practically see him weighing all of his accolades and tenure against such a black mark.

"What's *Bahía Paraíso*?" Peggy asks.

"An Argentinian supply ship trapped in 1989," I tell her. "It was struck by a 'berg and sank here in Antarctica."

"Spilled a hundred and thirty thousand gallons of diesel fuel all over the west Antarctic Peninsula coast," Grim continues, "and destroyed the local wildlife."

"I came here to do something good," I tell them, spreading what I hope is a compelling look over the entire team. "Something that could help in our fight to save this planet. I'll be damned if I'll be party to devastating one of the most pristine parts it has left."

"What good will it do for us to go down with the ship?" Dr. Larnyard demands.

"Not go down with it," I say, not even bothering now to hide my impatience and disdain for the man. "Save it. When the Americans call back, we have to at least try to negotiate a rescue for this ship. If not when they pick us up, as soon as humanly safe and possible."

The radio crackles, signaling incoming communication. I don't hesitate but grab the radio before anyone tells me I can or can't.

"*Chrysalis*, do you copy?" the voice on the other end asks over the sound of whipping wind and propellers.

"This is *Chrysalis*," I say, glancing at Captain Rosteen, who gives a reluctant nod of approval. "We copy."

"We're about a mile out," the pilot says. "We've identified the ice floe large enough for us to land. Have you marked it?"

"Roger that. The wind died down enough for the part of our team out on that ice floe to leave their tents and mark it with coffee beans." I wink at Grim, whose agile genius had led to that idea.

"Coffee, huh?" The pilot laughs, providing the only measure of comfort I've felt since ice pierced our ship. "As long as I can see it in the snow, we should be fine, but we gotta be fast. Satellite projects those storms will be swinging back soon. And with the size of your team, even with five helicopters, it'll take several trips."

"I know you're doing us a huge favor with this," I say carefully, "and at great risk to your crew, but I have to ask. Any chance you have the means to repair this ship at least enough so it doesn't sink before somebody can come back and retrieve it when the ice shifts?"

"We got a team of engineers with us," the pilot says. "If it's one thing we know how to prevent, it's oil spills, Maxim."

Maxim? How does he know me?

"That's good to hear," I reply, smiling and frowning, pleased and confused. "You guys are prepared. Who are you anyway?"

"Oh," the pilot says, surprise evident in his words. "I thought you knew. It's Cade Energy, sir. Your father sent us."

CHAPTER 31
LENNIX

"We have an update on that ship stranded in the Antarctic. An American oil company was able to fly in and has rescued the team."

Rescued.

The news anchor's words leave me slumped in my seat at the bar, limp with relief. Our team is having drinks after a day of barnstorming Oklahoma's most economically depressed rural areas. I've been checking for news constantly since the *Chrysalis* crisis was reported, but there had been little news and no change for hours. Now, surrounded by the people who have become as close to me as family over the past few months of the campaign, I hear the news that Maxim is going to be okay.

"Thank God," I whisper, pushing a trembling hand through my hair. Tears leak from the corners of my eyes and burn my cheeks. "Dammit."

I swipe at my face, trying to keep my composure, but I'm undone with the unfathomable relief of knowing Maxim has been rescued. I give up. I can't stave off the sobs that wrack me right in the middle of the bar. After Mama and Tammara and so many losses, I had braced my heart for another, but one I wasn't sure I could handle. To lose Maxim before I ever really even had him would have devastated me.

I may have no right, and he may not even want to see me, but I'm already devising a plan to find him, to go to him. To hug him and kiss him and slap him across the face for putting me through that hell.

"You okay?" Mena asks softly, sliding a glass of whiskey toward me. "Kimba told me about Maxim."

"Yeah, I just…" I struggle to evict the words from my throat, to pull myself together, but I'm distracted by the coverage on the large screen mounted over the bar.

LIVE from DFW International.

Dallas?

Two tall, dark-haired men emerge from a private plane, coming one after the other down a short bank of steps. A swarm of reporters closes around them. Shock rips through my body. How could I have been so blind?

I'm a fool, and Maxim is a liar.

Warren Cade, dressed in his tailored suit and wearing his usual privilege like a mantle, grins at the circle of cameras and microphones. Beside him is a man who, now that I see them together, looks exactly like him. Maxim is a younger, more casually dressed version of his father with his longer hair, Berkeley sweatshirt, and dark jeans. Little dots of blood show starkly leaking through the square bandage on his forehead.

"Mr. Cade," a reporter calls.

Both men look toward the camera, the same patina of arrogance stamped on the handsome set of features.

"Um, *Maxim* Cade," she says with a chuckle. "Sorry. How's it feel to be back in the States after such a harrowing adventure?"

Impatience flashes in those peridot eyes I thought I knew so well.

"Uh, great," he says, pushing a shoulder through the crowd.

"And you were scheduled to go to the Amazon next," another reporter shouts at his back. "After such a close call, will you be rethinking that?"

Not breaking stride, his long, lean legs taking him closer to the luxury SUV waiting on the tarmac where his father stands, he glances over his shoulder and shoots the crowd that pirate's grin. "Hell, no. I'm still going. Why wouldn't I?"

Too many emotions roil in my belly. Too many thoughts whisk in my head. *Betrayal. Fear. Relief.* Something tender, an unopened bud that I crush before it can fully open.

"That's him?" Mena asks, her eyes fixed on the screen as Maxim climbs into the vehicle behind his father.

"No," I say, blinking dry eyes and knocking back her whiskey. "I don't know who that man is."

CHAPTER 32
MAXIM

"I WANTED TO THANK YOU FOR EVERYTHING, DAD," I SAY, SIPPING the water served with the elaborate meal my mother had our chef prepare. I haven't been in this house in years and wasn't sure I'd ever return.

"No need to thank me, son." My father takes a bite of his steak and points to me with his fork. "Coming home where you belong is thanks enough."

I stiffen, knowing where this is going and how it will end. This détente will be short-lived because, as much as I appreciate my father's assistance, I can't give him what he wants.

"Yes," Mom rushes to say, her look bouncing between my father and me. "So good to have you home. We've missed you, haven't we, Warren?"

My father sips his red wine and nods. "I hope this last incident got all this Greenpeace shit out of your system. Cade Energy needs you."

His words fall into a vat of tension-laced silence. I finish chewing and carefully place my fork on my plate. "I'm not working for Cade Energy, Dad. You know that."

His jaw ticks, the muscle flexing along his strong jawline. My jawline. My cheekbones. My eyes. My *face*.

My stubborn will, 1.0.

I've never admired and resented one person so simultaneously as I do my father. When he looks down the table at me, I know he feels the same way.

"You ungrateful fool," he says through clenched teeth. His fist slams the table, clanging the glasses and silverware. My mother jumps and closes her eyes, resignation in every line of her body and on her face. "I rescue you and your conservationist friends. I fix your stupid boat. I fly you home, and what do you give me in return? Defiance and rebellion."

"No one asked you to," I fire at him, my voice tight with anger.

"And what should I have done? Let you die?"

"If you saved me only to control me, then yeah."

"Maxim," my mother protests. "Don't be ridiculous. Of course we'd save you."

"Maybe if he'd known I wasn't going to toe the line, he wouldn't have bothered," I say.

"That's a fucking lie, and you know it, Maxim," my father says, his eyes narrowed and his body tense. "All I'm asking is for a little bit of gratitude."

"Which you have, but I'm not changing the course of my life to make you feel I'm sufficiently grateful."

"What course? Another useless degree? More wandering the world collecting mud samples? You call that a career?"

"I have a career. I have a plan that has nothing to do with you. You'll see, Dad. You have no idea who I am."

"No, *you* have no idea who you are," he bellows, leaning forward over the table. "You're a fucking Cade, and you're running around like you're a nobody. Well, *be* a nobody, Maxim. Meanwhile I'll keep running one of the most successful businesses in the world and your brother will become president of this country. You go save whales." He tosses a linen napkin over his unfinished meal. "See if I give a shit."

Long, powerful strides take him out of the dining room and into his office. The heavy door slams behind him, locking me out of the inner sanctum that used to be like a second home.

"He doesn't mean it," my mother says, her eyes filled with tears. "Please don't go again. I worry about you. I miss you."

"He meant it, Mom." I stand and cross around the table to pull her up and into a tight hug, knowing this may be our last one for a while. Her petite frame shakes against me while she sobs into my shirt. I swallow the emotion burning my throat and bury my nose in her hair. "He meant it, Mom, but so did I."

CHAPTER 33
LENNIX

"There's someone here to see you, Lenn." Portia pokes her head into the conference room. Her smile is megawatt. I've known her just a few weeks, but she's usually only this excited about donations.

"To see me?" I touch the *Nighthorse Now* graphic emblazoned on my chest. "You sure? Besides the team, I don't know anybody in Oklahoma."

"Well, he knows you." Portia purses the corners of her lips with suppressed satisfaction. "Why didn't you tell us you knew Maxim Cade? He's been all over the news."

I'm in the process of packing up a box of campaign buttons. Her words stop me mid-reach. I send her a sharp glance and then shake my head. "I don't know him, and I don't want to see him. Could you say I'm not here?"

The jubilation proclaimed all over Portia's face fades. She folds her arms across her chest and aims a look at me over the bottle-green rims of her glasses. "Look, I don't know what's going on," Portia says. "But he just made a donation to the campaign, and if he wants to speak to one of our staff, our staff will be available."

Donation. Money.

Of course. He *is* a Cade after all.

Without speaking, I tuck my T-shirt into the waistband of my skirt and walk past her out into the campaign headquarters lobby. Maxim sits on the shabby thrift-store couch. He makes it look like a throne, even wearing a simple white T-shirt and jeans. How did I not know this man was a Cade or some equivalent? It's so obvious now. Men like Maxim don't happen overnight. It takes generations to breed them.

He glances up and stands. I force myself to stay where I am. His eyes gleam bright between a dark fan of lashes. There's concern there and probably the closest thing to an apology he can manage. And desire. Oh, yes. I recognize that quick flare of want in his expression because it's igniting in me, too, at just the sight of him. My heart calls him the liar he is, but my body clenches, seeking a satisfaction it's only ever found when he was inside me.

"Mr. Cade," I say, my tone brisk and businesslike.

He grimaces and shoves his hands into the pockets of his jeans. He takes a few steps forward until only inches separate us. And that tiny amount of space hums with memory and hunger, but I ignore it.

"Nix," he says, his voice husky, rough. He reaches for my hand, and I step back, warning him with a look to keep his damn hands off. With his eyes never leaving my face, he nods. "Is there somewhere we could talk? Maybe grab a coffee or something?"

"Sorry, Mr. Cade." I gesture to the half-open boxes overflowing with buttons, bumper stickers, signs, and other campaign paraphernalia. "As you can see, we're preparing to hit the trail."

He grimaces. "I should have told you. If we can just go somewhere, I can explain."

"Anything you have to say to me, you can say out here."

The bell above the door heralds the entrance of two volunteers. Our scheduler sits on the floor nearby with a giant whiteboard and dry-erase markers.

"I really think we should discuss this in private," he says, reaching for my hand again.

I cross my hands behind my back, out of reach, and just stare him down, wordlessly warning him.

"All right." He gives a careless shrug. "That night in the alley when we fuc—"

I clamp my hand over his mouth and drag him by the arm into the conference room. He closes the door behind us and leans against it, a smug smile on his disgustingly handsome face.

"I'm still not sure why you're here, Mr. Cade."

"Would you stop calling me that?" He releases a frustrated breath and drags his hands through the hair that's even longer than it was the last time I saw him.

"Oh, I'm sorry. That's what they were calling you on television. Did they get it wrong, too? What should I call you? Kingsman?" A humorless laugh spills out of me. "We both know that's a lie."

"It's not a lie. All the men in my family have Kingsman as our middle name."

"Your daddy, too?"

He stares at me for a moment before dropping his eyes to the floor. "Him, too, yeah. I should have told you about my family."

"Oh, but you did." I hop up on the conference room table and swing my legs back and forth. "You said your family was wealthy, but you didn't have much money of your own."

"True."

"You said your brother was a senator."

"He is."

"You said you and your father were estranged."

"Yes, we—"

"But somehow neglected to mention he's the man I can't stand. That you'll inherit the company that trampled over the most sacred land my people still held."

"I won't. Inherit, I mean. I dedicated the last eight years of my life to researching climate change, Nix. Do you really think I want anything to do with my family's oil company?"

"I don't actually know *what* to think since you've misrepresented yourself to me this whole time." I shake my head and force my lips into a waxy smile. "While all of us wondered what would happen after the protest, how long we'd be in jail, if the charges would stick, you knew you were guaranteed bail. Guaranteed freedom. Protection. Wrapped all cozy in your wealth. How you must have laughed at us."

"I didn't laugh."

"But it was a game for you, one you played with absolutely no risk while we risked *everything*."

"It wasn't a game. I saw you, I heard you, and it's like I said before." He takes a few steps closer until he's mere inches from the table. "I knew I'd never forget you. When I saw those dogs headed straight for you…" He rubs the back of his neck and releases a harsh sigh. "I didn't think twice. I left my father in the car and took off running. I just knew I had to…never mind. You won't believe me. Just know it wasn't a joke."

"Every one of us was risking our reputation, our freedom, possibly our lives if things had escalated, and you acted like you had something to lose when Warren Cade would never let anything happen to his heir."

"I told you we're estranged."

"Were you then? That day?"

"No. I tried to convince him not to go forward with the pipeline. When he refused to change his mind, I left."

"You let me think you had come all the way from California specifically to protest with us. Was that true?"

His silence is thick with guilt and frustration.

"No," he admits after a moment. "I'd flown in with my father. I didn't know why we were there. Hearing what he had done and thinking I would never see any of you again, I didn't see the point of saying who I was."

"And in Amsterdam?" The words sour in my mouth. "The first night, could you have seen the point? Or maybe the second night before you fucked me? You could have mentioned who you were, but maybe you thought you wouldn't tap this ass if I knew."

"Nix—"

"And you were right. You wouldn't have."

"I won't let you cheapen what we had."

"*I'm* cheapening it? You told me because I had been so honest with you, you wanted to be completely open and honest with me."

"I did."

"And then you lied to me for the next week."

"I *omitted* it because it doesn't matter, dammit."

"If you really believed that, you would have told me, and you know it."

"I'm telling you now."

"No, I saw it on television with the rest of the world, and you came here for what?" I grip the edge of the conference room table. "To ensure if you ever make it back from the Amazon or whatever remote place you visit next, you'll still have some ass in the States?"

He moves so quickly, I jerk back when he's standing right in front of me, caging me with his arms on either side where I sit on the table. This close, I smell him. I feel him. His body, big and familiar and still a mystery, radiates heat. It makes me remember us curled around each other, naked in sex-scented sheets; to recall a day lying among half-opened tulips, sharing our dreams and ambitions.

"I'm losing patience, Nix," he says, so close his words rest on my lips.

"Oh, am I not forgiving you fast enough? How very privileged of you to expect it."

"I don't want it to be like this." He leans forward until only a sultry centimeter separates us. "I missed you. I came for—"

"What?" My will wavers and then snaps back into place. "What do you want?"

The look he pours over me is hot oil, burning me even through serviceable layers of cotton. His heated perusal caresses my face, sluices over my breasts and hips, and then pools at my feet.

"Oh, *that* you won't ever get again," I say, my voice a soft, certain promise. "I don't fuck liars. I'm particular that way."

"Never say never," he drawls, tilting up my chin with his finger.

"Nev—"

He crushes the word between our mouths. It falls apart in the scorching, sweet tangle of lips and teeth. With one hand, he digs his fingers into my hair. The other splays across my lower back, his grip on me almost convulsive, urging me up and closer. I'm in stasis. I'm completely startled by the kiss, unable to respond. I send a desperate message to my brain.

Move. Pull back. Push him away.

But the urgent glide of his hand down my spine to cup my ass melts my thoughts to liquid, and they swim in my head. I can't pull back, and all hope of resistance dissolves when he presses his thumb to my chin, prying me open. He stalks my tongue, hunts down a response, licking and sucking and groaning and growling. His hands tighten on me until I strain up to seek him, yanking his hair, pulling him even closer.

"Dammit, Nix," he mutters between kisses. His hand wanders down my neck and across my shoulder and cups my breast, twisting the nipple through flimsy barriers of cotton and lace. He shoves up my skirt, pulling my legs wider, and pushes my panties aside, his fingers invading me. My body remembers this mad craving that claws out of my bones—that wants out. That wants *him*. Under his rough touch, my body blooms, and my hips rock.

"That's it," he says, taking my earlobe between his lips.

My head falls back, and I moan. It's so damn good. His touch awakens me. His hands, his kisses bring me to life. It feels like I'm taking my first deep breath since we were last together, and it fills my lungs, seeps into my pores. He's all over me and inside me.

"I missed you," he says, sucking my lips and kissing the corners, quick, hungry. "I'm sorry. Baby, I—"

"Stop talking." I reach between us to loosen his belt, catching his zipper and dragging it down, dragging him out. "Shut the fuck up."

He's thick and rigid in my hand. The promise of stretching around him makes my body weep. I don't wait for him to move or ask but scoot forward to interlock our bodies. A harsh exhale clashes between our mouths, both of us losing our breath at this most carnal of reunions. For a moment, it's the perfection of us together, our bodies conduits to our souls. And then he moves, reducing the world to this mating dance. It's ancient, the beat of my blood and my heart. The way he takes me, it's new, fresh. Like it's the first time, the last time, he grips my thighs to hold me in place while he claims me, at first a deep, slow thrust and then increasing. Faster. Pounding. *Louder.* Our pleasure reaches the top of our lungs, heedless of who hears beyond the conference room door. I couldn't hold back these sounds if I tried—involuntary grunts and hisses and moans, too much for my body to keep private as I come hard and he soon follows.

I press my forehead to his, ghost my lips over his to taste his urgent breaths.

"Don't tell me never again," he pants. "I don't like that word."

His commanding words jar me. I jerk back and push him away. God, what have I done? What have I allowed? Yielded? Anyone could have walked in, caught us. I risked so much for what? A quick fuck with a man who lied to me?

I scramble off the table, standing and righting my clothes. Shame burns my face as the evidence of my weakness trickles out of me, dampening my panties. I'm weak. So weak. I can't resist him, but I can't have him. I won't.

"I need you to go." I turn away, struggling to regain my composure. "That was a mistake."

"That was what happens when we're together," he counters, behind me and closer than he was a few seconds ago. "That's why I came here, even knowing you'd be furious. Remember when you asked me that night in the alley if it's always like this?"

I turn to face him, watching him closely. "You said sometimes."

"I lied. It's never like this. I thought I could walk away, but I don't want to, Lennix. That was always my rule, but I'd never had *you*. I can't stay away from you. Don't ask me to. Yes, I have to go to the Amazon and you're going on the campaign trail, but we can try long distance. We can get past this misunderstanding and—"

"Misunderstanding?" I offer a disbelieving laugh. "You and your family, your father represent everything I want to spend my life fighting."

"I told you I'm not the company."

"*Not the company*. You're a liar and a thief, just like Warren Cade. He took things that weren't his, just like you did."

"Everything of yours I have," he says, anger burning in his glare, "you gave freely, and you know it."

"To Maxim Kingsman—not to you."

"It's all the same. It's all me," he shouts. "Maxim Kingsman Cade. That's who I am. I can't change that, Nix."

"You should have told me the truth and let me decide for myself if I wanted to be involved with you because that means being involved with your family, connected to your father. That's too complicated for me. And you lied."

"Let me tell you the truth now."

"It's too late."

"Too late?" He points to the conference room table. "That *just* happened. *We* are still happening. I can't be in the same room with you for ten seconds without wanting that to happen, so don't tell me it's too late. You still want this, want me. And I want you so fucking much. When I was in Antarctica—"

"Don't." I close my eyes and cover my ears. If I think about the way my heart broke when I thought he might die, I'll lose my anger, my indignation, and I'll hold him all night. I might try to hold him forever. "Don't talk about that."

"You don't want to hear that when I wondered if we'd be rescued in time, all I could think about was you?" he asks softly. "That after only a week with you, it wasn't my family or the memories from twenty-eight years on this Earth that kept me sane, but it was a matter of days with you? Reliving your kisses and our conversations. The hope that I could make it back to you and convince you we shouldn't walk away. That I was wrong. A stupid bastard to think I could."

"I'm glad you made it out alive," I say, such a pale reflection of the knee-weakening relief that came when I heard he'd been rescued. "But don't you get it?" I ask, blinking back tears. "You did the one thing I am so tired of everyone doing. You lied to get what you want."

"If you would just let me explain—"

"How will you explain? You'll use that bright mind and that silver tongue to convince me? To persuade me? You're all so good at tricking us, aren't you? If you care about me at all, don't convince me. Don't trick me out of my convictions. When you tell the truth now, it only reminds me that whatever we were before, it was a lie."

"You expect what? That I'll just walk away?"

"Wasn't that the original plan?"

"Before this, Nix. Before *us*. If you hadn't left Amsterdam early, I would have told you the truth. I would have told you I can't walk away."

My insides are melting again. The longer I'm around him, the longer I stand in this heat we generate when we're together, the harder it is to hold on to my anger. My fingers slip and slide around my indignation when he's inside me, when he tells me all the things I wanted to hear from the first night we made love.

I'm weakening when something bright on the floor by one of the boxes catches my attention. It's one of the neon fliers we posted searching for Tammara.

Tammara. Another girl lost. Gone.

Mama. Lost. Gone.

Our land, our traditions, our language—they're lost and gone. Stolen. A cycle of thievery and scorn and cruelty that began with an invasion, one act after another that evolved into the systems that never give us a chance.

Liar. Trickster. Thief.

That's who I was falling for. That's who I gave myself to. The son of our oppressor. The heir to our spoils.

Liar. Trickster. Thief.

I let the mantra reverberate through me, reach all the places Maxim claimed for himself, and I take them back.

He shoves his hands through his hair, away from his face, exposing the neat row of stitches at his hairline. I steel my will against the parts of me weakening, thinking of him in danger.

"Get out." Even I hear the new resolve in my voice, the starched determination of my words. "I never want to see you again."

"Nix." He strides over, his hands already reaching for me, but I evade him and open the conference room door.

"Go," I say. "This was the plan from the beginning. We said we'd walk away, and I'm sticking to it. Go to the Amazon, the Antarctic. You go off and change your world." I point to the campaign logo on my T-shirt. "And I'll change mine."

"There's only one world, Nix," he says.

A harsh laugh burns my lips, acidic and cynical. "God, you *are* a fool if you believe that. Every statistic, every news story, every broken promise and dead girl tells me we don't live in the same world and we have different battles to fight. You go fight yours and leave me to fight mine."

Something changes in him, on his face. Anger and resolve harden his features. He walks up to me but doesn't touch.

"Since you found out that I'm a Cade," he says. "I don't have to hide anymore. There's something you should know about us."

"And what's that?" I ask, feeling hunted by the wolf gleam in his eyes. I want to deny what a thrill it sends through me.

"We get whatever the fuck we want," he says, dropping his eyes down the length of my body. "And I want you, Lennix Moon. I want the girl who chases stars."

"Well, you can't have her. You can't have me."

"I can't force you. I wouldn't want you like that anyway. You want time. I can respect that. I can't *make* you give me another chance."

He pulls in a tired breath and shoves his hands through his hair. "I have to leave now for this expedition, but we're not done."

"I say we are." My voice is shockingly steady, considering how I'm trembling inside.

"We're not. Do what you need to do. Change your world," he says softly, his eyes connected to mine so intensely there's no hope of looking away. "I have to go *make* my world, but when the time is right, I'll be back for you."

PART 3

"Let us put our minds together to see what kind of future we can make…"

—*Sitting Bull, Lakota holy man and leader*

CHAPTER 34
LENNIX

TEN YEARS LATER

"Never fuck the candidate."

No matter how many times I've said it, there's always some dewy-eyed girl still smelling like sorority who doesn't get it. Who just haaaaaaas to know what two hundred or so pounds of future Mr. President feels like between her legs.

"It's rule number one, Lacy." I sit on the edge of my desk and consider the young campaign technology director. "And you broke it."

"I didn't mean for it to happen." Fat tears stream from Lacy's eyes and she rubs at them just enough to look cute, but not smear her makeup.

"Cut the tears, honey," I say. "This act you're putting on, it's a rerun. I've seen every season."

Lacy freezes mid-weep, glancing at me from under a set of press-on lashes.

"I don't have time for tears or excuses," I continue. "Day one, I tell everybody, don't fuck the candidate. It's bad for business. It eliminates your objectiveness. Most of all, it gives the press, and therefore potential voters, something to focus on besides the issues. And nine times out of ten, it costs everyone: the candidate, the sweet young thing, and most importantly, the people that candidate could have helped had we installed them into the place of power. That is the main reason the rule exists because the people are our bottom line."

I cross my legs, swinging one bright-green Louboutin Pigalle sling-back in time with the second hand ticking on my wall clock.

"I have to let you go." I sculpt my voice into the shape and hardness of dismissal.

Lacy's shocked eyes snap to meet mine.

"Are you kidding me?" She shakes her head, setting her blond curls bobbing. "I could have run tech for fifty campaigns, but I wanted to work with the Kingmaker. I chose you."

I grimace at the ridiculous nickname the press started using a few years ago when a string of my candidates won high-profile races.

"Actually, I chose you," I remind her ungently. "Not the other way around. And I appreciate your special talents and your dedication to the job, but you're compromised. I'm running triage now covering your tracks and trying my damnedest to keep this out of the news cycle."

"We were discreet."

"Oh, is that what you call it? Susan's wife came home to find the two of you in *her* bed with their kids asleep upstairs. What part of that do you consider discreet exactly?"

"Kristin was supposed to be out of town," Lacy says defensively. "And it was so late, we knew the kids wouldn't come downstairs. I just…Susan's so amazing."

"They often are. In my experience, power gilds the goose. Makes it look like a peacock, but in the end, it's still just a bird that honks when it flies."

"I need this job, Lennix."

"And I need you off this campaign. Firing you is the first of several steps to keep Kristin at Susan's side, smiling for the cameras until Election Day. Susan may have a wandering eye, but she's got damn good ideas for getting women equal pay. That's all I care about. We need her to win in Denver."

"But where will I go?" Lacy cries, and this time I believe her tears. She doesn't bother being careful with the mascara. "What will I do? Can you at least give me a letter of reference?"

"Sure. The first line of my letter will read, 'Watch this one. She fucks the candidates.'" I pluck a couple Kleenex from the glass holder on the corner of my desk and hand them to her. "I wish this could be different, and I wish you the best."

"The hell you wish me the best." Lacy stands, her fists clenched at her sides. "Bitch. Do you know how hard it will be for me to find another job in politics without a reference letter?"

"Harder than keeping your legs closed, I'm guessing? 'Cause that proved really difficult for you." I lean back and press the intercom. "Karla, Lacy's ready for her escort."

The heavy glass doors swing open. My assistant, Karla, stands there with two security guards. They walk forward, and though they don't grab Lacy, it's obvious if she jumps, they're ready.

"This is ridiculous," Lacy screams. "I'll sue you for this."

"Try that. You signed an iron-clad contract that you wouldn't have sexual relations with any candidate Hunter, Allen represents. We've all signed that agreement with the understanding that violating it is grounds for instant dismissal."

"You'll regret this," Lacy grits between her teeth.

"You can clear out your things." I reach behind my desk and proffer a box already assembled. "Or Karla can do it for you. Either way is fine with me."

Lacy snatches the box from my hands and walks toward the door with her head held high and Karla at her heels. "I'll do it myself. I've done nothing to be ashamed of."

"Actually you had an affair with a married woman whose wife almost died giving birth to their triplets. So…yeah. The public would think you should be ashamed."

Susan should be ashamed, too, but she probably won't be. Concerned, yes, about whether we can convince her wife to hang around. Concerned that this never makes it to the public's greedy noses. She won't be concerned, though, that I just fired one of the most brilliant tech minds I've encountered in a long time.

"And now I need a replacement."

"Yeah, you do," Kimba says from the door, the "Allen" in Hunter, Allen & Associates. "And fast. This campaign is in full swing."

"Karla!" I say loud enough to carry to my assistant's outer office. She hurries in, running a hand over her purple pixie cut and with red in her cheeks.

"Lacy is not happy," she says, her eyes wide. "But the guards are with her."

"Good. I want her off the property in ten. Find Kristin Bowden for me, will ya? I need to speak to her ASAP."

"Got it, boss." Karla heads for the door but leaves a parting shot over her shoulder. "And ASAP number two needs to be getting outta here and down to the set."

"Exactly why I'm here," Kimba says. "We need to leave in ten minutes if we're gonna make it to the taping in time."

"Ugh." I massage my temples. "Remind me again why we're doing this *now*? I fly to New York tonight for that rally in Queens. This is the last thing I need."

"We're doing this because *Beltway* is the hottest new political show around." Kimba raises perfectly shaped brows over shrewd brown eyes. "You know I love stuff like this about as much as a Pap smear, but we got books to sell, baby."

"*Louder* is already a *New York Times* bestseller, no thanks to Bryce Collins. If he'd *actually* wanted to help, he would have had us on for release week when we asked. Why now?"

"Who said he wants to help us? I'm sure he has his own agenda, but don't kick a gift horse. Get that pretty little ass in gear."

I grin and wiggle the pretty little ass in question at her, walk behind my desk, and then flop down into my chair with a whoosh of tired breath.

"And the publisher wants us to do it," Kimba continues. "The studio's sending a car over to take us."

"Fancy."

The intercom buzzes on my desk.

"Lenn," Karla says. "I have Kristin Bowden on the phone."

Kimba and I exchange a harassed look. I sigh and pick up the phone, leaning back in my chair and kicking my feet up onto the desk.

"Kristin," I say, ready to beg and mollify. "Thanks for taking my call."

"So she's still in?" Kimba asks once we're in the car *Beltway* sent for us.

"Barely. She was angry and hurt, of course, but she does believe in Susan's vision. And she loves her and wants to save her marriage, so hearing that Lacy is no longer working for the campaign went a long way. Good luck getting Susan to stop long enough to focus on fixing the marriage, though."

"Is every politician a narcissist?"

"Pretty much, with few exceptions. We work with whom we're given."

"You know how everyone talks about that once-in-a-lifetime candidate?" Kimba asks. "We've put some incredible people in power and done a lot of good, but I'm still waiting for that."

"Me, too." I sigh. "Until then, we keep doing our best with what we get."

Our best has been great, and we've gotten a lot. In the five years since we started our political consulting firm, Allen, Hunter & Associates, we've gotten a lot of people who champion the causes of marginalized people elected.

"You look great," I tell Kimba when we arrive at *Beltway's* downtown studio.

"Ya think?" She fluffs the cloud of her naturally textured brown hair, highlighted with gold. "That Orangetheory must be working. Gotta keep this ass in check."

Several men and a few women watch said ass in Kimba's body-hugging fuchsia dress.

"I think you're doing just fine," I say wryly.

"You look great, too." She nods to my dress. "Is that another Wiona original?"

"Yup." I smooth the fitted azure dress and scarf at my neck. "I try to wear her stuff when I have appearances."

Wiona is an incredibly gifted Indigenous fashion designer I met in North Dakota. I wear her clothes every chance I get, declaring my heritage when I can.

We're in the dressing room getting our makeup freshened when Alice, the producer, comes in. She's sharp, and I respect her despite the fact that her host is a bit of an ass. He postures himself as a moderate who maintains professional objectivity, but I think it thinly veils his implicit bias and misogyny. Kimba says I find bias and misogyny in houseplants. She's not wrong, but come on. That shit's everywhere.

"So did they tell you who's on with you today?" Alice asks, splitting a glance in the mirror between Kimba and me as the makeup artists apply color to our cheeks.

Beltway's format is similar to old-school late-night television in that the guests stay as others are added. It's kind of Bill Maher-esque with the host encouraging conversation and interaction between the guests.

"It's Rhonda Mays?" Kimba asks. "The special education advocate?"

"And Senator Biggs," I add. "Republican from Ohio, right?"

"Oh." Alice's brows pull into a careful crinkle like she doesn't want to fully frown. "We had some booking changes. Only one other guest today. I'm sorry you weren't apprised."

I stiffen. I don't like walking into situations blindly. Anyone working for any length of time in DC knows that about me. Kimba and I think quickly on our feet, but I don't like to be caught flat-footed. I've been ambushed more than once by some reporter trying to make their name off my possible gaffe. Preparation is key.

"Who?" I ask curtly.

"Owen Cade."

Motherfucker.

Not Owen personally. He's not a motherfucker, as far as I can tell. He's actually proven to be an excellent senator. Moderate in some of the ways I'd prefer him to be progressive, but not a douchebag. He's compassionate, seems to put his constituents first, has never been associated with any scandal, and has that "it" factor most politicians would give their left nut or boob for. He has stock in that "it" factor.

Like his brother.

"That's fine," Kimba says. "Thanks, Alice."

"Oh, good," Alice says, relief on her face. "See you out there. Someone will come get you when it's time."

The door closes behind Alice, and I catch Kimba's eyes in the mirror.

"You know I don't like surprises," I say through a thin opening in my lips as the makeup artist traces the outline of my mouth.

"I know you don't like Cades," Kimba says, her eyes obediently to the ceiling while her tech applies mascara.

"I think that looks great," I tell the makeup artist, gesturing toward her bags and brushes and colorful palettes. "Thanks, but we're done." I look at Kimba's tech in the mirror. "You, too."

"I'm almost done," she protests. "I just need to—"

"You're done," I say with a smile that barely moves my freshly painted lips.

Once we're alone, Kimba and I share a long look in the mirror. The name Cade always makes me feel ill at ease.

"You know he's in town, right?" Kimba asks.

"Who?" My muscles tighten, braced for her answer.

"Maxim. Testifying before Congress about climate change."

"Oh." I look away from my friend to the safety of my own reflection in the mirror, finding stray hairs to smooth. "How nice he remembered he's an American and graced our shores."

"He's in America all the time, but a lot of his business is overseas."

"Sounds like you've kept up with him a lot more than I have, which is not at all."

"It was ten years ago, Lenn. I know he lied to you—"

"Right. Ten years ago, which is what makes this conversation completely unnecessary."

I last saw Maxim face-to-face in that Oklahoma conference room. His threat of "coming back for me" has proven an idle one, though he did try to maintain contact at first. His text messages—unreturned. Postcards from faraway places—tossed in the trash. Voice mails—deleted before I could hear the plea in his words. The incident—okay, the *fucking*—in the conference room demonstrated that I'm vulnerable where Maxim Cade is concerned, so I had to shut down every attempt, cut him off at every pass, and keep him out of my life. He was so busy risking *his* life in the Amazon or where the hell ever, it wasn't hard to do.

And then it all just…stopped.

I was left to assume his threat to come back for me was indeed an empty one. Each time he's been in DC to testify before Congress, I half-wondered if he might show up at my office. The element of surprise and all that, but no. Over the past decade, he's seemed completely focused on building his clean energy empire, just like he said he would. The crusader and the capitalist, too busy to come back. Or maybe he just moved on.

Like I have.

The door opens, and a production assistant pops in.

"They're ready for you, ladies." She opens the door wider and gestures ahead with her clipboard. "If you'd follow me."

Bryce Collins is who I thought he was, with questions ranging from subtly condescending to blatantly sexist.

"So they call you the Kingmaker, Ms. Hunter," he says. "But it seems you like to focus on making queens. About 60 percent of your candidates are women."

"It's actually closer to 70 percent," I offer with a wide, proud smile.

"What do you have against us guys?" he asks, his humor lined with invisible barbs.

"As we discuss in our book *Louder*, Kimba and I decided we wanted to amplify muted voices—wanted to position in places of power those most concerned about marginalized groups, especially women, people of color, LGBTQIA, and those with disabilities."

"Seems like we add letters every day for being gay," Bryce says with a caustic laugh.

"Try to keep up," Kimba says. "It's the least we can do."

"Yes, well, you're running a candidate now who hits on several categories," he says. "Susan Bowden, a gay woman, married with three children. How's the Denver race going?"

If he's sniffing around a story, we can't afford to give anything away, not with Kristin barely contained.

"Susan is an exceptional leader." My smile comes naturally. "We expect big things from her—things that will benefit people who need better representation, especially women seeking equal pay."

"I keep hearing about women not making as much," Bryce says with a shrug. "But you ladies seem to be doing really well, and a lot of other women, too."

"We command the same rates as our peers," Kimba replies. "Every woman is not in a position to demand. Those are the ones we fight for."

"Yes, well," Bryce continues. "You mentioned your book, *Louder*. In it, you're very critical of some of this nation's forefathers, Ms. Hunter. Men widely recognized as heroes."

"Recognizing their contributions without exposing their short-comings, the discrepancies between rhetoric of freedom and systemic mistreatment and exclusion of marginalized groups, is a disservice," I say, trying to check my irritation. "As for them being heroes, how could I consider Andrew Jackson, a president who ratified the death of my ancestors, a hero? A man who sent them on the Trail of Tears? Is he my hero? The men who stripped us of our heritage, stole our language, forbade our customs—they aren't my heroes. My ancestors, the people who *resisted* them, those are heroes to me."

"Forgive me." Bryce leans forward, his eyes gleaming, obviously relishing the rise he gets out of me. "But your sentiments don't sound very patriotic."

"Dissent is the highest form of patriotism," I quote. "I love this country too much to settle for the lies written in our history books. I love the Constitution too much not to hold the men who wrote it accountable for the truth of its principles."

"Some would call your perspective radical."

"Some would be right," I say with my sweetest smile. "I'll continue loving this country on one hand and exposing the government's kleptocratic practices on the other."

"What are we supposed to do with that information, Ms. Hunter?" Bryce asks. "Feel guilty for something our ancestors did? Doesn't this line of discussion simply perpetuate the divisiveness that's tearing our country apart? How is this productive?"

"Not only is it productive, it's essential. Most Americans don't really know the full truth of what happened to Native people because our history books don't tell it. We have to *know* what happened if we are to ensure that it never happens again. And it's not just what occurred in the past but what's still happening. We're still living with it, and there are things that can be done now. This is not about blaming for the past. It's about us *all* being responsible for the future."

Bryce blinks at me, apparently at the end of his combative line of questioning, and turns his attention to Kimba. The light of battle in her eyes tells him he doesn't want any of that, and he offers a softer version of the thrust and parry for the next few minutes until we break and add Owen Cade to the set.

"You're doing great, girls," Bryce says, patting Kimba's hand.

"We're not your girls," I say mildly. "We're your guests, and thanks for having us."

He watches me for an extra few seconds, picking through what is admittedly backhanded appreciation. "Thanks for coming at the last minute," he finally replies.

I want to ask why the last minute. He doesn't seem particularly interested in our book, our causes or us in general, but I'm distracted by Owen Cade taking the seat next to me. They're checking his mic, which gives me a chance to check *him*.

I've seen him before, of course. He's a California senator, but our paths have crossed very little. Maybe that was intentional on my part. I've never allowed myself to think too much about it. About him. Or about his brother.

He couldn't be more unlike Maxim. Where Maxim is dark-haired and green-eyed like his father, Owen looks very much like his mother, fair with blue eyes. Truly and literally the golden boy of politics. He reaches across the aisle, manages to remain civil in the most vitriolic political climate, and, at least as far as I've heard, never cheats on his wife.

"Ladies," he says to Kimba and me once he's settled. "Glad to be on with you today. I don't think we've ever actually met, but I know of your father and grandfather, of course, Ms. Allen. Their contribution to the civil rights movement is invaluable. So sorry for your family's loss."

Kimba's grandfather died years before, but her father passed away from a heart attack just a few months ago. Pain tweaks her expression for a second, but she clears it and pulls the professional mask in place before most would notice. "Thank you, Senator Cade," she replies.

"Please," he says. "Call me Owen."

She won't. Neither will I.

"And you, Ms. Hunter." He turns that piercing blue stare on me. "I've wanted to meet you for a long time."

"Really?" I keep my voice neutral and am relieved when Bryce asks for our attention to review the next segment. It's mainly questions for Owen, but Bryce wants us all to be prepared.

"We're back," Bryce says into the camera, "and joined by Senator Owen Cade. Thank you for being with us, Senator."

"Thank you for having me," Owen replies. I wonder if his humility is an act. Has to be. His father and brother certainly aren't humble. Maybe he's just the best actor of the family.

Bryce is much more solicitous with the fine senator than he was with us. Even if Owen wasn't one of the most powerful members of the Senate, he'd still have the famous Cade pedigree on his side. That always garners attention and respect. Bryce's opening salvos are pretty standard, inquiring about Owen's recent votes and positions he's known to hold on safe topics. But *Beltway* wouldn't be as popular as it is if Bryce didn't go for the jugular and ask the questions everyone wants to know.

"And can we soon officially add presidential hopeful to your titles, Senator?" he asks cagily.

Owen laughs, his posture relaxed, and sits back in his chair. He crosses an ankle over one long leg with the same physical ease and strength as his brother.

"I'm not ruling it out," he says. "I'm not prepared to make any announcements quite yet, though."

"Your family has a history in politics," Bryce continues, "but is even better known for business. Cade Energy, led by your father, and CadeCo, led by your brother, who are famously estranged from one another. Where do you fall in the spectrum of their beliefs?"

"I'm not my father or my brother." The affable smile dissolves from Owen's face, and I see traces of the ruthlessness his family is known for. "I represent the people of California and have for the last ten years. My brother is, as most know, a strong proponent of clean energy, and my father is in oil and gas. I believe climate change is one of the most pressing issues we face now and assuredly in the foreseeable future. However, I'm a pragmatist and understand change doesn't happen overnight. We are an oil-producing and dependent country. Millions of jobs are tied to fossil fuel production. I believe in responsibly transitioning this nation to less fossil fuel dependence as we cultivate green-energy solutions like wind and solar."

"Your brother's made quite a lot of money from these energy solutions he's so passionate about America adopting," Bryce says. "He was added to the *Forbes* list of billionaires this year. Quite convenient that the measures he recommends are the very ones that line his own pockets."

Owen's smile reappears. "My little brother has risked his life in places most of us barely know exist collecting data in the fight to save our planet. He's an adventurer, a capitalist, and an overachiever, but he's not an opportunist. An opportunist wouldn't sign the Giving Pledge, committing half his wealth to charity over the course of his lifetime."

"Spoken like a loyal big brother," Bryce says wryly.

"I'm loyal to the people I care about," Owen says, "including the people who vote for me. I work for their interests."

"And when the interests conflict with those of the many oil lobbyists your father employs?" Bryce asks, impressing me with his journalistic tenacity.

"I love my father," Owen says carefully, allowing a slight smile. "But I don't work for him."

"Ms. Hunter," Bryce says, jolting me by introducing my name into the conversation. "I'm interested to hear your thoughts. You've challenged Cade Energy over several pipeline projects through the years."

"The ones that would cross protected grounds, yes," I say,

recovering quickly enough to respond. "So many cities in this country have been built from subterfuge and land grabs that broke treaties and promises."

"You've actually stopped some of them," Bryce says, glancing between Owen and me.

"Win some, lose some." I turn my attention to the senator, too. "I'm curious, though, Senator Cade, to hear your thoughts about corporations stealing land for these projects. Should companies like your father's be allowed to commandeer property that doesn't belong to them, sacred lands, for instance, for the sake of their own interests?"

"Check my record on pipeline construction, Ms. Hunter," Owen replies, holding my eyes in a steady stare. "On more than one occasion, I've voted to block pipelines that potentially violated a treaty with tribal leadership. I've actually worked with Senator Nighthorse, whom I believe you helped elect, on this and MMIW legislation."

"MMIW?" Bryce asks. "All these acronyms. Could you clarify for the uninitiated?"

"Murdered and missing Indigenous women," I say.

"Right," Owen confirms almost gently. "I've worked with Senator Nighthorse and his wife, Mena, on MMIW as well as on the issues of pay equity and criminal justice reform, which I know is of special interest to you, Ms. Allen."

"Certainly," Kimba says. "I've been following the legislative developments around reduced mandatory sentences. Great work that I hope will prove fruitful."

Owen Cade is impressive in his own right. By the time the taping concludes, I think he'll actually get my vote if he decides to run.

We're taking off microphones when a knock comes on the dressing-room door.

"Come in," Kimba and I call in unison.

Owen Cade pokes his slightly tousled blond head through the door. His security detail is in the hall, and he stands half in, half out of the small room. "Ladies, could I have a moment?"

Kimba's eyebrows raise to the same level of speculation I feel. "Sure. Yes, sir. Of course."

"No sirs, please," he says, stepping into the room and closing the door behind him.

"I grew up in Atlanta," Kimba says dryly. "You'll have to excuse my Southern roots knee-jerk manners. They're hard to shake."

Owen leans against the wall with a half-smile. "I'm going to run for president."

Maxim predicted it years ago, but hearing it from *Owen* still takes me by surprise. I clear my throat and reply, "Good luck. I'm sure you'll make a fine candidate."

"I think I can with the right team running my campaign," he says, looking between the two of us. "How would you like the job?"

For a moment, I'm too shocked to respond, and then I do in the most inappropriate way. I snort...as one does in the face of a powerful senator.

"Sorry." I cover my mouth and shake my head as if clearing it. "You're just not our usual client, and I'm not sure how we could help you."

"Why is that?" He frowns and tilts his head.

"Because rich white boys don't need our help," I say flatly. "In case you hadn't noticed, our mission is to put people in power who will champion the marginalized."

"Which I plan to do," he replies without missing a beat. "Did you not hear me discussing my plans for criminal justice reform, women's pay equity, and missing and murdered Indigenous women? Where better to install an ally than in the Oval?"

"I don't think—"

"All I'm asking you to do right now *is* to think about it," he cuts in and hands Kimba a card. "That's a direct line to me. I hope I'll hear from you soon."

And with those final words, he leaves.

"Can you believe that guy?" I ask once the door closes behind him.

"Yeah. The nerve of him, offering us the biggest opportunity of our lives," Kimba says, an irritated note in her voice. "That man is probably the next president of the United States, Lenn. You know that, right?"

I remember his smooth answers, recall the open, honest face that has the added bonus of being movie-star handsome.

"Maybe," I concede. "But that doesn't mean we should represent him. We can't compromise our mission."

"He may *embody* our mission. Look, I'm all about putting women and people of color in power as much as you are. You know that, but ultimately, we want changes made in the system to help them. A friend at 1600 Pennsylvania can only help."

"I just don't know that it's the right fit for us."

"And I just don't know that it's only your call to make," Kimba fires back. "We're fifty-fifty in this thing, boo. My fifty says we do it. In addition to advancing the causes we care about, we will have elected a president. Do you know how much business will come our way if we pull that off?"

"A lot," I mutter without much enthusiasm.

"A lot. We can't *not* consider it." Kimba props one rounded hip against the makeup table, watching me closely. "Hey, this is me. Let's talk about the real reason you don't want to work with Owen Cade. His brother."

I slingshot a baleful look at her. "That's ridiculous. You think I'm still in my feelings for that man?"

"I saw you two together," Kimba reminds me softly. "In the words of m'girl Sade, it was no ordinary love."

"It was no love *at all*. It was a week."

"He was your first."

"Everybody has a first."

"Everybody's first is not Maxim Cade. And you may not have been his first, but it was obvious you were special to him."

"So special he lied to me," I spit, clinging to the righteous indignation I wrapped around myself like armor. "He knew how I felt about his father."

"Ever thought him being afraid to tell you about his dad is an indication of how much he wanted it to work? That maybe he thought you wouldn't give him a shot if you knew?"

I don't answer, but just stare at her. It's too much. Maxim coming to town. Seeing his brother and getting this offer. I've studiously avoided all things Maxim Cade for the past ten years. I've built the life I dreamt about, and he's built his. We both got everything we wanted.

A tiny rebel part of me has the nerve to whisper.

Not everything.

CHAPTER 35
MAXIM

"I CANNOT OVERSTATE THE NECESSITY OF DEVELOPING A CIRCULAR economy—one that minimizes waste and maximizes our natural resources."

It's a different way of saying what I've been telling this panel for the past hour. This isn't my first time testifying before Congress, but it may be my last.

"Could you elaborate, Mr. Cade?" A narrow-faced man speaks into his little microphone, peering down at me from his perch.

"Yes. In a circular system, we minimize waste, emission, and energy leakage by slowing and closing energy and material loops," I say as patiently as I can. "Not like in a more linear, traditional 'take, make, dispose' model. Economic circularity not only reduces resources used and waste and leakage created and conserves resources, but it also reduces environmental pollution."

"According to the studies you provided," says one congresswoman, glancing down at a sizable stack of papers, "China and Europe are taking the lead in this."

"It's true that most of the forward movement in circular economics is occurring in Europe and China," I say. "Europe tends to focus more on the environmental implications, but China is very much concerned with the economic by-products, too. Circular economy has been national policy for the Chinese since 2006."

In other words, we're lagging behind, guys.

"Concrete examples?" the first congressman asks, one brow elevated.

"There are many," I answer. "But I think one of the best examples is in the textile industry. In fashion, it's recycling clothes and fibers so they reenter the economy instead of ending up in landfills as waste. Designers like Patagonia and Stella McCartney are high-profile examples of how this can work."

"And you've ventured into this yourself, correct, Mr. Cade?" another asks. "You're making money through this circular economy." It sounds almost like an accusation.

"Hand over fist," I confirm unapologetically. "Shoes, leggings, sports bras. You name it, and my company Wear It Again is making it over and over and over. We're not only regenerating materials but profit. We need these new ways of thinking if we expect to deliver on the emissions reductions commitments we and our global partners have made."

"This is all a lot to take in," one of them says. "A lot to process."

"Exactly, which is why I'd rather be discussing how we can reeducate America's populace and retrain our workforce for green jobs instead of convincing you the sky is indeed falling. We need to make this *real* for people. Like telling farmers global warming is contributing to desertification, which means lower crop yields. They'll get that."

I spend another thirty minutes breaking down things most of the interns in my companies could easily explain to these politicians. Their ivory towers have chimney stacks, carelessly puffing poison into the environment. I hope I'm not wasting my time "educating" them, but they haven't delivered in the past at the rate and level I had hoped.

"If we don't address these issues," I say, "the socioeconomic implications are even greater than the ones we've already discussed. Shifting ecosystems and natural disasters will cause poverty, hunger, homelessness, and disease and will disproportionately affect those countries already most vulnerable. Quite frankly, in some instances, I believe we're already too late and have to begin thinking of how we'll *survive*, not reverse, the consequences of what we've done."

They ask more follow-up questions and look for ways to skirt the truth, but I don't give them outs, and I counter every shortcut they want to take with hard facts.

"Let's go," I mutter to my assistant Jin Lei once the final question has been answered. "Quickest way out of here with as little press as possible."

"As little" proves relative since a small cadre of reporters gather at the side exit we find.

"Maxim," one reporter shouts, his iPhone shoved in my face. "Are you glad to be back in America?"

"I'm in America all the time," I reply neutrally, eyeing the strip of sidewalk between the door and the SUV waiting at the curb. "I just don't announce my comings and goings, but yeah. Of course, it's always good to be home."

"This is your fifth time testifying before Congress," another yells. "And you serve with the president's special counsel on climate change. Any chance we might see you venturing into politics?"

"Uh, no." I laugh and start inching toward the car. "I'll leave that to my brother."

"Lots of rumblings about a presidential run for him," the reporter says. "You've been very clear that you're an Independent, not affiliated with either party. If your brother runs, can we expect you to support him?"

"I may be a little biased, but this country would be lucky to have my brother as president." I take Jin Lei's elbow and press forward. "I don't pretend to know what he'll do, but he'll have my full support no matter what."

I nod to the car and reheat the smile I've been using all day with the stalwarts in Congress. "Sorry. Gotta go."

I allow their persistent questions to harmlessly bounce off my back while we stride to the car.

"Why are they always so interested here?" I ask Jin Lei, dropping my head back against the seat. "I walk outside in London, Paris, Milan—not a peep."

"For one," Jin Lei says, "they don't see you as much. Two and three would be your brother and father. One is a soon-to-be presidential front-runner, and the other owns one of the largest oil companies in the world. Americans don't have royalty, so they're interested in anything that comes close. Apparently, the Cades come close."

I miss anonymity. Those days when the only people who really took notice of my existence were the students in my class when I was a TA getting my doctorate. My Kingsman days were simple, sweet. Though too few, my fondest memories from that season of my life are in Amsterdam.

"Is the new office set up?" I glance at the passing scene of downtown DC.

"Yes, sir."

"Apartment upstairs?" It's temporary, but I need my workspace within striking distance of where I sleep, considering how *little* I sleep.

"Yes, sir. Both are ready."

"Good." I rub my hands over my face. "Hell, I'm exhausted."

"This was your last commitment for the day," she says, her dark eyes concerned. "You hit the ground running."

"I'm used to it. I'll be fine."

The hotel's penthouse is marble floors, a wall of windows, and the height of modern minimalism. The elaborate arrangement of orchids on the foyer table is the only thing alive in the place. Everything else feels lifeless, impersonal, and outrageously luxurious.

"It's perfect," I say.

In the office, a plasma wall displays multiple screens—CNN, CNBC, MarketWatch, and news from international markets. I widen the feed so the entire wall displays the show I recorded.

"It was that political show *Beltway* you wanted the recording of, right?" Jin Lei asks.

"Uh, yeah," I say distractedly, watching the show's title package. "I'm expecting my brother. Tell them downstairs the senator and his detail can come up as soon as they arrive."

The door closes behind Jin Lei, and I watch this Bryce asshole interview Kimba and Lennix, who is impossibly *more* than she even was before. More beautiful. More confident. More passionate. Everything about her appeals to me on a level few things ever touch. She views Bryce through knowing eyes, remaining composed when he tries to fluster her. Undaunted when he tries to intimidate. Dignified when he patronizes. She is exactly who the past ten years have made her, and I regret missing the journey.

I tried. I had hoped the months I was away in the Amazon would soften her position—give her room to cool off and reconsider. The unanswered correspondence didn't deter me, but when I returned to the States, Wallace Murrow did. A few well-placed inquiries revealed Lennix was dating Vivienne's brother. Nix had been very loud and clear about not wanting me in her life. There is a fine line between going all out for a woman you believe wants you as much as you want her and stalking, harassing. I couldn't land on the wrong side of that line, not with Nix of all people. Controlling her own destiny means everything to her.

There always seemed to be something. If it wasn't another man in her life, it was a hill to climb in mine. Those first few years, many of the things I did were with my father in mind—to show him how wrong he was about me, but eventually it became about who *I* wanted to be and what *I* wanted to do.

Once it was buying a company with little hope of surviving but with endless potential. Pulling that company out of the ditch consumed every waking moment for three years, but it became the foundation for the CadeCo conglomerate.

Another time it was fending off a hostile takeover. They regretted crossing me. I performed a backflip takeover, turning the tables on them and acquiring that company for my holdings instead of being gobbled up. Every challenge seemed to take me closer to my goals and further away from Lennix, the girl I could never forget.

But I'm here now, Nix. And you will deal with me.

"Getting to the good part, I see," my brother says from the door. I turn and smile, glad to see him for the first time in months.

"Can you please leave your guard dogs outside?" I ask, nodding to the two dour-faced men who look on high alert. "And tell them this place is basically Fort Knox. They can relax."

He grins and says a few words to them before closing the door.

"You've got a guard dog of your own." He removes his suit jacket, undoes his tie, and flops onto the leather couch facing the plasma wall.

"Jin Lei's growl is worse than her bite," I say, taking a seat across from him. "But her growl is pretty bad."

"So what'd you think about the interview? Was it worth the favors we had to call in to get them on?"

"That Bryce guy is an asshole. He should be glad Lennix agreed to come on his sorry show."

"It has great ratings."

"So did *Jersey Shore*. You asked her?"

He kicks his Italian boots up onto my coffee table. "I asked them, yeah."

"And?" He's doing this on purpose, drawing it out.

"Kimba's interested."

"And Lennix?"

"She said she doesn't help rich white boys." He grimaces, and I laugh.

"That sounds like Nix."

"You better be glad I agree they'd be the best ones to run my campaign." He picks up a glass of water Jin Lei left in easy reach. "Or I wouldn't be doing this."

"You want to be president? Hire them. They're the best. You'll already get moderates and progressive white voters. You need black women, Latinas. Those voters will have choices and be looking for very specific things in the candidate they support. And no one knows marginalized groups like these ladies do. So does it really matter that I suggested it?"

"But why? You've barely shown any interest in my political career before." His smile widens. "But then it's *her* you're interested in. Am I right, brother? You know Ms. Hunter?"

Intimately and not at all.

"We've met."

"Don't bullshit me. This is my future, possibly the future of this country we're talking about. I'm not your matchmaker. I need to win, and I need to know everything about your history with Lennix Hunter."

I knock back a swallow of the bourbon Jin Lei knows I like and stocks in every residence.

"Want some?" I proffer the decanter.

"No, thanks. Tell me about you and Lennix."

"What do you want to know?" I walk over to the wall of windows, taking in the view of the city. Glittering lights overlay the grime of politics. It's a city where ideals climb in a corrupted bed with compromise to get things done. One of my least favorite cities in the world, and I need to be here to get what I want.

"Did you fuck her?" he asks.

"That is not the important part of this story." I chuckle and shake my head. "I've fucked a lot of women. You should be asking why this one. What makes her so special that I'd go to the trouble of finally involving myself in your political career? Of dealing with that greaseball Bryce to arrange your meeting with her? And

setting up shop in DC, of all places, when my business is everywhere but here?"

"So why?"

I take a long swallow of the sense-numbing liquor before answering. "I have to know if she's as good as I remember. Did I convince
myself we were perfect together before I screwed it all to hell?"

"Give me a minute to digest this." Owen leans forward and
props his elbows on his knees. "So you have a history with Lennix
Hunter."

"Right." I roll my eyes. "That's what I just said."

"You've never talked this seriously about a girl, except for once."
He turns wide eyes to me. "Amsterdam. Lennix is the girl from
Amsterdam."

"So." Brilliant response, but it's all I can come up with on such
short notice. I didn't expect him to make that connection this quickly.

"So you're still hung up on her? How'd you screw it up before?"

I slam my glass down on the desk and rub my eyes. "I kind of left
out the fact that I was a Cade. And that my father is, for all intents
and purposes, the man she hates maybe most in the world."

"The pipeline."

"Yeah, among other things. She said I lied to her."

"Which technically, you did."

"There was nothing *technical* about the connection we had
before I left for Antarctica. I intended to tell her when I came back,
but Dad's daring rescue got so much airtime and outed me on every
news outlet before I could explain."

"So you gave up?"

"Not exactly," I say defensively. "I put things on hold."

"For what…a decade?" he asks with a frown. "Amsterdam was
like ten years ago, wasn't it?"

"Look, she sent me away. I tried, and she turned me down. She
had shit to do, and so did I. Neither of us was ready to stop what we
were doing." I shrug. "Maybe she made the right call. I can't even

imagine managing a long-distance relationship considering what the last ten years of my life have been."

I've been planning this for some time. Events coalesced perfectly—Kimba and Lennix opening their political consulting firm, Owen following through on his precious ten-year plan for the presidency, and me hitting my milestones, allowing me a little room to breathe for the first time in years.

"And now you've decided you want her, so it's time?" Owen asks, skepticism in his expression. "And she should just fall in line with your wishes?"

"I think she'll wish it, too. Or at least she will once I remind her." I smile slow and wide. "We couldn't keep our hands off each other."

"Spare me the details, brother," he says with a disgusted grimace. "I don't need the complications of your love life screwing things up for me. I just want her expertise."

"You can have her expertise." I toss back another much-needed swig of my bourbon. "I want everything else."

CHAPTER 36
LENNIX

"THIS WORKED OUT PERFECTLY," I say, grabbing my luggage from the conveyor belt.

"Yeah, you know I hate traveling alone," Wallace says, grabbing his, too.

"I made it to the rally in Queens."

"And I made my keynote speech at the conference."

"And we both got to see the baby." I turn heart-eyes his way. "Madison is the most adorable baby ever. She has your eyes. Vivienne's eyes."

"And Stephen's red hair. Mom doesn't know what to do with herself. She's just glad one of her kids has reproduced." He playfully nudges me as we make our way out of Reagan International and into the crisp fall air. "She was counting on you to marry me and give her grandbabies." He laughs when I cross my eyes and poke my tongue out at him. "You ruined everything breaking up with me."

"What would have ruined everything," I say, craning my neck to see if I spot the car Karla sent for us, "is divorcing after like three months and making it hella awkward with my best friend."

"I thought I was your best friend. That was my only consolation when you ended things."

"Of course you are." I pat his hand reassuringly. "Just don't tell Viv and Kimba, 'kay? It'll be our little secret."

"There's the car." He points toward a waiting Lincoln Aviator.

We settle into the back seat, and I just want to close my eyes for a few minutes, but of course, Wallace keeps up a constant stream of chatter.

"I thought biochemist types were supposed to be introverted, withdrawn creatures," I say, faking exasperation...kind of. "You're yammering like a chick at a sleepover, Wall."

"Is that why you dumped me?"

"I broke it off," I correct deliberately. "Because the sex was weird." I say it to shock him, but it's the truth. I can barely suppress my grin.

"Ah, yes. Now I remember," he says, tongue in his cheek. "You said it felt like kissing your foster step-cousin."

Our laughter bubbles over at the same time and fills the car. It feels good to laugh as hard as I do when I'm with Wallace. If only the sex hadn't been weird and I hadn't cared too much to let him settle for someone who didn't want him the way he deserved.

"You dodged a bullet, baby." I give him a quick peck on the cheek.

"Is that what you're doing by not taking on Owen Cade?" he asks. "Dodging bullets?"

I regret telling him everything. He knows my history with Maxim, since Vivienne warned her big brother off dating me. She said I was rebounding from a guy I met in Amsterdam. It had been months by then, so I'd assumed she was wrong.

She wasn't.

I'm just glad Wallace and I only dated a few months and I didn't waste any more of his time. Just long enough to know we were better as friends. He did have the unfortunate honor of being my second lover, and Maxim was a hard act to follow. I don't think anyone could have satisfied me right after being with him. I needed the effect he had on my body to fade, and it wouldn't. As much as I hate admitting it, Maxim left an imprint on me, and other hands felt wrong. No one else inside me fit the same, *felt* the same.

"You're gonna miss the opportunity of a lifetime to avoid some guy you slept with for only a week ten years ago?" Wallace scoffs. "You're better than that. Smarter than that. Too ambitious for that."

"Speaking of ambition," I say, smoothly pointing the finger away from me. "Congrats on this promotion. Kimba and I love having you here in DC now."

"I've always wanted my own research team." Wallace grins. "But I didn't expect to have it for years. I'm pretty stoked about this opportunity with CamTech. Moving closer to you guys was a bonus for sure."

"Good things happen when you're brilliant and work hard."

He shrugs off my praise with a lift of his shoulders and a modest smile. "Whatever. Now stop distracting me with flattery. Back to you and Maxim Cade."

Ugh. It was worth a try.

"There is no me and Maxim Cade."

"Sounds like avoidance. What does your therapist say?"

I release a two-ton sigh. "I haven't talked to her about it. I will. I just…"

"You just what, baby girl?" He pulls my head down onto his shoulder. "Go on. Tell foster step-cousin Wally all about it."

I snort-laugh and turn my face into the comforting scent of his sweater. "He lied to me," I say, and I hate that hearing it still makes me a little sad. "And he played me for a fool."

"Did he really, Lenny?" Wall kisses the top of my head. "Or do you tell yourself that so you won't have to deal with how he made you feel? Maybe still could make you feel?"

My head pops up, and I stare at him in the thin illumination lent by the city's bright lights passing outside the car window.

"Not you, too," I say, making a disgusted sound in my throat. "You sound like my therapist. And Mena."

"I think maybe they're *both* right." Wallace searches my eyes, a concerned frown on his dear face. "There's some part of you that's afraid to trust happiness because of what happened with your mom."

"It's not happiness I don't trust. It's *him*. And his lies. He made a fool of me."

"Okay. Then don't sleep with him, but don't pass up the chance to manage the next president's campaign."

"Who knows if Cade will even win."

"He will if you and Kimba get a hold of him," Wally says with a smile.

"There's still the matter of Owen's *father*." I spit the unpleasant word out. "I need to know he won't interfere and that I won't have to deal with that bastard."

"These seem like things you can talk through and work out. Senator Cade isn't his father. Don't miss out on this, baby girl. They call you the Kingmaker now. What will they say when you make a president?"

"I don't care what they call me. I just want to do the things that are important to me. To my people and other groups that have been disenfranchised, overlooked, and dismissed."

"If you get Cade elected, you can write your ticket. Campaign managers for winners end up White House staffers, cabinet members, real power players. It could catapult you and Kimba."

"I'm not sure I have a choice anyway," I reply somewhat petulantly. "Kimba wants to do it. Everyone thinks I'm the bulldog, but behind closed doors, she makes me look like Bambi."

"Just think about it." Wallace kisses my knuckle. "And who's to say he'll even be involved? Maybe he'll keep his distance. He has for a decade. Why stop now?"

When the time is right, I'll be back for you.

Those words remind me of how he looked at me that day in the conference room. Like we were inevitable. That hum that was always just beneath my skin when I was around him is back even though we haven't come face-to-face. I can't help but wonder if somehow he feels it, too.

CHAPTER 37
LENNIX

"HE HAS ARRIVED, *GLIKO MOU*."

Iasonos's words are unnecessary since I see the two bodyguards who always accompany Owen Cade seated in the main dining room. They're already digging into the taramasalata and bread spread on the table in front of them.

"Thanks, Nos." I smile warmly at the man who's been my friend since I moved to DC seven years ago. In search of good Greek, Kimba and I stumbled into this classic unassuming "hole in the wall" that ended up serving the best baklava I've ever tasted. It was near closing that first night, and Kimba and I shut the place down. It only took a few times for Nos to "adopt" us.

His restaurant, Trógo, is closed on Mondays, but we've conducted more than one covert meeting in his back room when he wasn't open for business. Today might be the most important to date.

Iasonos pauses at the closed swinging door. "Just you today?" he asks.

"Yeah, Kimba's at the office, but you know there'll be hell to pay if I don't take back some of your spanakopita."

"I'll have it ready," he says, a pleased smile creasing cheeks. "For you, too?"

"Nah. Just a salad for me." I roll my eyes at the obvious disapproval in his expression. "If it was up to you, I'd be popping out of all my clothes."

"You need meat on the bones."

"I've got plenty of meat on the bones," I say, laughing and heading for the back room. "Salad, please."

Owen sits at one of the few tables in the back room. It's covered with a red-and-white-gingham tablecloth and topped with unlit candles. He's on the phone but smiles when he sees me enter.

"Okay, Chuck," he says. "I need to go, but I'll see you back up on the Hill before the meeting."

I take the seat across from him and reach for the carafe of water. "Hope you didn't cut your call short on my account."

"I did actually. I know how valuable your time is and didn't want to keep you waiting."

More considerate than most candidates. Plus column for him.

"Did you order already?" I sip my water. "Want something stronger than water?"

"No, I have a subcommittee meeting after this and need a clear head."

"Makes sense."

"I was glad to hear from Kimba." He pours water for himself. "She sounded excited about working with me, and I was curious when she mentioned you wanted to talk before finalizing."

"Yes, she's excited." I offer a genuine smile, something I reserve for genuine people. "*I'm* excited. I know it may not seem that way, but I like all my cards on the table, so I wanted to talk with you before we go any further."

"A woman after my own heart." His smile is the real thing, too, and puts me at ease. Selling him to voters will be like handing out free candy apples at a county fair. He's the perfect candidate waiting to happen.

"There are a few things we need to discuss before I sign on," I say, tic-tac-toe-ing in the squares of the gingham tablecloth with my index finger. "Your father being the first."

"And my brother being the second?"

I snap my gaze up from the table to meet his. Of course, he would have had Kimba and me vetted before approaching us.

"Either your research team has been busy," I say wryly, "or Maxim told you himself."

"Both," he says, his voice quiet and eyes steady. "My team's good, but they probably wouldn't have dug up that one week in Amsterdam. Maxim told me that."

"He did?"

"Yes, he didn't tell me much, but I know it ended...badly."

There could not have been a good ending to what we had. I'd thought it would end because of the truth Maxim told me from our first night together—that he would walk away no matter what. Ultimately it ended because of the truth he withheld.

"It was only a week." I lower my lashes, protecting any secrets my eyes might share without permission. "But we didn't part on the best of terms. I'd like to know what role you see him playing in your campaign."

"Well, I'm hiring Hunter, Allen because I trust your judgment." He angles a frank look from under a lock of blond hair that has defied styling. "But my brother is very popular and well respected."

"Yeah. Handsome. Forward-thinking. Environmentally and philanthropically aware. A little too rich and privileged to trust completely, but then leaving your father gives him that bootstrap narrative. People like and trust him."

"Sounds like you've given it some thought."

"I give everyone some thought when they're connected to one of my campaigns."

"One of yours?" He lifts his brows. "So we're good?"

"Not even close." The comment has no real teeth, and we share a quick grin. "I still need to clarify how we'll deploy your brother. I agree that he could be possibly your most valuable surrogate, but I don't want to work with him."

Owen's speculation and my unbending will squeeze into the tight silence my comment leaves behind.

"Kimba or another staffer can accompany him when he goes on the trail," I say. "We'll assign someone who is not me to prep him for interviews and appearances."

Iasonos comes in with my salad and Owen's païdakia. Our conversation idles while Nos serves the food.

"Need anything else?" Nos asks.

"No," I say with a smile. "I'm good."

"So am I," Owen says. "Looks delicious. Thank you so much."

Ever solicitous and sensitive to the private nature of my business back here, Iasonos backs out quickly.

"So you want no contact with Maxim," Owen says, picking up his fork and the thread of our conversation. "Got it."

"I want to avoid any awkwardness, and a personal relationship, even former, could prove awkward, but I understand there may be times when we…encounter each other."

"I get it," Owen says around a steaming bite of food. "I'll tell him."

It feels cold, Owen delivering this message to Maxim, but I want as little contact with him as possible.

"The other issue may actually prove more difficult." I heave a sigh and then dive in. "I don't think your father should be seen as connected to the campaign at all."

He looks at me for several seconds before laying down his fork.

"My father first mentioned the presidency to me when I was seven years old, Ms. Hunter. He will not take kindly to being completely cut out."

"Please, call me Lennix."

"Lennix," he says pointedly, "my father is one of the most power-ful men in the world. Having his support can only be a good thing."

"Oh, really? When you've distanced yourself from him on half the votes his oil lobbyists pushed?"

"Well—"

"When your brother, whom we've just said will be one of your most important surrogates, has been estranged from him for nearly fifteen years based on deeply entrenched philosophical and political differences?"

"True, but—"

"When *I* have led several protests against him when Cade Energy infringed on restricted tribal property?"

"I know, but—"

"Him speaking for you makes the three of us look like hypocrites." I lean forward and defy Emily Post to prop my elbows on the table. "And I haven't been in politics long enough to be okay with looking like I don't mean what I say."

"He has connections we could use."

"Some of them, if uncovered, could lead to unsavory places." I hold up my hand when it looks like he'll protest. "I said unsavory, not illegal. We've already started digging. Just because something isn't illegal doesn't mean the public will like it."

"You're saying I should cut my father out altogether?"

"I'm saying if your daddy is pulling any strings, I don't wanna see them."

"He's not pulling my strings," Owen says, the closest thing to anger I've seen showing in his eyes.

"Then this is a moot discussion."

"Isn't there some middle ground between him representing the campaign and not being involved at all?"

"I didn't say he couldn't be involved at all. I think aligning yourself with him publicly too closely will backfire. I said I don't want to see the strings, not that he couldn't work backstage."

"Let's get something straight, Ms. Hunter," he says, pointedly ignoring my invitation to address me informally. "My father is not a ventriloquist, and I'm no dummy. You're running my campaign, but never forget it is *my* campaign. I understand the differences you have with my father and that you don't want anything to do with my brother. I won't hesitate to put distance between me and either of them if necessary, but I won't disavow them simply for being who they are."

His expression softens. "They're family. We don't always agree on every single thing, but we support each other and set aside differences when it matters most. I'd say me running for president qualifies as 'most.' I hope voters will relate to that."

Perversely, his pushback solidifies that I do indeed want to work with Owen Cade. I drew my line in the sand, and he didn't move his to satisfy me. If he can be that principled fighting for the causes I care about, I'll count his victory as ours.

"Senator Cade, I think we can work it out. Let's lay some ground rules and take exceptions case by case." I nod and offer a pleasant smile. "How about dessert? The baklava is divine."

CHAPTER 38
MAXIM

"Owen tells me you have a crush on his new campaign manager."

At my sister-in-law's words, I stiffen before handing my coat over to the young woman waiting to take it.

"He said what?" I try to play it off with a quick laugh, but Millicent's no fool. Foolishness is one of the few luxuries Cades can't actually afford.

"Lennix, right?" Millicent adjusts flowers in the arrangement dominating the foyer of their Georgetown townhouse. "I haven't met her yet, but I hear she's brilliant."

"Well, you'll get to meet the entire team they've assembled," I answer, re-steering the conversation. "Isn't that the point of tonight? To have the family meet the team?"

"Yes, O thinks it's important we feel comfortable with the people who'll play such a big part in our lives for the next eighteen months." Apparently satisfied with the floral arrangement, she turns to me and slips her arm through the crook of my elbow. "I especially can't wait to meet your new girlfriend."

I drop my head back and groan. "I'm gonna kill my brother."

"It's just been so long since you liked anyone." She squeezes my arm. "I want you to be happy."

"I am happy, Mill. Don't worry about me."

"Of course we worry. You're always off risking your life in some godforsaken place, and for what? Algae? Plastic samples?"

"I haven't been anywhere truly dangerous in a long time." I smile down at her. "I kind of miss it, and I think you're oversimplifying complex scientific research that could possibly reverse global warming."

"Ahh, it must get so heavy."

"What?"

"The whole planet on those big, broad shoulders of yours." She widens her eyes innocently. "How will the world keep turning without you and your recycled sports bras?"

"You love those sports bras," I say, walking her into the dining room. "We can't keep that racerback in stock, and I think you buy half of them."

She punches my arm harmlessly, painlessly. "You were supposed to bring me the new one, you big oaf."

"I'll have some shipped." I chuckle and glance at the formally dressed dining room table. "Wow. You really broke out the heavy artillery for this one."

"It's important we start with a show of strength," Mill says, her sweet mouth firming. "They're all riding the Cade train to the White House. They should see what it means to be one of us."

Funny. I couldn't run from my name fast enough, and Mill couldn't wait to marry into it. She's completely a Cade. The perfect political wife. Anything about herself and her life before Owen that didn't fit, she cast off without a second thought.

Owen and Mill don't have an arranged marriage. I believe they love each other, but it's a power match without a doubt. Her father, a former governor, has been grooming his pretty daughter for the White House for as long as our father has been grooming Owen. It doesn't hurt that she's probably smart enough to run the country herself in a pinch.

"So back to this woman, Lennix," Millicent says. "Maybe having her around will calm you down some."

If there is one thing that I'm not around Lennix, it's calm. At least I wasn't before. Who knows now? We haven't been in the same room in ten years, and the last time we were together, I fucked her on a table.

"That's doubtful," I reply.

"What's doubtful?" Owen asks from the dining room door.

"That Max's new girlfriend will calm him down."

"Girlfriend?" Owen frowns. "Who?"

"She's talking about Lennix," I say, tugging a strand loose from the disciplined pleat of Millicent's hair.

"Maxim!" She shrieks and jogs over to the framed mirror taking up half a wall. "Now I have to fix it."

"You know we talked about this, Max," Owen says, his "big brother" face in full effect. He practically wags his finger at me. "You know Lennix's conditions."

"Conditions?" Millicent asks, turning from the mirror. "Which ones? What are they?"

Owen doesn't want to know where he and Lennix can shove their conditions. It's very dark there.

"She doesn't want to work directly with Maxim because of their torrid past," he says, pulling her into his side. "You look beautiful, Mill."

"Why, thank you, O." She beams up at him, all silky blond hair and limpid blue eyes. They're basically POTUS Ken and Barbie. "But tell me more about these conditions and their torrid affair. I had no idea."

"It wasn't torrid. How many are we expecting?" I ask, deliberately sidestepping the irksome subject of Lennix's conditions and our past.

"Well, it's just the nucleus team," Millicent answers, winking at me and mouthing, *We'll talk later*. "And we wanted it to feel personal, so we said they could invite a significant other."

"That's nice," I say, only half listening and a quarter interested while I check stock numbers on my watch.

"Most of them aren't bringing anyone," Owen says, hesitating for a moment before continuing. "But Lennix is."

My head jerks up and I stare at my brother for an elongated moment while I make a conscious effort not to bare my teeth at him. I finally ask the question pounding at my temples. "Who?"

CHAPTER 39
LENNIX

"Are you sure about this?" Wallace asks, the question in his voice reflected in his expression.

"I told you a dozen times that tie is fine," I say, reaching up to adjust the knot. "But good Lord, when I gave it to you, I never thought you'd mangle it. Where'd you learn to tie these? The Boy Scouts? This tie is Armani, and you made it look like I picked it up at the five-and-dime."

"Not the damn tie, Lenny." Wallace grabs my hand and pulls it away from his neck. "Me coming with you to this campaign thing."

"Of course." I slide my glance to the perfectly manicured bushes flanking the front porch of Owen Cade's townhouse. "They said we could bring someone."

"Someone? Like a random friend?"

"Random?" I overstretch my eyes and mouth with outrage. "You're not random. You are the most on-purpose friend I have. Joe's bringing Erin."

"They're married."

"Howard's bringing Bill."

"They're married." He points to himself. "I'm not your husband."

"Not for lack of trying on your part." I grin up at him. "Come on, Wall. I neeeeeed you."

"I'm your beard, aren't I?" he asks, suspicion and realization lighting his eyes. "You're betting Maxim Cade will leave you alone if he thinks you're taken."

"Exactly." My smile comes and goes, and then I shake my head. "No! I mean, no. Not at all."

He dips his head and looks at me knowingly.

"Okay. Maybe a little." I put my hands over my ears. "Stop looking at me so loud."

"If you expect Maxim to believe you're an old married couple," Kimba says from the bottom of the steps, "your bickering will convince him."

"Would you shut up?" I hiss, looking at the bushes like they might be bugged.

"Also that startling lack of sexual chemistry you two got going on?" Kimba points between us. "Reeks of trudging through matrimony."

"Can we please just put on our big girl panties and show Senator Cade why we're the best in the business?" I ask.

"I'm already wearing my big girl panties, honey," Kimba says, practically gliding up the steps. "They're La Perla."

"I'm not comfortable at all with this turn of conversation," Wallace mumbles. "I've been telling myself, 'Wall, you need male friends.' Too many girls."

"Shut it. You love us." Kimba reaches up to hug Wallace around the neck. "How the heck are ya, Wall? Welcome to paradise. Good to have you in DC. Congrats on the promotion."

"Thanks," Wallace says, returning her hug.

"Now if we could persuade your sister to accept a promising opportunity every once in a while," I interject. "Who leaves the *LA Times* on the table?"

"That was a decade ago, Lenn," Kimba says. "You still riding Viv about that?"

"I'm not *riding her* about what happened ten years ago," I say.

"Not when we only have to go back a year to her turning down a great assignment in Paris."

"She was pregnant with Madison," Wallace reminds me. "Please don't begrudge me my niece, Mary Tyler Moore."

"Mary Tyler Moore?" I ask, not connecting any dots.

"Yes, Mary Tyler Moore," Wallace says patiently, like we should know this. "Career woman from the seventies. Threw the hat up in the air."

"What have I told you about watching those seventies reruns on *Nick at Nite?*" Kimba swats Wallace's arm. "What's next? Blow-up dolls? How the *hell* am I supposed to find you a normal girl with you watching *Mary Tyler Moore?*"

"I don't like normal girls," Wallace says sullenly. "Find me someone like Lennix."

"Hey," I pipe up, offended. "I'm normal."

They exchange a meaningful glance before looking back to me.

"You're not normal even a little bit," Wallace says. "It's why I love you, Lennix."

He says it just as the door opens and we come face-to-face with none other than Maxim Cade.

I should have prepared for this moment better. I vaguely recall experiments where continued exposure to certain stimuli desensitized the subjects to the impact of it. I should have spent last night playing footage of Maxim nonstop on a loop so I wouldn't have this reaction to him.

I've seen him over the years, of course, on television, but that screen and distance diluted the full impact of those gemstone eyes and the burnished dark hair. I couldn't smell him, couldn't feel like I'm standing in the shadow of a great wall. My body clenches reflexively, reminding me just how long it's been since he was inside me. The blood melts in my veins, slowing to a languid crawl under the fixed heat of his stare.

Leaves crackle under someone's feet down on the sidewalk.

Autumn wind whistles through near-barren branches. My surroundings feed me sensory information to ground me in this moment where I can't seem to look away from Maxim and he doesn't even seem to be trying to look away from me.

"Ahem," Kimba clears her throat and shatters the charged silence, moving toward Maxim for a hug. "So good to see you, Maxim. Been too long."

He pats her back, his eyes still set on me. When he looks down at her, my breath whooshes out, and I realize I haven't breathed since he opened the door.

"Good to see you, too." Maxim's smile for Kimba is warm and sincere. "You've been shaking up the world, I see."

"Had to." Kimba laughs and tips her head. "Me and the Kingmaker over here. Can you believe this one?"

Maxim's smile dissipates, and he turns his attention back to me.

"I believe it, yeah," he says, his voice quiet. "I've always known Nix was exceptional."

The painfully awkward silence stretches until I'm sure my ears will bleed.

"Hello, Maxim." I don't make any move toward him, and he makes no move toward me. "Good to see you again."

"Same," he mutters. His eyes chill when they rest on Wallace. "Introduce me to your…"

No way in hell am I completing that sentence for him.

"This is Wallace Murrow," I say, slipping my arm through Wallace's. "Wall, Maxim Cade."

"So pleased to meet you," Wallace says, extending his hand. Maxim just stares at it for a few seconds, waiting just beyond polite and shy of rude before accepting Wallace's outstretched hand.

Wallace shoots me a glance, equal parts bewilderment and irritation. "Um, I saw you testifying before Congress a few weeks—"

"It's cool outside," Maxim cuts in over Wallace and opens the door wider. "You guys come on in. Everyone else is here."

I walk in first, evading the hand Maxim extends for my arm. Without looking at him, I follow the sound of voices.

Our hand-selected core team is spread across couches and tucked into corners, drinking and nibbling from trays of hors d'oeuvres. I walk over to Joe, our field director, and his wife Erin. They're standing with a woman I recognize as Millicent Cade, one of the most powerful political wives and hostesses in the city. An invitation to one of her parties cements one's place in DC society, and a snub from her solidifies one's place *outside* it.

"Good evening," I greet the three of them. "Mrs. Cade, I'm Lennix Hunter. Nice to finally meet you."

"Oh, I've heard so much about *you*, from Owen *and* Maxim," she says, her cornflower-blue eyes sharpening with speculation. "We need to chat real soon."

"Yes, we have a lot to talk about. There's a team member assigned to you for the campaign trail," I say, deliberately misunderstanding her. "I think you'll love June."

"I'm sure I will," she purrs, her smile deepening to pop dimples in her cheeks. "Be warned. I choose my own clothes."

"You have perfect taste. June will just make sure it's displayed perfectly on the trail."

Our smiles reach a mutual understanding before she drifts off to check on her other guests.

"Impressive, these Cades," Joe says. "Thanks for bringing me in."

"I loved your work in Maryland for the governor's race. Voter turnout was record-breaking, and I know that was your doing."

"We'll do that for Senator Cade and then some." Joe glances over at Owen and Maxim standing by the fireplace chatting with Howard, our volunteer coordinator. "Quite the one-two punch, those brothers. We've got an embarrassment of riches to work with."

Wallace joins us, a drink in each hand. Joe drifts off to join his wife Erin.

"Here's your martini, um…darling," Wallace says, handing me a glass.

"Be still, my heart," I whisper. "That was so convincing. Can't believe you're not down on your knees proposing yet."

"Thanks to you," Wallace grinds out, "Maxim Cade has been treating me like a pariah all night."

"And by all night, you mean in the fifteen minutes since we've arrived?"

"He's staring daggers at me." Wallace demonstrates with a pseudo-scary glare. "Like this."

My involuntary snort-laugh morphs into a gut buster, which often happens with Wallace. I lean into him, burying my face and chuckling against his shoulder.

"Thanks a lot," Wallace says, but I hear some answering humor in his voice. "I'm getting even more daggers now."

"Has he been rude to you?" I glance up at him, still leaning on his shoulder. "I mean, since he looked at you like you were a bottom feeder and practically refused to shake your hand?"

"I tried to talk to him about his work with recycling systems in developing countries, and he walked off."

I wince. "He's being ridiculous. I don't get it."

"I think he heard me say I love you."

"Which is none of his business. *I'm* none of his business."

"You're going to have to talk to him." He chews on something delicious-smelling wrapped in bacon. "How long do we have to do this pretend relationship?"

"Would you just shut it?" I glance around to make sure no one heard. "You're the worst beard ever."

"Am not."

"Are too. He's more likely to believe I'm dating Kimba at the rate you're going, falling at his feet and shit."

"I just admire him and would like to have actual conversations with him about real-world issues."

"Would you also like long walks on the beach with him?" I take a much-needed sip of the martini. "Maybe wear his letterman jacket? Date to the prom?"

"If I didn't love you so much…" He fixes a deer-in-headlights stare over my shoulder. "Uh, Maxim. Hi. We were just… That new electric car you're developing. I think it's great."

A chilly silence meets Wallace's comment. I don't look over my shoulder to acknowledge Maxim.

"Thanks," he replies to Wallace after a few more frigid seconds. "Dinner's about to be served. I was wondering if I could talk to you for a second, Nix?"

"I don't think so," I murmur into my martini glass. "But thanks for the heads-up on dinner. Ready, Wall?"

Wallace looks at me like I kicked his puppy for a second and then grits out, "Yes, dear."

I drag him to follow everyone else into the dining room. Wallace and I are seated at one end of the table with Kimba and a few others from the team. Maxim sits near Cade and Millicent at the other end, and they're joined by the Cades' towheaded twins, both of whom have excellent table manners and infectious laughs. "Uncle Max's" rich baritone drifts down to my end of the table more than once, punctuated with childish giggles. The shield over my heart almost slips at the sight and the sound of Maxim connected to his family. In Amsterdam, I could tell he missed them. From what I know, his relationship with his father remains strained, but it's good to see him with Owen's family.

"So what do you do, Murray?" Maxim's question winnows all the way down the table and through the varied conversations like an arrow. "For a living, I mean."

An awkward silence spreads over the group, everyone unsure if they should wait for Wallace's response or return to their own conversations.

"Uh, it's Murrow." Wallace clears his throat. "And to answer your question, I'm a biochemist. I specialize in vaccine development."

"Wow," Bill says with elevated eyebrows, obviously impressed. "Smart guy, huh?"

Wallace shrugs, self-conscious and never comfortable being the center of attention. "Everyone has their specialty, I guess," he mumbles.

"But they're not just handing out doctorates in biochemistry over at MIT," I say.

"Duke," Wallace corrects softly.

"Duke," I say, the pride I feel for my friend something I don't have to fake. "Wallace is brilliant. He focuses on making vaccines more effective in developing nations."

"Admirable," Millicent says from the north end of the table, sending Wallace a kind smile.

"Lennix and Wall are actually going to administer vaccines in a few months," Kimba adds, winking at Wallace. "This is what? Your sixth service trip together?"

"Seventh," I correct. "And don't worry, guys. *I'm* not doing anything that involves a needle."

"What *will* you be doing?" Millicent asks.

"Our team is helping with some building projects," I answer.

"Where?" Maxim asks, a frown between his dark brows.

I meet his eyes directly, as I've rarely done at all tonight. My single lifted brow asks what the hell it has to do with him, but I answer. "Talamanca. The Bribri reserve there has the largest Indigenous population in Costa Rica. Over ten thousand."

"Lenny's taking a group of students from the San Carlos Reservation in Arizona with us," Wallace adds.

"It's great for them to see another Indigenous community," I say. "One with so much of their culture and language intact. They think we're going to serve the people of Bribri, but honestly, these students will gain more than they give. At least that's how it always is for me."

"It's safe?" Maxim demands, forcing me to meet his eyes again.

I shouldn't have looked at him because an invisible stream of memory passes between us. Every kiss, every touch, every time we laughed and made love flashes on a superhighway from my eyes to his. It's a head-on collision that leaves me shaken, exposed, with everyone at the table witnessing the wreckage.

I lower my eyes and draw a deep breath.

"Very safe," Wallace answers, his voice quiet and sure. "I would never do anything to put Lenny in danger."

He takes my hand on the table and squeezes, bathing me in the warm affection of his smile. He bends to kiss my forehead, and I know to others, it looks intimate, and it is. It's the intimacy of a decade-long friendship that has survived bad sex with each other and broken hearts with other people and still managed to hold fast. I blink rapidly, moved by Wallace's unconditional friendship and still breathless from the direct look I shared with Maxim, like the airbags have deployed and punched me in the chest. Will I be bruised tomorrow?

"Well, that's really cool," Owen says, smiling at Wallace. "Sounds like you're as passionate about helping people as Lennix is."

Wallace and I lace our fingers tightly, and I know he hopes they will move on to something else as much as I do. It doesn't take long for them to turn back to discussing the latest gossip on the Hill and dissecting every season of *Game of Thrones*. We share a quick chuckle, and when I look up, Maxim's eyes are fixed to the point where Wallace and I still hold hands.

"Guess I'm not such a bad beard after all," Wallace whispers in my ear. "Maxim looks convinced. Maybe he'll move on and find some other girl to fill his time while he's here in DC."

"Probably," I say around a knot in my throat. "We did good."

I thought I'd feel relief that he believes I'm taken, but I don't. I'll have to examine the contrariness of my emotions when I'm alone. I've already shown too much.

We make it through the next two delicious courses before Owen stands and starts speaking.

"Eat." He waves at the table, urging everyone to continue with their meal. "This isn't a formal meeting. I'm sure Kimba and Lennix will have plenty of those ahead of us."

Everyone chuckles and keeps eating, dividing attention between their plates and their new candidate.

"Thank you all for coming. Mill and I wanted to have you here in our home," Owen continues. "To have you meet our kids, Darcy and Elijah, and my brother, Maxim, who'll be pivotal in our strategy. For some reason, people love this guy. I don't get it."

Maxim shoots him a wry look before dropping his eyes back to his plate, his mouth set into a firm line. For a second, I feel awful for ignoring him, deceiving him, but I have to protect myself. I know how it feels to hurt for that man. I won't do it again.

"Lennix and Kimba," Owen says, jerking me out of my thoughts. "anything you'd like to say?"

Kimba hates public speaking of any kind. She gives me a nod and the look that says, *Girl, don't even.* With a sigh, I take a deep gulp of my water and stand. I search the faces of the men and women assembled around the table, and I search for what I should say.

"My mother once said injustice never rests, and neither will I." A sad little twist of my lips is as close as I can come to a smile. "She was an agitator. One of my earliest memories is of her hoisting me onto her shoulders at a protest. It's in my blood."

I find and hold every set of eyes on my team. "I'm counting on it being in yours, too. We have a remarkable candidate in Senator Cade, one I know we can all get behind. It's no secret that Kimba and I have made our life's work empowering candidates who will champion the causes of the marginalized. That's what gets me out of bed every morning. It has been my complete focus for the last ten years, since I left college."

Maxim's stare singes a hole in me, but I ignore it and go on.

"On this journey, there will be times when we think we're losing. Things will happen we never saw coming and aren't sure how to negotiate. There will be times when we want to give up, but I descend from a long line of warriors. The Apache were the last to surrender. I take a certain amount of pride in that. I embrace it as part of who I am and how I fight."

I look down the table to Owen. "I'll fight for you, Senator Cade, because I trust you to fight for the people I dedicate my life to serve. Every person sitting at this table was selected not only for their brilliant mind but for their fighter's heart. You're a dream candidate, but we're a dream team." I allow the smallest smile to bend my lips before softly saying, "Don't let us down."

My team cheers. Owen offers a solemn smile from his end of the table, and his wife studies me with new interest, her eyes darting between her brother-in-law and me. I sit and reach for my glass of water, praying this will end soon so I can go home.

It's only a blessed half hour before things start breaking up. A nanny comes to take the twins upstairs. The staff clear away the remnants of our last course, and everyone starts collecting their coats and saying their goodbyes.

Wallace is sliding my coat onto my shoulders when Maxim walks over. He just stands there. I sense him, even though I don't look up from my Stuart Weitzman pumps. The silence encompasses the three of us, wrapping around and restraining me like barbed wire biting into my flesh.

"Can I have a word before you go, Lennix?" Maxim finally asks, his voice subdued.

A word. He means to bundle me off to Owen's office or to the library. He'll whittle my resistance down to a nub. He'll make me forget he lied and that I shouldn't allow him within ten paces of my body or heart. He wants to remind me how he feels and smells and tastes. He used to camouflage the wolf, but not anymore. He's tamed his hair, cut the burnished waves that used to nearly kiss his shoulders, but his spirit is still wild, howling on some frequency I shouldn't be tuned into but I am. He's now completely wolf and unashamedly Cade. He's still the rebel, and I'm afraid I'm no more able to resist him than I was in that conference room a decade ago.

Afraid. I'm afraid. That's an emotion I hadn't allowed myself to acknowledge in this scenario with Maxim. Is this self-awareness? My therapist will be so proud.

Without lifting my head, I answer before I turn to leave. "No."

CHAPTER 40
MAXIM

LAST NIGHT DID NOT GO WELL.

I'm not sure what I expected, but it wasn't for Lennix to bring a damn date. Not just a date, but a *relationship* apparently. One where they go on service projects and build wells together and generally make the world a better place. I grudgingly admit Wallace Murrow is not a bad guy. Not at all. I made sure of that when they dated before, but they're *back* together? In the decade we've been apart, I took heart in the fact that Nix never dated any one guy for long. Wallace was the longest relationship I knew about, and for her to go *back* to him?

I stepped back before. The wounds were fresh. Her anger still burned hot, and she'd ignored every attempt I made to contact her. Not to mention I was in the fight of my life trying to save my company, but a lot of time has passed. We're both in different places now, and I'm done waiting.

I'm not sure how serious she and Murrow are, and…this makes no sense, but I don't know if I buy it. There's something missing with them. I'd never felt anything like the hot, addictive urgency that surged between Lennix and me, and I haven't experienced it since. I guess I wanted to believe she hadn't either. Maybe that is just the arrogant part of me—which I freely admit is a good portion of my personality. Whatever I expected, it bothers me that she isn't available.

How'd Grim miss that? His security firm was one of the smartest investments I ever made. It pays dividends that have nothing to do with profit. Information is often just as valuable, and Grim deals information like a king pen.

After the last argument with my father, I continued seeking answers on climate change but also turned my attention to doing what Cades do best: building a fortune. What really exploded the coffers was innovation. Finding inventors interested in creating the things we use every day more sustainably. Not just sports bras and clothing, but tiny parts in electric cars that I now hold a patent on to make that entire industry more efficient.

Grim has, through the years, kept loose tabs on Lennix for me. That wasn't hard. Her star in the political world rose steadily and spectacularly, which didn't surprise me at all.

What do I want from Lennix? To know if my memory tricked me and she wasn't as fantastic as I remember? Do I need that reassurance to move forward? I can't call this love, the near-obsessive burn in my gut when I think of her, when I saw her last night. She was a candle lit and extinguished too quickly, but the smoke of what we had has endured, lingering in the air all these years.

I wouldn't call it love, but it's something I've never found elsewhere, and I need to know if I could have it again.

If I could have *her* again.

I'm not famous, generally speaking. There are no squealing girls or awestruck fans when I venture out, but in certain circles I'm well known. DC would be one of those circles, especially with my brother rising the way he has. I pull the brim of my Astros cap a little lower and adjust my sunglasses. When I enter the Royal, the LeDetroit Park coffee shop where, according to my sources, Lennix has breakfast each morning, I don't cause even a ripple of interest.

She's seated at a table tucked into a back corner. Sunlight shines golden on her high cheekbones. She's reading, her dark brows bunched, and she chews on her bottom lip. I stand there for a second watching her. It feels good to simply be able to look at her again. She reaches for the steaming teacup beside her and takes a sip.

"Morning," I say.

"Shit." She startles, hissing at the burn and tugging her bottom lip. She sets down her steaming cup of tea and aims a look caffeinated with impatience up at me. "Good morning. Too much to hope this is a coincidence?"

I crook a half-grin and nod to the empty seat across from her. "Can I sit?"

"I mean, you went to all this trouble to find me."

I sit and lay my sunglasses and hat on the table. "Not too much to figure out since you eat breakfast here every day."

"It's creepy that you know that."

"One man's creepy is another man's determination."

"A new business venture for you. Inspirational quotes for stalkers." She pushes away the untouched croissant in front of her. "Print that over an ocean scene. It'll be gorgeous on the wall of some Peeping Tom."

"Nice one." I chuckle and sink lower into the seat. "This could have been avoided if you'd just talked to me last night."

She glances up from under a sweep of midnight lashes but slides her gaze away, out the window to the people passing by. There was a time when this woman's body begged for mine, and now she'll barely look at me.

"I didn't think we had anything to discuss," she says, eyes still trained outside, voice pitched to a level of indifference. "I'm assuming Owen told you my conditions for accepting the job."

"You mean that Kimba is my handler?" I infuse some amusement into the words, but I didn't find it funny when Owen told me. I still don't.

"Your contact." She looks at me directly. "It's not unusual for us to divide responsibilities."

"Is it unusual to have slept with your clients?"

Her eyes and mouth pinch at the corners. That's what I wanted—the fire I know is there, not these cold ashes she's giving me.

"This is exactly why I didn't think we should work together," she says.

"Because you're scared? Or would Wally not like it?"

"I'm not scared, and it's *Wallace*. Please stay out of my relationship."

"Your relationship." I stretch the word out as if examining it syllable by syllable. "So when did you and *Wallace* start seeing each other?"

Back then, Grim reported that they were dating, but it wasn't clear when they started.

"The first time it was not too long after college graduation," she answers.

I tense at her words. "Were you seeing him when I came to the campaign office in Oklahoma?"

"No." She clears her throat. "What happened that day was a mistake, but it never would have happened if I'd been in a committed relationship."

"So you like to think."

"I know so. I would never cheat on Wallace." Truth rings in her voice, and I'm even less sure of what's going on between them.

"If there's a point, could you make it?" She asks, glancing at the slim watch on her wrist. "I need to get to the office."

"You obviously believe my brother can win," I say, lowering my voice and glancing around. Owen hasn't announced yet, and this city is crawling with eyes and ears.

"I believe he will win. I wouldn't have taken him on if I didn't believe that."

"But he's a Cade. Same blood. Same last name. Same father as mine."

"You still don't get it?" She leans forward, holding my eyes in a steely stare. "Who knows if I would have gotten over who your father was? You didn't give me the chance to decide. You did to me what they always do."

She tilts her chin up to a proud angle. "You thought you knew best and decided *for* me. You took away my choices, let me get involved that deeply with you knowing how I felt about your father and Cade Energy. You deliberately withheld the truth to get what you wanted."

"I should have handled it differently," I admit through tight lips. "You have no idea how many times I wish I had told you from the start, but I didn't."

"You lied."

"Yes, I think that's been well established over the ten years you've held it against me."

"You think I've been pining for you? I haven't."

That grates because I can't count how many times I've rolled over in some bed in some city and remembered her hair spilled on my pillow. Imagined I could smell the sheets again after the first time we made love, a heady blend of our bodies together and the subtle perfume that kissed her neck. Every time I see a windmill I remember her low, sweet laughing voice calling me Doc Quixote as she rode a bicycle ahead of me.

"If you want to tell yourself what we had was nothing special," I say, "then lies must not bother you as much as you say they do. I can't lie to you, but it's okay for you to lie to yourself?"

"It's not like that."

"We both had our own agendas, dreams, and goals. It's good we took time apart to pursue everything we wanted." I reach for her hand resting near her tea, lacing our fingers together. "But I told you I would come back for you. I never forgot you, Nix. And I always hoped there would be a time when we could repair things between us."

"You shouldn't have come back." She pulls her hand away, fixes her eyes on her tea. "Not for that. Not for me. If you're really here to help your brother, I've laid out my terms, and we can both help elect him. If you're back for me, you'll be disappointed."

"I'm back for both, and I don't intend to be disappointed by either outcome."

Her eyes flash, gunpowder gray and just as explosive, when they meet mine. "I told Owen I won't work with you."

Last night, Lennix committed her entire team to Owen's campaign. Kimba won't let them pass on an opportunity this good. The stakes are too high for a personal wrinkle like a past relationship to get in the way. Owen's in.

And so am I.

"Do you really think I came back for the thrill of working with you on a campaign?" I chuckle. "I don't give a damn who 'handles' me on the trail. What's happening between us is completely separate from Owen's bid for the presidency."

"Nothing's happening between us."

"Damn, I just got back." I fake an exasperated sigh. "Give me some time. I'm going as fast as I can."

"You know that's not what I mean. I told Owen—"

"I know what you told Owen, and I'm more than happy to have Kimba as my contact. What the hell does that have to do with us?"

She frowns. "You agreed to the conditions."

"I did, but your conditions said nothing about what I do outside the campaign."

"Bastard," she says, her tone calm, her eyes flaring.

"We both know my father. I'm not a bastard. Asshole, yes. Prick, may—"

"What do you want?"

"The same thing I wanted ten years ago." I soften my tone. "A chance with you."

"Why?"

"Because no one else has done what you did for me. Not before you and not since. I want to see if what we had, what we *should* have had, is still there."

"It's not."

"Liar." Her lips part like she's about to speak, but I don't let her get that far. "I felt it last night. I feel it now. Since you value the truth so much, tell me you don't."

The muscles tense beneath her clear golden-brown skin, disrupting the fine line of her jaw. "Wallace and I—"

"Yeah, how do I get rid of him?" I ask abruptly.

"You're asking how to get rid of my boyfriend?" Dark brows wing over the scorn in her eyes. "You don't."

"Do us all a favor. When he asks you to marry him, just let him down easy."

"He hasn't—"

"He will, and when he does, tell him no."

"Why would I do that?"

"Because."

"This isn't second grade, Maxim. 'Because' isn't a sound or compelling argument."

"Because *me*. Better?"

"Your arrogance is truly astounding."

"Thank you for that."

"Not a compliment."

"I make my own compliments. How does it feel knowing you could bring a man like me to my knees?"

"I don't want to."

"Oh, don't worry. You'll be on your knees, too. Should I tell you what you'll be doing when you're down there? Or do you remember?"

I lean forward a little, lower my voice.

"Do you ever think about how it felt to have my cock in your mouth, Nix?"

"Stop." She grinds the word out, not looking at me, her fingers trembling around her teacup.

"To know that in that moment, I was completely at your mercy. That I belonged to you."

"I don't—"

"Because I think about you like that all the time. I want you like that again. Every night. Naked in bed and completely mine."

"In what world could you possibly think I would belong to you?"

"In the one we make together."

When I say it, whatever guard she had in place slips. Just for a second, and I see something in her eyes that tells me I'm not crazy. That tells me I'm not wasting my time. That tells me there's more to her resistance than Wallace and our past and my mistakes and lies. I don't know what's behind that guard, but I'll be damned if I stop pursuing her until I do.

"You did this on purpose," she finally says. "Waited until the whole team was in place and we'd officially signed with Owen to show your hand."

"Yes."

"Because you think I want to win so badly I won't back out?"

"No, because now you believe in Owen and you won't let the inconvenient fact that I want you derail his candidacy."

"You're right. You're not worth me giving up on someone who can advance my causes." A bitter, brittle smile appears on her lips and then shatters. "But if you think you get a second chance, you don't."

She stands, and so do I. I don't bother being discreet with the glance I rake over her in the bright-red dress molded to her body from shoulder to hip, tracking the curve of her thigh. Her stilettos bring her to my nose. I tease her scent out from all the others wafting through the coffeehouse. Hers is spicy, studded with sage and honey.

I want to pull her onto my lap, bury my face in the curve of her neck like I did once before. Nibble at the silky skin until she trembles against me. I'd do indecent things to her in broad daylight if I thought I could get away with it.

She moves to walk around me, and I gently grasp her elbow. The contact with her skin affects me. She's a jolt of electricity, and my body is a live wire, struck by the power she probably doesn't even know or care that she holds over me.

"It's a shame you'll set your resentment aside long enough to elect a Cade," I say, "but can't find it in yourself to forgive one."

She flicks a glance from my hand on her elbow and up to me. "No, I don't forgive you, and you can't make me. You can't *will* me to."

"I've spent the last ten years getting what I want, not because I'm a Cade but because I work harder than everyone else. I keep working after everyone else has gone home. I take risks no one else even considers. I don't give up on seemingly lost causes. When I want something, really want something, I'll do whatever I have to until I have it."

The strengths of her resistance and mine collide. No one looking would know this charming coffee shop is actually a battlefield and our weapons are drawn.

"I know I can't *will* you to give me another chance, but remember this, Nix." I bend my head so close my breath stirs her hair and her scent stirs my pulse. "The harder I have to work for something, the harder I take it."

CHAPTER 41
LENNIX

IT'S BEEN A MONTH SINCE MAXIM AMBUSHED ME AT THE COFFEE shop. I know he and Kimba have kept in touch, but there isn't much for him to do right now. We're the ones working our asses off. We formed Owen's exploratory committee and have been discreetly raising money from interested donors, of which there are many. We're strategizing, gathering data, preparing to formally announce that the committee has been formed. In the year or so between now and Iowa's February caucus, there is a lot less for Maxim to do than there will be later.

Not a day has gone by when I didn't think about our confrontation in the coffee shop. I keep waiting for Maxim to jump out from behind a bush and try to kiss me or something. He made all those declarations about wanting a second chance, getting rid of Wallace, getting me to forgive him, and then…nothing.

You sound almost disappointed.

This from my inner voice.

Well, inner voice, you can shut it.

I'm *not* disappointed. I'm just braced for his next move. If he's not going to make one, why is he still in town?

I can't tear my eyes from the large flat-screen mounted on the wall across from my desk. It's *Beltway*'s "Night on the Hill" segment showing Maxim out with some DC socialite seventeen years his junior. The man is thirty-eight. What's he doing out with a twenty-one-year-old?

Okay. Even I hear the petty in my judgy.

"Why are you still here?" I ask my empty office, plopping a carton of Indian takeout on the desk.

"Why is who still here?" Kimba asks from my office door.

Our space is industrial meets modern and is located in DC's center city complex. We were so proud to open Hunter, Allen & Associates. We chose every piece of furniture, all the paint, the fixtures, and the rugs ourselves. It was a labor of love. This whole operation has been a labor of love.

"Oh, hey." I poke around in my tandoori chicken. "Thought everyone had left for the night."

"I forgot something." She holds up a folder.

I nod and scoop up some rice. "Gotcha."

"Why is who still here?"

Inward groan.

"Mmm, no one," I mumble, my mouth deliberately stuffed with savory meat.

"Oh, cool." Kimba leans against the doorjamb. "Because I thought you were asking the television why Maxim Cade is still in DC. Or even why's he dating a gorgeous woman ten years younger than you."

I stop mid-chew, my mouth hanging open in a way that cannot be flattering. I glare at her over a forkful of food, clear my throat, and set the takeout carton back on the edge of my desk. "So they're actually dating?"

Kimba rolls her eyes up to the ceiling before walking deeper into my office. It's a Friday, our casual day, and her jeans hang loose everywhere but her ass. She's wearing her Black Girl Magic T-shirt, and her hair is pulled up to show off the regal lines of her face. My best friend is pretty damn gorgeous.

"Do you really want to know?" She sits in the Queen Anne chair I chose for its sturdiness, comfort, and loveliness.

I reach for the glasses and bottle of wine stowed under my desk and start pouring. "Do tell."

"Maxim has set up shop here in DC."

Red wine splashes onto the desk and my hand. "What? Why?"

"He says he can do business from anywhere," Kimba says, watching me mop up the mess I made with a napkin. "The man's got business interests all over the world. He says he believes entrenching himself in DC society will be beneficial to the campaign, but I have my own theory."

Which I do not want to hear.

"Want some?" I tip the chicken toward her. "Got plenty."

"No, thanks. You don't want to hear why I think Maxim's still in DC?"

I tip my head to the side and squint one eye. "I do know how to ask follow-up questions when I actually want to know something, but thanks."

"I think he's still in DC for the same reason seeing him with Miss Teen USA bothers you so much."

"It does not bother me." I do a double take. "Wait. Is she really Miss Teen USA?"

"No, but she is young. My *point* is I think he's here for you."

My heart somersaults foolishly in my chest, and I take a long draw on my wine. "I don't care about Miss Teen USA, and I don't care why he's here."

"He still thinks you're dating Wallace, ya know."

A satisfied smile spreads over my face. "How do you know that?"

"Because he asked me if you were still dating Wallace."

I slam my glass on the desk. "What did you say? Tell me exactly what you said."

"I said that from what I knew—" Her sigh is disgusted. "—nothing has changed."

"Great answer. You didn't lie, but you didn't betray me. Very good."

"Are you horny at all?"

I choke on my food and pound my chest at the whiplash change in conversation. "'Scuse me? Come again?"

"Yeah, when's the last time you came again?" Kimba's grin is salacious smeared on a sassy bun. "I had back-to-back orgasms last week, and it was incredible."

"Not counting Mr. Feelgood. Anybody can put in batteries."

"Oh, no, honey. Not my vibrator. This was flesh and bone." She waggles her eyebrows. "Lots of bone."

"Who?"

"Don't you worry about who."

"Oh, my God, *who*, you shameless hussy?"

"That new corn lobbyist we met last month."

"Oh, he was dreamy."

"Yes, ma'am, and generous. He took care of ya girl." She closes her eyes and sighs. "Woo child."

"Well I'm very happy for you, but don't worry about me."

"Studies show that women who have frequent orgasms are significantly more productive."

"Really?"

"No, but I betcha."

"Out." I point a finger toward the exit. "Be gone and leave me to my delicious, if solitary, meal."

"Seriously, though, Lenn," Kimba says, standing and walking to the door. "I know how much you value honesty. You need to have an honest conversation with *yourself.* Do you remember what it was like with Maxim?"

I bite my lip to keep from moaning. I relive that week in my wet dreams. Not just the first and best sex of my life but everything else. An intimacy so sheer Maxim and I could see each other clearly, completely through it. Lying in a field of half-opened tulips. Our eyes meeting over an underground candlelit dinner. Racing through rain-splashed streets, chased by his heavy footsteps and the low rumble of his laughter.

My heart burns in my chest, and I set my fork down, praying for indigestion but afraid it's something else.

"If you can forgive him," Kimba says, "and I personally think you already have but are just scared to risk yourself again, then don't waste more time. He's not dating Miss Teen USA now, but keep him waiting much longer, and he might."

CHAPTER 42
MAXIM

"*Ya by khotel sosat' tvoy chlen.*"

I keep my surprised laughter low enough for only the woman seated beside me to hear.

"My Russian is patchy, Katya," I murmur, slicing into the perfectly prepared lamb chop on my plate. "But I think you just asked to suck me off. Am I right?"

"You remember." Her brown eyes smolder over a glass of Sangiovese. "I taught you well."

"I actually remember very little from your lessons, but I do know enough to say, *Nyet, spaseebo.*"

"Turning me down?" Her sultry expression dives to crestfallen. "But we had so much fun in Moscow."

She slides her hand under the table and into my lap, finding and gripping me hard.

I'm enduring the tedium of this dinner party in the heart of Georgetown to make connections, not only for Owen's upcoming campaign but for the legislation I want to push forward in the future. I didn't expect the daughter of a Russian ambassador I met five years ago to be in attendance.

And yet here we are. My dick in her hand under a table beside the leader of the Budget Committee.

"Move your hand, Katya." My voice is calm but firm. "Now."

"You don't mean that." She slides her hand up and down. "Ah, see, he wants to come out and play. Remember the night we had together? And then the morning?" A husky laugh drifts past her lips, and her brown eyes are dark with humor and horniness. "And the afternoon."

"I won't ask you again. Move your hand."

Her hand slides away, and she pouts. "You're less fun in your old age."

"I like to think wiser." I glance over to find her lashes lowered, blinking rapidly, and the color high on her cheeks. "Hey. I'm sorry. I didn't mean to hurt you. I just…" The truth will make her feel better. "Katya, there's someone else."

Her eyes flick up to meet mine. "You're *with* someone else?"

I shake my head, an ironic smile tipping one side of my mouth. "No, I want someone else, and I'm waiting for her to want me back."

"That's all very noble," Katya says, her Russian accent thickening, sliding her hand back to my thigh. "But while you're waiting…"

I catch hold of her hand and push it away but offer what I hope is a kind smile. "*Nyet, spaseebo.*"

She nods and cuts into her own lamb chop. "So who is this madwoman who does not know what she's missing?"

"Oh, she knows. She's had it before, but I screwed things up."

"You cheated?" she asks, her eyes condemning slits.

"No, I lied."

Katya nods sagely, turning down the corners of her mouth and shrugging. "Lying is simply cheating on the truth."

"Yeah, well, I did that about something that was important to her. She's with someone else for now."

"You'll take her from him, though, *da*?"

I shake my head. "She'll have to leave him. I need her to come to me."

Lennix freely given was the most intoxicating thing I've ever tasted. She spilled down my throat like wine, warm and wet and full-bodied. Unbuttoning her blouse, offering me her breasts. Leaned back on her elbows in my bed, morning sunshine beaming between her long, firm legs spread open. Begging me not to stop in the chill of night, in the rain.

Shit. My dick didn't get hard with Katya's little hand wrapped around it, but the thought of Lennix's kisses from ten years ago has me stiff as a tree trunk.

"Someone's taking photos for tomorrow's papers," Katya whispers, leaning over. "Let's make her jealous."

"What?"

Before I can stop her, she kisses me.

CHAPTER 43
LENNIX

"This will be fantastic."

Millicent fairly glows reading the plans we've drafted to announce Owen's exploratory committee on New Year's Eve. Take-out cartons, coffee cups, laptops, and iPads crowd the glass surface of our conference-room table. The faces around the room look tired, but her response makes the hard work worth it.

"I agree," Owen says absently. "Fantastic."

He's been reading the draft of a bill during the meeting, negotiating the challenge of still serving in the Senate while running for president. That will only intensify the further we get into this process.

Millicent gives him a heatless glare and rolls her eyes. "He'll be no fun until that bill goes through. Now I do have some questions about the menu and decorations. It *is* still New Year's Eve. It has to be festive."

"It'll be at our house," Owen says, still not looking up from the massive stack in front of him. "Our Christmas decorations are up from Thanksgiving 'til St. Patrick's Day. You don't get more festive than that."

"He exaggerates," she says with a smile. "They're down by Valentine's Day."

She crosses her arms and begins what resembles a military march. "But that is neither here nor there. We need to discuss menu, additional decorations, entertainment, fireworks—"

"Fireworks?" Owen, Kimba and I ask simultaneously.

She lifts one haughty brow, her general's face on. "Are we going to have a problem with my fireworks? It's the least we can do to launch one of the greatest presidential administrations in our fine nation's history. A Cade finally sitting in the Oval? We need to blow some shit up."

Silence hangs in the air. Everyone exchanges nervous glances. Then there is a snicker from the far end of the conference-room table. It's Maxim, who hasn't said a word the entire meeting. With his head and shoulders hunched over his iPad, I assumed he was barely paying attention. His humor seems to uncork everyone else, and then we're all laughing. Owen laughs loudest and pulls his wife down onto his lap.

"My girl wants fireworks," he says, kissing the top of Millicent's head. "My girl gets fireworks."

She giggles and burrows into his neck. "Thank you, O."

I stand and put on *my* general face.

"There's something else we need to discuss," I say, waiting for the laughter to settle down. "This announcement is taking place at your house. Your Pacific Heights mansion in San Francisco, to be more precise."

"It's our home," Owen says, his voice stiffening. "I thought we agreed that would personalize it rather than at a city hall or something."

"I think the party at your place is great," I say. "And Millicent's known to be an incredible hostess, so treating it like a party is perfect. We just need to be cognizant of the optics. Republicans will paint you as elitist, and speaking frankly, there's a lot about your background that screams wealth and the dirtiest buzzword of all right now—privilege."

"We can't change who we are," Millicent says, a little defensively.

"I'm not asking you to change who you are," I reassure her, keeping my voice calm. "I'm asking you to manage how they see you. We don't want struggling working-class voters to feel like they could never relate to you. Seeing all your rich friends gathered around the sprawling ballroom in your mansion does not exactly communicate 'I feel your pain.'"

"Okay," Millicent says with a small frown. "What do you suggest?"

"I think we need to make sure you don't look like the one percenters you actually are if we want the middle class pulling the lever for you next year, Senator Cade. Most Americans don't even really tune into politics until we start gearing up for elections. Do you want their first impression of you to be the elitism your opponent will surely accuse you of?"

My words land with a *thump* into the subsequent quiet. I give it a beat and am about to elaborate, but Maxim speaks before I can. "She's right, O."

I look up to find his stare fixed on me, but he quickly shifts it to his brother. "Not many people grew up the way we did or live the way we do. We want them to know we may have a lot, but we want to use what we have to help."

"Exactly," I add. "I'm not suggesting you hide who you are or fake poverty. That would be disingenuous, and your authenticity is one of the most appealing things about you."

"Then what?" Owen asks.

"Your political positions and your personality, everything about you polls really well with millennials," I say. "You feel like a breath of fresh air to them."

"Well, that's good to know." Owen laughs. "Did you hear that, Mill? This old guy polls well with millennials."

A few of the team chuckle, but they're also typing on their iPads and laptops, jotting notes, grabbing data. They've started tracking down leads before I've had to ask for them.

"Let's invite them," Kimba says, excitement sparking in her dark-brown eyes. "Students, community organizers, Instagram influencers, leaders from marginalized groups—all of them."

"Yes!" I agree. Kimba and I basically share a brain, so I see where this could go. "Bus caravans."

"By car, by train," she picks up. "We send out invitations now to campus leaders, folks who volunteered for campaigns, all key figures in those crucial demographics. We don't leave them with their faces pressed to the window."

"Right," I say. "We open the doors. Yes, I have a big house, but it's *your* house, too. At least for tonight."

Everyone laughs again, and the brief tension that had infiltrated the room flees completely. I pace, my brain like a beehive, every idea causing another and chasing that one until I'm buzzing with thoughts and I can't get the words out fast enough.

"Not just a party to celebrate a New *Year's* Eve," I say, my voice climbing, "but a new era!"

"A new era's eve party," Kimba laughs, high-fiving me. "Ooooh! We're cooking with hot grease now, honey."

We continue spitballing ideas and assigning actionable items. It's another hour before we break, but I feel much better about this soiree we're throwing.

"Big plans for Thanksgiving, Lennix?" Millicent asks, gathering some of the dinner debris while the team packs up to go.

"Lennix doesn't celebrate Thanksgiving," Maxim says from the other end of the table, his words quiet. He looks up from his iPad to meet my eyes. "Unless that's changed?"

He and I stare at one another so long I feel other people noticing.

"No, I don't celebrate," I say.

Thanksgiving is one of those distinctly American *traditions* that has problematic origins for American Indians.

"I don't begrudge other people celebrating," I tell them, shrugging. "Even some from my tribe celebrate. It's fine. I just don't." I smile to lighten the mood and my words. "But I do go home. My dad and I order pizza and watch parades and boring football games."

Everyone laughs, keeps packing up and heading out. I'm still processing that Maxim knows I don't celebrate Thanksgiving. I must have forgotten we discussed it. I thought I remembered everything about that week.

"Maxim, Lennix," Owen says. "Could you two hang for a minute?"

Maxim glances at the Richard Mille watch on his wrist. "I can give you twenty of them. Jin Lei has my car downstairs and a flight waiting."

"You're leaving DC?" I ask before I catch my damn tongue.

Maxim goes still in the middle of pulling on his leather jacket and glances up at me, one brow lifted.

"I mean," I say hastily. "I just wondered in case we need anything or have questions."

He pulls his jacket on and grabs his iPad from the table. "Kimba has my itinerary and knows how to get in touch with me."

One of my conditions. He doesn't say it, but the silent truth travels the length of the table.

"Yeah, I've been in contact with Jin Lei," Kimba affirms, smiling. "I know how to find you."

He smiles back with an ease that doesn't exist between the two of us anymore. He hasn't made any attempts to contact me. Everything I've heard of Maxim comes through Kimba or the gossip columns. There seems to be a report about him on DC's social circuit every night. The latest morsel involved him kissing a Russian ambassador's daughter. I've been convincing myself all week that I don't care. He *does* think I'm with Wallace. Maybe he decided to give up?

And shouldn't I be happy if he has?

"Well, my mama has started cooking Thanksgiving dinner," Kimba says, rubbing her stomach. "I can already smell the turkey and dressing."

"Oooh, and string bean casserole," Howard groans.

"Mac and cheese," Kimba bounces back as they leave the conference room.

"I'm gonna go check on the twins," Millicent says. She pauses at the door and turns to me. "Thanks for not backing down in the meeting, Lennix. Some people blow smoke up my ass because of who I'm married to."

"First of all, if I blew smoke up your ass," I tell her, "it would be because of who *you* are, not your husband. And second of all, I got no smoke, lady."

We exchange slow, genuine smiles. She nods and leaves the room.

"So what's up, brother?" Maxim asks. "I got a plane to catch."

"Where are you going?" Owen asks, frowning a little.

"Berlin, Prague, Stockholm," Maxim says. "Then it gets fuzzy and you'll have to ask Jin Lei."

"When do you come back to the States?" Owen asks. "Will you be home for Christmas?"

Maxim's face shutters. "You already know the answer to that, O. I'll make sure to send the twins their gifts and—"

"And your mother?" Owen demands. "When will you see her?"

"I see Mom more than ever," Maxim fires back. "Just not with him. He doesn't want to see me."

"And he says you don't want to see him." Exasperation and frustration war on Owen's face. "You two are the most—"

"My flight, Owen," Maxim interrupts. "I've adjusted everything for your campaign. The least you can do is not give me hell when I need to get back to my life every once in a while."

"You know that's not..." Owen takes a deep breath. "Anyway, okay. Do what you need to do, but we'll be at Mom and Dad's. Our kids need to know their grandparents *and* their uncle."

Maxim remains silent, the muscles of his body seemingly drawn tight and preternaturally still. Owen finally nods and steeples his fingers in front of him on the table. I feel like an interloper witnessing this family discord. I wonder if they've forgotten I'm here, but then Owen turns his attention to me.

"My father will be there when I announce the exploratory committee." His words brook no argument, and I don't give him any.

"Yes, sir," I say. "I expected as much, but I hope you don't want him to speak or—"

"No, nothing like that." Owen frowns. "He doesn't want that. He actually has steered pretty clear of everything. He's probably afraid if he gets involved, he'll run you off, Max."

"Perceptive," Maxim intones. "We'll be fine."

Millicent pokes her head back in, her cell phone held to her chest. "Sorry, but could I borrow you for a sec, O? The kids want to say goodnight."

"Of course." Owen rises and leaves the room, already wearing that smile reserved only for the three people who live under his roof.

The walls push in as soon as I'm alone with Maxim. The air throbs with awareness like smoke filling my lungs, choking me. I allow myself short, shallow breaths so the smell of him doesn't overwhelm my senses. I grab my bag and head toward the door, deciding not to even speak. At the threshold, though, curiosity gets the better of me, and I turn back to face him.

His eyes are waiting for me, intense and hungry. Fully wolf. The naked emotion on his face snatches my breath and my thoughts and my words for a second. It's familiar. This look hovered above me when he drove into my body with commanding sensuality, but it seems different on this matured version of him. It's even more dangerous, more appealing.

I clear my throat, needing to break the tension arcing between us. "When did I tell you I don't celebrate Thanksgiving?"

He frowns and turns down the firm, full lips at the corners. "That night at Vuurtoreneiland."

"Really? I don't remember. I guess we talked about a lot of things that night."

It comes back to me now, though. Both of us leaning forward across the table, pushing in closer, straining to catch each other's voices, like archeologists digging around in each other's heads, searching for answers. I wanted so badly to bottle those moments—not to miss a word he said.

"I can't believe I forgot I told you," I say, leaning my back against the doorjamb.

"It was a great night." He chuckles and sits on the edge of the desk. "I think we were both talking a mile a minute, and by the end of the meal, I couldn't wait to get out of there."

My cheeks heat with the memory of our hurried departure. We couldn't stop touching each other on the ferry back to the city. I confessed my virginity in the moonlight, and we sprinted through the streets to reach his house. Everything that followed once we were inside rushes back, and I see myself again, spread on his bed, offering myself to him.

"Such a great night," he repeats, holding my gaze captive. "I think about it all the time."

Me, too.

It's an unspoken whisper singeing my heart with its hot breath and secret sentiment. I search for my anger, resentment—anything still lurking around because of the things he didn't tell me that week—but I can only remember the things he *did* say. And time folds on itself, blending Kingsman, the young adventurer with a head full of dreams, and Cade, the unimaginably successful man standing in front of me now who brought that young man's ideas to life. Two men not so different when I think about it. Not different at all. What we had that week, that night, it was true. I think I've wanted to run from that because the implication of forgiving Maxim, accepting him back into my life…

"You better catch that flight," I say, turning to walk out the door.

"Nix," he says from behind me, his voice getting closer. "I've been giving you space, but I haven't given up. I've decided to use a different tactic."

I pause but don't turn. "And what tactic is that?"

"Letting you miss me," he says softly. "Letting you remember what we were like together. Is it working?"

Every single day.

Every single day some memory of our time together disrupts my peace of mind, but I won't tell him that.

"I'm trying to respect your wishes." He steps in front of me so we're facing each other. "To respect your decision and your..." He twists his lips and they tighten at the corners. "Your relationship, but I told you I would come back when the time was right. I think the time is now. I love my brother, and I would support his run, but I wouldn't be living in this city for him."

He brushes a knuckle over my cheek and pushes my hair back. "I'm not here for Owen, Nix. I'm here for you."

"Maxim," I say, my breath trapped in my throat. "I don't think—"

"What do I have to do?" he asks, bending so our mouths line up, so the question waits on my lips for an answer. "What does a man like me, used to getting anything he wants, do when the woman he wants more than anything won't forgive him for a mistake when he was too stupid and too young to know better?"

I close my eyes against the urgency in his stare, dark green like a forest I'd get lost in. My chest heaves as if I'm running, but the only exertion is staying out of his arms, is not throwing myself on top of him and kissing him like it's been ten years since I had anything as good as what we had. It takes everything to remain still, mute.

I want to tell him there's no relationship to respect. There's nothing to forgive, but if I say any of those things, there will be no barrier between us—nothing keeping the wolf from my door. And if he gets in...

With swift steps, I make my escape to the elevator, duck in, and press the *close doors* button. I probably won't see him again until the announcement. When I look up, he stands there, frustration clearly painted on his strong face.

"Happy holidays, Doc," I say as the doors close.

CHAPTER 44
LENNIX

"MERRY CHRISTMAS, MAMA."

I say it every year here in this place where I whispered her name. It's not much, but it's all the closure I have. No body and no grave. A story with no end. I can only hope she found peace because I'm not sure I ever really can.

"Rest in peace, Liana," my father says, his sober gaze fixed below.

I'd almost forgotten he stood beside me, I was so turned in on my own sadness. He comes every year, though I haven't asked him to in a long time. They never married and weren't together when she died.

Guilt stabs at me.

"Dad, you don't have to keep coming." I take his hand and squeeze. "You should be home with Bethany. I could have come alone."

"Bethany's fine," he says of the English professor he married after dating a few years. "It's just an hour, and she understands."

She is pretty awesome. Since she came into my father's life, Christmas has become festive again with trees lit and tables laid.

"Besides, Liana was a woman who deserves to be remembered."

I nod. She was indeed. A warrior. Fierce and principled.

"You're so like her," Dad says, a gentle smile quirking his lips even though his gaze is trained on the sky, not on me. "She would be proud of you—of how you fought to protect this place."

"And failed," I mumble, misery making my eyes burn. "I couldn't save…"

Her. The land. Tammara. Too many losses to name over the years. It makes me tired. I stare at the smooth expanse of dry land, with the pipeline trail cutting over it like a scar, healed but jagged.

"You can't save them all, Lenn," Dad says, slipping an arm around me and pulling me in tight. "But you're your mother's daughter, so I know you'll always try."

I nod against his shoulder, tears stinging my eyes.

"Just promise me you'll stop fighting for everyone else long enough to find something for yourself," Dad says. "Liana never did that, but you can."

He's right. It usually feels like everything I want most is for someone else.

Not everything, that damn voice reminds me again.

I clench my eyes closed against the images that flood my mind—images of Maxim and me. My desire for him was a living thing that writhed and screamed and demanded for itself—took what it wanted. Took him however he came. Wanted him with no holds barred, even if it hurt.

But then it *did* hurt, and I ran away.

The barren land mocks me, an open casket holding nothing more than a whisper and my pain. God, so much pain. Pain I don't think I can live through again.

Mena says I cut myself off so I never have to feel this again—never have to lose like this again. Does never having someone to lose mean I'll never have someone…at all?

CHAPTER 45
MAXIM

"And *then* Lennix says, 'Happy holidays…'" I pause for emphasis. "…*Doc*.'"

David and Grim don't look as impressed by this last bit of information as they should. They actually look slightly disinterested.

"You get the significance of that, right?" I demand. "Remember I told you she used to call me—"

"Doc Quixote," they both finish flatly, arms crossed over their chests. They're slumped into the sumptuous sectional that takes up a quarter of the room. We're at my place embedded in the slopes of the Aspen Highlands. Neither of them have immediate families, and mine… Well, it's obviously complicated.

"Not all the time. Mostly she would just call me Doc, but there was that one time we went—"

"Bike riding," they say together again, exasperation creeping into their voices.

"I told you guys about that?" I frown. "About the windmills when we went bike riding in Amsterdam?"

"Holy shit," David groans, running a hand through his hair. "I don't know about you, Grim, but if he says 'Amsterdam' one more time…"

"Yeah." Grim reaches for the heavily spiked eggnog my chef has perfected over the years. "I'll figure out how to chew my own ear off."

"Good one." David chuckles and clicks his mug to Grim's. "Now, Max, you say Kimba is your main contact for the campaign, right? She still got that great ass? Did she ask about me? I mean, she and I also had a great week in the city that shall not be named."

"Really?" Grim turns to him, his brows lifted. "You tapped that?"

"Dude…" David closes his eyes and tips his head back into the cushions. "Like one of my top ten fucks of all time."

"Top ten?" Grim does look impressed by that. "Wow."

"I'm sorry," I interrupt. "But I was kind of in the middle of asking for your advice."

"Are we still talking about you?" David frowns. "I didn't want to say it, man, but Kimba and I had a week, too, and you don't hear me going on and on about it."

"Because it meant absolutely nothing to either of you. She passed her goodbye through me on the street and *told* me it meant nothing."

David cocks his grin to the side. "But I bet she remembers my dick fondly."

He and Grim bump fists, and their bawdy laughter echoes through the room.

"I was *trying* to ask if I should call Lennix," I tell them. "She hasn't called me Doc since I've been back. Hell, she's barely looked me in the face."

Through the floor-to-ceiling window, I contemplate the mountains. Nearby properties glitter with Christmas lights, and the moon hangs low in the sky like an Earth-sized ornament, illuminating the snow-dusted rise of mountains. It's a scene from a holiday postcard, but it doesn't feel like Christmas. Not really.

I talked to Owen and Millie and the kids yesterday before they left for my parents' place in Dallas. The kids loved the gifts I sent, and I could hear their squeals of laughter and their cocker spaniel barking in the background. It reminded me of Christmases growing up, Owen and me running downstairs at one minute past midnight and tearing into our gifts. My mom and dad would get up with us to watch.

I had a fantastic childhood. I can appreciate that now. Not for the reason people would assume, for all the money, but for my family. I think I blocked some of it so the separation from my father wouldn't hurt as much, but tonight, I feel it. Dad was busier than I could even comprehend then, but I caught him once assembling our bikes himself so they'd be under the tree when we woke up. He stood there with my mom, bleary-eyed in his robe, grinning when we rode the bikes up and down the halls.

I miss my parents. I miss my dad. I don't allow myself to acknowledge that most days. The enmity has calcified between us—hardened into bone that might now prove too painful if we break it.

"If you don't call," Grim says, pulling me away from past holiday mornings, "you'll just keep thinking about it."

"And, God help us, *talking* about it," David says. "So just call."

Dammit, they're right. I step out onto the veranda overlooking a string of pearl-topped mountains. I dial the number, waiting while the cold pierces through my thick sweater.

"Maxim!" my mom says, her voice breaking over my name.

Maybe I'm a coward. This was the easier call to make.

"Mom, hey."

"I was hoping you'd call. I planned to call you in a few minutes, so I'm…" A silence thick with emotion builds between us.

"It's good hearing your voice," I say, forcing a lighter tone. "Those kids of Owen's driving you crazy yet? They're the loudest little monsters I've ever met. They drive me bonkers in DC."

"I'm pretty sure if I survived my own two little Kingsman monsters," she says, her voice warm, "I can survive Owen's."

I hadn't thought of that in years, how she used to chase us around the house yelling, "I'm looking for all the king's men!"

"I'm so glad you're with Owen while he's running," she continues. "He needs someone he can trust, and politics is a dirty game."

"One he's been playing for ten years," I remind her dryly.

"Yes, but this is another level. It requires even more ruthless-ness." She pauses to laugh. "And we both know you're ten times as ruthless as your brother."

"Not sure how I feel about that, Mom. Thanks?"

"You get it from your father," she says, humor and affection in her voice. "You both play dirty when you have to. I'm glad Owen has you at his back. Take care of your brother, son."

It should be an odd request considering I'm younger, but she's right. Owen has a heart of gold, but I've always been the fighter of us two.

"I will, Mom," I promise. "I got him."

"Would you, um…like to speak with your father?" she asks, her voice trying to sound normal.

I try for normal, too, as if my father and I talk every day instead of once every few years. "Sure."

It *is* Christmas.

"Okay," she says, clearly happy and relieved. "Let me get him. I love you, Maxim."

"Love you, too, Mom."

"Maxim." My father's deep voice booms over the phone, and I'm transported back to sunlit days standing in water past our knees, him yelling down the river while we cast lines fly-fishing.

"Dad," I reply, keeping my voice even. "Merry Christmas."

I remind myself that I'm not that college kid he reamed for not being ruthless or focused enough. Not the one who wondered if my father was right when he said I'd never make it without the protec-tion of his name. I'm the man who fled his father's shadow and flew on his own.

"Merry Christmas," my father says. "I hope it's been good for you so far."

"Yeah, great."

"You're in Aspen?"

How the hell does my father always know where I am? "Uh, yeah. With David and Grim."

"Be sure to give them our best." A long pause neither of us seems to know how to fill follows before he continues. "It's good you're in DC with O."

"Yeah," I reply, grabbing hold of something we can agree on. "I think he has a real shot. Actually, according to all the numbers, the best shot. He leads in every early poll."

"I don't trust polls, and I don't trust that *girl* he has running his campaign. Under the expensive clothes and fine education, she's the same bothersome baggage who tried to stop my pipeline. And she *keeps* trying to stop them, little nuisance."

I clamp my teeth around the sharp edges of the words I want to hurl at him.

"She's the best in the business, Dad," I say, my voice stiff as a mannequin. "They don't call her the Kingmaker for nothing."

"You think I don't know about the soft spot you have for Lennix Hunter?" he asks, a bitter note entering his voice. "That dick of yours is gonna lead you somewhere you don't need to go one day. Oh, wait. It already has. Amsterdam, wasn't it?"

I grip the phone until I think it might snap in my fingers. "Stay out of my business, Dad."

"Tell *her* to stay out of mine."

"You know I can't control Lennix. Every time you try to lay a pipeline on tribal ground, she's coming for your ass."

"Well, she better hope I never come for hers."

A block of ice solidifies in my chest. I know what my father's vendettas look like. Ruined careers. Lost fortunes. Shattered lives.

"Let me make something abundantly clear to you, *Warren*," I say in a low rumble of danger I don't even recognize as my own voice. "You think things have been bad between us the last fifteen years? Touch her and I will make the worst you've ever done look like child's play. Do you understand me?"

A frigid silence accumulates across the miles, as cold and densely dark as the Antarctic winter. Snow starts falling, huge crystalline flakes that land on my hand and melt before I can touch or appreciate them.

"You'd choose that little bitch over your family?" my father asks, his voice tight and furious.

"I'd choose her over you."

He replies with a disgusted huff of breath. "The only reason I'm tolerating her at the announcement is because Owen seems to believe she knows what she's doing and won't listen when I tell him to fire her ass."

"I don't want to see you within ten feet of her on New Year's Eve."

"You won't see me within ten feet of her *ever* if I can help it," he says, his voice taut with rage. "Goodbye, Maxim, and merry Christmas."

The line goes as dead as any affection I thought I'd salvaged for him. Every time I think we might be able to fix all the things that have gone wrong between us, my father does something to remind me why I left in the first place.

This isn't how I saw Christmas going. Somewhere in my mind, I hoped Lennix and I would have worked things out by now. She said each Christmas she goes to the site where she whispered her mother's name and laid her to some kind of rest. She probably sees the Cade Energy pipeline there and remembers all the reasons she shouldn't trust me. My father. My family's business. My lies.

None of those are things I can fix or change. How I hurt her, deceived her, is in the past, but standing out here in the cold alone under a Yuletide moon and falling snow, I wonder if we'll ever find our way to the future.

CHAPTER 46
LENNIX

"Everything's incredible, Mill," I say. "And the house looks beautiful."

An army of servers circle the room carrying trays laden with champagne. Christmas lights sparkle overhead and along the stairwell banister. The branches of a huge tree in the corner stretch toward the ceiling, its decorative cheer adding to the festive atmosphere.

"Even more beautiful with all these students here." Millicent scans the room, packed with the faces of so many young leaders from all over the country. "This was such a great idea. Everyone's excited, even though they don't know what's coming."

"I'm sure some suspect. CNN, MSNBC, Fox, and every major news outlet are at this party. They know we wouldn't have them here just to ring in the New Year."

"After tonight, everything changes, huh?" Her blue eyes find mine, and they're sober in this festive scene. "Once he makes it official, our lives change forever."

"We're just announcing the exploratory committee tonight. He'll announce he's running in February, and then we're off."

"You wouldn't have taken him on if you didn't think he'd win," she says, her smile knowing. "You bet on the winners, don't you?"

I think of all the battles I've lost. All the pipelines that got built anyway. All the young men still languishing in prison despite Kimba's and my best efforts.

"Not always, no," I reply, staring into my champagne. "I just fight for the ones I think *should* win."

"Hey," Kimba says, appearing beside us. "CNN wants an interview after."

"Excuse me, ladies. I need to go find my children," Millicent says by way of exit. "See you in a bit."

"What time do they want to do the interview?" I ask Kimba.

"'Round midnight, and you know I don't do that shit."

"Okay." I laugh and roll my eyes. "But one day you'll get shoved into the spotlight, so you better be ready."

"Not if I can help it." She pulls an iPad from where it's tucked under her arm. "So Owen starts his speech at eleven thirty. He makes the announcement. We do the countdown to midnight and then the interview."

"Right. I'll be ready."

I search the crowd for Maxim. He's been working the room all night. I know it's for Owen, but he freely admits he has his own agenda, the same one he has been advancing for the past decade—to wean this country off fossil fuels and direct our resources to cleaner, more sustainable energy. He's a single-minded man. It's hard to remember how it feels having all that power and intensity focused on me since he hasn't looked at me all night.

He's striking in black, perfectly tailored pants and a button-down shirt. There's a satyr-like look to his dark hair and brows, the sensual curve of his mouth, the wild, wicked light in his eyes.

"Who invited the Russian?" Kimba asks.

I shift my attention from Maxim to the woman at his side. It's the Russian ambassador's daughter. The one who kissed him. He's laughing down at her, easy affection in his expression. She reaches up to cup his face, the gesture familiar and intimate. My breath gets hung on irritation like a dress on a nail. A sharp, tiny thorn pricks my heart, but before the pain has time to take root, Maxim pulls her hand away from his face and shakes his head. His smile is gentle, but it's a firm dismissal that reassures me. He said there had never been anyone else like me. I believe him because for me, there's never been anyone like him.

My father told me to want something, to take something for myself.

I want Maxim. Will I take him tonight? After hiding so much *about* myself *from* myself, lying to myself, can I tell him the truth?

"We're thirty minutes from the announcement," Kimba says, her face taking on a serious set.

"I'll go check on Owen. I think he went upstairs to review his speech."

With one last glance at Maxim, now laughing with a congressman from North Carolina, I make a dash for the stairs and toward the guest room where Owen is supposed to be. The two men who are always with him stand outside the door, wearing identical impassive expressions. I stride down the long hall, anxious to make sure he's prepared for the biggest speech of his life to date. He has an excellent speechwriter, but he drafted most of it himself. Maxim, Kimba and I weighed in and offered suggestions. The speech is loaded to a teleprompter we brought in, so he should be set, but I want to make sure. I lift my fist to knock, but the door opens before I get the chance.

Filling the doorway is the man who is almost the exact, albeit older, physical replica of Maxim. Our eyes narrow and our shoulders stiffen at the same time, the only things about us in synch. He closes the door behind him.

"Miss Hunter," Warren Cade drawls. "I wondered when you'd turn up."

Turn up like a bad penny if his disdainful look is any indication of how he feels about me.

"I've been around," I tell him, keeping my voice as neutral as possible. "There's a lot riding on tonight. We all want Owen to do well."

Any polite pretense disintegrates from his face. "You better not ruin one damn thing for my boy."

"I want Owen to win. I'm willing to set aside our personal differences long enough to get your son elected because I believe he will take this country in a direction that benefits those most vulnerable among us."

"You're so concerned about the most vulnerable, yet every time I turn around you're ingratiating yourself with extremely powerful men, specifically my sons. Why is that, Miss Hunter? I think you're as hungry for power as the ones you claim to hate."

"Your sons came to me, not the other way around. I don't want power. I want what has been promised to my people for centuries. I only want what is ours to remain ours. What was stolen from us, where possible, to be returned. You're the one constantly collecting things that aren't yours as if you don't already have enough."

"Enough?" His laugh is dark and twists between us. "What is this concept of *enough*? It sounds wholly un-American. There's never enough. Ask my son if he ever gets enough."

He leans down to look directly into my eyes. "Not Owen. The other one. Maxim's just like me. You do know that, right? Under all that clean, Greenpeace shit, he's as ruthless and insatiable as I am, though he doesn't like to admit it. You think some girl from the reservation will ever be *enough* for him?"

Never be enough for Maxim? For the man who put himself between me and a pack of dogs before he even knew my name? Not enough for the man who shook me awake from my nightmares and held me all night? The man who begged for my forgiveness, admitted he was wrong and came back for me…just like he said he would?

"You hate it, don't you?" I ask, my voice low and taunting. "That I'm the one he wants?"

His confident smile flickers, slips.

"You know him so well," I say. "Not Owen. *The other one.*"

I take a bold step closer so my words have less space to travel.

"You know Maxim well enough to see that he didn't come back for Owen. He came back for me."

"You're wrong," Warren says with an ease belied by the hard glimmer in his eyes.

"Am I? God, it must grate that your son wants…how did you put it? Some girl from the reservation? The girl who can't stand you and gets in your way at every turn?"

"You should be very careful," Warren says, his voice a threat.

"Or what? You'll destroy my career? Come against my friends? My family? You don't scare me." I laugh with sudden realization. "I scare *you*. Because you know that if you hurt me, Maxim will never forgive you."

"That's ridiculous." His laugh scoffs, but I see something in his eyes—the same thing Maxim doesn't want me to see in his. Longing. He longs for a relationship with his son the way Maxim longs for him. He misses Maxim, but he can't have him.

And I can.

"I know your secret, Mr. Cade." I tip up on my toes and whisper in his ear. "You love Maxim most."

When I step back, a vein bisects his forehead like a lightning bolt. The anger swirls around him, cyclonic and forceful. If Maxim's own words didn't convince me how much he cares for me, his father's response does.

"Now if you'll excuse me," I say, keeping my voice low. "Your other son needs me."

I open the door, step inside the room, and close the door in Warren Cade's face. A deep breath settles me and clears my mind of the unpleasant encounter before I approach Owen. He's seated on the bed, iPad beside him, and he looks perfectly at ease. He's a natural. He doesn't just poll well; he *is* a good man. He'll be good for our country. He'll unite us but still be uncompromising for the people who deserve defending.

"You ready?" I ask.

"As ready as I'll ever be." His smile is a little weary, but I've seen him in action enough to know when the lights come on, so does he. He'll bring the energy we need.

"Tonight has already been a huge success, and your announcement is gonna top it off in the best way possible. After this, it's a whole new ball game, and we're ready to play."

Owen nods, smiles, but there's a sobriety to his expression.

"Sure you're okay, Owen?" I touch his shoulder and frown.

"Yeah, I'm good." His smile is meant to reassure me. "It's a tremendous amount of responsibility, and I've been preparing all my life for this, but tonight it's more real than it's ever been. I've seen how power corrupts, and I never want to be that. You know?"

Still feeling the sting of his father's barbs, I *do* know what power misused looks and feels like. "The fact that you even think about this means you won't do it. Hold on to that and surround yourself with people who won't let you get away with it."

"I'm glad I've surrounded myself with you and Kimba. Keep me accountable?"

"That you don't have to worry about," I tell him with a smile.

The door opens, and Millicent and the twins stand there.

"Sorry to interrupt," she says.

"No, we're just wrapping up." I look to Owen. "Kimba and I and the whole team are here for you. Let us know if you need anything. We have about ten minutes before you'll take the stage."

When I return to the main room, I check with our producer that the cameras are set up and ready to record Owen's announcement. We'll push it out on social media immediately.

I glance up and find Maxim's eyes set on me. It's a cool night in San Francisco, but when our gazes connect, a blast of heat covers my entire body. His eyes leave mine to fall over me—my breasts and hips and thighs, all the way to my feet. He takes his time retracing the path back up and over each dip and curve until he's looking into my eyes again. I don't nod or smile, but I can't tear my eyes away from him.

He emanates power—the physical power of his muscles and strong body subdued by the expensive clothing made to mold his form. He carries a magnetic aura that draws senators, congressmen, ambassadors—all want a piece of him for the wealth he's acquired and the influence he wields. There's the power of his mind, that sharp tool he's honed to build an empire from scratch without his father's assistance through a series of risks only a buccaneer would hazard. And finally, there's the power he seems to have over me—a visceral, personal force that knows how to tempt me, that fascinates and mesmerizes me. All the others he's carefully cultivated, but the power he holds over me, I think it's effortless.

His assistant tugs on his arm, drawing his attention away, and I take the opportunity to move as if released from a trance.

"Biggest night of the campaign so far," I mutter to myself, "and you're mooning over the candidate's brother."

When the moment arrives, it's obvious Owen was made for it. He takes the stage, his wife and twins standing with him.

"I want to thank all of you for coming tonight," he says with a smile that encompasses the entire room. "I'm sure you had a dozen places you could have been to bring in the New Year, but you chose to be here with my family and me."

He turns to the right where we have strategically grouped most of the college leaders. I look to the back of the room and catch our producer's eye, silently signaling him to make sure we get all those young, eager faces on camera for B-roll later. He nods and speaks into his headset.

"And a special thanks to all the young leaders who came on buses, trains, in caravans from all across the country to be with us tonight." Owen gestures to the cluster of students who, as I knew they would, cheer as loudly as if Owen is scoring a touchdown instead of making a political speech. "Your energy and foresight and compassion are the things that will secure our future. I just hope we old folks don't screw it up too badly before you get it."

More cheers, and Kimba and I put our heads close together to whisper, identifying which of them it will be good to get reactions from after the announcement.

"When I started in the Senate ten years ago, I had that same energy and enthusiasm for getting things done," Owen says, a rueful grin tipping one side of his mouth. "It's easy to lose sight of our dreams and of the things that motivated us to public service in the first place when we get trapped in bureaucracy and political infighting. Being around you reminds me why it's so important we never stop striving for the best of ourselves and of this country.

"Many of you may have heard rumors of my possible presidential run," he says with a chuckle. "I know. Rumors in DC? Hard to believe. I'm confirming tonight that I have formed a presidential exploratory committee."

The room erupts and the energy skyrockets.. Even the more staid partygoers seem to be affected by the youthful enthusiasm the students emit.

"If we get this much juice from the exploratory committee announcement," Kimba says from the corner of her brightly painted mouth, "imagine when he announces that he's actually running."

I nod my agreement, about to speak when I notice Maxim standing against the wall watching me. Before I realize what I'm doing, I take a step in his direction.

"Lenn," Kimba says, jerking my attention away from Maxim and halting my steps. "Mark wants you in the back."

By the time I speed walk to the back and answer the producer's questions, Owen is wrapping up.

"So over the next few months," Owen says, "my team, my family, and I will continue to kick the tires and see how far this should go."

The students start chanting, "ALL THE WAY! ALL THE WAY!"

Owen smiles and holds up his hand to quiet the crowd so he can land the plane.

"There's a lot ahead," he says. "We hope soon to herald in a new era of politics in this, our great nation. Tonight, though, we're heralding a new *year*. Grab a glass of champagne and find the ones you want to be closest to. I'll be back in a few minutes to count in another great year. Thank you again for coming."

I search the crowded room for Maxim, finding him still leaning on the wall with his arms folded, the ambassador's daughter stuck to his side like flypaper. My hands ball into fists, my fingernails digging into my palms.

"Just staring," Kimba says from beside me, "won't get him."

I didn't even notice her come up, I was so fixated on them.

"What?" I drag my eyes away from the two glamorous people across the room, him a dark contrast to her fairness. "I don't know what you're talking about."

"Come on, Lenn," Kimba says, her usual no-nonsense tone somewhat gentled. "This is your girl. Talk to me."

For a moment, I plan to ignore the frank sympathy in my best friend's eyes, to tough it out and pretend I'm not in the midst of some kind of existential crisis, but I'm tired of holding this armor in place. It's slipping anyway.

"He asked for another chance," I say after a pause. "Maxim, he said he was young and stupid and made a mistake before. He asked me to forgive him."

Kimba nods slowly, dipping her head to catch my lowered eyes. "And have you forgiven him?"

My laugh comes quick and hollow. "Well, yeah. I guess somewhere along the way, I did."

"Praise Jesus. I was gonna give you 'til the end of this campaign, honey, and then smack some sense into you."

"That won't be necessary. At least, I don't think so." I glance across the room where he stands with the Russian princess. "If he's even still interested."

"Oh, he's interested." Kimba follows my stare. "He's a patient man."

"Not really," I say with a laugh. "Quite the opposite, but he's trying."

"Then why keep him waiting? Talk to him. Tell him tonight."

I glance at my watch. "The toast is in ten minutes."

"The hard part is over for now. Owen'll come back and do the countdown and then the New Year's Eve toast."

"And then the CNN interview," I remind her.

She rolls her eyes up to Millie's glittering chandelier and expels a lengthy sigh. "Screw it. I'll do the interview."

I press the back of my hand to her forehead.

"What are you doing?" she asks, her expression puzzled.

"Checking for fever."

Her laugh is hearty. "You better go get that man before I change my mind."

"You sure?"

"Girl, what'd I say?"

"Thank you." I smile and loop my arms around her neck. "Happy New Year."

I draw a deep breath and cross the room toward Maxim, growing more confident with each step. It seems to take forever, but finally I'm standing right in front of him. He glances up, his posture indolent, his hands in his pockets, but his eyes are sharp and questioning.

I don't look at the beautiful blond standing next to him but address him directly.

"How do I get rid of her?" I ask, borrowing his question about Wallace that day in the coffee shop.

She gasps and then chuckles, surprising me into glancing at her. She really is exquisite. Her brown eyes are amused, not offended, and her smile is natural and blinding.

Maxim tips his head to the side, watching me. "Katya, could you give us a minute?"

"Of course," Katya says, her accent thick and sexy. "Also, I told you. I knew what I was doing."

Conversations continue around us, but we stare at each other for seconds that stretch into a minute.

"What did she mean?" I finally ask. "When she said she knew what she was doing?"

A small smile crooks his full lips. "She thought I should make you jealous."

"Why would she... How does she know me?"

"She doesn't." He sketches a casual shrug with his broad shoulders. "She wanted to suck my dick, and I said no."

My teeth clench, and I swallow around the painful lump in my throat. "Why'd you say no?"

"Because I don't want anyone sucking my dick but you."

My eyes snap up to meet his, and they're completely serious. There's no sign of humor. "Is there somewhere we can talk?" I ask.

"The garden." He tips his head toward a large set of French doors. "Through there."

I nod, and he pushes off the wall, grabs my hand, and leads me across the room and through the door. I hope the press of bodies hides our clasped hands. I don't need any rumors getting started or to field dumb questions from snoopy journalists bored with politics and looking for more.

Once outside, we're swallowed by shadows. He's just an intimidating silhouette. I'd know the shape of him, his scent anywhere, but what do I really know about this man asking me to trust him on a new adventure? One that risks not just something of his but of mine?

My heart.

He pulls me deeper into the garden until a tall hedge of bushes shelters us on every side. We've entered a maze of sorts and continue a few yards more until we reach a small stone bench. He sits and leans back, supporting his weight with his hands flattened on the bench and his arms stretched straight.

"Talk to me, Nix," he says, watching my face closely in the moonlight. "Tell me what you're thinking."

I blink at the sudden hot wetness behind my eyes.

I'm afraid.

I want to tell him that I can face down Dobermans and tear gas and rubber bullets at a protest. I can give speeches broadcast to hundreds of thousands of people without a second thought. I can lead a team to elect governors and maybe even a president. But the thought of trusting him with so much of myself—again—scares me.

"Wallace and I aren't together." I start with the easiest of the things I need to say.

Maxim's brows lift, and a satisfied grin spreads across his handsome face. "When did this happen?"

"Oh, about three months after we got together." I pause for impact. "Almost ten years ago."

His smile disappears. "Excuse me? But you said… You *lied* to me?"

"Not exactly," I say, my voice offering no apology. "I did what you did. I let you believe what you wanted about the truth."

"The hell I did that. What do you mean?"

"I *did* start dating him the year I graduated from college. I just left out that we only lasted three months."

"You two still seem extremely close. Why didn't it work out?"

"We are the best of friends." I chuckle. "You'll laugh at this. I told him it was like having sex with my foster step-cousin."

He's quiet while I snicker.

"You thought I would laugh about you fucking someone else?" he asks, a serrated edge to his voice. "I don't find that funny at all."

My light laughter fizzles into a thickening silence. He doesn't crack a smile. "You're being really intense right now, Doc."

"I thought you knew I'm pretty intense when it comes to you." Our stare holds in the moonlight with only the faintest clink of glasses and music in the distance. "I already knew you dated Wallace before because I kept tabs on you through the years. Not in a stalkery way."

"Is there a non-stalkery way to keep tabs on someone for ten years?"

"Yeah, the way I did it."

"If you say so," I say with a tiny smirk. "Why'd you keep tabs on me in this non-stalkerish manner?"

"I wanted to see how your career was going. I knew you'd do great, but even I never imagined you'd do so well so quickly."

"Thank you."

"And I was curious if you married or had kids, a family." He pauses before going on. "What I had with you, I've never even come close with anyone else, and that was in only a week. Imagine if it had been more. Now it *can* be more if you give me another chance."

"I don't know, Doc." I let the words fall, unsure if I should pick them up again. I know what I want, that I want *him*, but the fear I hid even from myself still makes me hesitate.

"Give me another chance, Nix. That's all I'm asking."

"That's *all*?" I nearly choke on my disbelieving laugh. "You're a wolf in wolf's clothing. You'll want everything."

"Everything." His agreement comes softly, but his eyes turn hard as sea glass. "There'll be no one else for you."

"See what I mean? You'll be growly and possessive and demanding."

"Of course I will."

"You'll be all *mine, mine, dammit, mine* and—"

"Only when someone needs reminding."

"I'm embarking on the most important campaign of my life, Maxim."

"So am I, and I'm not talking about Owen's."

"Doc," I groan. "Maybe this isn't the right time. It's a lot fast."

"Fast? It's been ten years." He reaches up and caresses my lips with his thumb. "Anytime we can get our shit together is the right time."

"There's something else we need to discuss." I fix my eyes on the expensive boots peeking out from beneath his pants. "Wallace wasn't the only thing I hid behind. I think I hid behind your lies."

"What do you mean?"

"My therapist has a theory about me." I laugh humorlessly. "She has several because apparently I'm a basket case."

He doesn't laugh but reaches for my hand and pulls me forward a few inches to stand between his legs. I don't pull back.

"Tell me these theories."

"Mena agrees with her. She always says, 'You paid a stranger to tell you what I told you years ago.'" I lift my eyes to briefly meet his, but the intensity of his gaze is so much, I look back to the ground right away.

"Which was?" he asks.

"She said when my mother disappeared, I shut a part of myself off because I was afraid to feel. Afraid to hope. I understand myself better now than I did when I was younger. It wasn't hard for me to abstain from sex because I need an emotional connection for physical intimacy, and I allowed myself that with very few people after my mother died."

"I get that."

"But then I met you again in Amsterdam." I shake my head and squeeze the bridge of my nose. "And it was like someone took a stick of dynamite to a dam, and everything that had been held back gushed out. I felt everything. More than I had ever felt. When you told me you would walk away, I think I dealt with that prospect pretty well." A bark of laughter scrapes my throat. "What you *didn't* say is you might almost die a few times. I could handle you walking away a lot better than that."

A single tear skids down my cheek, and I swipe at it. "I hated that you made me hope, you made me pray again when you disappeared. No one could get to you. We weren't sure if you were dead or alive. And I just…"

I shake my head and heave a breath, searching for the strength to keep going. He squeezes my hand, silently encouraging me to continue. I reach down to touch his hair, pushing it back to expose the silvery scar where stitches used to be.

"I had poured all my feelings into protest, into activism, into my studies—those things never let me down. They never disappeared."

"But I did," he says, understanding in his voice. "I disappeared."

"Yeah, you did." I drop my hand from his hair. "You disappeared, and I hoped and hoped and hoped like I promised myself I never would have to hope again. I thought you would die."

"But I didn't," he reminds me, his voice rising. "Baby, I didn't."

"But you hadn't even gotten home and were already planning to go to the damn Amazon and then God knows where. You love danger."

"No, I don't love danger," he says, his frown fierce and marring the line of his brows. "I love knowledge, and some mysteries have to be pursued. The greatest innovations, inventions, and solutions don't just fall into our laps. Some answers have to be hunted down."

"And they're worth the risk, right? I heard the interviews after. You're a thrill seeker. You're reckless. I didn't have enough hope left for someone like you, and I couldn't have my heart broken that way again."

I close my eyes tightly, but the image of me whispering my mother's name into the wind won't go away. "Not like that. I can't live through that again."

"And my lie was the perfect excuse for you to give up on me."

"In retrospect, I think so." I run a trembling hand through my hair. "And it worked until you came back and started demanding that I feel again."

He wraps his hands around the backs of my legs and brings me even deeper into the *V* of his thighs. "We can do this, Nix."

"Can we? Is it worth it for someone I barely even know?"

His head snaps back. "Barely know? I've known you since you were seventeen years old."

"*Technically*, yeah, but—"

"I know your favorite color is blue–green," he says, tightening his hands on me. "Because they're just better blended together."

I bend my head, hiding my smile.

"I know you used to want to be a clown," he continues, "but then decided to pursue the more conventional path of being an astronaut."

He palms the curve of my waist with one hand and lifts my chin with one finger, holding my eyes when I raise them. "I know you're the girl who chases stars, Nix."

I smile and push an errant lock of burnished dark hair back from his forehead. The humor fades from his eyes, from his expression.

"I've seen the spot where you whispered your mother's name to the wind," he says, lacing his fingers with mine, drawing me down, unresisting, to perch on his leg. I snuggle into him, tucking my head into the strong slope of his shoulder and neck.

"I know you liked Bobby better than Jack," I whisper into his ear. His arm tightens at my back, and laughter rumbles through him. "I know the exact spot of the very first windmill you ever bought, Doc Quixote."

"Wind *turbine*, Nix. It's not a windmill."

"Whatever. I know where it is."

My laughter dies down, and I reach for his arm, pushing back the cuff of his shirt. I run my fingers over the small strip of silvery skin marking his forearm. "I know you got this scar protecting a girl you didn't even know in a fight that wasn't yours."

I bend my head and kiss the small reminder of how we met. "I know that your father is the biggest prick asshole I've ever met and I cannot stand him," I say, icing my tone and then gradually thawing my eyes. "And I know that you still love and miss him."

Shadows flicker in his eyes, the same green as Warren Cade's.

He presses his forehead to mine and cups the back of my head, releasing a heavy sigh. His fingers sift into my hair, and I feel his lips at my ear, ghosting kisses along my neck. "So do I get my second chance?" he asks.

This maze is as convoluted as our journey, as our circumstances. The winding path to this moment runs over sacred grounds turned to battlefields, through Amsterdam's cobblestone streets and canals, through a frozen tundra under midnight suns. Through our nation's capital. Every step led to me sitting here in Maxim's lap, letting him chase my fears away. Letting him tempt me into a second chance.

The corners of my mouth lift, and so does my heart. I feel lighter than I have since he came to town.

"I don't know," I tease. "You're not the simple graduate student I knew before. There's the problem of all that money you've gone and made. You know what they say. More money, more problems."

"I give a lot of it away, if that helps." He laughs and strokes one finger along my bare knee under my dress.

"You're a lot to take."

"I seem to remember you taking me just fine," he says, his voice husky. "It was a tight fit, but we worked it out."

I shift in his lap, my laugh echoing through the network of bushes.

"God, Nix. If you keep squirming like that, we'll find out right now if you can still take it. I'm dying here. Are we or are we not doing this?"

I pull back enough to look into those gemstone eyes, watching me so intently. "Yes."

The word is barely out of my mouth before his lips are on mine. It's a claiming kiss. I knew it would be. It declares that I'm his, and with every answering stroke of my tongue, I accept his terms and warn him that he's mine, too. He turns me so my legs fall on either side of his, and our chests press flush. There's a language between our heartbeats I have no translation for—no words, just a thumping communion.

I pull back and place my hand between our lips.

"Doc, wait," I say, a playful note in my voice when I glance at my watch. "It's not midnight. We're not supposed to kiss until midnight."

"Screw that," he says, leaning forward to mutter against my lips. "It may not be midnight, but it's about damn time."

It's finally our time.

His hunger is voracious, an open-mouthed consumption swallowing me. I feed him my whimpers and moans, my desperate pleasure. His hands roam over my body, deliberately laying claim to every part of me, squeezing my ass, cupping my breasts through my strapless dress, pinching my nipples, kissing my neck, and reminding my body of his possession. He slides his hand between us, reaching under my dress and into my panties, thrusting two fingers inside.

"Doc." I drop my head to kiss our temples together and start riding his hand.

He tugs the bodice of my dress until the chill night air kisses my breasts, and then he dips to suck them one at a time, never letting up between my legs.

"I'm gonna come," I pant.

"We both are," he says, his voice and body hard. "I plan to fuck you out here right now."

"Doc."

"Tell me no." He pulls back to search my eyes, checking to see what I want. "And we won't."

My father said I should find something for myself. Well, this man is for me. On the cusp of a new year, he's all I want. A future with him, this *moment* with him, is what I want most. I undo his belt and unbutton, unzip his pants.

"You're sure?" he asks, his eyes heavy-lidded.

The last time we made love, anger clogged the air, and I called it a mistake when we were done. There's no doubt in my mind right now that this is what I want.

"I'm sure." I bring my knees up on the bench beside his legs, positioning myself, raising up over him. "Let's see if you still fit."

Beneath my dress, he drags my panties aside and pushes in. The air whooshes between our mouths. His hands at my hips keep me still when I start to move.

"I missed this," he says softly and shifts to kiss my jaw. "I missed you."

"Same," I say, breathless from the way he fills me up, stretches me.

"Same?" He laughs and guides my hips into a rhythm. "Damn, that feels good."

I hook my elbow at his neck and deepen the wave of my body over him, arching my back and increasing the pace. I light up like he's flipped a switch no one else has ever found.

"It's never like this," I whisper, tears christening the corners of my eyes.

"It's never like this," he agrees, linking our fingers and pressing our hands between our chests, between my breasts. He finds my eyes in the weak illumination of moonlight. "This feeling belongs to you, Lennix."

"Yes." I lay my forehead against his again, thrust my fingers into his hair. "You're mine, Maxim Cade."

He kisses the curve of my neck and squeezes my ass. "Yours."

"Tell your Russian princess"—I tighten my thighs at his hips and ride him harder—"and your teenage pageant queen to back the fuck off."

His chuckle is breathless as our bodies battle, struggle to get closer, push for a deeper mating of flesh and soul.

"Only you, Nix," he says, leaving the promise in my hair. "No one else."

"And I'm yours," I offer before he has to ask. "Only you, Cade."

He stills, and I realize I used the last name that has caused us so many problems and may cause more in the future. That name in my mouth has always been a curse, but here in this convolution of hedges under a new year of stars, I make it mine. It's my way of telling him I want, I accept every part of him. Even the last name that represents everything I hate. Even the baggage that comes with his family.

"Maxim," I say, my thighs spread wide over him, my knees leveraged on the stone bench. "Kingsman."

I pull back enough to show him my acceptance of the part he tried to hide—to show him that the part that came between us before won't separate us now. "Cade."

It seems to set something off in him, his last name on my lips while he's buried inside me, and his hands tighten on me, the thrusts more urgent, deeper, faster. I hold on tighter, my body clamped around him possessively. He reaches between us to find the place where our bodies are joined and strokes my clit, his thumb fast and sure.

"Maxim," I scream, my hoarse voice tearing through the privacy of our night in this maze. Wave after wave of ungovernable pleasure overwhelms me, overtakes me, until I'm quaking with it, shaking and sobbing into the warm curve of his neck.

He keeps going, every thrust more aggressive and deeper, my bare breasts grazing his shirt, the nipples peaking while he takes his own pleasure. A growl tears from him when he comes, going impossibly harder and bigger and stiffer inside me.

"Shit, shit, shit," he chants, his hands like steel, his breaths harsh and fast. He groans long and rough, emptying himself inside me, a hot, wet rush of passion. I receive him, trembling with wonder at the blend of our bodies. I don't want to move because he'll run out of me. I want to keep him, to keep these moments and these emotions as long as I can.

He was my first. Ten years ago when we made love, I didn't know a passion like this was rare, something to be coveted and chased and clutched, but tonight, I know it's a comet shooting across the sky and all we can do is ride its fiery trail.

Now I know.

CHAPTER 47
LENNIX

"THERE'S BEEN A SLIGHT CHANGE OF PLANS," KIMBA SAYS.

I study her face on my phone. It's our third FaceTime of the day. She's been holding it down in DC, and I'm in San Francisco, about to fly to Ohio. Owen won't make his official presidential announcement until February, but I'm running ahead and laying tracks for our ground game in some purple states where we'll need as much of a head start as possible.

"Change of plans?" I frown and mentally review my meetings for the next day with volunteer coordinators in Ohio. "If we're gonna stay on track for February, we have to stick to the schedule."

"I'm well aware," she says dryly.

I'm handpicking volunteer coordinators in our most crucial battleground states and starting to strategize. We'll use technology to reach voters in as many innovative ways as possible, but I learned early on to never underestimate the importance of a strong ground game.

"I'm on my way to the airport now," I say. "I'm so confused, and you know I hate being confused about as much as I hate peanut butter."

"I'm not sure I trust people who don't like peanut butter."

"It sticks to the… Never mind! What is the change of plans? I need to tell this driver what to do."

"Oh, he already knows."

"Excuse me, sir?" I catch the driver's eye in the rearview mirror. "Where are we going?"

"We're here, ma'am," he says.

I look out the window of the SUV and realize we're at an empty tarmac. Empty except for a jet with CadeCo emblazoned on the side.

"I'm going to get you both," I tell Kimba when I look back to my screen and find her grinning. I'm grinning, too, though, so she can only take my threat so seriously.

Maxim was called away literally on New Year's Day almost as soon as the party was over because of some explosion at one of his Asia-based companies. A week into our "second chance" and we haven't been in the same room once, not since the garden, and I leave for my service trip with Wallace in a few days.

"Get me?" Kimba pretends to consider it. "I think you mean thank me later."

The driver, already carrying my suitcase, opens the door for me. I hesitate. Yes, the jet says CadeCo, but my Cade is nowhere in sight.

I'm about to dial Maxim when a hybrid SUV pulls up. Maxim opens the door and strides toward me with a grin I can only call wolfish—wide and wily and like he plans to eat me. Scruff shadows that protractor jawline, and his dark hair curls around his ears. I mentioned liking it longer. I hope he's not growing it out for me. I love the silky hair any way I can feel it.

He's wearing a cable-knit sweater the color of oatmeal, which should be illegal contrasting with his tanned skin that way. Dark-wash jeans and boots make him look so rugged and sexy, my thighs immediately clench with the need to clamp around him. I don't know what he has planned, but sex better be on the agenda, or I'm making a motion to amend.

His arms encircle me, and he dips his head for a kiss. His hands rove over my back, gripping low on my hips, just short of my ass, and urge me up onto my toes. He plunders my mouth, the heat of the kiss burning through my self-consciousness in seconds. I'm straining up, folding my arms at the elbows behind his neck, opening my mouth greedily under his, sucking his tongue in as deep and hard as humanly possible. I forget about our audience of two and grunt and moan and whimper the longer we kiss. He finally pulls back just enough to lay his forehead to mine, our labored breaths tangling between our lips.

"Hey," he says.

"Hey." I smile up at him and settle my hands on his shoulders.

"Keep kissing me like that and we won't even make it to the plane."

My cheeks warm as his words and our surroundings—the two watching, waiting men—sink in.

"You're in trouble," I tell him as sternly as I can feeling this turned on. "Nobody rearranges me."

"I did." He takes the handle of my suitcase from the driver and pulls it toward the idling plane. "I mean, with the help of Kimba, of course."

"I have to be in Ohio for a meeting at nine o'clock tomorrow morning," I say, trying to hold on to my sense of humor *and* adventure.

"And you will." He takes my hand.

I squeeze his fingers and decide to enjoy myself. "Where are we going, Doc?"

"On a date," he says, the boyish grin that unravels my heartstrings in evidence.

"I said where, not what, though thank you for *telling* me we're going on a date. Some guys just ask, which is so boring."

"Who are these guys who've had you making all those pesky choices about where you'll go and what you'll do? Don't they know you have better things to do than think about dates? I handled all of that for you. You're welcome."

"Something about that isn't right. I hate it when you charm the logic out of everything."

He shrugs. "It's a gift. And we're flying to Ohio because that's where you need to be. Our date will have to be in the air. I'm just getting you where you need to go and stealing some of your time."

"You flew here just to pick up li'l ol' me?" I bat my lashes at him. "You're supposed to be Mr. Clean and Green. I'm really disappointed in your carbon footprint."

"You know what they say about a man with a big carbon footprint," he says, toggling his brows suggestively.

"Oh, God. That was awful. Your conservation jokes suck."

"Who needs to make jokes when I can make money?" he asks, laughing when I roll my eyes. "And I'm manufacturing sports bras from plastic bottles. I think I'm okay flying every once in a while."

"You *are*? How did I miss this? I need a good sports bra."

"We can't keep them in stock. Mill loves them, but I'm gonna go out on a limb and say you won't be needing a bra tonight."

"Wow." I lift both brows and try to ignore how his words are flirting with sensitive spots on my body. "Aren't you confident?"

He drops his eyes down over me, and he draws his bottom lip between his teeth. "I like to think of it as hopeful."

"Who am I to steal a man's hope?"

We climb the short set of steps lowered from the plane. He snaps the curtain closed behind us, and I barely have time to absorb the luxuriously appointed cabin before he pulls me down into one of the oversize leather seats, across his lap. He thrusts one hand into my hair, guiding my face down to his, and licks hungrily into my mouth.

"Maxim." I laugh into the kiss. "We haven't even taken off yet."

"I'm making up for lost time."

"The last week?" I ask, kissing down his chin and to the strong rise of his throat from his sweater.

"The last week, the last decade. The last hour." His hand ventures under my blouse to squeeze my breast. I gasp, leaning deeper into his palm. "You hungry?"

"Very." I shift to straddle him, roll my hips over him, groaning at the way his hardness relieves some of the sexual pressure I feel but also stokes it higher. He holds me still while he thrusts up, teasing me through my clothes with what I want naked. I want to tear his clothes off, burn mine, and celebrate this new thing between us right on this leather seat.

The curtain pulls open, and I glance over my shoulder to find a blond flight attendant who looks completely shocked to see some strange woman straddling her boss.

"Mr. Cade," she gasps. "I'm so sorry."

She starts backing out through the curtain.

"It's okay, Laura," Maxim breathes heavily into the curve of my neck. He strokes my back and tucks my head into his shoulder, hiding my flaming face. "Dinner?"

"Yes, sir. Cook says it's ready."

"Thank you. Bring it in." He kisses my hair. "We're starving."

Once I hear the curtain close, I laugh and pull back to look at him. "Well, that wasn't embarrassing at all."

"She's paid not to be awkward."

I thread my fingers through his, looking at our hands instead of at him. "You mean when you bring women on your plane to make out?"

"I'm thirty-eight years old. I don't 'make out' anymore." He lifts my chin and holds my stare. "And I haven't brought a woman with me like this before."

I roll my eyes. "Tell me another one, Doc. You expect me to believe you haven't gone all mile-high club with other women?"

The humor fades from his expression, leaving a sober cast. "I do expect you to believe it. It's true. I learned the hard way to be really careful about whom I allow into my private space, into my private life. Even the most authentic people develop ulterior motives when they see just how much you could do for them."

"I feel honored then," I tell him softly. "Was there never a woman you thought might be the one? Your Russian princess maybe?" I pretend to study the cream-and-black leather and gold accents of the decor so he won't see the jealousy I'm sure brews in my eyes.

"Katya's a great girl. She really is, and I can't deny we had a wild couple of days a few years ago."

I stuff a feral scream and tamp down the urge to yank a handful of blond strands from her scalp.

"But she's never been here." He tips my chin up again. "Just you, Nix."

I search his eyes and find what looks like the truth. Some of the tension in my shoulders drains, and I smile. The curtain opens again, and Laura rolls in a large cart bearing several silver domes.

Maxim shifts me off his lap so he can get up and take the seat across from me. Laura rolls the table between us. There's chicken, seafood, potatoes, asparagus, salad, and even some rich chocolate ganache–looking thing.

"Thank you," I murmur to Laura.

"Thanks, Laura," Maxim says. "Can you wait to clear this when we land? We aren't to be disturbed again."

She nods, and I take a gulp from my glass of water, hoping to cool the heat rising from the center of my body and fanning out over every part of me.

"I hope it's okay she brought everything out at once instead of in courses," he continues. "My mother would die a thousand deaths. She thinks it's vulgar to eat food all slammed together."

"You want it all and at once. A man of big appetites."

"So you do remember," he teases. "You're right, but I also didn't want her coming in and out. I want to be alone with you."

As quickly as we shove the delicious food in, we can't seem to get the words out fast enough. I'd forgotten how each conversation with Maxim opens up something I'd never considered. His mind reaches for things most people would never imagine. Even while he's plotting how we could save this planet, he's wondering how we could survive on Mars if necessary.

I pierce the last bite of chicken and release a satisfied sigh. He nods to the empty plate I've practically licked clean. "I really wish you had enjoyed your meal more."

I toss a dinner roll at him, which bounces off his forehead. He flinches, fork pausing halfway to his mouth. "It's all coming back to me, why I never bring girls on my plane."

I toss my head back and laugh and can't remember the last time I enjoyed anyone's company this much. Once we finish our meal, he pulls my hand to his lips and kisses my knuckles. "I hope there won't be ten years between this date and our next one."

"Well, at the rate we're going, with me being on the campaign trail and you being all over the world," I say ruefully, "it may be."

"Nah. I won't let that happen again."

There's a serious note in his voice that makes me look up. His expression is completely void of humor.

"I deserved your distrust, Nix," he says softly. "I know how I handled things hit a particular nerve for you, and I'm sorry about that."

"It's okay. And I told you, thanks to my therapist, I now recognize there was more to it than what was on the surface."

"I understand your fear about me…" He shakes his head. "Over the years, I always needed to make sure you were okay, so I get you being concerned about my…how did you put it? Love for danger?"

I manage a smile because it still scares me on some level that his pursuit of the next thing, the thing that doesn't even exist yet, might one day put him in danger he can't get out of. I've picked up those pieces before, and I'm not sure I can do it again.

"I wanted to give you something." He lifts the lid from a small dome by his plate to reveal a small flat box.

"What is it?" It doesn't even matter. It's for me from him. It's him thinking about me when we were apart.

"Open it."

He offers me the jewelry box, and my hands tremble the slightest bit when I take it from him. Our fingers brush, and that same charge zips over my nerve endings in a way I've never experienced with anyone else. My body finds a thousand ways to tell me Maxim is distinct. It has refused to offer this response to any other man, and I'm finally accepting his place in my life. It's hard to imagine where I fit in his if I think about it too hard, so I've determined to just feel how good it is to be with him again.

"Doc, it's absolutely beautiful." Tears prick my eyes, and I touch the compass charm dangling from a platinum bracelet. "You didn't... You don't have to do this."

"I wanted to."

He takes it from me, wraps the delicate rope around my wrist, and does the clasp. I trace the points—north, south, east and west—and remember running in the four directions during my Sunrise Dance, gathering the elements to myself. This gift feels perfect and meaningful.

"It's because we found our way back to each other," he says, a self-deprecating twist to his mouth. "Or rather I got tired of waiting and demanded you back in my life. Maybe I'm more like my father than I want to admit."

He says it lightly, but I know he means it and, on some level, questions it, maybe even worries about it.

I stand and walk around the table. For once I'm taller, his face level with my chest.

"You and your father *are* a lot alike, but you're different in all the right ways. I sometimes wonder how did Warren Cade make a man like you?"

He nods and lets out a harsh laugh. "I wonder that, too."

"But he didn't make you. The ruthlessness, the ambition, the determination and sense of adventure—all those things come from your father, but you studied beyond what he taught you. You went out into the world to see what else there was to it. You *chose* those experiences, and they shaped you into the man you are. Into the man I..."

I can't say that word yet. Our reunion is too new. *We're* too new, this version of us.

I dip my head and hold his stare. "You're exactly the man I want."

CHAPTER 48
MAXIM

SHE CAN'T POSSIBLY KNOW WHAT IT MEANS TO HEAR HER SAY THAT.

I'm exactly the man she wants.

The way she looks down at me now is the same way she did when she thought I was a struggling student abroad. Before she knew my name or who my family was, she looked at me just like this, a double helix of curiosity and hunger. I thought I wanted her then, but it was just a struck match. What burns inside me now is rampant, a wildfire I'm tired of trying to contain.

She straddles me. Her skirt rides up, exposing the length of firm thighs and a tantalizing glimpse of pink panties. I slide my palms over her legs and under her skirt, cupping her ass and urging her closer. Her breath hitches when her pussy, covered only by a strip of silk, hits my cock. There's so little separating me from what I've wanted since that night in the garden. She closes her eyes and moves her hips, the muscles of her butt flexing in my hands.

"So no mile-high club for you yet?" she asks.

"Are you going to pop my mile-high cherry?" I laugh.

"I'll pop it if I can find it." She grins and slips her hand between us, gripping and squeezing my cock. "Oh, look. Here it is."

"Jesus, Nix." I drop my head back and groan at her touch. I reach for the buttons of her blouse, my fingers clumsy, but I'm determined to see her. Her bra is pink, too, and the brown discs of her nipples show through the windows of lace. I tug the straps from her shoulders, jerking the bra down to expose the plump nipples tipping her breasts. I can't tear my eyes away and reach out to thumb one. She inhales sharply, her eyes dazed, her mouth open and panting. I take one breast into my mouth and pinch the other.

She starts riding me, rhythmic and writhing. She presses me to her. "Suck harder."

God, she's a dream. I comply, sucking harder. "What else?" I ask against her breast. "Tell me what you want, Nix."

"I want…" She closes her eyes and licks her lips. "Finger me."

Hell, yes.

Still sucking her breast, I slip my hand into her panties, stroking her clit with my thumb and pushing three fingers inside of her.

Wet. Hot. Slick.

"Holy shit." She clutches the back of my neck, rides my fingers, and lifts the fall of hair off her neck. "Don't stop."

I'm mesmerized by the undulating line of her body, by the long, trembling sweep of her throat, by the bob of her breasts. Her dark brows pinch, and her moans fill the cabin.

"What else can I do for you?" I ask, my voice husky, my dick so very hard. Pleasing her turns me on almost as much as her hands on me.

She eyes me through an arc of dense lashes when she says what I hoped against hope she would. "Eat my pussy."

Fuck, that's hot. I'm gonna come in my pants if I don't get inside her soon.

I pick her up, and she loops her arms around my neck and locks her ankles at the base of my spine. With quick strides, I take us to the back of the plane and into the bedroom outfitted with everything I need to be comfortable even thirty thousand feet in the air.

I lay her down gently on the bed, push her skirt up, and pull her panties down past her ankles. Dragging her to the edge, I press my face between her legs, lick the inside of her thigh. It's damp, and I get drunk on the smell, the taste of her passion.

"Like this?" I pant into the plump, wet rise between her thighs.

"Oh, God, Maxim. Yes. Come on."

I lick her pussy, spreading the lips, tonguing her, sucking her clit. I don't know how long I'm down there, but it's like a fever dream. I lose myself. I've wanted this, her, for so long I'm afraid to stop. She spills on my tongue, the flavor so rich and even better than I remember. I groan, not wanting to stop despite the demanding throb of my cock.

She's limp, her eyes closed, her fingers twitching, her kiss-swollen bottom lip caught between her teeth, and her cheeks streaked with tears. I lift myself to hover over her and bury my head in the dusky cloud of hair spread behind her.

"What else?" I whisper in her ear. "I want to make you feel good. What else can I do?"

Her lashes lift slowly, her pupils blown wide with lust and emotion that swallow the foggy gray of her eyes. "Fuck me."

A shudder rips through my entire body. I don't know if she's begging for it or commanding it, but I want to give it to her right now. I impatiently shed my pants and briefs and jerk the sweater over my head. I settle between her legs, but she stops me.

"Wait," she says, the one word hanging between us. "I want to see you."

"To see me?" I can't even compute it for a moment, but then she starts touching me, tracing the muscles in my belly and at my hips. She caresses the tattoo inked over my left pectoral.

"Endurance," she reads. "I don't remember that being there before."

"It wasn't."

"Is that for Shackleton's ship? Or the quality in your character?"

I smile and dot kisses over her breasts, pleased she remembered the things I told her about my expedition hero. "Both."

She shivers under my lips and fingers, running her hand over my ass. I clench under her sensual exploration. She caresses the flanks of my thighs and urges me forward.

"You're a beautiful man, Maxim Kingsman Cade." A wicked grin lights her eyes and curves her lips. She opens her legs like they're the gates to paradise.

It's her willingness that is my undoing. She wants it as badly as I do. I prop myself on one elbow beside her head. I push in excruciatingly slowly, inch by torturous inch. My body begs to slam into her, but I want to relish these first few seconds when she's mine again. The way her body clamps around me is literally the best thing I've ever felt in my life.

"Oh, my God," she gasps, closing her eyes.

"Look at me when I'm fucking you, Lennix."

Her eyes open, flaring at the commanding, possessive tone I can't suppress any longer. She was right about me. I am a wolf in wolf's clothing, and I'll consume her if she'll let me. I won't leave even a crumb for another man. She is *mine*.

"I gave you what you wanted," I say. "Now you give me what I want."

"What can I do for you, Mr. Cade?" she asks, her voice teasing, husky.

I brush a few flyaway strands from her face. "Don't shut me out ever again."

Surprise flits across her expression. I move inside her, pushing deeper until we both groan and grip each other like this could end at any moment.

"Okay." Her breathing is labored and thin. "I won't shut you out."

That's all I want from her.

Oh, and this pussy.

"I want this." I hook my elbow under her knee and press our foreheads together as I burrow deeper inside, as deep as possible. "Just this."

I plow into her, and my cock is relentless in its pursuit of satisfaction. I lose my train of thought in the bliss of her body. Her legs tangle with mine. I kiss her, and it's so tender, the way she opens for me, the emotion in something as simple as the glide of our tongues together, it makes my chest ache. I slip one hand between us, stroking her, clasping her neck as the rhythm of our bodies turns frenetic, a churning chaos of arms and legs and pussy and cock. The rich intercourse of our scents and the sounds we make enshroud us in a world that blocks out everything but this. We make a universe of our own. It's just us, and this is where I want to be.

She is where I want to be.

I've spent my entire life chasing answers, solutions, truth, money, success—you name it, I've been driven to gain it. That drive is as much a part of my DNA as my father's green eyes. But right now, buried inside the woman who feels like a part of me, contracting around me, our heartbeats pounding in synch, my body spilling all its secrets to hers, I gain the one thing that has eluded me all these years. A perfect stillness. An end to the searching. A found-ness, a seen-ness I didn't even know to look for.

So this is contentment.

CHAPTER 49
LENNIX

I'VE HAD SEX, BUT IT'S BEEN YEARS SINCE I WOKE WITH A MAN IN my bed.

Much less a wolf.

A wall of muscle warms my back, and hard arms hold me tightly, possessively, and with the utmost care. I trace the bulge of Maxim's bicep, the golden skin and fine hairs dusting his forearms. When I find the tiny scar that introduced us, I smile. That seventeen-year-old-girl who gaped at this gorgeous man through clouds of tear gas and a rain of rubber bullets had no idea she would end up here with him. Naked between love-mussed sheets.

"You up?" Maxim asks, leaving tender kisses on my back, neck, and shoulders, his hand roaming my stomach and sliding between my breasts. His cock digs into the curve of my butt.

"I see *you* are up." I laugh.

His chuckle rumbles through my bones like a car, revved, idling. "Don't mind him," Maxim says. "He has a one-track mind."

I turn over in the decadence of million-thread-count silk sheets, in the biggest bed I've ever slept in. Maxim doesn't do anything on a small scale, and the plane last night and this hotel are no exception.

"Which track is that?" I smile into eyes that mirror my own satisfaction.

"The *you* track." His smile dims a little, but the contentment doesn't. "Pretty much just you, Nix."

"The *me* track has to get out of this bed if I plan to make my meeting. I'm in Ohio to work for your brother, buddy. Sorry we don't get more time together."

"I have an idea." He dips his head and nibbles my ear, sending a ripple of lust I don't have time for through my body. "You could skip the service trip to Costa Rica and come with me to Paris for this climate change summit instead."

"You *do* realize you just suggested I renege on my commitment to building schools in an impoverished village to run off to Paris with you?"

"And that's bad?" he asks with a straight face and sly humor in his eyes.

I slap his shoulder. "You know I can't. I committed to this trip before I took on Owen's campaign, so it's not the best timing, but I have to honor my word. If for no other reason than I can't let the San Carlos students I'm taking with me down."

"And Wallace?" Maxim runs a finger along my collarbone, not looking up when he asks the question.

"What about him?"

"Ten whole days in a hot jungle with your ex-boyfriend sounds sexy." A humorless smile pulls his mouth into a stiff curve. "Maybe old feelings stir. Things happen."

"Hey." I pass my thumb over that unnatural smile he's wearing. "Foster step-cousin, remember?"

His smile is genuine for the first time since we started discussing the trip.

"It's not like that with Wall and me," I tell him. "It never really was. We just…tried."

"Well, there's no trying with me." Maxim gently pushes me back into the pillows. "There's no stopping this."

His kisses descend from the curve of my neck to the tilt of my breast, melting my core, and my hips start circling, subtly finding an ancient rhythm of want. His fingers wander from my knee to inside my thigh and higher. My breath hitches when he strokes between my legs.

"Doc," I groan, giving the watch on my wrist a half-hearted glance. "My meeting. I have to get up. I have to go."

"Not yet," he whispers and kisses my neck, sucks my nipple, squeezes my ass. "Give me a little more. Two more minutes."

Two turns to ten. His tender, nibbling kisses devour me. Light touches ignite our bodies to burn. Our hearts pound, and our passion overwhelms us. *A little more* becomes *everything*, and before I know it, we're lost in a tangle of *I am his* and *he is mine*, insatiable, inseparable.

Perfect together.

CHAPTER 50
LENNIX

"So do you hate me yet?" Wallace asks.

The look I shoot him is part affection, part exasperation, and no hatred whatsoever.

"Of course not." I scoop a spoonful of rice and beans into my mouth, a staple here on the Bribri reserve, and chew before continuing. "It's been a great trip."

"Not too rough?" He takes a bite of potato wrapped in banana leaf and waits for my reply.

"The hardest part was getting here."

After we landed in San Jose with our group of twenty—a few doctors and scientists like Wallace, some adult volunteers like me, and ten students from the San Carlos reservation—we took a bumpy five-hour bus ride on rugged terrain into the mountains, swerving to avoid the occasional bull or chicken in the middle of the road. Then a raft carried us deeper into parts of the village only accessible by water.

"Paco said we're lucky it's not the rainy season," one of the students, Anna, says, her wide smile gleaming from the metal of her braces. "We might not have been able to cross the river."

I smile at the young women from the San Carlos reservation

who have conducted themselves with such dignity since we arrived. A few of them speak Spanish, which is what the people here speak primarily. I listen with fascination and some wistfulness when I hear the people of Bribri speaking their native language, too. I know some Apache and am constantly learning more, but I, like many of my generation, am not fluent. The devastating legacy of colonialism in America is so vast, but one of the worst parts is the gradual disappearance of our languages. We were forbidden for many years to even speak our tribal tongues, and many of our languages could be extinct within the next decade. The people of Bribri may not have much materially, but I love seeing that they still have their culture, their ancient ways, and their language, even as they attempt to embrace modern necessities.

Like vaccinations.

"How'd the shots go today?" I ask Wallace.

"Pretty good," he says. "Costa Rica requires vaccines, but it's harder to administer in some of these more remote places. Some people here have to walk hours to even reach a hospital. We're coordinating with the Ministry of Health to get as many of these kids vaccinated as possible. I'm doing more tomorrow in another village not too far away."

"I'll ask if they can spare me tomorrow so I can help you. I used to want to be a clown. That should count for something. I can distract them from the needles."

"Okay, Bozo. It's a deal." Wallace laughs and takes a sip of water. "So how's your boyfriend doing?"

I don't stop my smile in time, and Wallace, who knows me so damn well, points at my dead-giveaway grin. "Lenny's in love!"

"Oh, good grief." I try to erase the perma-smile that paints itself on my mouth every time I think of Maxim—of the night we had together and the morning after in Ohio. Of what we'll have when I return. "It hasn't even been that long since we started…"

The word *dating* teeters on my lips, almost falling out. I've gone from avoiding Maxim to tolerating him to sleeping with him and missing his arms around me. I'm afraid to admit even to myself how deep my feelings for him run. I'm certainly not admitting anything to Wallace.

"How are Viv and the baby?" I ask, hoping Wallace will let me change the subject.

He offers a *you don't fool me* look but launches into his latest tale from the uncle chronicles. The students and the rest of the team finishing up their dinner laugh louder the more animated Wallace becomes. Their good humor provides great cover for my less-than-happy thoughts. I miss Maxim. The little time we had before I left wasn't enough. My body longs for him, but it's not just my body. My heart aches and feels like it's barely beating with him so far away. I open my hands in my lap and follow the invisible map he sketched across my palms so long ago.

Now you have the whole world in your hands.

I caress the compass charm dangling from my bracelet. I know it's expensive and I should probably take it off while I'm working here. If I was smart, I would have left the obviously valuable jewelry at home. But there was no way that was happening. I needed this part of him with me.

"You ready to turn in, ladies?" I ask the girls, noting the faint lines of weariness on their faces. "We all have a really early start tomorrow."

We cross the reserve, walking leisurely over the lush green grass, the palm leaves casting shadows in moonlight. We climb the few wooden steps into our thatch-roofed hut. Five of us share it, each having a mattress on the floor and mosquito netting.

Once we're in our pajamas and under our mosquito nets, the conversation starts. I love their questions about boys and college, love hearing their dreams and ambitions and how they want to hold on to our culture, language, and traditions even while navigating the world beyond the reservation. The same things I had to figure out.

There is a unique duality to our experience that's sometimes hard for others to understand. Living on patches of land when all of it, by rights, belonged to our ancestors. Living in, loving a nation professing freedom, liberty, and justice for all when our traditions were suppressed and we were forced from our homes and endured unimaginable injustices. Things like Thanksgiving, Columbus Day, even Mount Rushmore, which is built on *our* sacred grounds—all are symbols of American tradition but also glaring examples of how we've been mistreated. Conquered. In America's transition from annihilating our people to assimilating them, we lost so much. These young girls have to reconcile making peace with that truth enough to succeed there but still agitating so we don't lose any more of the traditions and culture our ancestors entrusted to us.

If I wasn't here, I'd be home, curled up by my fireplace in a cashmere robe, clinging to a wine glass filled with my favorite Bordeaux. Probably reviewing data and policy papers for Owen's campaign. I love my life and can't imagine a path more suited to who I am and how I'm made. But these trips, these nights talking with girls like these about their dreams and how to hold on to and pass on our rich heritage—I wouldn't trade this.

"Can I ask you something, Ms. Hunter?" Anna asks after we've been talking for a while.

"Sure." I stifle a yawn and force myself to focus. "What's up?"

"Your, um…your first time," she says in a rush and with a deep breath like she's diving underwater. "Did you, well, did you love him?"

The question takes me by surprise. We've talked about boys, sure, and crushes, but I didn't expect this. Anna's sixteen, so I guess that's about right. Most girls don't seem to wait quite as long as I did, but most girls don't have Maxim Cade as their first. A reminiscent smile curves my lips in the dark. God, he was so careful with me, but then so completely out of control, like he couldn't get inside fast enough and wanted to stay there forever. I didn't have words that night for what I felt when he initiated me not just into sex but into this world that is just ours. Just our two bodies, sun and moon, just our souls, earth and water. We are the sky and the sea, and the horizon is where our hearts meet. Every part of that world is made by and from and for just us two. I couldn't articulate it then, but now I have no choice.

"Yeah, I loved him," I say, trying to keep my voice steady, the hot emotion in my throat nearly melting the words.

I don't have time to process those words and their meaning before the girls dig deeper and for more. More questions, harder answers. Finally the girls' words start slurring, and my eyes grow heavy. The stirring breeze through the open window keeps us awake a few moments longer, and then we sleep.

Morning comes quickly. It feels like I've barely closed my eyes before Wallace is gently shaking my shoulder, asking if I still want to go with him to the village. The sun isn't even up. The girls have another hour or so to sleep, so I dress as quietly as I can. I join Wallace and Paco at a jeep that has seen better days, climb into the back seat, and rest my head against the window.

"At least we get to ride," Wallace says wryly. "The village is about ten miles away. That would have been a long walk."

"Promise me I won't have to stick a needle in some poor, unsuspecting kid," I say on a yawn.

"Just be my clown, Lenny."

He reaches back to give one of my two braids an affectionate tug. We share a smile and then lapse into silence. For once Wallace doesn't keep up a running commentary about everything we see but allows me to appreciate it. It's hard to believe that a mere five hours away, there's an airport and a bustling city. Here on the fringe of it lies this wild, untamed jungle, the narrow road carved into the side of a mountain the only concession to progress. Paco is carefully negotiating the road, and I can't help but risk a glance over the side, the precipitous height making my belly dive and flop.

The jeep screeches to a halt and jerks my attention forward. A small, camouflage-spotted truck with a canvas-covered bed blocks our way forward on the narrow strip of road.

"What the hell?" Wallace asks, peering through the windshield.

A round of gunshots blast into the air, staccato and strident. My heart seizes, clamoring against my ribs at the violent sound. Wallace reaches to the back seat and shoves me to the floor.

"Stay down," he whispers. The flattened panic in his voice is only outdone by the terror. A half-formed scream jams in my throat. A flurry of Spanish words fly past my ears faster than I can process or translate. I force my body as low to the floorboard as possible, keeping my head down.

Paco's door is yanked open. I hear him begging, a series of *por favors* and confused pleas. I brace myself for the sound of the shot that could end his life, but it doesn't come. I bite my lip against a cry. I'm completely blind to what's happening. My fear has no shape or form—only sound.

To my right, I hear Wallace's door jerked open too, his body dragged out.

"This one," a man says in heavily accented English. "He the one."

"What?" Wallace asks, his voice slightly higher and confused. "No. There's been a mistake. *Un error. Vacuna.*"

"*Sí, sí,*" the man replies, satisfaction in the words. "*Vacuna.* Come. He the one."

There's no way I'm hunching down in the back seat like some timid rabbit while God knows who drags off my best friend. I've never been more frightened, but I couldn't live with myself if I didn't do *something*. If I didn't try. I've heard of tourists being kidnapped by extremists or mercenaries. This overgrown paradise will swallow any trace of Wallace, and I might never find him. That's not happening to me again. I can't lose anyone else that way. I'm working up the nerve to get out and do something, try *something*, when the back door rips open, and my choice is taken away.

"Ah ha ha," a man drawls. "What do we have here?"

His voice is so neutral it sounds like he ruthlessly scrubbed anything that could trace its owner from it. When I glance up in centimeters of trepidation, the mask covering the man's face matches the anonymity of his voice. It's a mask of Abraham Lincoln, incongruously comical, like a child would wear for trick or treat. He's heavily muscled, broad and tall, maybe six foot five, with blond hair rioting around his head in a cloud of paradoxically cherubic curls. A Kurt Cobain T-shirt tops his camouflage pants.

"Hi," he says, his tone infuriatingly calm for a man with a semi-automatic weapon slung over his shoulder. "Care to join the party?"

He orders me out with a curt flick of his head. My teeth grit around a torrent of curses and demands as his flippancy finally roots out the fury buried beneath my fear.

I uncoil from my hiding place behind the front seat and climb out. Several dark-haired men, apparently locals, stand behind him, armed and grim-faced. Paco huddles in the truck bed, his wrists trapped in plastic cuffs. Wallace stands on the barrel side of a gun aimed at his head.

"Who's this?" another voice asks from just beyond Abe's shoulder. A man, roughly Abe's height, maybe a few inches shorter, with hair not quite as blond, curls not quite as cherubic, and an accent firmly from the Midwest, walks toward us wearing a Richard Nixon mask.

"We don't know yet," Abe replies.

"Can I keep her?" Nixon asks, and even behind the slits of his mask I feel his eyes crawling over my body in my fitted T-shirt and jeans.

"We may need to dispose of her, brother," Abe says, apology in his tone.

Fear weakens my knees, and I struggle to stay on my feet. My chest goes so tight, every breath is torture. The threat of his words finds its mark in my racing heart.

Abe grabs my arm and drags me forward. "What a shame that

would be. She's a pretty little thing, but I need the good doctor here, not stowaways. Can't afford dead weight, even if it *is* lightweight."

"Well, let's see who she is," Nixon says, grabbing my backpack from the back seat and rummaging through it. He pulls out my passport. "Lennix Moon Hunter. What kind of name is that? What are you? Mexican or some kind of Puerto Rican?"

"Yavapai-Apache," I answer, trying to keep my voice from trembling. "What do you want with us?"

"Oh, I don't want anything with you," Abe assures me, his voice soothing. "I'm probably tossing you off the side of this mountain in a few seconds."

Oh, God. An ear-splitting scream is trapped inside my head, desperate to get out. I'm not sure I could even run. Terror weights my body and nails my feet to the path.

Abe tips his golden head toward Wallace. "He's the one I want."

"Me?" Wallace touches his chest. "Wh—I don't—why? I'm a biochemist administering vaccines. There's been a mistake."

"I know who you are," Abe says, a grin tipping his mask to the side, "but thank you for confirming you're exactly who I've been looking for. You're gonna make me lots of money, Doctor Murrow."

"I have no idea what you're talking about," Wallace says, his words and eyes frantic. "But Lennix has nothing to do with this. Let her go. She hasn't seen your face and—"

Abe cuts Wallace's words short with a backhanded slap. Even in the first-morning sun's heat, coldness emanates from Abe's arctic-blue eyes behind the mask.

"This is my operation, Doctor Murrow," he says as if he hasn't just drawn blood from Wallace's lip. "I'll tell you what I need from you, and I'll decide if Lennix Moon Hunter lives or dies."

He issues a low stream of Spanish commands, and two of the armed men grab Wallace by the arms and then shove him into the covered bed of the truck.

"No!" I surge forward, my fright for Wallace overcoming the fear for myself. Abe blocks me with the butt of his gun under my chin.

"You're not invited. Yet," he says, his voice harsh and pleasant. "I need to figure out who you are before I let you in the clubhouse."

"I've seen her before," Nixon says, studying me, his eyes narrowed in the mask's slits.

"We don't know each other," I say carefully, the butt of the gun digging into my neck. "I'd remember a face like that."

Abe's laughter booms through the trees, bouncing off mountains and scurrying birds from their branches.

"Oh, I get it. Because of the mask." He gestures to his covered face. "Clever little *squaw*, aren't you? Lucky for you I like my women feisty and foreign."

"I'm an American," I reply, tensing at the insult, "like you."

The cheeks of his mask drop with his disappearing smile. "You don't know what I am, who I am, and if you're a smart bitch, you'll make sure it stays that way."

"I got it," Nixon says, his voice eager. He shifts his weapon on his shoulder. "That political show *Beltway*. That's where I saw her. She was talking about her book."

Abe tilts his head, the blue eyes narrowing with interest and speculation.

"Politics, Ms. Moon?" Abe asks, I'm sure deliberately misnaming me. "The plot does thicken."

I wish he'd stop toying with his food and just bite so I can know what I'm dealing with. "Let him go," I say.

Before I can draw my next breath, he grabs me by the neck, lifts me clear off the ground, and, with a few powerful strides, takes me to the edge of the road. He dangles me over the side of the mountain by one strong hand. Hundreds of feet sprawl beneath my frantically kicking legs. Lush jungle, the curvature of a rushing river with rocks like fangs jutting from the water sprawls so far below they look like game-board pieces. Breathing is impossible, not just because of the huge hand cutting off my air supply but because of the helplessness and fear scrambling up from my belly, anaerobic and nauseating.

"Stop!" Wallace shouts from the back of the truck. "You'll drop her!"

He's silenced. I can't tell by what or whom, but his raised voice is swallowed in abrupt quiet.

"I don't care if she falls," Abe says, the cheeks of his mask lifting with a smile that infects his blue eyes with a diabolical gleam. "I'll hold her here until she learns who's in control or dies."

This is power at its worst. A madman who, by loosening his fingers, could end my life, hurling me to certain death. By tightening them, he could do the same, choking the very breath from me.

He squeezes, sick pleasure flooding his bluebell eyes. The irrepressible sound of me fighting for air, for life, fills my own ears. My hands fly to his arms involuntarily, even though if he drops me, I'm dead. I can't stop them from begging for relief from the iron manacling my neck.

I'm going to die.

The thought sprints through my head so fast I can barely catch it. I envision him dropping me, and my belly hollows out like I'm already falling.

The thick muscles of his arm bulge and strain with the effort of keeping me suspended. Despite his obvious strength, he's struggling to hold my weight, and I feel his fingers on my neck slipping. His skin peels under my clawing nails. Tears fall over my cheeks, my body's desperate response to the torturous grip at my throat.

My strength fails and my arms drop. Thoughts, images flood my mind. My father bent over his papers, glancing up, love in his eyes, to find me standing at his office door. Mena sprinkling sacred pollen across my cheeks and plunging me into the cold, cleansing river. Kimba and Vivienne, stretched out under spring sunshine, our laughter floating over the Amstel River.

Maxim.

Oh, God, Maxim.

"Doc."

His name sputters over my lips on a choking moan. Sobs rack my thrashing, gasping body dangling over a fatal fall. The tangled brush of the landscape below tilts as my consciousness surrenders. Behind my eyes dawns an unlit sky, a blanket of darkness that smothers all sight and every sound. A thousand images my mind and heart have hoarded tattoo themselves behind my eyelids as they fall closed.

Meeting Maxim for the first time amid a spray of rubber bullets in the Arizona desert. Finding him again on a moonlit night in Amsterdam. Lost with him, found with him in a labyrinth of hedges, rediscovering us after years apart. A squandered decade. Will I ever get to make up for lost time? To tell him I love him? God, I love him so much, and he doesn't even know.

And now… Now it's too late.

ABOUT THE AUTHOR

A RITA® Award winner and *USA Today* bestseller, Kennedy Ryan writes for women from all walks of life, empowering them and placing them firmly at the center of each story and in charge of their own destinies. Her heroes respect, cherish, and lose their minds for the women who capture their hearts.

Kennedy and her writings have been featured in *Chicken Soup for the Soul*, *USA Today*, *Entertainment Weekly*, *Glamour*, *Cosmo*, *TIME*, *O Mag*, and many others. She has a passion for raising autism awareness. The cofounder of LIFT 4 Autism, an annual charitable book auction, she has appeared on *Headline News*, *Montel Williams*, NPR, and other media outlets as an advocate for ASD families. She is a wife to her lifetime lover and mother to an extraordinary son.

Connect with Kennedy!

Website: kennedyryanwrites.com
Facebook: /kennedyryanauthor
Instagram: @kennedyryan1
TikTok: @kennedyryanauthor
Twitter: @kennedyrwrites